Chimera

"A touching story on the nature of family, trust, and love lies hidden in this action thriller. . . . Thurman weaves personal discovery seamlessly into the fast-paced action, making it easy to cheer for these overgrown, dangerous boys."   —*Publishers Weekly*

"Thurman delivers a fast-paced thriller with plenty of twists and turns. . . . The characters are terrific—Stefan's wiseass attitude will especially resonate with the many Cal Leandros fans out there—and the pace never lets up once the two leads are together. . . . Thurman shows a flair for handling SF/near-future action."   —*SFRevu*

"A very enjoyable and engaging book that kept me turning the pages."   —*BSCreview*

"*Chimera* is a kick-ass story about characters that will steal your heart and a plot that will keep it pounding."   —*The Book Lush*

"A gut-wrenching tale of loss and something so huge that the simple four-letter word 'hope' cannot begin to encompass it. . . . *Chimera* grabs the reader's attention and heart immediately and does not let go through the many adventures, twists, and betrayals on the long ride to redemption. . . . Rob Thurman has created a haunting and eloquent testimony to the power of love and brotherhood, as well as a mystery that enthralls and keeps the reader on the edge of his seat ALL the time. The characters are so solid and vital, they almost walk off the pages and into your home. This is a masterpiece of . . . great storytelling."   —*Bitten by Books*

"The end of *Chimera* is a brilliant Machiavellian twist that surprised, saddened, and elated me."   —*Smexy Books Romance Reviews*

"If you enjoy powerful stories of intense relationships [and] diverse challenges, you'll enjoy *Chimera*, as well as Rob Thurman's other books. Her first series, which centers around two brothers, one of whom is half monster—literally—is a wonderful story that includes the perfect mix of action, adventure, horror, and the love that can exist between two brothers placed in dire circumstances through no fault of their own."   —*HubPages*

"This was a very entertaining book with plenty of action, a character-driven plot, and a surprising twist at the end. It was one of my favorite books of the year."   —*Fiction Kingdom*

continued . . .

THE CAL LEANDROS NOVELS

Blackout

"Thurman delivers in spades. . . . As always, a great entry in a series that only gets better with each new installment."   —SFRevu

"*Blackout* is a snarky and entertaining page-turner. Cal Leandros is an engaging hero who draws you into his story from the moment he awakens. . . . Funny, adventurous, and appealingly irreverent—the semidead cats got me every time—*Blackout* is one for the to-be-read pile."   —Romance Reviews Today

"If you're looking for a powerful dark noir urban fantasy that promises an excitable read but delivers so much more, then look no further than the Cal Leandros series."   —Smexy Books Romance Reviews

Roadkill

"Readers will relish this roller-coaster ride filled with danger. . . . The unexpected is the norm in this urban fantasy." —Alternative Worlds

"Thurman has broken new ground, expanding the mythology of her world in new and ingenious ways while offering new challenges to her heroes. . . . The finale of the story is perhaps the most emotionally moving bit of writing I've read this year. . . . *Roadkill* is a great addition to the series and will delight Thurman's growing legions of fans." —SFRevu

Deathwish

"Fans of street-level urban fantasy will enjoy this new novel. . . . Thurman continues to deliver strong tales of dark urban fantasy."
          —SFRevu

"The action is fast-paced and exciting, and the plot twists are delicious."   —Errant Dreams Reviews

Madhouse

"One of *Madhouse*'s strengths is Cal's narrative voice, which is never anything less than sardonic. Another strength is the dialogue, which is just as sharp and, depending on your sense of humor, hysterical."
          —Dear Author . . .

Moonshine

"[Cal and Niko] are back and better than ever . . . a fast-paced story full of action."   —SFRevu

"The supernatural elements meld seamlessly into the gritty urban setting. . . . Cal continues to be a wonderful narrator, and his perspective on the world is one of the highlights of this book. . . . The plotting is tight and fast-paced, and the world building is top-notch."
          —Romantic Times

Also by Rob Thurman

Basilisk

Rob Thurman

A ROC BOOK

ROC

Published by New American Library, a division of
Penguin Group (USA) Inc., 375 Hudson Street,
New York, New York 10014, USA
Penguin Group (Canada), 90 Eglinton Avenue East, Suite 700, Toronto,
Ontario M4P 2Y3, Canada (a division of Pearson Penguin Canada Inc.)
Penguin Books Ltd., 80 Strand, London WC2R 0RL, England
Penguin Ireland, 25 St. Stephen's Green, Dublin 2,
Ireland (a division of Penguin Books Ltd.)
Penguin Group (Australia), 250 Camberwell Road, Camberwell, Victoria 3124,
Australia (a division of Pearson Australia Group Pty. Ltd.)
Penguin Books India Pvt. Ltd., 11 Community Centre, Panchsheel Park,
New Delhi - 110 017, India
Penguin Group (NZ), 67 Apollo Drive, Rosedale, Auckland 0632,
New Zealand (a division of Pearson New Zealand Ltd.)
Penguin Books (South Africa) (Pty.) Ltd., 24 Sturdee Avenue,
Rosebank, Johannesburg 2196, South Africa

Penguin Books Ltd., Registered Offices:
80 Strand, London WC2R 0RL, England

First published by Roc, an imprint of New American Library,
a division of Penguin Group (USA) Inc.

First Printing, August 2011
10 9 8 7 6 5 4 3 2 1

Copyright © Robyn Thurman, 2011
All rights reserved

 REGISTERED TRADEMARK—MARCA REGISTRADA

Printed in the United States of America

To my characters—I am so damn sorry for the things
I do to you.

But what the hell? I do have to pay the bills.

Acknowledgments

To my mom, who suggested why not give my old dream of writing a go. Who knew she harbored such inner rage toward her own child? To Shannon, best friend and sister with a black belt in tough love; to my patient editor, Anne Sowards; to the infallible Kat Sherbo; to Brian McKay, ninja of the dark craft of copy writing; to Agent Jeff Thurman of the FBI for the usual weapons advice; to talented artist Aleta Rafton; to Lucienne Diver, who astounds me in the best possible way at every turn; and to great and lasting friends Michael and Sara, as well as Linda and Richard (who give new meaning to "Been there, done that, then went to China and did it again during a total eclipse of the sun").

"Fantasy abandoned by reason creates impossible monsters. . . ."

—Francisco Goya, 1799

"Genius might be described as a supreme capacity for getting its possessors into trouble of all kinds."

—Samuel Butler, 1835–1902

Prologue

On the day a nine-year-old boy killed Stefan, he didn't see his life flash before his eyes.

It's what they say you'll see, but not him. Clichés, who needed them?

That this was the second time in his life he'd thought the same exact thing would've been worth mentioning . . . if it hadn't been for the actual process of dying. That tended to be distracting from pithy observations. He was aware that he was lacking in the last-thoughts, much less last-words, department. He knew . . . but what could a guy do?

Life is like that. Sooner or later, it boils down to "What the hell can you do?"

His brother, Michael, once told him that when he had no hope, he dreamed of sun, wind, and horses. They were a part of his past—in a way, the best part. Every night he had dreamed of them—sun, wind, and horses. When Stefan had no hope, because dying doesn't leave a person much, he saw the same.

Sun, wind, and horses.

Stefan felt his heart stutter and skip. He wouldn't have thought that one or two missed beats would hurt that much, but they did. Invisible fingers of agony fastened around that beating hunk of muscle and squeezed once, twice, as his lungs staggered in sync. Then red, as scarlet as a field of poppies, bloomed behind his eyes, and he was on the beach. There were pounding waves, pale sand, and a sky so blue it couldn't be real. It was a child's painting, carefully covering every bit of the paper; it was blue and dense enough that you could probably scrape a thick peeling of color away with a thumbnail. He could smell the salt that stung his nose, feel the water that soaked his legs, and the warmth of the horse beneath him, the coarse mane he hung on to as he galloped through the surf. The wind in his face made him feel that he could fly. It was one of those moments no one forgets; the exhilaration, the sensation of wind, water, and sun branded forever in the mind of the fourteen-year-old kid.

He couldn't see his brother, but he could hear him laughing in the way only a seven-year-old can laugh—with all his being. He was on his own horse behind Stefan, sharing the adventure. It was a great memory, there, then—before the blood. Before the red coated the rock and sand, it was better than great—it was the perfect memory. Time spent with the strippers in his old *Mafiya* haunts didn't beat that. Even the first time he fell in love didn't conquer that. Didn't come close.

The next flash was when he'd saved his brother ten years after his abduction on that same beach. Stefan didn't see him through his own eyes this time. He wasn't Stefan anymore. He *was* his brother. He saw himself from his brother's point of view—a stranger all in black standing in the doorway of his prison, then pulling him out of a place of horror. He felt his confusion, his lack of trust, but years of brainwashed obedience had him allowing the grip on his arm and the tug and the run to freedom. The gravel and glass under his bare feet, the pain of the cuts, the ear-ripping explosions of firing guns, and the stars; Stefan felt and saw it all. Pain, blood, and flying bullets; he'd thought that would be what would stick with the kid—Michael—but it was the stars he remembered the most. The students— the prisoners—of the facility weren't allowed to wander the grounds at night, and they didn't have windows in the small cell-like rooms. Death behind him, and, for all he knew, death in front of him, but it was the stars that he saw. Far from any city, deep in the Everglades, the sky might be the color of the Grim Reaper's cloak, but Death's robe did make the ideal background for a hundred stars.

Brilliant light that shone down on you and could almost make you believe in miracles.

A light that could almost make you believe escape could be real and life was more than being trained to kill, turned into a weapon with no will of your own.

A light that was worth dying to see.

Only Michael had it in him to think that, which was unbelievable too. A wonder. He was a good kid. A damn good kid. The best. Even while dying, Stefan knew that as well as he knew anything in the goddamn world.

Michael left the bullets and the stars behind. The next was a string of emotions: fear, confusion, exasperation, more confusion, bewilderment, denial, annoyance, finally a reluctant acceptance, contentment, and a sense of belonging. All those emotions had been caused by Stefan, and while he wished the ones at the beginning could've been avoided, he was damn proud of the ones he felt . . . that his brother felt at the end.

Aside from emotions, there was also life in the world outside a concrete/razor-wire wall of the worst of prisons. Movies, TV, books, people that weren't instructors or torturers, restaurants, pizza, girls, a smelly ferret, making his own decisions—a life. A real life, something he'd thought impossible. And family, something he thought a fairy tale. Michael had been stunned by that. Amazed. He had family, a concept that even a genius like him could barely comprehend and could never have imagined applied to him. Someone cared about him. Someone told him he belonged. Someone would give up everything for him. Someone would give up *their* life for him. He wasn't alone.

He had his brother. He had Stefan.

Almost impossible to believe, but it was true.

If someone could like dying, Stefan liked that he was reliving Michael's life and not going through a rerun of his own. This way he didn't have to wonder if he'd done good by the kid, done good by his brother; he knew. He absolutely *knew* he'd done good. No doubts. Not a one.

The kid could've done better than him, he thought in disjointed chunks as he faded further into the darkness, but it was something; it truly was . . . what Michael thought so fiercely as that Grim Reaper's cloak from the Everglades came to wrap tighter around Stefan. *Family. Brother. You always watched out for your brother, no matter if he was the older one. You held on to your family because having one was a luxury no one . . . goddamn* no one *could afford to take for granted. You didn't let your family down and you didn't let your brother down, no matter how many times he called you a kid.*

How did Stefan know that? How did he know what his brother had experienced thought by thought years ago? What he was thinking now? How did he know Michael felt that way—even down to his annoyance at being called a kid? His absolute fury that Stefan would dare die on him? How did he get that last gift?

That was easy.

Because on the day Stefan died, that kid proved what his brother had known about him all along.

That damn kid . . . he was a miracle.

Chapter 1

"Hey, kid. I'll take a black coffee, large. I need something to keep me awake in this boring-ass town."

I didn't bother to look up from my book resting on the counter. "I'm not a kid." I repeated that every day to my brother, not that he listened. I turned a page. My name was actually Michael, but I couldn't tell the customer that; I couldn't tell anyone. "And it's already waiting for you at the end of the counter. That will be three fifty." I'd seen him come in, a flash in the corner of my eye, and heard his loud voice from the sidewalk long before he'd entered. If he had been a regular, I'd have given him my immediate attention and the service-friendly smile that exactly echoed that of the former employee of the month, whose picture was framed on the wall. It was the right kind of smile . . . friendly but not stalker-friendly. It said, "I make minimum wage, but it's a nice day, and you seem like a nice person. How can I help you?" It was natural, nonnoteworthy, and appropriate for the job. It took me two tries in the bathroom mirror to copy it, and I'd used it for every patron since the day the coffee shop had hired me. It was the expected smile—the normal smile.

It was important to be normal.

At least, it was important that people think that you were normal.

I wasn't normal.

This tourist was my first exception to pierce my mask of prosaic, run-of-the-mill normalcy. He'd come in every day for a week, ordering the same thing, tipping the same amount—nothing—and saying the same insult: boring-ass town. Cascade Falls was not a boring-ass town. It was a nice town. It was small and inconspicuous and no one had tried to kill me or my brother here, not yet. That made it the perfect town really, and I wished that this guy's new wife—it had to be a new wife; he wasn't the camping type—had planned their honeymoon elsewhere, because I was tired of hearing him carp every morning. I was tired of him, period.

Also, only my brother could get away with calling me kid.

The man was five foot ten, about forty to forty-three, mildly thinning blond hair greasy with the sheen of Rogaine, hazel eyes that blinked with astigmatism or too much alcohol the night before, twenty-two to twenty-five pounds overweight, and with a small crease in his earlobe that indicated possible heart problems due to his body's inability to cope with his diet. He glared at me over the top of sunglasses he hardly needed on a typical Oregon day in the Falls and tossed down three dollar bills and two carefully fished-for quarters. He snorted and flicked the tip jar with a finger. "Like you caffeine pushers do anything worth a tip."

He made his way down to a cardboard cup of coffee, still steaming, that was waiting for him, grabbed it, and headed for the door. I could do something worth a tip, quite a few somethings, if that was his complaint, but I doubted he wanted to experience any of them. Although, making him impotent on his honeymoon would be a poetic punishment. . . .

I shook my head, clearing it. Simply because I could do certain things didn't mean it was right. I knew right from wrong. My brother, Stefan, had commented on it once—that I knew right from wrong better than anyone raised in a family of Peace Corps pacifists descended from the bloodlines of Gandhi and Mother Teresa. Considering how I'd actually been raised, what I had been molded for and meant to be, he said that made him proud as hell of me. Proud. I ducked my head down to study my book again, but I didn't see the words, only smears of black ink. Stefan was proud of me and not for what I could do, but for what I refused to do. It was a good feeling, and while it might have been almost three years since he'd first said it, I remembered how it felt then—and all the other times he'd said it since. It was a feeling worth holding on to. I concentrated on that rather than on what I wanted to do to the rude tourist.

Stefan also said that despite his former career, he knew right from wrong too, but before he found me, he was beginning to lose his tolerance for it. It was a lie—or maybe a wish that he could do away with his conscience, because what he'd once done had to weigh on it. He'd worked for the Russian *Mafiya*. He'd done bad things to . . . well, probably equally bad or corrupt people, but the weak too. The weak always got in over their heads in dark waters. What Stefan had done, he didn't want to tell me and I didn't push, but I did my research. You didn't work as a bodyguard in the Russian mob as Stefan had without doing some serious damage to people who may or may not have deserved it.

Regardless of that and regardless of the things Stefan had done for me, under that ruthlessness to protect, and the willingness to kill if that was what it took to keep me safe, there was a part of him that wanted to believe in a world that was fair. He wanted to believe that concepts like right and wrong could be viable. Despite all he'd done and had been forced to do, he wanted to believe, though he knew better. Stefan had a heart and he didn't realize it. Why else would he search for a kidnapped brother for ten years when his—our—own father had given up?

Older brothers, especially ex-mobsters, weren't supposed to be more naïve than their younger ones, but Stefan . . . sometimes I thought he was. We had both been trained to be killers, but I thought I'd learned far more than Stefan. He would deny it, but he was wrong.

If he hadn't spent almost half of his life looking for me and doing what was necessary to finance that search, I wasn't sure what my brother would've been. Not what he was, I did know that. When I had been taken—such a simple word—it had ruined lives, and when it came to Stefan, when I had been abducted, it had done more than ruin. It had done things I wasn't sure there were words for. And when it had happened, it had changed my brother as much as it had me— which wasn't either right or fair. But true as that was, we were both alive and free now, and that was a thousand times more than I'd ever expected or dreamed. Where I had spent most of my life, freedom wasn't a concept, only a meaningless word to be looked up in a dictionary.

My brother had made it mean something. Cascade Falls was part of that, which only made me wish again I had made that tourist pay for his contempt. And that was a slippery slope. I focused on my book and the words swam into focus. I was close, very close to what I was trying to accomplish—it was only a matter of weeks or maybe days, I hoped. I'd had seven years of a normal life before I'd been kidnapped, Stefan said, although I couldn't remember a single second of them; ten years of captivity, which I remembered with stark, vivid clarity; and nearly three years of freedom, freedom to do research; and now the time was almost right. I was almost there. All the more reason to learn more and do it faster.

A finger poked at my book on neurosurgery. "Parker, you're always studying. If you're not going to college, why bother?"

Parker wasn't my real name, but Sarafynna didn't know that. Then again, Sarafynna didn't know how to spell her own name and that made me doubt she cared that my name was actually Michael. Or Mykyl. When it came to Sarafynna, I wasn't too sure that wasn't how the letters popped up in her brain. Truthfully, I wasn't sure Sarafynna had a brain at all without an MRI to back that up. All that Sara—the nickname was much simpler and it didn't make my mind twitch—knew was how to put whipped cream on top of the lattes and how to flirt. To "mack" or "hit on" guys. Since I didn't know who Mack was, I went with the other one—"hit on." That was more modern than "flirt" . . . to "hit on" guys. Whatever. I had more significant things to concentrate on.

Saving brain cells for important information outweighed saving them for teenage slang—which was mostly uninteresting anyway. Besides, in another month I wouldn't be a teenager anymore.

In almost three years I'd learned about flirting and sex, but now, at nineteen closing in on twenty, I liked intelligence in girls or women. Sara was entertaining and she let me know my hormones were working at top capacity—she was gorgeous. . . . Hot, I mean— "hot" was what someone my age should say. But she didn't have it all. I'd come to find out that I needed resourceful and smart too; Sara had everything except that. She had sunshine-bright blond hair—fake; big, turquoise eyes—fake; and she bounced wherever she went. That meant certain things on her, those things also fake, bounced with her as she went and rarely stopped bouncing. The first time Stefan had met her, he waited until I got off work that night and took me to the drugstore for a box of condoms.

I told him I didn't need them, and he told me I was an idiot if I didn't want to play in that sandbox. I was nineteen, he said with a grin, and that was what nineteen was all about. Nineteen and friction—knock yourself out.

But I didn't. I saw her fake-colored contacts and thought about the one I wore that turned my one blue eye mossy green to match the other one—two fakes don't make a reality; I thought about her lack upstairs of anything but whipped cream, and it seemed like a waste. Stefan and I had lived in Bolivia for two years before we came to Cascade Falls. I'd played in sand-boxes there, whatever Stefan had said. It wasn't as if I were a virgin. I'd had the experience . . . experiences. I'd been seventeen before I'd gotten to make my own choices, even a single one. Now that I had almost three years of making decisions for myself, I wanted to be sure that each one I made now was the best I could make.

Sara did bounce in a very intriguing way, though. It might be worth thinking about. Hmm.

"I might go to college someday," I said, turning another page. What I didn't tell her was that I was going to the equivalent of college and then some. I had the knowledge base for a medical degree with a specialty in biogenetics with an emphasis on polymorphism and pseudogenes, and a PhD in biochemistry and neurology.

Theoretically.

Nineteen and a doctor three times over, but it was amazing what you could learn when you could hack into the computer system of any university in the world. Computer hacking had actually been the easiest thing to learn compared to many other things. In fact, it was pretty boring.

Yes, I'm smart. I know.

The question was whether I was born that way or made that way.

"College sounds like a lot of work." Sara's voice brightened. "Except for the parties. I'll bet frat parties are fun. Maybe I should go. My parents keep bitching at me to since I graduated." She pushed up to sit on the counter—against the rules—but I was reading. Technically I shouldn't notice.

And technically my eyes didn't wander to technically not watch her bouncing—lying to yourself can be entertaining—when I saw past her to the television in the break room. What I saw on it made Sara's whipped cream skills and bouncing vanish. The sound was turned low, but I could still hear it. I could still see him on the small screen. I saw a man I'd never expected to see again. His face had that enigmatic smile that could save your life or far more likely put you in your grave; he was Stefan's father.

Or our father, Stefan would say. . . . Anatoly Korsak.

And they were saying he was dead.

I told Sara I felt sick, and then I went to the bathroom and threw up, nice and loud—no finger needed. Genetic skills, I had them in spades. And you don't tell stories you can't back up. You always do what needs to be done to provide evidence to support your deception. I hadn't learned that from Stefan. I'd learned it at the Institute—the place Stefan had rescued me from. The Institute had thousands of lessons and some hung around, lingered—when I was awake, when I was asleep. They most likely would my whole life. When it came to making people think what you wanted, a small number of those lessons were harmless, the rest considerably less so, but all were efficient.

I was nothing if not extremely efficient.

My trip to the bathroom got me a "Shit, Parker, sweetie. Are you okay?" from Sara and a call to someone else to replace me. Ben Jansen. Ben liked the bouncing as much as I did—or as much as Stefan said I should.

Stefan . . . he should know better. He shouldn't have done this. There was protective and overprotective; then there was something so far beyond that—a word hadn't been invented for it yet—and that was what Stefan practiced. Anatoly was dead; it was all over the news, and Stefan hadn't told me. He hadn't called me to let me know. How could he think I wouldn't find out? I didn't know, but I did know it had to stop. Nearly three years free and twice I'd saved his life; it was a two-way street now. He had to trust me with the bad as well as the good. I wasn't a kid anymore, no matter what he called me. I could more than carry my own weight.

The coffee shop door shut behind me and I started down the sidewalk with my hands in my pockets, heading to my car. It was seven years old, gray, and a Toyota. They were virtually invisible. That was mob and Institute knowledge, oddly coinciding. Low tech meets high tech, with the same purpose: clean getaways. Of course, the Institute expected no getaway would be necessary if you did your job adequately. I guessed we'd fooled them, because Cascade Falls was a clean getaway so far.

In the distance I could see through the trees the silver glint of the Bridge of the Heavens crossing the Columbia River. When we'd picked this place to live, Stefan had quirked his lips. "Bridge of the Heavens," he'd said. "How about that, Misha? That must mean this is Paradise." Sometimes he could be a little thick, my brother. He didn't always get that everywhere I went outside of the Institute was Paradise. If there was actually a Hell, the Institute would make it seem like Paradise too. Hell would be a walk in the park. Hell would be nothing.

"Hey, smart-ass. You get tired of ripping people off with your high-priced shit?" The words, tainted with bile, came from out of nowhere, or nowhere if your attention was not in the here and now, and mine wasn't.

Stupid. How could I be so careless and stupid? Anatoly was no excuse. You were always ready. *Always.*

It was the tourist. He was sitting on the wrought-iron bench, always freshly painted bright blue, outside Printz's Bakery. I noticed that every day. The swirls of iron reflected the exact same color of the sky overhead. It was one more detail about Cascade Falls that made me . . . happy, I guess, and made it my home. The tourist wasn't one of those warm, small-town features. There wasn't anything warm about him at all, except his sweat. He had a cheese Danish the size of a four-year-old's head in one hand and a smear of buttery cheese on his chin as he glared at me. As I'd thought earlier—his body had its work cut out in taking care of him.

But it wasn't my job to take care of him, unlike his unlucky heart, and I ignored him and kept walking. That was normal too and being normal was the best move I could make now. Do as a normal teenager would do. Only I was barely still a teenager and I was nothing close to normal. But I played the game as I'd been taught. Normal teenagers usually aren't polite to annoying people—or assholes—and that meant I walked on as if I hadn't heard him.

Stefan would definitely say this guy was an asshole. He wouldn't be wrong.

"Shithead, I'm *talking* to you." I'd only just passed him when there was a hand grabbing my arm to give me a shake. From the smell, he'd put something in the coffee after he'd left the shop. Cheese, alcohol, coffee, and natural halitosis—I'd smelled better things and I'd smelled worse. People almost always smelled worse on the inside than the outside.

The Institute had had anatomy classes and enough cadavers to make Harvard Medical School jealous. The Institute taught its students to hurt people, taught them to use what had been stamped on their genes. But I hadn't wanted to hurt anyone. I hadn't wanted to kill anyone. The thought of it, in self-defense or not, had made me sick. That didn't mean I wasn't forced to learn and it didn't mean I hadn't killed.

Once.

I didn't plan on ever doing it again.

In addition, the Institute had biology classes. One thing they taught us there was that as adolescent males grow, the production of testosterone increases, and so do levels of aggression—the natural kind that gives you the instinct to protect yourself if attacked. Three years ago I wouldn't have hurt this on-my-last-nerve irritating tourist. I wouldn't hurt him now, although the jolting surprise of his voice and his shaking me made it a very close thing. But I caught myself. He wasn't a threat, despite being bigger than I was. No, I wouldn't hurt him, but it didn't mean I wasn't more tempted now than I would've been when I was younger. My temper ran hotter now than it had then. Nature—it can't be stopped—usually.

Slippery slope, I was repeating to myself, same as I had in the coffee shop, when he shook my arm again, harder this time. Slippery, slippery slope.

But then again, what was one ski run, really? Just the one?

This once, I gave in to nature. I looked at the tourist and tried not to smile. I didn't think I was successful and I doubted it was a friendly smile. Not that that employee-of-the-month one. "Alcohol is harmful to your liver and not all that great for your stomach either," I said, pulling my arm free. His eyes widened, he dropped the Danish he was holding in his other hand, and I backed away quickly. I made it in time as he bent over and threw up on the sidewalk. I'd done the same to myself earlier in the coffee house bathroom, but not quite so . . . explosively. I should've been sorry, but I wasn't. He deserved it. Out of range and unsplattered, I turned my back on him and kept walking toward my car. I heard him vomit one more time, curse, groan, and then vomit again. He would keep it up for approximately the next fifteen minutes until he was empty of everything, including yesterday's breakfast. He would chalk it up to strong coffee, whatever alcohol he'd put in it, and the Danish. After all, what other explanation could there be?

Well. . . .

Other than me?

He was fortunate I wasn't more like my former

classmates. If I had been, that one touch of his hand to my arm, that hard shake he'd given me—I could've ripped holes in his brain, torn his heart into pieces, liquefied his intestines. After all, that was what I was: a genetically created, lab-altered, medically modified child of Frankenstein, trained to do one thing and one thing only.

Kill.

All with a single touch.

Isn't science fun?

Besides, vomiting didn't hurt. It was only annoying, like the man who was doing it.

Mr. Fat-ass Danish would never know. I climbed into the car, pleased for a split second. Mr. Fat-ass Danish . . . the phrase had come out naturally, no work at all. Cursing was one thing that had proved difficult to learn. I was getting better at it. Then I remembered Anatoly, and the pleasure popped and disappeared like a soap bubble. Stefan and I needed to talk. I started the car. His babysitting days were over. That took me to the most simple of physics lessons: immovable object, unstoppable force. I sighed and pulled the car away from the curb.

All right, his babysitting days were mostly over.

Fifteen minutes later I was telling my brother the same thing that I'd told the tourist when he'd asked for his coffee.

"I am not a kid."

And I wasn't. My brother called me that daily at least, but since he had lost me when I was seven years old and only gotten me back when I was seventeen, I understood. Calling me a kid was his way of trying to ignore or reclaim those ten lost years. It was an emotional and appraisal-based mixed coping skill.

Again, still smart.

As I denied my inclusion in the kid category, Stefan wiped the back of his hand along his forehead, not that there was any sweat. Moisture, but no sweat. I'd spent most of my life in Florida and so had he. But when you were living in Oregon, when there was water dripping down your forehead, it wasn't often sweat. It was the air. You drank your air in the Falls; it was that heavy on every molecule. It was July now and around fifty-five degrees today. I didn't mind the drop in temperature compared to Florida and Bolivia. It was green here in Cascade Falls, everywhere green, and it was cool on the river. I was surprised to find I liked that. I was usually surprised when I liked anything. "Prepare for the worst and get the worst." That had been an unspoken Institute motto among the students. I'd been raised there with suspicion as my very best friend since my first memories. That meant everything I saw, touched, tasted, heard—it was all evaluated through a filter of wariness. But in the time since the Institute I'd had more pleasant surprises than unpleasant ones.

That, ironically, surprised me too.

I liked Oregon and I was lucky to be able to have an opinion one way or the other, which made me like it more. I didn't mind the lack of ocean. I'd seen it in South Carolina for a short time, and I'd have liked to have seen more, but if I needed water, there was also the river. But more than that, there was Stefan.

He was overprotective and he called me kid, but he

was my brother—mine—and I sort of loved him. Not that I'd say that. You couldn't just go and say things like that aloud. TV said so. Movies said so. General guy culture said so—I'd learned that from close observation. Everything said so.

Almost three years with him and the possibility of losing him said so.

Funny the things you don't want to say and tempt fate, the things you don't want to admit to yourself, no matter how often you think them. We were free and alive now, but that might not always be true.

"I'm not a kid and that ladder is too high. You could break a leg," I said. Yet there I was, thinking it again. People were fragile. They were like ancient glass found in Roman ruins waiting to shatter into pieces at one simple touch, thousands of pieces that could never be glued back together. Easily . . . extraordinarily easily broken, those normal people.

I wasn't normal. I tried to be, but I wasn't. The Institute had made certain of that.

Stefan was painting Mrs. Adelaide Sloot's house today. Every morning before he left, I made him leave a schedule pinned to the refrigerator with my Albert Einstein magnet. Fine. I was forced to admit it: the babysitting thing went both ways. Now with my showing up, he let the brush fall back in the can of mint green paint and looked the ladder's entire ten feet plus half of his own size down at me and my scowl from where he perched on top. "Okay, that's out of nowhere." He meant the kid part, not the ladder complaint. He'd made it clear I was profoundly overprotective lots of times before. Profound was an exaggeration, as was pathological. I thought he'd been carrying around a dictionary that particular day—stuck on the letter *P*. I was cautious, that was all. Besides, considering what he'd done to protect me in the past, I wasn't sure I came anywhere close to falling in the same category.

Anatoly's death and Stefan's not telling me about it proved that, didn't they?

He ran a hand through his short, wavy black hair, leaving flecks of green. "I promise to be extremely careful with this Tower of Babel–tall ladder." He said it solemnly enough, but I had my doubts. "Why aren't you at work? You fought kicking and screaming to work in a public place, and now you're skipping?"

"I did not kick or scream. Are you mocking me?" And I had to be out in public eventually. I couldn't live my entire life sitting in the house, afraid I'd be spotted by employees of the Institute. I wasn't letting them take more years away from me. They weren't taking any more of my life. This wasn't about me, though. This was about Anatoly, what Stefan had done, and how to approach the subject without making him dig in his heels harder. He was stubborn. I was too.

As I thought about it, I swung a bag in my hand that I could easily throw up to him or *at* him, depending on his mentioning kicking or screaming again. I added, "And, I repeat, yet again, I'm not a kid."

"I would never mock you. Make fun of you or tease you, maybe, but never mock." That was twice as solemn and earnest and a flat-out lie. Maybe his head. I could hit him in the head with the bag. No. Then his chances of falling that treacherous ten feet only increased. Revenge was tricky that way. "And what's up

with the kid thing? Am I wearing a T-shirt that says
you're a kid?" he went on with a grin. "Did you hear
me talking in my sleep last night and going down the
hall to the bathroom, calling you cute names? Things
like 'puppy' or 'skipper'? Something that made you
resent me enough to chase me down while I paint gingerbread?"

Cascade Falls was a long way from Miami, or Bolivia, where we'd spent two years before coming to this
tiny Oregon town of "homey" but expensive restaurants; small artsy stores; happy, pleasant people—or
unhappy, unpleasant people with excellent acting
skills. I was still debating the last part. Caution and
suspicion—they kept you alive. There were also tourists, the newlywed or nature type—and the puking
type, thanks to me—but definitely not the mob types
Stefan was doing his best to avoid. The town also had
several bed-and-breakfasts, as did the surrounding
small cities.

Bed-and-breakfasts, like Mrs. Sloot's, seemed odd to
me. It didn't matter that all the Web sites and brochures
talked about your "home away from home." Why
would I want to stay in the home of someone I didn't
know, didn't trust, and didn't have a thorough background check on? At least, *theoretically* didn't have a
background check on. White lies didn't hurt when your
brother thought you spent too much time on the computer.

Despite all that, there was one positive to bed-and-
breakfasts—they always had gingerbread trim in need
of painting. Stefan now had more than enough money
in offshore accounts his father—our father, he kept tell-

ing me—had given him before we'd left for Bolivia. Anatoly Korsak had made a massive amount of it in his time running the majority of the Miami mob for twenty or so years. Now, part of that money let Stefan work as a handyman and still afford to feed us.

Plus, he'd told me, he had a bachelor's degree in general studies from the University of Miami, which translated to "Do you want fries with that?" Then he'd explained why that was both funny and sad. I got the funny. Sad? I didn't tell him it was one of the furthest things from sad there was. Stefan was living with a guilt he'd never be rid of thanks to my kidnapping. I wasn't going to go prodding at it, especially as he didn't deserve it, not any of it. It turned out that Stefan liked the work, which was good and he deserved good. He said it gave him a helluva lot more sense of satisfaction than beating up people for the *Mafiya*.

"Helluva." That was one of the curse words I kept meaning to add to my vocabulary. I could add it to "fat-ass." To fit in. Stefan liked his job and Stefan painted a helluva lot of gingerbread. Good. That sounded correct. It sounded like something a real person would say. A real boy . . . just like that old children's cartoon, *Pinocchio*.

Except I wasn't a boy. I was a man and I wasn't real, thanks to the Institute. Not real, not quite yet, but Stefan was and always had been—more real than he should've been forced to be. Choosing real-life decisions in a life he wouldn't have chosen at all if it hadn't been for me. Being in the *Mafiya* had been Anatoly's calling, not Stefan's. When he ended up wearing cotton candy pink, sunshine yellow, or mint green paint on his jeans these days, I knew he didn't mind. His masculinity would survive pastels, I'd pointed out helpfully, or it wasn't much masculinity to begin with. He'd balled up his jeans and thrown them at me, and he'd laughed. I'd made him laugh. Stefan didn't laugh much. I was proud of every laugh I'd been a part of.

And it was good work, what he did—the handyman job. Good, and except for tall ladders, mostly safe, and, better, he didn't need a gun to paint the trim on a house. But he carried one anyway—there and everywhere else.

It made sense when we were on the run from the Russian *Mafiya* and another organization so secretive and grim that James Bond producers would've pissed themselves just reading the script—I knew that for a fact because I'd seen men piss themselves in fear in real life, and I liked James Bond movies. In any case, when you had all that chasing you, you wanted reassurance—as much as you could hope for. Oregon weather was good too for layering your shirts, and that in turn was good for covering up a discreet gun tucked into the back of a person's jeans. As for me. . . .

I didn't need a gun.

"You forgot your lunch," I said, before repeating for the third time, "and I'm not a kid." I'd had the bag in the car and had planned on driving it over to him at noon. Now it was an excuse for a few more minutes to stall and think how to go about this. He was only protecting me, or thought he was. I had to get him to see that he wasn't. Not anymore, not by holding back vital information. It was time to treat me as an equal, not as a little brother.

He caught the bag I tossed up to him. I made him lunch every day. I'd considered writing his name on the side in marker, but my newfound sense of humor might get my hair ruffled with that one. And raised in the Institute or not, trained for an obedience and passivity that, in my case, never really took, I was not putting up with that at all.

Lunches were only part of it. I tried to take care of Stefan for all he'd done for me. He said I was an idiot and that it wasn't necessary and something else after that, but I'd tuned him out by then. He was as overprotective of me, physically and emotionally, as he accused me of being of him. When it came to arguments over who didn't owe anyone anything, I ignored him and did what I wanted—I gave him what he did deserve . . . or the best I could.

He could talk forever, but he wasn't going to change my mind about that. Besides, it made me happy, and he liked his brother happy, so he huffed and let it go. I'd discovered peanut butter and Marshmallow Fluff sandwiches were the very best things in the world and that was what I made him every day—two of them in a brown paper bag. I didn't think people carried their lunches in brown bags anymore, but I'd seen it once in an old movie at the Institute and the image had branded itself onto my brain as the ideal family moment—the handing over of the brown-paper-bag lunch before sending Junior on his way. That was the way it was done and that was the way I was going to do it.

Movies were how I learned a good deal about life in the Institute—where there was no peanut butter or marshmallow. Three years in the real world hadn't changed movies or me as much as I'd thought it would. Stefan said there was nothing wrong with that. I liked movies and real life . . . though it wasn't always one hundred percent likable. I didn't blame myself for preferring the fake version once in a while. Stefan wasn't actually thick. He was smarter than I was in a lot of ways.

He opened up the bag I'd tossed and caught the whiff of peanut butter and Fluff. I know, because I did too. The smell made me hungry. His lips twitched with a particular amusement I hadn't quite figured out yet before he rolled the top back shut to wait for lunchtime. "Thanks, kiddo."

"For the fourth time, I'm not a kid. I'm an adult." I folded my arms and gave him a grim frown. "Nineteen. Almost twenty. A goddamn adult."

" 'Goddamn,' huh? We're having a serious moment here. And legally maybe you are an adult, but you're kind of scrawny." He grinned. He always grinned or smiled or bumped my shoulder. He kidded about calling me a puppy, but you'd have thought he was the most harmless, puppylike grown man with matching puppy brown eyes if that was all you saw—him with me. When you saw him with other people, he was different—harder, cynical, not to be messed with. When you saw him with people who wanted to hurt us, he was lethal. Period. And his smiles then were nothing near puppyish. They were the smile of a wolf before its jaws closed on its prey, and those brown eyes went pure rapacious amber.

Stefan could go from puppy to predator in a heartbeat and then end yours.

Right now he looked like a happy Labrador. The scar that ran along his jaw from his chin almost to his eyebrow only made his grin look wider. He yawned, up and out to work before dawn, and looked me up and down with a dubious snort. "If adult were measured in pounds, I don't know . . . it'd be close."

I let my frown deepen. I'd grown since I'd been with my brother. I'd gone from five foot nine to five foot eleven, the same height as Stefan, but I was . . . not skinny, but light, built like a runner. Considering our lives, that was a good thing. I was just your average teenager with average brown hair and slightly less average green eyes. One of my eyes was blue and the other green. Far too distinctive, which was why I wore a colored contact lens to give me matching green eyes. To the people in town, I was nothing out of the ordinary—as we'd planned and as being in hiding required.

I was stalling, but I had to stop. It wasn't going to be pleasant, but it was time for the truth. "This *is* serious. I am an adult and you have to accept that. I mean it. Stop being so overprotective."

"I swear," he said, a puzzled furrow appearing between his brows. The Institute had a class on reading facial expressions. I was seventy percent effective at it—not that great among my peers, but passable. I could tell if someone was uncomfortable by a crease, whether it was physical or emotional distress by a line, and the cause of it by a flicker of their eyes toward the source. I could diagnose an STD faster than any doctor and without having to see one single crotch scratch.

"I don't have a clue why your panties are in a wad," Stefan went on.

"Did you think I wouldn't find out?" I tilted my head, trying to figure it all out. "Unlike you, who just reads the comics"—a lie; that was only every other day—"I watch the news every day." As well as reading it online . . . every day, several times a day, alert for any pertinent fact that someone was on to us.

"And?" he asked, looking more confused than before.

Oh, shit.

That cursing came naturally for the third time today. I didn't have to check my mental folder for it. I'd made a mistake, a big one. I stopped frowning and ran a hand in unconscious imitation of him over my brown hair. I could've kept my face from tensing—in the acting class at the Institute we learned that perfect assassins are perfect actors—but I didn't. Because that would have been a lie and I wouldn't lie to Stefan. Not unless it was for his own good. "You don't know. About Anatoly. You don't know."

Because he was painting. Because he wasn't by a TV. Because he didn't listen to the radio that often while working.

Maybe I wasn't smart. Maybe I was as idiotic as they come.

I took a step backward, the longtime natural instinct of a former prisoner, then reversed to take one forward, a new instinct, hard won. "He's . . . gone. I'm sorry, Stefan. They found his body. He's been dead for about four weeks. Anatoly's gone."

The lunch bag didn't drop from his hand, but I saw his fingers loosen. He was stunned and why wouldn't he be? Anatoly was dead. His father was dead.

Then his fingers tightened and the paper bag crumpled under his hand. I could guess, sort of, what he might be thinking, his first thought. We'd talked about Anatoly since my rescue and I'd gotten a fair picture of Stefan and his relationship. Anatoly and mine, not as much, but I knew Stefan and his father—our father—as much as I could. What do you think when your father dies, when he never was a father at all but an imitation at best? How can you love and respect a man who ordered people killed as easily as he ordered dinner in a restaurant? You pretend, I guess. Pretend, and when that man dies, you mourn what should've been . . . what you wish could've been, not what actually was.

Stefan had said he'd never killed anyone in the mob and I believed him, but if it had come down to it . . . if it had been kill them to have the money to save me, I knew what his decision would've been. He would've killed his own soul for me. He thought that made him and Anatoly not so different. He was wrong. Anatoly had done it for the money and the power. Stefan would've done it to save me, because Anatoly wouldn't give him the money then to chase ghosts. To Anatoly, that was what I'd been. He'd given up on me when Stefan never had. No matter what Stefan thought, he was nothing like our father. And I only called Anatoly our father aloud and in my mind for Stefan.

Stefan had told me once that he didn't know that Anatoly didn't love his sons, because he didn't know for sure that he didn't. Murderers could love their own—couldn't they? I didn't know, and I didn't think Stefan knew for sure, but I agreed they could. It was what he had wanted to hear. That was something I'd learned on my own, not at the Institute.

"Stefan?"

He blinked at the sound of his name, his real name, and corrected me automatically—"Harry." Here we were Harry and Parker Alonzo, not Stefan and Michael Korsak. Stefan and Michael Korsak were on at least two kill lists. Fake names kept it that way, because you came off those kill lists only when you were dead. I'd picked the names . . . from another old movie, *Butch Cassidy and the Sundance Kid*. It was my favorite, though it was older than I was.

Stefan had snorted when I'd suggested it and promptly said that if I wanted to call myself Sundance, he supported my bold and very personal decision.

I'd called him an ass, another curse word I'd learned to use, and gave him Harry. It was Sundance's real name and I used Parker, Butch's last name. He was the smart one after all, I'd told my brother smugly, although I wasn't being too bright right now. Harry was also the name of Stefan's horse that was shot and killed on the beach the day I was taken by the Institute. I thought that might bother him, but he'd said no . . . that we leave memorials scattered through our lives in different ways. Gravestones were frozen in time, but memories you could take with you anywhere. Names too—you could keep them with you always. He hadn't thought Harry would mind.

"Harry," I corrected myself with my frown returning, this one directed at my own forgetfulness. I was better than that and had been trained to be exceptional in all areas of deception. I wasn't being exceptional now. "We should go home. I'll tell Mrs. Sloot that a pipe burst. It's flooding the bathroom. You have to go home and fix it." I turned to go inside the house, but then I hesitated long enough to say over my shoulder, "I'm . . . as I said—I didn't think . . . I'm sorry." It was the most awkward handful of words to come out of my mouth probably ever. It was self-conscious and tongue-tied five times over, but it seemed to mean something to Stefan. The darkness in his eyes lightened a little.

He cleared his throat and replied, "Thanks, but he was your father too, even if you don't remember."

I nodded silently and went on into the big house with trim the color of half-fresh mint green and half-faded lavender. As I did, I heard the lid being hammered back onto the paint can. Anatoly was gone and there was Stefan covered with paint, doing a job his father would've had hired someone to in turn hire someone else to actually do. If it didn't involve a gun or a knife, manual labor was far beneath him, I imagined. But he was the man who'd bought Stefan his first bike or at least had been the one to give it to him after having his own handyman put it together. Stefan had mentioned the bike. Anatoly probably wasn't there for school things . . . whatever school things there were— plays or football. But he'd been there for Christmases, Thanksgivings, birthdays, at least half the nights of the week. I'd seen the pictures when recuperating in South Carolina. I doubt he'd hugged Stefan much, though, except when he was younger than three. A web strung together from what Stefan had told me and what logic trumped. That was what I thought and with years of being near the top of my class in psychological training, and, with a failing grade being a failure at survival, I thought I guessed right.

Stefan had once said Anatoly thought I'd hung the sun and the moon—that I was special. I honestly didn't care what Anatoly had thought about long-ago Lukas. Contrary to popular belief, it isn't the thought that counts. What did count was a rescue ten years later by a brother who had refused to give up.

I knocked on the door to the house and as the sign, painted in loops and whirls with tulips and roses, told me to, I went on inside. There, Mrs. Sloot—"Adelaide, sweetie. Call me Adelaide"—tried to stuff me with sugar cookies. "Such a skinny boy." I might be almost six feet, but I didn't look nineteen. Seventeen was the best I could hope for, but I could've looked fifty and still had grandmotherly women trying to shove food down me. It happened all the time.

I learned to live with it, take the cookies, and be grateful I was too old for them to pinch my cheek—although the lady in one of the tourist shops in town had, only a different cheek. I hadn't told Stefan. He would either laugh or break her arm, and arm breaking wasn't part of the whole lying low thing. "Yes, Miss Adelaide, water's everywhere. Harry's going home to fix it."

Her poodle jumped at my feet, then nipped me on the ankle as she *tsk*ed about our bad luck and gave me another cookie. "Oh, Parker, sweetie, look at my new tchotchke. I know you like animals. Sookie-Sue loves you. You'll think it's cute as can be." I did like animals and Sookie-Sue was the first one to not like me back, but. . . .

It was too late. She'd shoved a small statue into my hand. It was an armadillo, I guessed dubiously, dressed like a clown, with a happy pointy smile, soulless red eyes, and balloons held in a gloved hand. It was the ugliest thing I'd ever seen. "It's nice," I lied effortlessly. I hadn't been an enthusiastic student at the Institute, but I had been a good one. Sookie-Sue nipped me again. I sighed patiently, but I did like all animals, including the ones that made it a challenge, and I didn't nudge her away. "What is it?"

Adelaide pursed her lips, coated with bright orange-red lipstick to match her hair, and her drawn-on eyebrows arched. "I told you, dear: it's a tchotchke."

My own eyebrows, and I actually had some, went up at the answer.

She scooped up Sookie-Sue. "Teenagers these days. Don't know a thing. A gewgaw, knickknack, bit of frou-frou."

Stefan's hand landed on my shoulder and he said with the friendly handyman's persona he'd perfected, "Useless dust collector, Park. Don't you start collecting 'em."

"Ah." I handed it back to her with as much care as I would for something not nearly as hideous and worthless and corrected my mental file of Adelaide Thomasina Sloot from mostly harmless with three unpaid parking tickets to bizarre, dusty, possible automotive maniac, with the 'harmless' designation to definitely be reevaluated at a later date.

Background checks were useless if you didn't update them frequently.

"Let's go home and get that mess cleaned up." Stefan steered me toward the door.

My mess. It wasn't all over the bathroom floor, but it was all over just the same. All that training . . . I wonder if the Institute knew how unreliable it was. Sometimes it worked and sometimes it didn't, and you never were quite sure which would be which. The Institute's students didn't fit in, no matter how many classes they gave us. We couldn't always act like normal people. We could manipulate them, but not act like them . . . not *be* normal people. Of all the training they'd given us, in the end we were good for only one thing; we could excel at only one thing over those normal people.

Killing them.

Chapter 2

"Michael."

The classroom was gray. Everything was gray at the Institute. There were no windows in the room. There were thirteen students, including two more Michaels—Michael Two and Michael Four. But I was the first Michael. I didn't need a numbered designation. Our creator, Jericho—that was what he called himself—our creator, had thought it humorous to name us after the lost children of Peter Pan. In the story, Michael, Peter, Lily, and Wendy hadn't been among the lost. In the Institute they were. Every child here was as lost as he could possibly be.

"Yes, Instructor," I said promptly. You were always quick and you always performed above average or you wouldn't be around much longer to fail at both of those things.

"Name the proper technique for avoiding suspicion in scenario twenty-seven."

Scenario twenty-seven was smiling wide and shaking the hand of the president like a good Boy Scout, essay-writer, or boy who'd saved the lives of a burning preschool full of babies. Whatever story it took to get you within touching distance of a man someone, it didn't matter who, wanted to die. "After inducing a fatal heart attack or aneurysm, he falls, and I cry and ask for my mother."

"Mommy. At your age, you ask for your mommy," the Instructor corrected me.

I nodded. "Yes, Instructor. I ask for my mommy."

My hands were folded and the desk was cool under my skin. I was eight or close to eight. I didn't know for sure. I'd say young, but there was no such thing as young at the Institute. I had no idea what an eight-year-old in the outside world would do after killing a head of state, but the Instructors told us what to do, how to emotionally manipulate, how to imitate the real thing—a genuine person. Imitation—it was what the best predators did. The biology Instructor told us that.

It would turn out that nothing they'd taught us had been as effective as they'd thought. Killing they hadn't had to teach us. Killing had been stamped on our genes. Killing was as easy as breathing.

Being human was a hundred times harder.

"Misha?"

Misha, the Russian nickname for Michael, was my real-life name, no matter how much I sucked at real life today. Actually, Lukas was my birth name, but I didn't remember it. Since I had lived with the name Michael for all the time I did remember, Lukas was one thing too many when Stefan had shown up. I'd been rescued, dragged into a world that I didn't know from true experience but only through books, movies, and field trips. I'd been told I had a brother . . . every second there had been something new, something strange, something frightening. And although a monster had given me the name Michael, it was the only familiar thing I'd had then—on the run as I was. I was stubborn and kept it, like a security blanket. Stefan had seen I'd needed it and had gone along. Lukas's memories were gone. In the time since my brother had found me, I hadn't gotten a single one of those memories back, so Lukas himself was basically gone. I did my best to make sure Michael was the next best thing.

Stefan had started his pickup truck, ladder and paint loaded in the back, but he hadn't pulled out of the driveway yet. His hand was on my shoulder, giving me a light shake. I left the Institute and came back to the here and now, almost as emotionally lost as I'd been then. "I'm sorry," I said. "I should've known you wouldn't have seen the news. I shouldn't have thought you'd be keeping it to yourself . . . I should've thought and not thought a lot of things." I managed to shut up and dive for the glove compartment.

Since Stefan had brought me out of Willy Wonka's Assassin Factory, as his friend Saul called it, he'd always stocked the cars and trucks we owned with Three Musketeers. He'd said they were my favorite before I'd been snatched and they were my favorite now—a seven-year hole in my memories didn't make a difference there.

Comfort food was always comfort food. That was one of the first things Stefan taught me and, unlike the teachings of my old instructors, his lessons were always right and true. I held on to the candy bar and felt the chocolate and filler squash under my fingers. "I'm sorry.

I screwed up. He was your father. I don't remember him being my father, but he was yours and I'm sorry."

"He was, but you're my brother." He wrapped his arm around my neck and pulled me close enough to rest his forehead against mine. After all this time, I still felt a knee-jerk reaction to tense up, but I didn't. Stefan had taught me I didn't need to and if I did, it would make him feel like shit. I wasn't going to do that.

"Some family you're born with," he said, "and some family you're goddamn lucky to have. You'd better know which one you are. Got it? And you didn't screw up. Burning down our garage, now that was a screwup, but this . . . this is just family shit. Nobody gets that off the bat and it's always messy." He bumped his head against mine, a light knock for every word. "You . . . did . . . not . . . screw . . . up."

"Burning down the garage was a possible side effect of my experiment. An acceptable risk," I muttered, trying to sound annoyed and failing, before straightening to hand him the Three Musketeers. "Comfort food," I explained.

He accepted it and curled his lips. "You're a good kid, Misha. The goddamn best."

I could've said, again, that I wasn't a kid, but this time I was a little smarter and kept my mouth shut.

And I didn't burn down the garage—only half of it. Big brothers—they couldn't let the little things go. I almost managed to smile to myself at the thought. Life I might not ever get a handle on, but the brother thing— that I would. I refused to believe anything else.

*   *   *

People are strange.

That's a polite way of saying people are nosy, snoop-
ing, and meddling. I didn't consider myself those
things merely because I'd used the Internet to gather a
file on every citizen in town. It was a small town, so it
didn't take long, and I had an excuse. It was a good
excuse. People wanted to kill me.

Other people though, those without targets on their
backs, they didn't have that justification for their why,
where, who, when, what, and on and on. Stefan had
rented the small house on Fox Creek Road because it
would be hard to explain how a handyman could buy
it outright and worse trying to pretend we needed a
mortgage. Saul Skoczinsky in Miami, Stefan's link to
all things convenient and criminal, sent us good fake
IDs. I'd since learned to make better, but banks like
their background checks as much as I did. It was best
to just rent the run-down ranch house with no neighbors in sight, but that didn't stop our landlady—
Adelaide Sloot's doppelganger, only with bleached-
blond hair—from asking where we were from. Why
had we moved? How old was I, because Cascade Falls
had a wooooonderful high school. There had been so
many o's in that "wonderful," I automatically knew
she had a relative who taught there, a grandchild who
went there, or received a commission for every teen
she scooped up and dragged clawing through their
doors.

That was one subject the Institute had been somewhat dead-on about: psychology. People walked
around turned inside out. If you knew enough to look,
everything you wanted to know about them was there

to see—things you didn't want to know too. The way she clutched Stefan's arm and hung on every word of his made-up story; the way her eyes didn't leave his, not once, as she led us through the house on the showing. She'd lost someone who looked like my brother. Maybe they had just had dark hair and an olive complexion, maybe only the brown eyes. They might have died or left her just because people leave. If Stefan had wanted, he could've gotten her to rent the place to us for half or maybe a third the price. He could've used the woman's loss, as I'd been taught to use weakness against others. But he didn't.

Mr. Ex-Mob paid full price and even painted the place, because it could use it. Patches were peeling off everywhere. I called it the Leprosy House until he finished painting it yellow—yellow paint was on sale that week. Then I called it the Bumblebee House and eventually the Bumble for short. "Are we going back to the Bumble for dinner?" On the inside, I called it home, but home was another word that made the universe notice and then crush you. There was no saying that aloud either—no tempting fate.

When we pulled up out front on the patch of gravel that was the driveway, Stefan passed through the door first. If we were together, he always did—a somewhat less than bulletproof vest. He was my own Secret Service, only without the cool wardrobe.

Inside, Stefan went straight to the kitchen table where my laptop was and opened it up as he sat down more heavily than usual. It would be quicker than finding the story on the television. His voice was heavier too. "Any best site or should I just Google 'dead dad'?"

I was surprised those words didn't fall out of the air to scuff the well-worn tile of the floor.

I exhaled and reached around him to type in the most informative news site. "Was that a joke?" I asked uncertainly. I didn't always get jokes, especially dark or grim ones. And just when I would think I was getting better at playing human if not actually getting back to being human, I fell flat on my face. Stefan reached over and took my arm and pulled me down into the chair next to his. The table was round and covered with scratches. I wished I could've looked at them instead of Stefan. He didn't look twenty-seven now. He looked fifteen years older and as tired as if he'd been up for days. If I'd not jumped to conclusions, if I'd figured things out, and told him better, told him right, he wouldn't look like this. He would look better and feel better, because I would've done better.

For a brief second I wished I'd done more to that asshole of a tourist, because then I might have felt better, stronger, more able to cope. But that was wrong, more than wrong, and I knew it. It didn't change the feeling, however. It did manage to add to the guilt, though. Wonderful.

"It was a joke," he said, squeezing my arm lightly. "A very bad gallows humor joke, and I'm sorry I made it. In my former line of business, it was the only humor we had. Not-so-good humor for not-so-good people. Smack me if I do it again." He squeezed again, then let go to start typing and then to read, eyes staring unblinking at the screen.

As he did, Godzilla came slinking across the living

room floor and climbed my leg to perch in my lap and rest his chin on the table. All those scratches on the wood were from him, but there was no food there now, which meant he had no interest. I stroked his back with one finger; he made a contented *mrrrp* sound and casually gnawed the edge of the table with his sharp teeth. Stefan pretended to only tolerate the ferret. Hmm, that wasn't quite right. Stefan did only tolerate Godzilla, calling him a stinky psychopathic carpet shark, but he did tolerate him for my sake and that said more than if he'd genuinely liked him.

Godzilla, naturally, didn't care if Stefan liked him or not. Neither did Mothra, the blue jay with the broken wing, or Gamera the snapping turtle that was so old he might have been here before the town itself had been founded. Mothra pecked Stefan's head if he went too close to the storeroom, which Mothra had claimed as his own, and Gamera, who I would have thought was too ancient to be aware of people or his surroundings, slept in Stefan's closet and snapped at him every day when he reached for his shoes.

Stefan would glare at me, mutter, but finally nurse his sore finger and say, "Maybe you'll be a vet." He thought I was trying to make up for the lab animals I'd been ordered to kill in the Institute to hone the skills they'd forced on us, and I was . . . in the only way I could. Fixing up strays right and left, saving lives to make up for the ones I'd been compelled to take. As if you could ever make up for even a single life you'd snatched away . . . but I tried, knowing it wasn't good enough. It wouldn't ever be good enough; yet it was all I could do.

But that wasn't my only reason for the animals . . . for playing doctor. No, not by a long shot.

Sometimes being smart wasn't enough. You had to be smarter.

You had to be better.

You had to evolve.

Sometimes you had to be the very best or your days on the run would be short. My time with Stefan was the only real life I'd known, but I wanted more, and to get that, I would do what I had to. The animals were part of that—a huge part.

Maybe later, if I had a chance, I would be a vet. Animals had ulterior motives, same as people, but theirs were much easier to understand. "Misha? You might want to go to your room or outside while I read this." Stefan's grin was long gone and his face . . . I didn't want to say what I saw on his face, so I was a coward and I went outside with Godzilla draped around my neck. I'd watched the news piece on Anatoly. He hadn't died quickly or painlessly, from what the autopsy had said. The saw marks on his bone had been made before he died. That said more than enough. The time we'd spent in South Carolina—the few months I'd known him while Stefan and I recovered from gunshot wounds—he'd looked so much like Stefan. Bad father, bad human being; it didn't matter. He had saved us both by shooting Jericho. More important, he had saved my brother. I didn't want to see his fate when it was reflected in Stefan's face—a younger mirror of Anatoly—so I left.

Outside, I sat on the small front porch, cracked as it was and tilting, and looked at the trees across the road.

They were soothing. Green green green. Nothing but green. Green was my second-favorite color.

Years ago I'd been asked that question.

"What is your favorite color?"

The Institute wasn't a school, not the kind most people knew about, and Dr. John Jericho Hooker wasn't an instructor. I hadn't doubted then that he was our creator. Now maybe I thought he was part creator of some, corrupter of others—like me—but in the end it didn't matter. He'd been the most frightening son of a bitch on the face of the earth. Cursing was automatic at that memory. When Jericho asked you to do something, you did it. When he asked you a question, you answered it. Years ago in that prison, Jericho had asked me my favorite color.

I'd thought carefully. This was a year or so after the question of the Instructor on what to do when I killed a president. I couldn't see how giving my true feelings could hurt in this one case. "Blue." The blue of sky, the blue of ocean. The blue of my dreams.

Jericho's ebony eyes stared unblinking at me. His prosthetic hand, replacing the one taken by one of his students—one of his creations who was much braver than I'd been in those days—rested on his desk. "What is your favorite color?"

I'd shown no fear. Those who showed fear were weak, and the weak did not often "graduate" from the Institute, although they did graduate from life . . . early. I thought again. I'd seen the movies, the books. I'd seen the trees and the grass on the screen and in the pictures. "Green."

Those frozen artificial fingers clicked against the top

of the desk and the eyes narrowed. "Michael, what is your favorite color?"

Third time was the charm. I'd read that before in those same books. But third time was never the charm here. That I was offered a third time was beyond the best I could've hoped for. Yet here it was, my third and last chance.

It was so simple. I couldn't believe I'd been fooled twice before. I knew the answer—the right one this time. I knew what he wanted to hear. "I don't have a favorite color."

"Good. You're learning. You have no thoughts but the ones I give you. Do not forget that." His lips curved, the creator pleased that his experiment had performed adequately. That was what I was—an experiment; less than human, different from human, but made to be a reaper of them.

I was glad he was dead. If Stefan's father had ever done anything right, it was in killing Jericho. Franken-stein had died on a beach like the one where I had been ripped from the real world. It didn't get any more fit-ting than that.

It was a story I hadn't made Stefan repeat time and time again, as much as I wanted to in an effort to get back those vanished memories. He told it once, and once was enough. He'd . . . fractured when he'd told me, like winter ice cracked and shattered by the first warm spring day. It was days before he was back to his usual self. How could I ask again? I'd memorized what he'd said, though, the whole thing and the bits and pieces added throughout the next few years, of what my life had been before the Institute. Anatoly had been big in the *Mafiya*. He and his wife, Anya, had emigrated from Russia and we were born here. Anatoly had brought the mob with him or the mob had brought him, but whichever, their children had lived a privileged life. When Lukas—I could think of that long-ago child only as Lukas, not me—was seven and Stefan was fourteen, they'd lived in a big house on a private beach near Miami. They'd been given horses for their Christmas presents and when the adult all-day Christmas party started, they'd taken those horses and gone to that beach to race the wind.

He said it was his idea . . . as if that made it his fault. A fourteen-year-old kid wanting to ride horses on the beach with his brother and he said it as if it were a capital crime. Whatever he'd said, it had probably been my—Lukas's—idea—a big adventure to a seven-year-old. It didn't make it my fault either. It was only Jericho's fault. He made killers out of chimeras and that was what I was—a chimera.

Chimeras started out as twins in utero, but then something would go wrong and one embryo would absorb the other. If you were fraternal twins, you could end up with two sets of separate DNA. Human squared. It didn't mean anything, normally; you just had two sets of DNA, not comic book superpowers. That was true until Jericho came along and made a difference that nature had never intended.

Stefan said he didn't know how he found out about Lukas—through hospital records most likely; blood tests from his birth—but he had found out and he'd come for his chimera. The surprising part, unbelievable in a way, was he'd waited so long before adding a new one to his collection of other children, the majority of whom had been fetuses implanted in surrogate mothers for pay—drug-addicted and hopeless people no one would miss when they didn't show up again. Marcus Bellucci, the man we'd thought was his academic rival, had told us that. He hadn't been a rival, though, or the fountain of information we'd thought he'd been; he'd been a combination of silent partner and silent alarm. He'd warned Jericho when we'd tracked him down and shown up asking questions; then when Jericho died, he'd disappeared.

The Institute had to have a creator.

The Institute was still out there and we knew where. We hadn't forgotten those left behind. Ten years or the seventeen it had felt like, I wouldn't leave anyone there to be discarded if the twisting and brainwashing didn't take hold. And the brainwashed needed to be saved as much as the potentially expendable who fought it off. Nearly three years later we hadn't made a move to save anyone yet, because what do you do with the brainwashed?

Not all of the students were like me. I'd hated what I could do. Not all others had. What do you do with genetically manipulated killers who have been taught to enjoy killing? When they'd as soon kill you as take your hand to be rescued. . . .

What do you do?

Godzilla *mrrrp*ed again and then bit my thumb for attention. I sucked the blood away, then watched as the puncture clotted immediately. In less than a half hour it would be gone. We healed quickly, Jericho's children—a much better talent than killing. I rubbed the ferret's head with the fingers of my other hand. With just that touch and a thought, I could've shut down the vessels to his heart, his brain. Or I could've opened them so wide that there wouldn't be enough blood pressure to keep his heart beating. I could've weakened the walls of his organs until they ripped open, or could have caused them to literally explode. Only a touch and a thought. That was what Jericho had made out of me . . . and every child in the Institute. I could kill but I couldn't undo a lifetime of conditioning with that same touch.

So what did you do to save those who didn't want to be saved?

It was a hard question and blind hope was not much of an answer. Neither was a leap of faith. Jericho's children weren't built for faith. Not that it mattered, because we *were* built for determination—success no matter the cost. "No weakness, no limitations, no mercy" was the credo we repeated aloud at the beginning of every single class.

No weakness. No limitations. No mercy.

That, not that it was meant to, was going to help me now, because despite those who might not want to be saved, there was a way, whether they knew it or not. Look at me.

I was saved.

I was smart.

And I was working on it.

Not a born killer, but an engineered one. Taken. Rebuilt. Changed. That was what Stefan knew had happened to me. I'd wondered what Stefan would be if his brother hadn't been kidnapped. I didn't wonder the same thing at all about me, because it was beyond imagination. I couldn't picture it or fantasize about it. It was impossible, and it was for the best, I thought. If I could have dreamed up an alternative to the life that I had lived under Jericho, the memories of the Institute would've done what it couldn't do now—crush me.

Godzilla wrapped around my arm and sniffled, puzzled, for the vanished blood from where he'd bitten me. Like me, he had a bit of a killer in him. When Stefan found that out, about the Michael Korsak compared to the Lukas Korsak—the killer part of me, when he'd found out what I was—he hadn't been afraid of me or what I could do. Not for a moment. I would've known it if he had; I'd have seen it on his face . . . in his eyes, but I'd seen nothing but acceptance. To him I wasn't an assassin-in-training or a human bullet all the way down to the genetic level. I was his brother, pure and simple, and nothing else made a difference.

He'd actually been a little exasperated that I wouldn't use what I had in me to protect myself. The drunk outside the bakery was one thing. But when someone attacked me with every intent of murdering me or, worse, taking me back to the Institute, it wasn't the same. With that kind of adrenaline running through me, starting something was easy. Stopping it wouldn't be. Stopping it could be impossible.

It had happened once, before Stefan pulled me out of the Institute. As a test—to them it had been only another test—a guard had been sent to kill me. Instead, I had been the one to kill . . . if only once. Wasn't once far more than enough? It wasn't going to happen again.

Jericho had changed me in biological ways, but I wouldn't give his dead corpse the satisfaction of ever having changed who I was as a person. He gave me the genetic skills to be a psychic executioner, but that didn't mean I had to use them. And, as far as I was concerned, he could rot in his grave for eternity before I became the assassin he wanted.

"Hey, kid." Stefan sat beside me on the porch. "Have a Fluffernut sandwich."

He handed me one of the two I'd made for him that morning. I took it out of the plastic sandwich bag and fed a bite to the ferret. The kid issue I simply gave up on for the day. I was nineteen for God's sake, nineteen and made to kill, but when it came to Stefan, I wasn't sure he'd let himself ever see me as anything but a little brother. "Do you know what happened . . . to Anatoly?" I should've phrased it better. I knew very well what had happened. According to the news report, someone had taken an electric saw to various parts of him. If Anatoly had been alive, and he most likely had been, since the saw had probably been just an interrogation tool, he'd most likely considered anything that happened besides that as merely incidental.

Stefan knew what I meant, though. "No. No idea who snatched him. *Mafiya* or the Institute trying to track us down." By "us," he meant me, but it was nice of him to spread the blame around. "It wasn't the FBI. They wanted him the most, but, despite Gitmo, no one at the government's using power saws to get info." He

fed a bite of his own sandwich to Godzilla too. A first—
but it was hard to have an appetite when someone had
cut up your father with the equivalent of a chain saw
while he was still alive.

He cleared his throat. His voice had gotten thick on
the word "saw." "But he couldn't have given us up.
Just as when he was on the run from the FBI and
wouldn't tell me where he was . . . for my own good."
The smile was both hard and regretful. "I didn't tell
him where you and I were. I was more honest, though.
I told him it was for our own good, and it turned out I
was right."

"The saw makes me think the mob. There were several *vors*"—mob bosses—"who'd lost a helluva lot of
their territory and power if Anatoly had come back.
And that place you were . . ." He hardly ever said "Institute." It was worse than the foulest word out there
for him, from the way he acted. He went on. "It doesn't
seem their style. Torture, yeah, but not with something
you could buy at Home Depot. More something scientific and a damn sight worse probably."

He offered another bite to Godzilla, who considered
him and this gesture of goodwill with bright black eyes
before biting Stefan's forefinger and taking the morsel
of sandwich. He purred contentedly as he ate the
slightly bloodstained bread and peanut butter. I
plopped the ferret on the other side of me, but Stefan
didn't seem to notice the slow drops of blood hitting
the concrete, scarlet on gray, like the sun setting into a
cloud-shrouded, tornado-spawning storm.

I had a feeling that one way or another what had
happened to Anatoly would start that storm.

"I called Saul. He's on some tantric sex yoga retreat or something. Trying to keep up with some women twenty years younger than him," Stefan said with a darkly amused twist of his lips. "Not that that would have him disconnecting from the outside world and the money that goes with it. He didn't know anything more than we did, but he's looking into it—if he can untangle himself from whatever knot he's tied himself into. Probably has his foot stuck up his own. . . ." He coughed and ate a bite of the sandwich.

I narrowed my eyes. "*Nineteen*—Jesus, going on twenty. I know about sex, tantric and otherwise."

He shrugged and swallowed the bite. "Face it, Michael. In some ways you'll always be the little brother." His words echoed what I'd thought only seconds ago.

In some ways, always the little brother. In some ways, always seven years old and laughing on a beach. I didn't need any psych class flashbacks to the Institute to know that wasn't healthy for either of us. But before I could say anything, Sheriff Kash Simmons drove up in front of the house. The first time I met him, he'd shaken my hand solemnly and said his name was Kash for Johnny Cash and it was my privilege to call him sir. What it was about this town that accounted for no one being able to spell their own names was going to have to remain a mystery, but why the sheriff was idling his gold and brown official car in front of our happy yellow house wasn't one. The blobby tourist was in the back pointing at me, his mouth moving a mile a minute.

Sheriff Simmons turned off the car and stepped out,

giving that same automatic hitch to his belt that all law-givers in every movie or every TV show did. He had the Stetson, the shades; it was like one of those hyper-realistic video games. Was the Law here to kick ass and take names? No. They didn't need any names—just more ass to kick. I'd learned a lot of slang and cursing from certain games. But when I'd earned points from accidentally backing over a prostitute, I decided to take all of the experience with a grain of salt.

When we'd first come to town, Stefan had laid down certain rules and sayings for keeping me safe. One of them had been regarding the cops, two total, in Cascade Falls. He told me, "No matter what you do, Misha, no matter absolutely fucking what. . . ." I'd waited for the epic brotherly promise, *Dead or alive, I will come for you. I will save you. If I have to claw myself out of my own grave, I will save you.* Something like that. I watched a lot of movies, owned a lot of movies. Hundreds. Maybe that was too many, but they did give me great expectations.

What Stefan had actually said had been, "No matter what you do, Misha, no matter absolutely fucking what . . . we can always get bail in this podunk town. So don't sweat it."

It was good advice, straight from his mob days.

I'd been a little disappointed. There was a certain lack of *No matter what, I will find you!* or *They can take our land, but they can never take our liberty!* Movies do leave you with certain anticipations in some instances. He'd more than made up for it back in Bolivia when he'd told me that if anyone in a uniform grabbed me, I was to kill every last motherfucker wearing one and run for my life. He'd been less concerned with the conse-

quences to my morals than to the consequences to my
physical body I carried them around in. And logically
he'd been right.

But I wouldn't have done it, and he knew that too.
That was the reason it was a long time before I was able
to go anywhere by myself. He'd been my shadow until
Cascade Falls, which he eventually deemed safe enough
for me.

My background checks on every citizen and the
homeless man who lived down by the river with his
dog helped. I also got a background on the dog, whom
I took a can of Alpo to every day. He was a nice dog.
His name was Ralphy, obtained at the pound two coun-
ties over—mixed breed, neutered, approximately five
years old, and he smelled, but none of us are perfect.
This was true of background checks too—they were effective when it came to dogs but useless when it came
to tourists. There were too many, too little warning, and
not enough time.

Now, here we were . . . about to find out if he'd been
right about that bail.

Stefan stayed sitting, and I stood, looking innocent
as a lamb—I knew I did as I'd practiced that expression
in the mirror many times too. I'd had to. Innocence
hadn't come as easily as the coffeehouse employee-of-
the-month expression. Innocence took a great deal of
work; it was something no student from the Institute
could ever claim. The tourist got out of the car behind
the sheriff, his mouth moving. "It had to be that punk.
He put something in my coffee. He's been giving me
attitude the whole week. Little bastard probably tried
to poison me."

People—always jumping to the wrong conclusions. Okay, jumping to the wrong methods. And I hadn't hurt him. I hadn't. I had inconvenienced him, but I hadn't hurt him. It was an important distinction. I . . . had . . . not . . . hurt . . . him.

Whether he deserved it or not.

Sheriff Simmons hefted his belt again with one hand and rubbed his mustache with the other. He was young for a sheriff. The mustache, skimpy at best, was over-compensation. He didn't appear that concerned, however, which was good. I could all but see the thought running through his mind: Of course mild-mannered, well-behaved Parker Alonzo hadn't poisoned this whiny-ass tourist and if I had, maybe I deserved a medal. But he had a job to do or at least go through the motions of doing.

"This fella—excuse me, sir—Mr. Mitchell says he became violently ill after drinking the coffee you served him, Parker." The sheriff yawned and continued to question me in a tone more bored than any that could be found in the world. "That's not so, is it, Parker? You trying to poison this fella? Mr. Mitchell, I mean."

"No, Sheriff, sir," I said, shocked—terribly shocked. Goodhearted Parker whom every parent in town knew and wished their kids were like? Never. "I was walking down the sidewalk to take Stefan his lunch when this guy started yelling at me. I didn't want to get into trouble, and I was kind of worried, you know. Sort of. He's twice my size." Three times was more like it, but I was playing nice, although too little, too late. That slippery slope had me now, but I kept the teenage talk flowing. "I kept going, but, like, I could smell the alcohol on him. I hate to say it . . . er . . . sir," I added earnestly. Hand to God and light a candle for the tourist's alcoholic soul, I was that earnest. "But I did. He smelled like Old Bob down at the river."

"*Bullshit.*" Mitchell, the tourist—with vomit fumes instead of alcohol now, snarled. "I wasn't drunk." Which could be true. He could've only been buzzed? . . . Yes, buzzed was what they called it. "And I grabbed the spiteful little shit. Shook him good. You be rude to me, that's what you get. And then he told me—"

Stefan cut him off. "You touched my brother?" The sheriff's car hadn't gotten him standing, but that did. "You grabbed him? You *shook* him?" I slanted a glance to see Stefan's eyes go that wolf amber . . . slits of pale brutal brown. "You called him names that I'll bet your mother should've put on your birth certificate? Is that what you did, shithead?" He seemed to get bigger somehow. "Well? Is it?"

Before the sheriff's sunglasses had a chance to slide down his nose more than a fraction at "Harry's" sudden change of temperament, Stefan was punching the tourist in the nose, which resulted in an explosion of blood. He then aimed the same fist at the man's oversized gut, causing yet another episode of vomiting, which he had to be tired of by now—before waiting until the man dropped to the ground and following up with a hard, solid kick to the ribs.

I looked up to see Sheriff Simmons peering over the top of his reflective glasses, his eyebrows raised. He didn't reach for his gun or move. He didn't look wary . . . but he should have. He was seeing Stefan, the real Stefan for the first time. Harry, the gingerbread-

painting, fence-repairing, gutter-cleaning, toss-back-a-
beer-on-Friday-nights-at-the-local-bar-and-talk-
football, all-around laid-back guy, had just added ass
kicking to his resume. And not ordinary ass kicking. In
the split second of speed and very purposeful brutality,
the sheriff had seen Stefan Korsak of the *Mafiya*. He'd
seen the man who hadn't wanted to choose a life of
violence, but when he had, he'd made sure he was extremely good at it.

What he'd done in that second was only a fraction of
what he could do. But then he remembered he wasn't
Stefan here. He blinked, and the bared teeth and wolf
eyes were gone and he was Happy Harry again—the
gingerbread man. "My old man was in the marines."
He gave a sheepish shrug but didn't back down. "He
taught me a thing or two. He also taught me you don't
pick on kids or family. This guy did both."

"And I think he'll regret that—once he stops puking." The sheriff pushed up his sunglasses and let it
go—what he'd seen and what he had to suspect, because it had turned out a few weeks ago that Stefan
was right.

In Cascade Falls you could get bail for anything.

Two weeks ago, Stefan had gotten in a bar fight on
his usual have-to-be-ordinary-to-fit-in-Friday routine.
I'd told him that wasn't the way to avoid notice, the
same thing he was always telling me to do. But he'd
shrugged and said, "It was the whole damn bar going
at it. If I hadn't swung back when that guy punched
me, I would've stood out. Exception that proves the
rule." The bail had been only five hundred dollars.
When I'd paid it and picked him up, he'd shrugged,

wadded up the receipt, and tossed it in the backseat. "'Harry Alonzo' now has a record. Actually, that's my first time behind bars, believe it or not, which means no worry about comparing fingerprints," he'd said.

This time there was no bail. The folks of Cascade Falls liked their tourists for the most part. But they didn't like ones that messed with their citizens. The sheriff waited until the one on the ground stopped puking, handcuffed him, and shoved him into the back of the car. "Assaulting a minor is no way to spend your vacation, son." Before he pushed his sunglasses back up, he winked at me to let me know it was a good time to pretend to be as young as I looked—seventeen instead of the twenty I almost was. "You call us next time you have some out-of-towner giving you trouble, Parker. Harry," he said, tipping his hat, "nice moves. You done your daddy proud." Then he was in the car and gone.

Maybe he'd recognized one of his own—a soldier of sorts. Although, from the premature beer belly on Sheriff Simmons, it'd been a long time since he'd kicked anyone in the ribs, which was, if you thought about it, great cardiovascular exercise. I'd have to look into the sheriff again. I'd underestimated him and his skills, former or not. I was really beginning to lose faith in my background checks.

Stefan folded his arms. "If I had a woodshed you hadn't blown up, I'd take you behind it and beat some sense into you."

I didn't bother to roll my eyes, the threat not worthy of a response.

"Seriously, what did I tell you, Misha? Don't let anyone see what you can do. Although making that fat bastard puke his guts up in the street. . . ." He swallowed the grin that surfaced and went for a more somber tone. "If it's to save your life, do what you have to do. Absolutely anything you have to do. If it's just a jackass messing with you, come get me and I'll make him sorry his father bought that on-sale cheap-ass expired condom. But if it's not life or death, keep what you can do secret, okay? Or we'll have more than the *Mafiya* and that hellish place that took you after us."

I said pointedly, "Because pounding him to a pulp was much more subtle."

"No, but it's not science fiction, so do what I tell you, all right? Now, are you done testing those teenage boundaries? The ones you missed while you were under that bastard who took you? Get it all out of your system, defying the big brother?"

Yeah, my brother was smarter than I have given him credit for sometimes. In matters of emotion, he was five Mensa levels smarter than I was. "He was a dick," I said stubbornly.

"Michael, in life you'll discover there are a million times more dicks in the world than there are shitheads to fucking hang them on," he snorted. "It's not right. It's not fair, but we have to work around it. You keep your Superman powers out of sight and I'll beat the crap out of anyone who messes with my family. Illegal, sure, but not science fiction."

Superman . . . that was so far off base, I didn't bother to go there. Like any other nineteen-year-old, I wanted to take care of myself. But unlike any other nineteen-year-old, I *could* take care of myself. I could take care of myself in a way that could leave the streets littered with bodies. My brother was right. He usually was. And like any other nineteen-year-old, that made me sulk for a while.

But, hey, the word "dick" had come to me naturally. That was something.

Chapter 3

"**Y**ou be kind to Stefan. He deserves that."

"Kind" was an odd word to come from a man who may have killed as many as the man who'd kidnapped his son, but he'd meant it. It was the only thing he'd meant as he'd talked to me the time when both Stefan and I had been shot by Jericho and his men. I was different then . . . and now. . . . I'd healed much faster than Stefan, although I'd been shot in the chest and he'd been shot in the leg. The bullet had broken his thighbone, which caused him to limp in cold weather. Me? Who they'd thought would die long before the AMA-booted doctor would show up? I barely had a scar.

It had been when I'd been closer to healthy and whole and Stefan knocked out on pain meds in that South Carolina safe house that Anatoly had said that to me.

"Be kind to Stefan. He deserves that."

He'd been right and I hadn't had to hear it from him. Stefan did deserve it. Stefan hadn't given up on his brother—he had saved me, and he didn't lie to me. Anatoly had done none of those things. He never even said my name, either of them, not Lukas or the "Michael" the Institute had given me. He'd been polite, for a killer, but weren't we all killers in that beach house/ makeshift hospital? Stefan had said that Anatoly was my father, but I hadn't trusted the older man for a second.

Now, though, looking at what was left of him on my computer screen, I wished I'd tried to find out more of who'd been behind the killer. Was there more to him? I'd had the skills at reading people, same as now, but I hadn't used them. Everything, the entire world, was so damn new then that Stefan was all I needed and all I could handle. I didn't want or need a father, I'd thought at the time, especially one who'd given up on me.

"Be kind to Stefan." I remembered those words.

I looked at the bones and chunks of decomposed flesh on the screen. He'd been in a lake. Lake Michigan. Floaters aren't pretty and I honestly couldn't remember if I'd learned that at the Institute or on one of the thousand TV cop shows since. Wherever I'd heard it, it was right. He was roadkill marinated in a swampy Everglades ditch. He was in pieces and the pieces didn't fit together to make anything that looked human. They'd identified him by dental records. I clicked on the next picture. These weren't the kind available to your average Internet surfer, but I wasn't your average anything. If there was a place that cybertendrils didn't extend into, I hadn't found it yet. Chimeras were trained to fool people. I'd found that fooling machines was far easier. If there was a data stream, I rode it; a path of pixels, I walked it. I saw it all, saw through everything as if it were made of glass.

Not like Anatoly.

"Be kind to Stefan," he had said. He hadn't been

much of a human before or after he died, I'd thought, but he'd loved his son. He hadn't loved me; I could tell. I didn't read him, but I didn't have to search his face or catalog his movements and words to know that. Love is easy to see; no effort required. Other emotions took effort, but love was simple. I didn't know why he hadn't accepted me like Stefan had. Maybe I'd been gone too long. Maybe he'd wiped me out of his heart and mind. The reason didn't matter.

I did know it now, but it didn't matter. Anatoly had ceased to matter to existence itself.

I couldn't read him emotionally any better today than then—it was hard to read pieces. But I could read what had been done to him. Brutal, vicious, and messy, but effective. I could've done it more quickly and neatly, but there weren't many of my kind around. Others had to make do with chain saws. This hadn't been done for punishment or fun. It would've taken too long. Psychopaths, such as the *Mafiya*, as much as they liked chain saws, were generally into immediate gratification. This had been done methodically by someone looking for information.

I searched the screen. I'd seen Anatoly and what had been done to him. It was what was behind his tangible, rotting memory that I'd noticed: a man. He was in all the pictures. In the ones where they'd pulled Anatoly's remains from the lake, loading him into the coroner's van, in the autopsy room—he was always there. The suit, short fringe of dark hair, opaque sunglasses, and inscrutable expression said government, but his dedication in following the body from place to place implied more dedication than FBI or IRS, the major bloodhounds on Anatoly's tail according to Stefan.

I clicked on the next picture and zoomed in on those deep-set black eyes in the one picture where he'd removed the glasses. Not entirely inscrutable. There was interest there, a deep and passionate desire. But for what? Anatoly was beyond indictment and prison. What was left that could be that fascinating?

The knock on my bedroom door had me automatically switching to another computer window. Stefan stuck his head in. He looked at the computer screen and groaned, appearing more than a little worried. "Again? Seriously, kiddo, you've got that live girl at the coffee shop made of mostly human parts, you've got porn at your fingertips, and you're wasting your time on that?"

I glanced at the Lolcats site. "There has to be a logic to it. It's idiotic, but people say it's funny. Unless all people are idiots, I'm missing something. I'm going to figure it out." It wasn't strictly a lie. It was not volunteering information and . . . waiting. And waiting wasn't wrong, not if you thought of it in the correct way. My mind was an Olympic gymnast at twisting and bending to see things in the manner that benefited me the most.

"Cats are intelligent." It was a diversion, but it was also true. "If they could talk, then I'm quite sure they could spell." My eyes were drawn back to the screen and the idiotic *U haz hareball on fut* under the picture of an evidently highly annoyed cat biting someone's ankle. There had to be something to it . . . but what in

God's name it was, I couldn't figure out. "Maybe their owners can't spell, but they could."

"Misha." His lips quirked. He was tired and darkness was in him, shadows filling up a flesh and blood pitcher. "Thanks for taking one of the more crappy days and making it better."

"By making a tourist vomit and giving you a chance to take out your frustrations by kicking him in the stomach?" I asked curiously, tearing my eyes away from the screen before it burned my retinas with its idiocy.

The grin was quick and fleeting, but it was there. "Don't do it again, but, yeah, I enjoyed it. I shouldn't have—a few of my old ways creeping back. But sometimes you need a distraction, and you, little brother, are always that. I needed it today. Now, get your ass off the computer and go to bed. It's past midnight and we both have to go back to work tomorrow as if nothing happened." Because as far as anyone knew, nothing had, but it didn't stop the darkness in him from beginning to overflow. He needed time to remember, time to put those memories in all those tiny boxes we have inside us. To put them away for another day—a day when they would be bearable again.

"Go." He pointed at my bed where Godzilla was curled up on my pillow. "And . . . thanks."

He closed my door. I didn't sleep, though Godzilla snored through a tiny deviated septum. I was nineteen and far beyond curfews and bedtimes, but Stefan's trying to take care of me made him feel better about Anatoly, so I didn't argue. I simply didn't obey, and by the morning I had more than enough reasons for Stefan to take back that thanks he'd given me.

I iz up shit crick, haz no paddle.

I now liked all animals except cats, which, if they'd allowed this travesty to go on, weren't as smart as I had thought they were. Kind of like me, I thought grimly before correcting myself. Self-blame, so sayeth Jericho, was destructive to the mission, any mission, including staying free and alive. I should've seen it sooner. I hadn't. It was time to move on to more constructive thoughts.

Stretching, I yawned, but only lightly. We healed faster, and as I got older, I started sleeping less too. Four hours were as good as eight to me. Less downtime, double the assassinations—Jericho had Walmart beat hands down for sales efficiency. I hadn't told Stefan yet about the change in my sleep patterns. I wanted to be as normal as possible in his eyes and with all the other genetic baggage I had, that was not easy. I got out the chair, showered, fed Godzilla, Gamera, and Mothra, and was waiting for Stefan in the kitchen with breakfast and a stack of pictures I'd printed off my computer.

He stopped in the doorway, which was also freshly painted—the mobster who'd traded his gun in for a paintbrush, or had switched hands with them anyway. Paint with the right, keep a weapon in your left. He didn't look much better than yesterday, especially with the addition of dark stubble that his scar ran through like a road to nowhere. "You cooked?" He rubbed the sleep crust from his eyes and took another look. "And it's healthy. That can't be good."

Cheese omelet with butter-fried potatoes, sausage,

toast, coffee, and orange juice. Compared to my usual chocolate chip pancakes or cinnamon-banana waffles, it was healthy. He sat down and started digging in, every fork stroke a testament to massively overacted resignation. "I'm rebuilding the garage, you know," he mumbled around a mouthful of food. "Poison ivy. Splinters. You couldn't have waited until winter to blow it up? When all the poison ivy, oak, and whatever else was dead?"

"You are such a drama queen," I said drily.

His eyebrows shot up and he almost choked on his eggs. "Sara at the coffee shop taught me that one," I explained. "It seems to fit."

"Glad you're picking up all the slang, but cut me some slack and at least give me drama king." He put down the fork and reached for the coffee. "Go on, spill. Let's get whatever it is out of the way. What could be worse than the garage, because I have houses to paint and you have tourists to *not* piss off today."

"Eat first," I ordered. He wouldn't feel like eating after, not for a while.

"Misha . . ."

"Eat." I folded my arms.

"Michael, I'm serious."

I looked up at the ceiling. There were cracks there. Three formed a completely perfect equilateral triangle. I'd measured it one day just to be sure. If there was a God, the bipolar one who was wrathful and vengeful in the Old Testament and raining fluffy kittens of love in the New Testament, it wouldn't be in the sky or the sea or the inexplicable saving of a life. It would be in a perfect, equal-sided triangle. God would be the uni-

verse; the universe is physics; physics is science. Therefore God would be science. I wondered if I could cut it
out of the ceiling and sell it on eBay. People did that
with tortillas all the time and you couldn't measure the
Madonna, Mother of God. I had proof. Surely that
would get me a higher price.

"Fine. Jesus. You are such a brat," he grumbled. I
lowered my gaze and narrowed my eyes. "Okay, okay."
He threw up his hands. "You've got me. You're not a
brat; you're not a kid; you're an adult. And one who
pushes me around as if I were a toy car and half the
time I don't realize it." He snorted and started finishing
off the breakfast.

"I am the puppet master," I said with appropriate
darkness and doom in my voice. It should've been a
joke, but unfortunately it was appropriate in real life
this morning as well.

"You're Darth Vader without the asthma and black
cape," he countered, scraping up the last forkful of potatoes.

"That too." I didn't mind. I liked Darth before he
became a whiny mama's boy. The whole choking people without having to touch them hit a little close to
home, but it was a big pop culture thing I'd missed at
the Institute and it was entertaining. I had all the Star
Wars movies—the good three and the blasphemy-
against-nature three. I'd watched the first three at least
twice each. At least I'd stopped before I bought a light-
saber to hide in the closet, although I still firmly stood
behind the view that Han had shot first. The man
wasn't an idiot. Of course he shot first. I'd been younger
then, by two years, and I had missed the excitement of

everything being new and engaging. Things had popped up now that were new, but not engaging.

Not in a good way at least.

Stefan got up, dumped his empty plate into the sink, and said, "Okay, you've made sure I'm fed and watered just like your little monsters, so tell already."

Tell I did. As he braced his hands on the back of my chair and looked down over my shoulder, I brought out the pictures I'd had hidden under my plate and laid them out. "I went back to look at the news on Anatoly." I didn't wait for a reaction, rushing on. "I thought something had seemed peculiar."

"Weird," Stefan substituted absently. He tried to help me get the language right for someone my age and my pretense of a lifelong coffeehouse career ambition.

"Weird. Something seemed weird." I pointed at each photo. "This man. He's in every one of them. Where they found Anatoly, when they put him into the coroner's van, at the autopsy." Stefan knew better than to ask where I'd gotten the autopsy photos. I could tell you who killed JFK if you wanted to know, but you really didn't.

"I was curious," I said. "There's nothing Anatoly can do for the FBI or IRS now, but he looks like government. Then I ran him through my facial recognition program."

That one did get to him. "You have a facial recognition program? You've got to be shitting me. Like the government and the TSA?"

"No, nothing like theirs. Mine is ninety-nine point nine percent accurate. They *wish* they had my program." I pointed at the last picture. "This is him coming through the Miami airport the day after you broke into the Institute, grabbed me, and they moved. I hacked into the rental car place he used—video cameras are everywhere in airports—it's great—found the car he rented under his own name, which definitely makes him government. Overconfident. I downloaded that car's GPS information and guess where he went."

Stefan didn't have to guess. There was only one place that would have me going to this much trouble. He had gone to the Institute. "Who is he? Who is the son of a bitch?"

"Hugo Raynor. He's been with the CIA, NSA, and now Homeland Security. He's forty-two, five foot ten, best marksman at the Farm." This was where CIA applicants trained when they were young and relatively untarnished. Raynor was far beyond the Farm and as blackened with tarnish as fifty-year-old tin. I'd bet he was still a good marksman, though. You're never that good at something unless you love it, and if you love it, you don't give it up.

"He speaks five languages," I continued, "amateur" running through my mind, "and repeated a course in advanced psychological and physical interrogation. He got the top score both times. I guess it was like a good book; once isn't enough." I leaned back in the chair and said what had to be said, although Stefan probably already knew it by now. "The mob would've been quicker with Anatoly. The autopsy report says what was done to him was slow. Someone wanted to know something. The mob wants to find you too. King Anatoly is dead. . . . Long live King Stefan." The man who'd taken Anatoly's place in the mob would want to make sure Stefan wasn't coming back to stir up old loyalties. "But they're not patient, not like this."

"Raynor. Goddamn it." He sat back down. "We knew the Institute had to have some sort of government contact to get away with what they did, but that he tracked down Anatoly when even I couldn't have." He shook his head. "That makes him one dangerous son of a bitch. Pack your shit. We're going. If this bastard is involved with the Institute, and he obviously is, what he wanted from Anatoly is you. Anatoly didn't know where we are, but it's too close. This motherfucker is too close." He stood. "Go on. Get your stuff. You know the drill. Hell, you wrote the drill because mine wasn't efficient enough. Fifteen minutes and we're in the car. *Go.*"

I had mildly tweaked the drill, but that wasn't the point. He was right, but . . . I didn't want to leave. This was home. The first I'd had. "But—"

"Fifteen minutes," he said, cutting me off, "and I toss you and your smelly, evil pets in the trunk of the car and drive until dark. If you don't want to live in those clothes for the next week, I suggest you start packing. Don't bother with the pictures of Raynor. Keep one; I'll take care of the rest." True to his word, fifteen minutes later, Stefan did take care of the rest.

He burned down the house.

Burning down the house had not been in my emergency drill. It should've been as it was the most efficient way of eliminating evidence and wayward genetic material such as hair or skin particles. I turned to watch out the back window as the Bumble—as my home—burned a cheerful red-orange against the green of the trees. Stefan had already called 911. They would get there in time for the house to burn to the ground but not for the fire to spread, which was good. I'd turned Mothra loose. He'd pecked me on the head and flown to freedom, wing as good as new. Gamera I'd put in the woods where he crawled off with a speed twice that of when I'd found him and eyes bright and open to the world. He was still old; he'd die sooner or later, but now it would be later.

You do what you can to make up for what you've done in the past.

We followed the bend in the road and there was only smoke to see then, a black fist hanging in the gray sky. No more rusty water out of creaking taps. No more raccoons squabbling in the attic every night. No more crickets or fireflies, the smell of free coffee from work soaking the air every day, no more wall of shelf after sagging shelf that held close to five hundred of my movies and old TV shows. Bottom line. . . .

No more home.

And no more "Harry," the friendly but not overly friendly in a pedophile kind of way handyman. Harry was gone and while Stefan was always himself when Harry was officially out of sight of the townspeople and off duty, now Stefan was back all the way and then some, full-time. Almost three years had done a lot for me. I'd learned more things than I'd imagined existed; I'd developed social skills—of a sort; I became whole. Not normal, but as whole as I could hope to be, and that was good enough for right now.

That same amount of time had done something for

Stefan too. I'd progressed and he'd regressed, but that wasn't a bad thing for him. He'd lost some of the guilt he'd been drowning in. When I remembered Stefan first coming for me, it wasn't a man in a black mask or a crazy guy shoving Three Musketeers bars at me as he tried to convince me that I was his brother. I remembered an ocean, dark as a universe without stars—black with guilt, despair, rage, violence, self-loathing. All I could see was his hand reaching out of the water; the rest of him was buried in a liquid Hell he couldn't escape.

All of Jericho's children could see, because we'd all been trained to look. I'd seen every one of Stefan's weaknesses and vulnerabilities—I'd seen him as a target long before I'd seen him as a person.

But the past years had taken his hand and pulled him up, pulled him out. He hadn't been on the shore, but he'd been in the breakers, close to being free. If he laughed, he meant it. If he was happy or at least content, he didn't have to fake it. Now he had to step farther back into the water, if only for the violence. I watched the smoke disappear behind us, because I didn't want to watch Stefan. He was a good man and when good men have to do bad things, that ocean will never let them go.

Be kind to Stefan, Anatoly whispered . . . because life hadn't been.

"Where's Raynor now?"

I didn't turn, the road unspooling behind—the same road to nowhere as Stefan's scar. "Gone. He lives in Washington, D.C., a house, so I was able to get into the utility companies there and take a look. His electricity and water use has been pretty much nil for the past two weeks, which means he left one light on and has a dripping faucet. I used Google Earth and his car is parked in the driveway, no airline has his name for that time, so either he had a nasty bathroom accident, statistics rank those very high on the scale, or he bought another car—a used one, with cash, because it hasn't been registered yet."

"He's smart. Fuck."

"I know. I think he might be as smart as me." I did turn this time, offended as they came at the notion. No, offended as . . . hell. Right. Offended as *hell*. "Do you think that's actually possible?"

"That he might know you're keeping an eye on your back trail to see if he might come following? Yeah, I think he's that smart. But as smart as you? Come on. Where's that ego I know and put up with?" He shoved my shoulder with one hand. "Although the earplugs really help with that last part."

We'd passed through town—there wasn't much to pass through; blink and it was gone—and we were headed for the Bridge of the Heavens. Kicked out of Paradise and I didn't even like apples that much.

Didn't that suck?

The plan called for driving through Washington, crossing the border into Canada and then we would keep going until we were lost in Banff National Park. Our fake IDs would pass border patrol; I knew that. I'd made them, but camping in the wilds of Canada wasn't going to help me continue my research to help save the rest of Jericho's children, all of them—to take away their power to kill. Saul had found their location two years ago and I'd been working on a way to fix them since then. I hadn't needed to be fixed. I didn't like to kill, but I knew the same wasn't true of all the rest. Some might be like me—it was a possibility—but some loved to kill. Where we were going there wasn't even the most hideous of creations—dial-up—much less WiFi. I'd never be able to continue talking with Ariel about my fake "paper," about the cure. And I needed to keep in contact with her—even if that was my business and no one else's at the moment. Maybe "suck" wasn't a strong enough word for this. "Bites"? "Blows"? "Sucks balls"?

I had to get a dictionary for these sorts of situations.

"Holy shit!" Stefan spat, and slammed on the brakes.

I automatically braced myself with one hand on the dashboard and with the other tossed Godzilla into the backseat. He hissed and I felt him crawl under my seat. He'd been through this type of thing before. He had his own drill plan.

As we three-sixtied off the road onto the grass and dirt side, I saw an unfamiliar car and an annoyingly familiar face through our windshield. The tourist—Mitchell, the sheriff had called him—was sitting on the hood of a car, gape-mouthed with a half-eaten sandwich dropping from his hand.

There is no such thing as coincidence in the known universe. This blobby ass didn't come close to the failing end of that grading curve. If nothing else, it was nice to know that stress improved my cursing abilities.

Stefan was out of the car with a fistful of the guy's shirt and slamming him repeatedly into the windshield of the man's car before I managed to get my seat belt unbuckled and get out myself. I was quicker, stronger, had trained for this for all of my life that I could remember, but Stefan hadn't only been trained. He'd lived it in the *Mafiya* every day, and that made him better than me. I wasn't envious of his skills. I was only sorry it had turned out that way.

"What are you doing here, asshole?" Stefan snarled, and banged him against the glass again, this time cracking it. It formed a spiderweb pattern around Mitchell. He was a tourist—a fake tourist—caught in a web of violence and rage that I didn't think he'd escape. "When I give people the kind of beating I gave you, they don't tend to stick around. They damn sure don't park by one of the two ways out of town and eat goddamn sandwiches. Who *are* you?"

Suddenly, the hand that had held the sandwich now held a gun, the dazed and stupid eyes sharpened, and what had seemed like fat now looked like something much more solid. The muzzle of the gun didn't have far to go to end up jammed under Stefan's chin to blow a hole through it, his brain, and out the top of his skull. Stefan stiffened before falling on the grass and road, a spray of blood and brain matter fanning the pale worn asphalt widely behind him. Eyes, neither brother brown nor aggressive amber, instead mirrored the gray of the sky.

Life changes just that fast.

People . . . they die faster.

And your desire to live can change from fierce to absent in that instant.

But that wasn't what happened.

It was what I saw in a split second of dark imagination, a calculation of the odds, the preparation for every possible outcome, and the Institute-honed, razor-sharp logic of predator prediction. We all had it, inherent, and were trained to see the deadliest of potentials on top of that, but Stefan proved it wrong. The man's gun was not far, but not far was too far. Harry used a paintbrush—his alter ego, Stefan, used a Steyr 9mm. A bullet from that could destroy a man's heart as easily as I could. And it did.

"Shit." Stefan stepped back from the body that sprawled on the hood of the car. He had blood on his shirt from the blowback of being so close when he'd pulled the trigger. "Shitshitshitshit."

I echoed the sentiment mentally, because right then I was as verbal as a goddamn rock.

Hey, more cursing. Look at me.

I dropped onto the hood of our own car, which was slick—Stefan waxed it as if practicing to represent his country in waterproofing in the Olympics. It was slick enough that I slid and went down over the bumper without feeling it—wax, wax, wax—and hit the ground, which was considerate enough to be gritty and solid. No car fanatics had gotten it yet, and there I sat. I would've thought my mouth was hanging open like the dead guy's, gaping in eternal surprise, but I tasted blood, so it was more likely that my teeth were buried in my lower lip.

It was the Institute all over again. The escape. The blood.

Once you thought you were out, they pulled you back in. Stefan should be saying that, though—it was from a mob movie.

Funny. Wasn't I funny?

But this wasn't the Institute repeated. This was almost three years later. And I wasn't obedient Michael

trained thoroughly enough to sit on his single bed
smelling of industrial bleach, unmotivated to move
until they came to take me for graduation or down-
stairs where they took the failures and dissected them
to see where they'd gone wrong. I wasn't that Michael
anymore. I was Misha, claimed son of a dead Russian
mobster and brother of a live one, and Misha wasn't
going back to Jericho-land fucking ever. Stefan had en-
couraged me to live the life of a teenager, a kid, to catch
up on all I'd missed out on. But that time was over. Just
as that logic-defying, contradictory book said: It was
time to leave childish things behind. I was not a victim
any longer. I was a man. I'd been saying it for a while
now, and it was time to start acting like it.

"Michael?"

"Misha," I corrected him as I stood up, solid as a
rock, inside and out. "You touched the hood of the car
with your left hand. Wipe off the prints, finger and
palm," I ordered.

He gave me a skeptical look but did so, using the
long sleeve of his shirt. "You're sure you're okay? Because I don't feel too goddamn great." He jacked in
another round and put the gun back in his shoulder
holster—one thing the fifteen-minute-escape plan had
allowed him to grab. "At the end, when we finally finished Jericho, I know I killed his homicidal thugs, but
not this close up." And with that, his eyes went a little
colder. "I guess if they're going to up the stakes, so will
we." He rested his foot against the bumper for a second
and said, "All right. Help me push the car and our
lying-ass tourist into the river."

"What about his ID?"

"It'll be as fake as he is. He's not a tourist and he's not a civilian, and he fooled us both, which made him smart, tough, and highly trained." Stefan was already pushing the car, the sleeves of his shirt pulled over the heels of his hands to keep it print free, as the dead man's slack legs scraped the ground.

"I know they'll be fake, but who made them will tell me something. Different methods, different materials." I moved past him as he stopped pushing the car, rolled the dead body to its side with no sympathy for the bastard who'd almost killed my brother, and pulled his wallet out of his back pocket. "All right. Now we push." I followed Stefan's lead and in less than a minute the car plunged down a nearly straight embankment into the river below.

He had fooled me, the son of a bitch, and that took a great deal of training . . . and a shitload of laziness on my part. But hadn't I gotten lazy in Cascade Falls? I did my background checks, and I was properly suspicious of what lay behind all the friendly faces—at first. Then I'd gotten complacent. I filed this one under asshole tourist and didn't use anything the Institute had taught me, didn't take a second glance, much less the third and fourth he deserved. I'd thought earlier that you could read anyone if you bothered to look . . . but I hadn't bothered to look. I, the shamefully stupid fucking asshole, had almost gotten us killed.

"That is a lot of frigging curse words from someone who has to study up on just how to say them." Stefan had my arm and was dragging me back to the car.

"Did I just say all that aloud?" I found my footing and ran with him.

"Yeah, it was damn impressive, but you did not almost get us killed."

"Right. It must've been that other Michael. The idiot." I slammed the car door and buckled up. "I'm guessing no Canada. We fool Raynor or whoever into thinking we went there, but head south? We'd better head for the new Institute before they get nervous with our being so close and move it. The cure is more or less done anyway." I looked through the wallet. The ID was fake all right, and shoddy. That had government subcontracting all over it.

"I'll call Saul and get the troops lined up then," Stefan responded. We'd been planning this for a long time. Saul and about twenty mercenaries were on call, more or less, for when they were needed. They could meet us there. They'd be hours behind us, but that would give us a chance to check out the place close up and not just from satellite pictures.

Stefan had left the car running. He jerked the steering wheel and headed back the way we came, adding roughly, "And it's not your fault."

It was definitely my fault, but I'd fix it. Kids let someone else fix their mistakes. Adults fixed their own. It was time Stefan had an equal now, not a responsibility.

Time to grow up.

There were actually more than two ways out of Cascade Falls, but the third way was known only by locals or handymen the locals trusted. It also would rip out the bottom of your car by the time you made it out, but destroying—no, trashing; that was the more apt word—trashing a car was better than meeting Raynor face-to-face before we were ready. An adult, but an adult with a completely average vocabulary to go with completely average brown hair, eyes made as average by contacts—camouflage, you have to work at it. If we were ever free, then I could talk like the genius I was—if I stopped making mistakes and made it back to genius status.

I started to reach for my computer but stopped to dig a shirt out of Stefan's bag in the backseat. "Do you want to get into something less . . . ummm . . . covered in ex-tourist?"

Anyone and everyone he'd killed he'd killed to save me, and as he'd said, I don't think he'd ever done it literally face-to-face, mere inches away. Wearing the evidence of it probably wasn't pleasant. Saying thanks, he let me grab the wheel as we bumped over the narrow excuse for a dirt road, and quickly took off his jacket and holster and changed the shirt. Once he was armed again and back in his jacket, he took the wheel. "Now, go e-mail your girlfriend."

I was going to deny that I was intending to e-mail her, although I had been planning to, and certainly say that she wasn't my girlfriend. I hadn't met her in person yet. She lived across the country in New York, not to mention many other obstacles. I didn't have a chance to get any of that out, however, as Stefan, instead of going with "holy shit" this time, went with "mother-fucker." He was looking in the rearview mirror. So much for locals giving out private town info only to their good-old-boy handyman.

The SUV behind us was built for this type of road

while our used, low-slung Toyota wasn't. It gobbled up the dirt and rocks behind us. It was black and I couldn't see more than a shadowy shape through its tinted windows. Raynor? The Institute? Raynor working for the Institute? It didn't matter. I couldn't do to him what I'd done to the dead tourist—make him vomit up his breakfast or cut off the blood flow to his brain for a few seconds. The latter would cause unconsciousness, and maybe he would veer off the road, and we could leave him behind. But I had to be able to touch the person to do those things. We all did, Jericho's legacy. All but one. And she wasn't here now, although if she had been, she would've gleefully had his brain melting out of his ears, blood spurting from his eyes, ears, nose, and mouth. Then she would've done the same to us.

Even the Institute had been glad there had been only one Wendy. She'd be ten this year. I'd seen what she could do at seven. I didn't want to know what she could do now.

But I could do something too. It was more mundane and might not work as well, but if it got the SUV off our trail, that was good enough. "Hold the wheel again," I heard Stefan say as I dived back into the backseat for one of my bags this time. "Let me take a few shots at the son of a bitch."

With this being more of a hiking trail than a road, we were bouncing roughly up and down. Stefan was a great shot, but under these conditions, it would be hard to make a shot that would count. Luckily, I had something that took less accuracy than a bullet. "Wait," I said as I unzipped the bag and pulled out two gray cylinders. "I have something better." I dropped one

into my lap, rolled down the window, leaned out, set
the detonator, and tossed the first one. It blew up one
of the back tires of the SUV. The second one took out a
front one. First, the vehicle spun, sending clouds of dirt
and clumps of grass into the air, before tipping over on
to one side. No one got out as long as we were in sight,
but the shadowy figure inside was moving. If he was
Hugo Raynor, with his impressive resume, I assumed
he'd have more guns and be better with them than the
sandwich guy who obviously had worked for him.
Without a better view of what Raynor was doing and
how he was armed, we were best to leave it and be
happy with one SUV dead in the water.

I smiled in satisfaction. "Guns are for boys. High explosives are for men."

Stefan didn't seem as satisfied.

"Bombs? You were making pipe *bombs*?" he demanded incredulously as he drove on.

"Garages don't blow themselves up," I pointed out
with some exasperation at his lack of gratitude. "And
they're not pipe bombs so much as proactive explosive measures. Little pipe bombs," I emphasized.
"You know . . . just in case." With electrical detonation
devices—very simple. Military detonation cord wasn't
as quick as I might need it to be. "They're really quite
easy to make. Too easy. They should be more respon-
sible with the information on the Internet. . . ."

"You told me that equipment was for your genetic
research"—I think he hit a rock on purpose as my
head smacked the inside roof of the car—"to find a
cure for the rest of the kids. You lied to me, Michael
Lukas Korsak."

"I didn't lie," I shot back. "I said that the equipment was to help me find a cure. I didn't say *all* the equipment was to help me find a cure. Some of it could be used to save our lives too."

"And you didn't think that was worth mentioning? You running an armory behind our house?" Stefan gritted his teeth. "I swear, when we switch cars, I'm going to take a minute to beat you like a redheaded stepchild."

"I didn't not mention it. It didn't come up, that's all." Yes, a fine line, but it was my line and I was stubbornly walking it. "And why do people have a dislike for people with red hair? I've heard that saying once or twice since moving here. Why would their hair color make them the targets of violence?"

"Not the time, and you know it's just some old saying. Don't think I don't recognize your version of smart-ass, Michael."

"Misha," I insisted again.

"And what's with that? We're running from who the hell knows and you're worried about your nickname?"

"Michael is the Institute. Misha is free. I'm free and I'm staying that way. I'm a man now, a new person, and Misha will remind me of that. I don't want their name anymore." But I couldn't go back to Lukas. That would be as wrong. I wasn't ever going to get my memories of Lukas's first seven years back, not to mention what I'd discovered in my research. I couldn't be that person. I couldn't be Lukas. I was Misha and only Misha now, for good. I was me, finally finished, finally recovered from the Institute, finally real. They weren't getting me back and they could keep their damn Peter Pan name.

"Fine. Misha the Mighty." The car bounced again and I heard the muffler hit one rock too many and it was gone behind us. "You got it. Now put that mighty brain to use and figure out how Raynor, and whoever the fuck he works for, found us."

I didn't have to put my brain to work. I knew. In a flash of inspiration . . . and subconscious brilliant deduction—a given—I knew. "Anatoly and you, Stefan. You both told him where we were."

Raynor was smart all right. Too smart. And we hadn't tried to finish him off when we had the chance. It was a thought I wouldn't have had three years ago—when I hadn't known what it was to have a real life. I wasn't ashamed I had the thought now. I'd learned a lot since that time. Life and death . . . It was the cycle of the world. For someone to live, someone had to die—especially if that person was trying to take your life, be it mental or physical.

And me?

I wanted to live.

The hell with the Institute and their lies about what I was and what I could never be.

I wanted to live.

Chapter 4

"We need to take the 84. We're heading southeast toward the Burns Paiute Indian Reservation," I told Stefan. I had the route memorized, but I handed him the map from the glove compartment. Stefan didn't like GPS. He thought all the voices were annoying, and when I programmed in HAL from *2001: A Space Odyssey*, he tossed it out the window and drove over it. I'd known Stefan wasn't technically . . . adept. That was the best and politest way to put it, but I didn't know he was afraid of killer computers.

I thought they were rather entertaining myself. There was no explaining taste.

He snatched the map. "Burns? Why the hell are we going to . . . wait. What the fuck. How did Anatoly and I give away our location? How the hell did you come up with that?"

Burns was one of my nine—technically, ten—backup plans if Canada didn't work out, but Stefan didn't seem in the mood to appreciate that right now, and I couldn't blame him. "Raynor must've found Anatoly," I said. "And as smart as he appears to be, Anatoly was smart too. It must have taken Raynor about"—I calculated—"up until four weeks ago to find him. Almost three years."

"But I told you, kiddo, I made sure Anatoly never knew where we were. Never knew where our money was, didn't know our account numbers in the Caymans. Raynor couldn't have found us through him." The car bumped again and I thought I heard something else fall off. I let Stefan's "kiddo" go. He was running on autopilot, but that would have to change in the future.

"But he did know one thing . . . all the properties he owned and used to hide in. He knew about the beach house where we were shot. Raynor must have gone to every one of them once Anatoly told." And anyone would tell eventually, no matter how *Mafiya* tough, when a saw was cutting through their bone. I cleared my throat. "Raynor would've gone to every single one and dusted for prints, then entered them in AFIS." This was a collection of fingerprints from a number of criminals and certain occupational workers.

How he became fixated on Anatoly to begin with was a mystery, unless he hung around Miami at the time of my rescue. While Jericho chased us, he'd investigated how the Institute had been discovered to begin with. With his clearance, he could've gone from the police to the FBI to see if anything peculiar had happened at the same time Stefan had taken me. He could've heard about a certain mob assassination, a missing mobster named Stefan Korsak. Stefan hadn't killed his boss, but everyone thought he had. There would be boards covered with pictures, family connections, and maybe the mention and photo of another Korsak brother, long gone—a little boy with bicolored eyes.

Blue and green, like all of Jericho's children.

If Raynor was as smart as I thought he was, he might have taken a chance on a wild-card hunch like that. "He would've kept them classified," I went on about the fingerprints. "He's Homeland. He can do that. But he would've had them, just waiting for one to pop up."

"Ah, shit." Stefan pounded his head once against the steering wheel. "And my stupid ass fucks up trying to blend in and be Harry-the-Handyman, good guy, up for a bar fight, who gets arrested and printed. Two weeks. Two goddamn weeks and he's probably been here watching us at least half that time. Brought along a buddy, not Homeland, but trained. That shithead was trained to fight and kill. He sends him in to annoy you day after day to see what you'll do. Make sure he has the right kid." I had changed a lot in the past three years—I had my contact that changed the color of my one blue eye to match the green. I was taller, my hair darker, enough for there to be some initial doubt, although with my living with Harry/Stefan as my brother, not more than a molecule of it. "He did it to see if he could trigger you."

"And he did," I said quietly. "That means I fucked up too and maybe worse than you."

"I don't think so"—he gave my shoulder a light push—"but if you want to share, let's say we both screwed up and you tell me why the hell we're going to the Burns Indian Reservation. Assuming the car holds together to make it to the interstate. The pipe bombs we will talk about later—I haven't forgotten. But why the reservation?"

"Oh, the reservation?" Actually, he probably was

going to forget about the pipe bombs. "That's where the plane is. Didn't I mention that before?"

"Plane? What plane?" he demanded.

"Our plane."

"Our plane? Since when do we have a plane?" His fingers were slowly beginning to whiten as his grip tightened on the steering wheel.

"Since I bought one," I replied as if it were the most obvious of answers.

I could see his jaw tightening now as he tried to hold on to his temper. In the beginning, when he'd rescued me, taught me how to live in the real world, taught me . . . hell . . . everything (even cursing), he was nothing but patient. He was the most patient, protective ex-mobster you could find, because he knew how damaged I was, which I think might have been only marginally more damaged than he was from guilt and despair. Not once in almost two years did he ever snap or lose his temper with me, even if I deserved it— *especially* if I deserved it. But after two years, he went from treating me as a phantom brother who would disappear at any moment and started treating me like a real brother.

It turned out that I liked that. After two years, I wanted to be given a verbal ass kicking when I deserved it, I wanted to pay off the half-blown-up garage with my paycheck from the coffeehouse, despite our having money in offshore accounts, I wanted all of that. Why? Because that meant no matter how annoying I was and how quickly Stefan would make sure I paid the price, he always had my back. He protected me from anyone and anything.

Blood is thicker than delinquent behavior.

And while that wasn't one hundred percent correct, I took it. Good, bad, and all that came between, Stefan would always be my brother, my family, and that was something. . . . That was really something.

"Since you *bought* one? Why did you buy a plane? How did you buy a plane? Who's going to fly the plane if we need a plane?" Stefan demanded. Now I could hear his teeth grinding at the end of the last question. I tried not to smile, but it was entertaining . . . just a little. That didn't make me a bad person. I simply found amusement where I could. That made me emotionally healthy and I could write a two-hundred-thousand-word paper to prove it.

"I bought one in case some of our other backup plans didn't work, and Raynor cancels out at least three of them. I bought it with the money from the Caymans. Who does our banking, remember? You're horrible with numbers. That was why that old lady hit you with her cane when you were in the ten-items-only line with sixteen items." I crossed my arms and Godzilla came slithering out from under the seat to paw at the glove compartment. He knew where the goodies were. "Besides, it's only a Cessna."

"Only a Cessna? Damn it, Michael, Misha, whatever. The government tracks that sort of thing, especially since 9/11."

"No problem. It was a totally illegal and untraceable purchase. I have quite a few friends of that sort on the Internet, but that time I went to your friend Saul. I told him not to tell you, that it was a surprise. He thought that was pretty hilarious." "Goddamn fucking hilarious" was what he'd actually said. "Then I found one of my friends from the Net who said there were a few people with flexible morals at the Burns Indian Reservation who would hide it for us in case we needed it." Like now. With Raynor, we definitely needed a plane, because he was going to the same place we were: the Institute. Not that he'd think we'd go there. I imagined he thought that was the very last place we'd go. A man like him wouldn't understand trying to save what you could own instead. No, he knew it was the best place to get his own fresh-from-the-oven baked assassin, a special one, because he'd seen what I could do when merely annoyed by a fake tourist. He wanted to be prepared. He didn't know I wouldn't use what I had in me to kill . . . that I wasn't like him or Jericho.

I hoped.

"*What?* They're hiding a plane? Jesus, they'll think we're terrorists, and hauling around pipe bombs isn't going to help with that impression." His knuckles were bone white now, and he was going to get hoarse soon if his voice became any louder.

"No, don't be ridiculous. I thought about that, so I told them we're drug dealers," I said with the complacent certainty I had in any of the plans I'd thought up. The Institute had taken my life, but they had taught me to plan like a son of a bitch. More cursing. It seemed I only needed adrenaline to bring it out in me. I probably shouldn't have been pleased by that accomplishment, but I was.

"Drug dealers? And they believed you?" Now he was looking at me, not at the road, which wasn't the best way to drive, and that amber I'd never seen directed at me was beginning to glint in his eyes.

"Why wouldn't they?" I reassured him. He no doubt thought I'd made a mistake. Big brothers were like that . . . always questioning the younger ones and never letting them grow up. "I pay them to grow marijuana. It took them a while to get . . . the hang of it? Right, the hang of it, but last month they finally said they'd figured out the correct temperature, hydration, where to get better grow lights, and they said they have a great crop now."

He blinked, his darker skin turning nearly as red as a sunburn. Pulling the car over into the emergency lane, he turned back and rested his forehead on the steering wheel and said nothing. I waited about five minutes. It was just a plane and some barely illegal drugs, which I thought should be legal. It was no worse than beer. Of course, I wasn't allowed to drink beer yet as I wasn't twenty-one and Stefan was as strict as a TV grandmother with things like that. Plane, drugs, only just illegal . . . and if I could've gotten a doctor involved, maybe not illegal at all—surely five minutes was enough to recover from my "surprise."

I slapped him on the back and went on to be, admittedly, an utter ass. "Are you okay? Was the healthy breakfast too healthy? Did it upset your normal intestinal workings? Do you want a Three Musketeers to counteract the health?"

"*Tui nemnogaya dermo*," he said without lifting his head.

I frowned. "You little shit? You called me a little shit. I am as tall as you now. I am not little."

"But you are a shit. What happened to that agreeable kid who used to be afraid of grocery stores? Who only scared me when he wanted the sex talk? Where did the pipe bomb–building drug lord come from?" He leaned his head back against the headrest and covered his eyes. "Where did I go wrong?"

I wasn't offended. In fact, if I'd known it would be this entertaining, I'd have told Stefan about all my plans—although some of the others might give him a heart attack—at least a year ago. I grinned, though he couldn't see it, and punched him hard on the shoulder. "I grew up. I'm a genius, I was raised to be an assassin, and I'm trying to figure out a way to bring down an entire Institute of assassin-makers while curing the assassins they made. What did you think I did in my spare time? At least I didn't build a nuclear bomb in the garage, which, by the way, is so beyond easy you wouldn't believe it. . . ."

Stefan sat up and clapped his hand over my mouth. "Michael . . . Misha, you're my brother and I love the hell out of you, but I think right now it would be a good thing if you didn't talk. For a while. A couple of hours at least."

I scowled at him, but this was brother stuff and I got it. I did. Stefan, despite killing a few people—a lot of people—to save me and being an ex-mobster on top of it, was delicate, apparently. I'd have to dole out the information in smaller bits so his brain wouldn't explode. He knew emotion; I knew everything else—together we were unstoppable. Again, I hoped.

He took his hand away from my mouth. "I have only one more question and then silence. Okay? Silence, so I can escape having a stroke and not take that damn stinky-ass ferret and beat you with it. One question."

I raised my eyebrows and looked interested. I genuinely was. What could he think I possibly left out of the plan?

"Do you know how to fly this plane? They taught you that at the Institute?"

Please. As if I would forget about that. I restrained myself from an annoyed snort. "No. I taught myself. There are classes for everything online. You can also order instructional videos, although of course they say those are only supplementary study materials and you can't learn to fly a plane just from watching one." Those who said this were nongeniuses. I had absolutely no doubt about that. "So yes, I can fly. Plus it's a Cessna. It's barely an airplane. More like a roller skate with wings." I gave Godzilla, who did not stink . . . not too much anyway, a PayDay candy bar, and he crawled back under the seat.

Stefan was starting to turn redder. I needed to check his blood pressure. He wasn't old enough to be worrying about that yet, but some of these things are genetic. "You really think you can fly a plane by watching something on the damn Internet?"

I grinned again. "Theoretically."

He didn't hit me with Godzilla, but he did seem intent on not speaking to me again for the conceivable future. I used the time on the computer, when I could get a connection . . . and when you hack into a satellite to control its orientation, you'd be amazed at how much your Internet connection can be improved. Others might suffer, but they could go to their local coffee shops. That wasn't an option for me right now. I contacted Ariel in New York. We'd been in contact for two years now. She was twenty-two and went to the Weill Cornell Medical College. Well, she didn't go; she was like me, a genius. She already had her MD and had started college at fourteen. She was a researcher at the college and after much surfing and looking and the thorough checking out of people at medical research sites, she was the one I thought who could help me the most. She had access to all the equipment that the money Stefan and I had couldn't buy. She could do the experiments on the genetic material I provided. She could help me look for a cure, though she thought she was only helping another researcher at a facility with far lesser equipment write a paper on one of the wilder theories she'd heard.

She was pretty too. Not that that had anything to do with anything. She wasn't blatantly sexy like Sara at the coffeehouse. More . . . cute. And I could talk to her because she was smart enough to understand me; sometimes I thought she might be smarter than I was. And that was hot. She had sleek pink hair that fell to her jaw, pale skin, and the tattoo of a tiny mermaid beside one of her blue eyes. When I asked her about it when we talked over webcam, she'd laughed and said being smart meant you had to try extra hard to see the fantasy in the world—the magic. And what was a world without those things?

See? Smart.

I found my fantasy in movies and she found it in mermaids, but we both knew you needed something.

The smarter you were, the more you saw the world for what it was, people for who they truly were, those inside-out people, and if that was all you saw . . . you'd be in therapy 24/7. You needed to make your own reality because the real version could make you doubt humanity, except for your brother and someone you could've maybe thought of as a . . . ah . . . friend you'd made online. Just a friend. Either way it would be nice to think that there were people in the world worth anything at all—not just Jerichos.

It would be nice.

She wasn't there the first time I tried. But the second time, four hours later, she was. There was no video this time, too risky, so I didn't know if she was wearing her favorite freshwater pearl choker dyed in blues and golds and purples—the same as a mermaid would wear. She'd changed her name, she'd said, to the Disney mermaid to remind her to not only believe in fantasy but to always stay a child when she could. She wouldn't tell me what her name had been before. She said she was saving that for our honeymoon.

Now I could feel my face getting hot and maybe not as red as Stefan's had been, but definitely not my normal color. Luckily he was concentrating on driving or meditating on not killing me and didn't notice.

I typed in *Hey, so what did you think of the theoretical overriding of the genetic code on the extra DNA strand for my paper?* I'd discovered, with Ariel's help, that the gene connected to the psychic ability to kill—not that that was what I told her its function was—was on only one of the DNA strands, while chimeras like me possessed two. It might be why all the assassins were chimeras. If a person had only one type of DNA as was customary, Jericho's manipulation could very well not work or could destroy the subject altogether. But to know that, I'd have to create a chimera embryo to see exactly what could happen. I wasn't going to do that. I wasn't the Frankenstein that Jericho had been.

She sent back her response in a flash; she was one fast typer. *I think theoretically that a viral explosion with some type of injection would lyse the target genes and inactivate them. I tried it on a few of those gene samples you sent and it definitely did something to them. If not complete disintegration, then close. If you·re talking about doing it to a live person, there'd definitely be bruising at the injection area and no sure guarantee that it would work, much less immediately, but in the realm of theory, it's conceivable.*

She called me Dr. Theoretical for as often as I used the word. She said it was my superpower, but I was being accurate. There was nothing wrong with accuracy. More letters appeared before I could reply. *Bone marrow transplant would work much better.* I highly doubted I'd be able to pull off a bone marrow transplant on thirty genetic assassins. Any cure would have to be almost instantaneous. Her typing continued. *But it's your paper. Hey, why no webcam this time, cutie? Get a bad haircut? Or did you finally break down and get that tattoo I've been trying to talk you into?* She kept telling me to get a Cheshire cat tattoo from *Alice in Wonderland* as I was so theoretical I was practically nothing but a floating smile in midair.

Living life on the run was exactly what I was doing, and I thought best not to advertise it. *No,* I typed back. *I dyed my hair pink to be half the genius you are.*

"Tell her that her hair is the color of a rose," came the suggestion from beside me.

"It's not," I said absently. "It's more the color of cotton candy."

"A chick probably isn't going to find that romantic. Go with rose."

"Why would I want to be romant— Hey!" I glared at Stefan as I slammed the computer closed. "How about eyes on the road and your own business? And I thought you weren't speaking to me."

"Revenge is worth it." His grin was far more wolfish than any I'd managed so far—mirrors and practice don't lie. "And get ready to play a nineteen-year-old drug lord, *jefe*, because we're almost at the reservation. Maybe if you tried some dark sunglasses and stroked your stinky carpet shark like a James Bond villain, they would go for it."

"You don't think I can pull off pretending to be a drug dealer?" I knew I was hampered by my face. The Institute made or chose their assassins with faces that were attractive to both sexes but also not so much that we stood out to every eye. We were made to appeal but also to blend in. But we were also taught by them to pull on any mask and play any part or suffer the consequences. "Learn a little faith, Stefan." I did grab his spare set of sunglasses in the floorboards when we arrived and put them on before climbing out of the car. Stefan brought it to a stop by the first and one of the few buildings on the reservation—a store/tourist spot. The rest of the area was dotted with small wooden houses and the occasional trailer. "I'll be back."

"Right, Arnold. I'm sure you will," he drawled, sliding down in the seat as I slammed my door behind me. Inside the store, I went straight to the cash register, automatically reached for a Milky Way, and said, "I'm looking for Jacob and Johanna Cloud-horse."

The girl there looked me over before flashing her teeth in a white, happy smile. "Which makes you a troublemaker. Deep shit and all that. I should call the law on you, but since Jacob is my baby's daddy, I guess I won't." I had many names. Sebastian was the drug dealer one. Sebastian had money out the ass, a plane to go with it, and he was here to get it.

I hardened my face and tried for that killer twist of Stefan's lips I'd seen a time or two, and by killer, I meant the authentic definition. "I know you won't. Now get them over here. Tell them Sebastian's here, and I don't like waiting."

She looked me up and down more thoroughly this time, her black ponytail swishing over her shoulder. Then with eyes turned to impenetrable onyx, she went for the phone, turning her back so I couldn't hear her speak. "Look at you. You scared a teen mom, probably all of sixteen. Good for you. Are you proud, 'Sebastian'?"

I snatched a quick glance over my shoulder to see Stefan standing behind me with arms folded and without any dark glasses because, face it, he didn't need any. It was practice versus the real thing again. Stefan didn't have to pretend or put on a mask to scare people—Stefan had to put one on not to scare people. That was what "Harry" had been all about. The real Stefan had only to show his true self, what he'd done, and what he'd still do if necessary; it was all in his face if he let it be. Reality was always more convincing than a mask.

I wasn't the one who'd pushed the girl into making that call. It was one glimpse of what stood behind me. "You don't want to be like me, Misha," he whispered low enough that only I could hear. "I don't want to be like me either, but that's my bad luck there. If the means justify the end, let me be the means. It's nothing new for me. You be yourself, got it?"

That the "myself" he was talking about was an assassin taught and trained was something he never remembered or never believed—the same as I tried not to believe. He moved up beside me and laid a casual arm over my shoulder, making sure his gun showed as his jacket gaped open. "Brother, cousin, or bodyguard?" he murmured.

Oh, damn, the story. What had I told the Cloud-horses . . . ? "Bodyguard," I replied.

"We'll go with cousin bodyguard. Gives me more reason to look out for your skinny ass." I barely heard the words before he said aloud to the girl on the phone, "We don't have all fucking day. Are they hauling their shit or not? We have a lot of money invested in their asses, and if they don't give as they have received, like the Good Book says, we'll take that money out of their asses and anyone else's we can find, including you. Hell, conveniently located as you are, we'll start with you, little bitch."

He said bitch as lazily as if that were the only thing he ever called women. Stefan, who painted houses for free for needy landladies and undercharged Mrs. Sloot to paint her gingerbread; Stefan, who treated women with the utmost respect—he even hadn't hurt the one who'd robbed us at gunpoint years ago at a time when we could least afford it. Yet if I hadn't known him, I'd have believed every word, and I knew I couldn't have carried that off. He was right. I should stick to being myself—the myself where my outside reflected what my inner biology wished it was.

But was it fair that Stefan had to be the mean one all the time, no matter his past?

No. No, it wasn't, especially as much as he wanted to leave that part of him behind. Being a drug dealer was much easier online. The reality of being one or pretending to be one . . . I saw now why Stefan had been so upset earlier. Or pissed off—highly pissed off. Maybe there was a reason all Jericho's children were like me . . . and looked somewhat younger and guiltless at first glance. We were trained to plan if we had to, trained every day of our lives, but we were made to not need to. Our faces were our alibis. Touch, kill, and who would ever suspect a nineteen-year-old who would probably look like a nineteen-year-old until he was thirty?

On the other hand, one look at Stefan and you'd know what he might do. One look at me and no one knew what I could do and that it was much worse than anything Stefan had in him. It was the perfect disguise. Nature would've applauded.

It only made me feel like a freak—as if it were only right I should be labeled "Caution," "Dangerous," "Biohazard." That was as far as my thought process went before starting to spiral bleakly downward until Stefan pinched my shoulder hard—he knew; how did

he always know?—and went straight for the Cloud-
horse siblings the second they walked through the
door.

They had rifles, attitude, and sneers, all of which
went limp under Stefan flashing his Steyr in their faces
before they had time to move. The muzzle set gently
over the eye of one of them—that of Jacob, the brother.
"Playtime is over, kiddies." They were barely younger
than he was, by two years at the most, but, in experience, I guess kids they were. If they'd used those rifles
for anything but shooting rabbits, I'd be surprised.
"This is why you look at porn on the Internet, not how
to hook up with dealers, because you are not ready,
assholes. You're worlds away from swimming in this
ocean but damn close to being six feet under that dirt
outside. Now, take us to the plane. And if your girlfriend calls the cops, you'll just be lying on top of that
dirt in a pool of your own guts and blood."

Stefan didn't want me to be like him, but thanks to
him, we had our stuff and were on the plane in fifteen
minutes. The Cloud-horses had built a big barnlike
building behind a line of pine trees to hide it. I didn't
know where they were hiding the drugs and Stefan
didn't mention it. The two Cloud-horses thought themselves pretty clever, I'm sure, in not bringing it up
themselves. They weren't. What kind of drug dealers
show up and don't want their drugs? But if they were
smart, we wouldn't be standing here in the first place.
Smart people don't grow marijuana and hide planes for
strangers on the Internet, no matter how much they
have been paid.

"Now." Stefan stood in the large outbuilding concealing the plane and tapped one of them—Jacob—on top of the head with his gun. It was a friendly tap, if you didn't count the pain that twisted the lean, brown face. "Which of you is going to take a ride with us? You or your sister?" His sister looked tougher by half, but she stood back with her hands up at shoulder level. When it came down to the bottom line, she came way before her brother apparently. Their rifles had been left outside at Stefan's order.

Jason stumbled over his words. "What? What the fuck? We did what you said. What Sebastian said." He pointed at me. I'd given up looking tough and just looked like what I was: bored. I was bored. Stupidity bored me and there was a massive amount of stupid here. Oddly, this expression seemed more intimidating than the one I'd tried at the store. I was being me now and that, despite Institute training, could be the most frightening thing of all in a person.

I remembered what Wendy at the Institute did when she was bored. It wasn't a good time to be a rabbit or a guinea pig in the animal lab on those days.

"Be yourself," Stefan had said.

Let that Frankenstein child you were shine through, I thought.

Shit.

I folded my arms, but didn't look away from the brother and sister team. Stefan wouldn't need back up with these two, but better safe than sorry. Now he was saying, "My cousin is learning the business. I want him to know drug dealers can't be trusted. Too bad that's a lesson you don't already know, huh? But don't worry. It won't be a long ride and just until we get far enough

off the ground to make sure you didn't screw with the
engine. Then we'll boot you right back out. Fifteen,
thirty feet. You'll be fine . . . *if* we're fine. You might
break your legs or your spine, but I hear great things
about wheelchairs these days." Jacob moaned and his
sister gave it up.

"We screwed with the engine some," she grunted.
"Jake, stop being such a whiny bitch. They'll fix it.
They'll go and you can go back to knocking up sixteen-
year-olds."

That was my cue. I went over to the Cessna 350 and
opened the cowling to peer at the engine. You can't
learn to fly a plane via instructional video if you don't
know what parts go where . . . at least not safely. Luckily, my partners in crime didn't know anything about
planes of any kind. They'd only yanked whatever to
them seemed yankable—idiots indeed. Twenty minutes later and after a run-through of the electronic
checklist, we were in the air. And, yes, I might have hit
the top of one of the pine trees, but that was why I said
theoretically so often. It left room for the tiny errors, the
learning curve. None of that mattered when I looked at
where we were. We were flying in a blue sky, the world
and its dangers gone beneath us. It was . . . freedom. It
was glory. It was a wonder I'd never seen, although it
was an unsteady wonder.

Things are never as easy as they appear on the Net
or in instructional videos. I blamed an imperfect world
for that. I was a genius—I wasn't blaming myself, because it obviously was not my fault. Stefan didn't
throw up as I gradually turned theoretical into a reality.
I had to give him credit. He turned green, he closed his

eyes, he cursed nonstop, but he didn't vomit, and it was an extremely bumpy ride for at least fifteen minutes. Godzilla did throw up, down Stefan's shirt as he wrapped himself tightly around my brother's neck and shivered. He wasn't a fan of theoretical flying either. I was surrounded by critics.

That didn't improve five hours later when I landed at the new Institute. Stefan, who hadn't been at all interested in the details of maximum cruising speed, fuel capacity, maximum climb rate, called it crashing, but I think that was an exaggeration. Considering his lack of curiosity about all things plane related—except for the copilot's three-point restraint system, or as he referred to it, "Where's the goddamn seat belt?"—I didn't think he had much room to judge.

The ground's rapidly approaching brown dirt, the unforeseen difficulty in getting the nose up, the speed down, but not too far down, and the bouncing off a jutting rock camouflaged the same color as the dirt—it did get the adrenaline pumping. There was no doubt about that, but it didn't change matters.

"Gravity, genius," Stefan groaned, holding on to his seat so tightly with one of his hands that it would probably cramp for days. The other hand held something else. "Gravity leads to crashes."

Despite the bump on my head and the blood dripping down Stefan's forehead, it definitely wasn't a full-on, complete crash. It was at least a controlled crash and that was the next best thing to a legitimate landing. That was my opinion and I was sticking with it. Besides, it was not my fault. I didn't create the often-inconvenient laws of physics. "Gravity"—I waved a dismissive and slightly shaking hand at Stefan's bitching—"schmavity. It's all relative."

"I thought that was time, Einstein," he pointed out, wiping blood onto the dried ferret vomit already on his shirt, "not schmavity." Why did he have to be smart at the least timely moment? It was close enough to a landing, considering I'd taken off and flown the entire way via Internet instruction. A slight hiccup in the landing did not a catastrophe make. But what we had seen at the Institute with a bird's-eye view, what we found there at a closer—God, too close—look, wasn't a catastrophe. It was worse.

It was a nightmare—the entire, oblivious world's worst nightmare.

The bodies were everywhere.

The stench of rot made the air almost unbreathable.

This Institute had been set up about seventy-five miles out in the desert from Barstow, California. The first one had been in the Everglades outside Miami. Isolation was important when you were setting up a facility that looked like a prison—that was a prison.

Inside it was identical to the one where I'd grown up. Cheap tile, battleship gray walls, fluorescent lights, no windows—home, sweet home. Even the bodies were the same, in a way, only there were more—many more. I'd seen a few at my Institute. Sometimes a "student" would lose it, go flat-out psychotic, and break in a second. The crazed individual would usually kill a few instructors before the guards shot him—and the guards were everywhere. Two or three bodies a year was about average. You got used to it. You can get used to anything if you want to survive. But I hadn't seen anything like this before.

Instructors, researchers, guards littered the halls, the labs, the empty classrooms. Some were flat on the floor with blood that had dried around their heads after it had exploded out of their ears, noses, and mouths. Some were curled up, appearing as peaceful as if they were asleep . . . if they hadn't been in their second week of decomposition. They were bloated with green and brown stains showing through their clothes. That didn't bring "peaceful" to mind.

There were students too, about fifteen. About half were shot in the head and half were spread-eagled, surrounded by the stain of every cell of blood in their body. If it hadn't been dark brown and flaking on the tile, it almost would've looked like wings spread around them—as if they were angels. Only one student could do that to another: Wendy. Some students were more powerful than others, but to be good assassins, a good product, we all had to be fairly equal in power to be useful, to bring a good price, and not be competitive to the bidders.

That equality meant that if a student tried to hurt another student, it didn't work. We could protect ourselves. If one started to cut off the blood to my brain, I could keep those vessels open. If one tried to stop my heart, I could reverse it before it had time to take effect. Students could not hurt other students. One was an immovable object; one was an irresistible force, like Stefan and I emotionally. It was a waste of time.

But then Wendy had come along and no one else was half as powerful as Wendy. She was the exception to the rule when I'd been kept prisoner years ago. No one had been able to protect themselves from her then. It had been lucky for her maker that Wendy liked the Institute in those days. . . . Top of her class in every way, she couldn't wait to get out into the real world and do what she'd been created to do. She'd never caused any problems. The better she was, the faster she "graduated" and she knew it. If they gave out gold stars for being a good little assassin, she'd have had a wall full of them—a galaxy of the dead.

Things change.

People, made in a lab or the old-fashioned way, change too.

I couldn't take my eyes off the dead students. It was too bad those left behind hadn't thought of that.

"This is a rebellion. Looks like some kids finally got pissed off at their keepers and showed them exactly what they'd learned." Stefan's hand was on my shoulder, squeezing tightly as I stared down at two brown and broken angels. It was two girls, both with red hair. That was the only way to recognize them, the red hair. Lily and Belle. Tiger Lily and Tinkerbell. They'd needed enough girl names to balance out the Michaels and Peters. No one was good at the Institute. We couldn't be, I'd told myself long ago in my own sterile prison room. The best we could hope for was indifference to our fate if we refused to kill. But was that good? Truly good? I didn't know. Then Stefan came along and told me I was good. Too good, he emphasized from the self-defense point. It drove him nuts that I wouldn't kill to save my own life.

Except for the one time, when I was fourteen, when

I was surprised and attacked in that Institute test. I woke up some nights with the sharp sensation of his knife against my throat, the ephemeral feel of his heart turning to a useless sack of blood under my hand where it rested against his chest. I saw his eyes go vacant again and again. It was a memory that wouldn't let me take another life, not for any reason.

There had been others like me, although not as stubborn. They would've done what they were told, only without any particular enthusiasm. Not that that made a difference. Enthusiastic or no, their targets would've ended up just as dead. Obedience always trumped eagerness here. They wouldn't have rebelled against Marcus Bellucci, the second Jericho. There were plenty of other students who did have a genetic and psychological passion for spilling blood, unlike Lily and Belle, but they wouldn't have revolted either; they were too indoctrinated not to do as they were told.

Unless they had a leader.

Someone else to tell them what to do.

"We need to look at the video," I said abruptly, and headed down the hall to the stairs. The Alpha guard station would be located in the same place here as in the first Institute. Everything was. The walls were the same, the razor wire—I'd seen the Institute's mirror image when I'd flown over. Waiting for the arrival of Saul and our makeshift army at a safe distance, that had been the plan—that and a slight addendum: Stefan would shoot Raynor if we saw him approaching the Institute, because he was not taking a student, even Wendy—a victim herself, as lethal as she was—out of there. Everyone was going to have a chance at my cure and when it came to Raynor himself, as they said down South, he just flat-out needed killing. The last had been Stefan's addition, but it was hard to disagree with it.

But what we saw as we flew over changed all that. It was almost seven p.m. and light enough to see easily. In the courtyard—nice name for a huge square of dirt where we were able to go out to see the sun once a day and exercise—pale, flabby assassins might stand out. We had to look normal. Jericho had never been able to fix the assassin gene that resulted in the different-colored eyes, but in every other way we were to look normal.

There hadn't been any exercising in the yard when I'd flown the Cessna over it. There'd been ten dead guards, and that was a plan-changer if ever there was one. I'd landed—*landed*, not crashed—the Cessna while Stefan held on to his M249 machine gun with his free hand. It was surprising what people smuggled back from Afghanistan and more surprising how easy those things were to buy . . . if you knew the right people. When it came to weapons, Stefan knew all the right people. He had Saul make the purchase instead of making it himself, to keep us hidden, but it was surprising, all in all. It wasn't surprising, though, that he thought he might need it here.

The numbness I felt walking toward the Alpha station wasn't that unexpected either. I should've been experiencing a number of emotions, all of them bad, because I already knew what this meant, but at times, too much is too much. And I wasn't talking about the massacre here. Understanding that was simple enough. It was a rebellion, as Stefan had said. I never would've imagined it, but it was plain that was what had happened. But the rest of it . . .

They had killed the ones who didn't wholeheartedly embrace what they were. Although they would've done what they were told, obedient to the end, they'd killed them anyway. What did the army rangers say? The best of the best?

The worst of the worst had walked out of here and they were loose in the world. They were out there, able to do whatever they pleased. What pleased them most? Freedom? No.

Death.

Chapter 5

The station was empty. All the guards would've seen what had been unfolding on their monitors and had likely run out with guns and Tasers in hand, for all the good it had done them. I sat down in one of the three chairs and started typing on the computer. I needed the feed from approximately two weeks ago. It should be flagged. The guards would've hit the alarm when it all started to fall apart.

Or come together. It depended which side you were on.

"We'll be able to actually see what happened?" Stefan leaned over my shoulder as I sat in the chair before the console. "I'm not sure that's convenient; it's going to be pretty damn fucking horrifying."

I nodded at Stefan's question. "We're obedient. I mean, *they* were obedient." Being a genius could suck. Being a genius meant you couldn't fool yourself as often as you wanted to. But I was different now. I'd not been as obedient as was required while at the Institute, but I'd been too obedient in my eyes. I wasn't obedient at all now; Stefan would be the first to tell me that. "They wouldn't have done anything like this without someone telling them, pushing them. Someone only pretending to be submissive, which I would've said was impossible," I told him as I found the logs from when the alert had gone out. I was about to pull it all up when I heard a door slam against a wall. Stefan hit me hard, knocking me out of the chair to land on the floor on my back.

Of all those movies I'd watched, and horror movies were the best, zombie stories had never been my favorite. In my opinion, if you get eaten by something whose brain has decomposed, you sort of deserve it. Fast or slow, they remained the closest thing to brain-dead you could come up with. If you couldn't outrun or outthink them, it was hard to have sympathy when one started gnawing on your skull.

Now, in the position of all those victims I'd had little respect for, I changed my mind. When something that should be dead but isn't dead looms over you, the skin slipping from its muscle, pieces of it falling on you, its eyes blinded with a thick film, there were so many psychological reactions to have. Fight or flight. Catatonia. Reversion to screaming for a mommy you didn't remember. There were also the physiological responses . . . the least embarrassing being urinating in your pants. My body that was as frozen as my brain tried to pick one. I hoped it wasn't the urinating one.

A hand, darkened and squirming with maggots, reached down for me. "Go . . . back . . . to . . . your . . . room."

The voice was garbled, thick, and almost impossible to understand. Two weeks without water would do that to you. Some people thought you could last only three days without fluids. It wasn't true. Although I knew this bastard would've wished it were true if he had a brain cell functional enough to make a wish. It depended on your environment, temperature, exertion level, and general health. Two weeks was at the end of the scale, but it could be done. It was one of those "don't-try-this-at-home" situations. It was a horrific way to go.

His tongue was curled, black and dry as fire-scorched suede. The hand was closer now, the palm a disintegrating nightmare, and nearly at my neck, when the butt of an M249 slammed against the guard's head and he flew across the room to hit the wall. He slid to the base of it and didn't move again. "He came out of the storeroom. Someone got sloppy."

Stefan's words penetrated my last late-night movie fest and I sat up, his hand pulling me the rest of the way back to my feet. "Or they're making zombies now?" he continued. "Misha, I can handle an assassin factory, but an assassin slash zombie factory? Forget it. We are headed for the mountains and we are never coming down. I've seen the movies. The zombies always fucking win."

"No. You were right. Someone was simply sloppy." The guard was still alive. I didn't want to touch him, but the Institute had prepared me for that too. I'd seen human bodies in worse condition. To cause death, Jericho thought we needed to be acquainted with all aspects of death—from freshly killed to the next best thing to King Tut. I ignored Stefan's "Misha, don't you fucking dare," and touched the unconscious guard's face with three fingertips. There wasn't anything that wasn't wrong with him, nothing that wasn't dying in him . . . every single cell. It was difficult to trace back to where it all started. I closed my eyes and mentally sludged my way through a swamp of putrid decay.

There.

There it was.

I opened my eyes and wiped my fingers on my jeans. "Aneurysm in his brain, but they didn't quite finish the job. Shoddy work or in a hurry. He's been alive this whole time, but too brain damaged to do anything about it. Dying by inches. Then, without the ability to know he needed food or water and with his brain slowly disintegrating, he went into multiorgan failure. His body went into crisis mode and started feeding blood only to the organs that keep it alive—brain, heart, kidneys and liver. Muscles and skin didn't get their share anymore. Then the kidneys and liver failed." I stood from where I'd been kneeling beside him. "Which is why he's like this. Living people can rot too and it looks just the same as a corpse." I righted, then sat back in the chair Stefan had tackled me from. "I suppose . . ." I trailed off, hesitating, then pushed on. "I guess maybe you should shoot him to put him out of his misery." Because he was in misery—profound, agonizing misery.

And that had me asking my brother to do what I refused to do myself. Possibly I wasn't good, like Stefan said. Possibly I was only a hypocrite.

"After what this asshole has done?" Stefan shook his head. "He deserves every ounce of misery he can get and then some. Let him rot until his last damn breath. Nothing but justice in my book." My genetic code had been manipulated to allow me to kill as easily as breathing, but my brother knew a real monster when he saw one—a destroyer of children's lives. For him, the subject was over. "Now bring up the video."

I did. There were banks of video monitors and each one split into four pictures. In every one, all looked normal: students in the classrooms, hands locked before them on their desks; students in the cafeteria; students in the media room watching carefully selected movies and TV shows or reading books that would help them fit in with the outside world if they were ever called on to enter a conversation before assassinating their target. Thirty seconds later, the time stamp at the bottom of the screen hit three p.m. On the video you could hear the low-toned ring that meant time to change classes or report to one. Classes lasted until seven every day.

Every day except this one.

This time, at the very first ring, school was out.

On every monitor, students lunged at the nearest instructor, guard, screaming cafeteria server, and people began to die. Guards tried to shoot and some students they did hit, as they were trained—a bullet in the head. It was the only way to be sure, as quickly as we healed. According to legend, zombies were here after all. They were us. But the guards hadn't faced anything remotely like this before. One student going berserk, the mind shattering under the stress, was one thing. All the students in a coordinated attack—it had not been conceived. That meant the guards died. The instructors died, too, much more quickly. They were armed with Tasers and had one guard in each room, but they were complacent. Years of utterly obedient killer human robots had made them that way. They were slow to fumble for their weapons. Jericho's children, however, weren't. They were never slow, never unsure.

No weakness. No limitations. No mercy.

The Institute had taught us that, and now we—*they* showed them how well they'd learned that.

They ran—everybody but the guards, who had their guns and their surety that things rarely went wrong. None of them noticed, not in any video screen, how close a student had managed to position himself to them. Yes, some students did die, but not all; nowhere near all. The teachers and researchers were the ones who ran, not the students; to the students, it was nothing but a good time—not to every student, but to some. Could you blame them when that was what they were raised, taught, created to do? Could you blame them for learning *too* well?

When all the dead were on the floor, unmoving, and the screaming was over, the students gathered in the media room. It was a small metaphorical window to the outside world . . . a world that belonged to them now. That was when I saw him, the one who'd organized it all; the one who'd risen above training and brainwashing and blind obedience to make this revolution happen.

Peter.

As I'd been called simply Michael as I was the first Michael, Peter was called simply Peter, not Peter One. He was about the same age as me, close as I could guess, since he hadn't "graduated," so he was maybe a year or so younger. He had black hair, wavy and short, slightly darker skin, and the same bicolored eyes we all had. He looked more like Stefan's brother than I did. Funny that. Or maybe not so much. Peter was one of the eager ones. He liked to kill. Not as much as Wendy, but no one liked killing quite as much as Wendy. Genghis Khan, Attila the Hun, Stalin; they all paled before Wendy.

And there she was. . . . Wendy Five, but like Peter and me, no one called her anything but Wendy. Not because she was the first, but because all the other Wendys were only shadows of her. There were only twenty students left now, the rest shot by the guards. I could hear Peter's voice, determined, but pleased too—and too damn happy for what was coming. "Wendy." It was all he said. It was all that needed to be said.

Seven students dropped instantly and simultaneously, the angel wings of blood I'd seen earlier erupting from their eyes, their ears, noses, mouths . . . and from every pore. Ten-year-old Wendy moved closer to the bodies, putting a fingertip in her mouth and tilting her head to better judge her work. She smiled. The video was crisp and clear. I could see the healthy whiteness of her teeth, the pink of her lips, the faint outline of freckles across her nose. Her hair was as silver blond as it had been three years ago and fell like a mist of cool spring rain to her shoulders. She was a beautiful little girl; beautiful and happy. "Am I a good girl, Peter? I am, aren't I? Like a little sister should be. I'm so good." She tilted her head the other way. "They look like birds, don't they? Birds with bright red wings. Fly away birds. Fly away no more."

"You did well, Wendy, and you are a good girl. Like I always say. The best we have." Peter bent to give her a brotherly kiss on top of her head. After that, he looked up directly into the camera in the media room, speaking to me across two weeks' time. "Hello, Michael. We've missed you. Mr. Raynor told Bellucci that he'd found you in someplace called Cascade Falls." Bellucci would've shared that information all too quickly if asked in the right way, and every student left standing knew how to ask. "It sounds intriguing, but then everything on the outside sounds intriguing. He also said he'd be bringing you back soon, but we couldn't wait. We have too much to do." He smiled and his smile was almost as cheerful as Wendy's. "But I think we'll be seeing you anyway. Family should stay in touch."

Family? We had never been taught to think that way. It was highly discouraged. Bonding with fellow students could lead to . . . well . . . something like this. I hadn't thought of it once during my time there. Since I was barely obedient and unenthusiastic, it had taken Stefan to teach me something I thought a fantasy of the outer world. Santa Claus, the Easter Bunny, family—all were a daydream even out there. Something like that? It couldn't be real.

Somehow Peter had outstripped me easily and done what I couldn't. He'd seen the value in the concept, taught it to himself, realized what I couldn't without Stefan's help, and learned it well enough to spread it to the other students. Some might have embraced it and some might have seen him as only better than being sold to the highest bidder by the new Jericho, Marcus Bellucci. Whichever it had been, Peter had shown intelligence beyond my own and an overwhelming charisma with the other students that he must have kept hidden from the Instructors. And he had used all that to make himself a leader. He'd taught; they'd listened. Every student had transferred his submission to him and not to his new maker.

Peter was obviously smarter than I was, and Wendy, his "little sister," could kill in ways I didn't want to think about. We were in serious shit. And I hadn't thought it could get more difficult than only trying to rescue them.

My skills at seeing all the possibilities, every potential outcome had faded since I'd left the Institute—badly.

The video continued to show the rest. In an instant they filed out of the room. We could watch their progress as they went down the hall, upstairs, and out to the exercise yard. We had always had one bus, for field trips—to malls usually—to see if we could function, although heavily drugged just in case, in the real world among real people. Peter put his lost boys and girls on that bus and the last video shot was of it disappearing down a dirt road toward Barstow. I thought I saw Wendy waving enthusiastically from the back window.

"That was the little girl I saw when I rescued you, isn't it?" Stefan said. He'd seen Wendy face-to-face then and was more than lucky he was around to tell that story. Wendy must have been just curious enough to let him live, to see what would happen.

Wendy became bored easily. Many graves could attest to that.

I nodded and rubbed my eyes with two fingers.

"Wendy. Jericho's pride and joy. Although sometimes I think he was afraid of her as well."

"Why did he do it?" Stefan asked quietly. "Why did that guy—Peter?—why did he have her kill the other kids? They were in on it. Not that I blame them. Getting out of this hellhole, I'd have done anything too. But why did that one, Peter, the kid in charge, have Wendy kill the other ones?"

"Peter's not a kid. He's about my age," I said, thinking to myself that meant he was all the more deadly for it. "And there's a difference between obedience and enthusiasm," I said grimly, slumping in the chair. "The birds with the red wings," as Wendy called them, "were the difference. They did what they were told, but they didn't like it or dislike it. It was just something they had to do, like brushing their teeth. Apparently obedience isn't enough for Peter. He wants the varsity team." I used a sports term. Stefan had taught me a lot of those. Now I had to teach him. He thought he knew it all, what had been done to me, the life I'd come from, but I'd painted him a blurry picture. It was time to sharpen it. It was time for what I'd hoped I wouldn't ever have to do.

It was time to tell him about the Basement.

I was leading Stefan down the hall when he asked, "Where are we going? It stinks to holy hell in here and I'd think you'd have had your fill of seeing dead bodies today. I know I have."

"I've seen dead bodies all my life," I replied, then added for him, "All of my life I can remember, I mean."

I moved around one as I said that and opened the

door that led to a set of stairs. Stefan balked. "This doesn't go to another medical lab, does it?" He remembered the layout of the old Institute almost as well as I did. There would be nothing like the memory of getting your ten-year-lost brother back to etch a floor plan into a person's mind. "Because I've seen only one of those and I don't want to see another. I don't want you to see another either." Stefan had seen where they took samples of our blood and tissue, scanned us, where they implanted the tracking chips over the base of our spines, and where they took apart their failures— failures with names and lives, storing their organs in a large medical refrigerator. Luckily they kept that locked and Stefan hadn't seen the contents. The Basement was enough. I was glad he hadn't seen where I would've ended up—not obedient enough, not enthusiastic enough. It was common knowledge among the students what that refrigerator held.

Why wouldn't it be? Jericho told us.

It didn't mean I wanted Stefan to know, which made me the overprotective one this time. Taking turns was what we did. It was what real family did and what Peter's "family" had no interest in at all.

"No, it's not the med lab," I answered as I started down the stairs. "It's a lab, though, and I think you need to see it. The researchers called it the Basement. Some students"—Wendy, first and foremost, I thought to myself—"called it the Playground."

Stefan followed me, but the trudge of his feet on the stairs told me he wasn't happy about it. "I don't have a whole lot of desire to see someplace that girl called the Playground."

"You aren't . . . weren't the only one who thought that." I reached the bottom and opened the door. It was already unlocked and bore the thumbprint of a guard's hand, which was now lying on the floor. The guard was superfluous, heavy, and unnecessary. Only the hand had been needed. I stepped around it and into the lab to turn on the lights inside. Two weeks—that one guard upstairs had been an exception. I didn't think we'd find any pseudo zombies down here.

I ignored the room. I remembered its double in Florida, although I'd seen it only once. Large with five cells, the room held video cameras to record the "play" and computers to type in reports for Jericho—or for Bellucci after Jericho's death. Bellucci was here now, right here. I couldn't recognize his face through the rot, not from the other four researchers dead on the floor, but his once-starched and immaculate lab coat had his name stitched over his chest. It was easily readable through the stains. He had less confidence or more false pride than Jericho. Jericho wore a suit. He didn't need his name out there like a billboard. We knew who he was— the beginning and the end; the alpha and the omega of our lives. That didn't need a name tag. It would be the same as marking the Apocalypse on a puppies and kittens wall calendar.

Pointless.

I took what I was searching for from the flop and stink of Marcus Bellucci's hand. An eight-by-ten rectangle— I could picture him holding it between him and Wendy or Peter as the most useless of shields. It was only a clipboard, made to hang on a hook beside the door. It wasn't high-tech like most things in the Institute, but it was as informative.

Stefan, I saw from the corner of my eye, had walked forward to examine the cells. They were the same as jail cells basically: a toilet and a bunk. You couldn't be sure how long it was until someone earned their playtime. You had to keep the prisoners from stinking up the place. For hygiene, there was a hose and a floor that slanted down to a drain to let the soapy water pour away.

"What the hell is this?" Stefan moved from cell to cell and finally I let myself see. Two cells were empty and three others had a dead man in each. Unlike the "red birds" upstairs, they weren't ready to fly, fly away; they had virtually exploded. Torn apart, they covered the floor of the six-by-six cells in pieces. Did you ever wonder what would happen should every vessel in your body burst under enormous pressure, each one, down to the tiniest vein? Probably not. Why would you wonder something like that?

But if you did . . . Wendy was the answer, and now Peter, unfathomably, had her on a false familial leash.

I looked away from the human version of raw hamburger. "In the Everglades, they brought us the homeless from Miami. Here, I'm guessing they went all the way to Las Vegas. Barstow is too small. The disappearances would be noticed." I handed Stefan the clipboard. He read it aloud.

"Wendy, Peter, Peter, Peter, Wendy, Wendy, Wendy, Michael Three, Wendy, Wendy, Lily Four, Peter, Peter, Peter, Peter, Belle Three, Peter. What is this?" He dropped it on the floor. I didn't blame him. The paper was as stained as what was left of Marcus Bellucci.

"This is the Playground. This is where you got to go if you'd done especially well, scored very high on a particular test," most often of the killing sort, "and deserved to be rewarded. You were brought down here to pick a prisoner and play as long or as quickly as you wanted. As messy or neat. Down here was the only free-for-all in the Institute. And there should be two names that stood out on the list. Every time you saw their name, someone down here died." I bent down and picked the clipboard up to hand it back to Stefan. "Maybe you should count." I'd scanned the date at the top of the page, which looked to be the first of about fifteen pages in all. "And the clipboard covers only three months. You need to know, Stefan, who spent most of their time down here. I said some of the students wouldn't want to be cured. Peter and Wendy would sooner die than be cured."

"But they'd much rather we die than try to cure them," he said as he shuffled through the pages, either counting or seeing what he'd rather not know the exact numbers on. "Did they ever bring you down here, Misha?" His eyes were on mine. "Not because you were the killer they wanted you to be, but for accidentally doing too well at some other test."

Everyone was brought down here. Ninety percent of the time it was a reward; ten percent of the time it was a test in itself. "I never killed anyone down here," I replied. And I hadn't. I'd been brought down in the evening of the same day Stefan had rescued me, four hours before he'd shown up in the doorway of my room.

I'd made my stand in the mirror of this place. Obedient, but not obedient enough. Genetically altered to be a killer, but refusing to fulfill my scientific destiny. I knew what it meant, that disobedience, but I didn't care. I just couldn't bring myself to care about surviving anymore . . . not in this life. I was taken back to my room where I knew they would come for me. They always came for the failures in the middle of the night. It was less of a disruption. We all knew what happened to those who flunked out of the Institute, but telling us and showing us were different. It led to more students losing it and killing everyone around them in a psychotic fit.

Good discipline, but in the end not profitable, Jericho had eventually decided.

That was why, when Stefan had come for me and had opened the door to my room, I'd been sitting on the bed, waiting, but not for him. I hadn't known he'd existed or that rescue was possible. I'd been ready for them to come and take me to the other lab . . . where failures were taken apart, studied, and then tucked away in specimen jars. Stefan didn't know that. He didn't know that had he been a day or a few hours later, I would've been scraps on an autopsy table.

And he wasn't going to know. That was a "what if" no brother could live with.

"I never killed anyone in the Basement," I repeated. Unless you counted almost killing myself by breaking Institute rules.

"Never thought differently, kiddo," Stefan assured me, tossing the clipboard forcefully across the room and slinging the M249 across his back. Putting both hands on my shoulders, he steered me back toward the door. "Now, let's get the hell out of here, call Saul, and abort the mission. It's not as if we need an army now. We have no idea where these kids are."

I countered, "You have to stop thinking of them as kids. Whether they're nineteen or ten, Stoipah, they can kill you, and you won't be able to do a thing to stop them with that attitude. All right? Nothing. Think of them as what they are—killers. Killers who, unlike some of the others, love to kill. Live to kill. You have to be ready and never, *never* let one touch you or you'll die." "Stoipah," the Russian nickname for Stefan, had slipped out before I could snatch it back. But, damn it, I worried about him. The big brother, the protector . . . he'd seen the tape of the massacre, but he'd also lived with me for three years and, deep down, I knew, he saw all the students as he saw me.

Salvageable. Needing only my cure. Teenagers, kids, children.

He was dead if he continued thinking that way. I had to figure out a way to send home the fact that killers were killers, children or adults, and if seeing all he had in this place hadn't done that . . . hell. I didn't bother to marvel anymore at how easily the curse words came. "Cancel the army, but your friend Saul—he might be able to help. Have him come. And we do know where the students are, or did you forget the tracking chips?" I'd had one in my back until Stefan had had a very shady doctor remove it. All my former classmates would have the same. "I'll grab one of the Institute's GPS trackers upstairs."

"Tell me what it looks like and I'll get it. You'll be

better off down here doing your computer thing. They might have information that'll help. You keep saying your cure is almost ready or should work . . . theoretically." He mimicked the last. "It's been almost three years. Who knows what these shitheads have come up with. They might have something to help us."

He was right. They might, but not in the way he thought. The Institute wasn't interested in cures, but they could have come up with a way to disable chimeras for a time. Wendy's abilities to kill with only a thought had always been a worry for them, although seeing what had happened upstairs and down here, I rather doubted they'd accomplished anything. It wouldn't hurt to check, however. Before I could start toward the bank of computers, Stefan handed me a gun. It was his backup—one of his many backups, rather, a small revolver. A .38? Guns didn't much interest me. I knew the types Stefan favored above all, the same way you know someone's favorite color, but that was it. Other than when I had been shot that time, guns were pointless in my life. I had the ability to perform better than any handgun. Now, a pipe bomb . . . that was a different matter. I respected my limitations.

"It's a thirty-eight Special," Stefan said. I'd been right as I usually was. But today wasn't a day for being proud of that. "It's light, not much recoil, no safety, and it's double action. All of that means you just have to point and pull the trigger over and over until you run out of ammo. Hopefully by that time you won't need any more ammo."

I held it and it was heavier than it looked. "Stefan, everyone down here is dead."

"That's what we thought about Zombie Bob upstairs. Since you've not shot a gun before, stubborn bastard, aim for their torso. It's your best bet of hitting them." Stefan had tried to get me to learn to shoot for the past two years. It wasn't that he wanted me to have to shoot someone. It was the last thing he wanted for me and told me so, but he was also a strong believer in better safe with the other guy dead than sorry with you dead.

I'd refused. I'd made it clear time and time again I wasn't going to kill anyone. I simply wasn't. That was the choice I'd made and I was comfortable with it. Stefan pointed out I could limit myself to shooting people in the legs, and he was right, but it was one more layer of lethalness to me I didn't want to add. I was all the lethal my psyche could deal with. The pipe bombs were for killing SUVs and other vehicles, not people. They were also an interesting experiment and I was a sucker for interesting. "No." I gave him back the gun. "You know I'm not going to do it. And if there is a Zombie Bob down here, I'll touch him and cut off blood flow to his brain long enough to knock him out."

"Stubborn. Goddamn stubborn." But he took back the gun, muttering under his breath that he'd rather shoot one of these rotting monsters than touch one any day.

As I'd said before, it was anatomy class all over again. Bodies were bodies; nothing new or unusual. I didn't spare them another glance, stepped over one on my way to the computers, and went to work. I didn't find anything especially helpful, but I did find one thing I'd suspected for a while. Life: Expect the worst and be pleasantly surprised. My life in the past day: Expect the worst and find out how lacking in imagination you really are.

I bowed my head, exhaled, and closed my eyes for a moment. Then I straightened, retrieved several travel drives of Institute information, and headed toward the stairs. Life was life. You either gave up on it, as I had while imprisoned in the Institute, or you made the best of it, as I had every day since I'd made it out of those walls.

Now that I was free, the best was all I'd settle for.

Two hours later we were in Barstow. We'd taken an SUV, tan to blend in with the dirt and sand, from the Institute and gone back to the plane for all our equipment. The Cessna's nose had been only slightly crumpled. One wheel bent sideways a bit. Stefan, who would be considering the day we'd had—I'd had, seeing my fellow students dead—had said nothing. Big brothers know when to give you a hard time and when to let it go. I learned that in the first six months I'd been on the run with Stefan.

After packing up everything, including Godzilla, we'd driven into Barstow and parked at an outlet mall. Mixed in with all the other vehicles, we may as well have been invisible. It would've been dark if not for the parking lot lights, but the lot was still packed full of cars.

In the driver's seat, Stefan was arguing on his cell. "Saul, just park your ass at the Las Vegas airport, send the mercs back, pay them full price . . . *pay* them full price, I said, same as if they'd done the job. The last thing we need in the middle of this is pissed-off mercs. We'll pick you up there." From the loud squawking, Saul didn't sound enthused at joining us without his army to chase after a band of killer kids. And Stefan's further excuse of we'd only attract attention with a caravan of mercenaries, perhaps government attention we definitely didn't want, didn't calm the squawking any. "Saul, just shut your yap. You're coming and you know you're coming. Wait for us. It'll be about three hours. Okay, Jesus, fine. We'll pick you up at the craps table at Caesar's. And, yeah, yeah, I know your fee will bankrupt me and three Third World countries." Disconnecting, he smacked his forehead lightly with the phone. "I know he helped save our lives God knows how many times, but breaking my foot off in his ass would be damn satisfying."

Under Stefan's eye, I had finished double-checking the two cases I had stowed in the SUV with several injection systems that looked like bulky guns. These were designed to be the mode of delivery for the cartridges. Those cartridges, plastic cylinders, had been made to be filled with a drug I'd started working on two years ago to alter the genetic makeup of the other chimeras. The cylinders could also be filled with enough tranquilizer to take down a rhino for a week or a chimera for an hour. Everything was intact in the foam packing despite the slightly less than smooth landing.

"Is it all good there?" He continued to smack his forehead with the phone.

"Nothing is broken," I said, evading with the truth.

"And you're not going to do your forehead any good banging on it more."

"I'm hitting it now, my choice. The windshield of your plane chose to hit it earlier." He had a two-inch cut, crusted with dried blood, and a dark bruise surrounding it. I determined to hack into that training video Web site and take my money back. As instructional tools, they were all but worthless, even to a genius. With proper videos, I was positive the landing would've been perfect.

The bump on my forehead was naturally already gone. Quick healing shouldn't make someone feel guilty, but occasionally it did. There was something I wanted to bring up to Stefan about the healing matter, but now wasn't the time. I wasn't quite sure when that time would be. "We need to get the first aid kit. I took it from the plane and put it in the backseat," I said.

"He's right, you know. That's a nasty cut you're sporting there, mate."

I had rolled down my window to get a flow of cool twilight air. It could've been to air out Godzilla's musky smell; that would've been reason enough. I'd stuck my head out when I had to make a cursory check to make sure no one was close enough to hear Stefan talking to Saul, but that hadn't kept someone from crouching and moving their way up beside my window to now rest a muzzle of a gun against my temple. "By the way, Michael, I've been with the Institute long enough to know you can't heal a bullet in your brain, and if you try to touch me, I'll put one there."

I couldn't turn my head, but I could see Raynor from

the corner of my eye, and I recognized him from the photos. He had a pleased smirk that revealed startlingly white teeth. Up close, I could also see the short dark hair and the satisfied glint in his black eyes. His face was cheerful with victory, but I had a feeling it would turn dark and toxic if he was crossed. "And Stefan Korsak. Nice to finally make your acquaintance. You were better at hiding than your father was . . . for a while. And please don't go for your gun, if you had any such rude inclinations. You might get me, but how gratifying would vengeance be when you're splattered with Michael's brains? Or should I say your brother's brains?" The smirk became more mocking. "Or should I not?"

I kept what vision I could on Raynor, but I didn't feel the air stir or hear the seat squeak. Stefan was doing as he was told. He was not moving and he wasn't speaking either. With an unknown element like Raynor, it was his best instinct, honed by his time in the mob. My time had been honed elsewhere and that led to a different approach. "You have a slight accent, Mr. Raynor. New Zealand. Christchurch, I think. But you came to the United States when you were twelve? Thirteen?"

The glitter in his eyes brightened as the muzzle ground harder against my temple. I felt blood vessels breaking, causing an incipient bruise. A fraction of a second later, I felt the blood vessels slowly knitting themselves back together. As I slept less now, I healed faster too. The difference almost three years could make in my abilities was staggering. When or if he pulled the gun away, I wouldn't have a bruise—the damage having healed before it had a chance to fully develop.

"You know me, then, and you're good with accents," Raynor commented, unfazed by my guess. "You are as clever as them all, aren't you? My mum's American. Would you like to see my papers? I've dual citizenship. I'm even human, which is more than I think can be said about you, Michael." The muzzle pressed harder against my head as that cheerful dark glint was snuffed out. "But enough about me. I'd like you to tell me what happened to the whole bloody lot of them, humans and freaks alike, back at the Institute."

He'd been there, probably not long after we had. We had guessed he would be heading there after we escaped him, looking for Wendy, his own "freak." If he was that involved in the Institute, he knew no other student could hurt me or contain me. He wasn't as smart as I'd originally thought. Wendy didn't hurt or control anyone. Wendy only killed, and Raynor could do that himself with a gun . . . like the one against my head.

"You know what happened." This time Stefan did speak, cautiously and slowly. "You saw the tape the same as we did. When there's slavery, there will always be rebellion. Only these slaves are walking, talking AK-47s, and that is on you." The caution faded. "You and every other bastard at that goddamn torture chamber. It's just too damn bad you didn't happen to be there when it went down."

That didn't make Raynor happy. "You're as mouthy as your father was, at least as he was at the beginning. But then again, a power saw will stop and have a man thinking better. It doesn't matter what happened at the Institute. I saw the tape, yes. I saw the ones who escaped and I'll have them back soon enough, plus"—he used his other hand to take a handful of my hair and give my head a light shake—"this one. Jericho didn't consider him worth graduating, but beggars can't be choosers, now can they? I'll take him off your hands 'as is.' A better deal you won't get and that's a fact. If you want a psychic assassin of your very own, you'll have to bid the same as everyone else."

"You're not taking him anywhere." Stefan's words were as dark as Raynor's eyes.

"Oh, but I think I am. I can take him, and I am, or I can blow out his brains and then do the same to you. You seem fond of your little killer pet. Ah . . . it must be the family thing and all that. Am I right? If that's so, I'd think you'd rather know he's alive than know he's one of two corpses in an SUV that smells of ferret." The smile was wider. "Now, this is what you're going to do. You're going to shoot yourself in each leg. I'm sure you have a silencer, so it won't be heard—no doubt this would be the case with a careful, cautious man such as yourself with your wide range of career experience in that area. Do try not to scream, if you please. And then, when you've done that, you will throw your gun—who am I fooling?—you will throw *all* of your guns into the back where you can't reach them."

"Then?" Stefan asked, the darkness suddenly gone from his voice. It was empty—lacking in emotion, lacking in inflection, lacking in humanity itself, and if Raynor had been half as intelligent as I'd thought he was, he would've dropped his own gun and run.

"Then Michael and I take a drive, but have no worries. I do want him alive. He's a valuable commodity, which oddly the two of you have never made use of, but no accounting for business acumen. Oh, and you can be certain my car won't have an Institute GPS tracker in it as this one you stole does."

I shifted my glance to Stefan and now he was smiling. I wouldn't have thought I'd see a smile that equaled Wendy's, but this one did. Sliding my gaze back to Raynor, I smiled myself. What it looked like, I had no idea. It wasn't one I'd practiced. It was genuine and sprang from a place of surgical blades and ice-cold metal and human flesh floating in jars. "Asshole," I said, "did you think we didn't know that?" Raynor's own smile faded into a split second of confusion. A split second was all he had time for.

The driver's window to the truck parked next to us slid down. Raynor turned swiftly at the soft sound and right into the short metal baton Saul slammed across his throat. Mr. Homeland Security fell to the asphalt instantly. He'd dropped his gun to grab at his throat with both hands. From the strangled sounds and the rapid color change from red to blue, his trachea had been shattered by Saul's blow. He was about five minutes away from death by asphyxiation.

I wasn't sympathetic. While I wouldn't kill, I did recognize that in the world we lived in there were people who deserved the ultimate punishment. Anyone involved in the Institute deserved it. Anyone who sent a sandwich-eating idiot to shoot my brother deserved it. Anyone who wanted to *sell* me as if I were nothing more than a sniper rifle deserved it.

Saul grinned, his white-streaked ginger beard a strange frame to such a homicidally happy flash of teeth. "Okay, I'd rather really be at Caesar's instead of faking it over the phone, but wetwork costs you double. That makes my bank account get a boner like there's no tomorrow." He started to open the door. "I'd better finish the job before he attracts attention, kicking and gasping like a headless chicken. Nice suit, though. I wonder where he bought it."

Before he could, there was a shout. "Hey, what's going on? What are you doing to that guy? What the fuck? Someone call the police!"

Good Samaritans more often for those on the run were Inconvenient Samaritans. "Shit. Civilians. I hate civilians." Saul swore, slammed his door shut, started the truck, and drove off, the vehicle's tires squealing. Stefan was right behind him. We'd been parked too close, as planned for the ambush of Raynor, for either car to swerve enough to put an end to the government agent without colliding with each other. He would have to take the full five minutes to die as no ambulance would get there in time. It wasn't as if things were ending differently for him, I told myself. If the rebellion at the Institute hadn't happened and Raynor had managed to get Wendy out to chase after me—free in the world as she was now, it would've been the same. Chases could be long and boring. Wendy didn't like boring. Eventually she would've had to find some way to entertain herself. Wendy would've eaten him for lunch.

We just saved her the time.

Chapter 6

We hadn't had to wait long at all for Raynor to show up in that parking lot. What we'd found at the Institute hadn't made us forget about him. He wasn't thirteen chimeras loose in the world, but he was smart and dangerous. He'd found Anatoly. He'd found us. He'd remained very much a threat, if the lesser one. We had enough on our plate to keep looking over our shoulders for him. It was another lesson that Institute and *Mafiya* teaching agreed on. If one threat is out of reach, take care of the one that isn't. Raynor had to be taken care of, one way or the other. I didn't know what had disturbed Stefan more when we'd both come to the separate but nearly simultaneous conclusion: that I could think like an ex-mobster or that he could think like a trained genetic assassin.

I'd have to ask him later, when he wasn't expecting it, to see how fiercely his brain would cramp. Brothers did that—joked around with each other. The three primary sources of information in my life now had taught me that: Stefan, movies, and the Internet. I'd gotten good at it in the past few years—so good that sometimes when I opened my mouth, Stefan's eye would twitch before I said a single word.

Now with Raynor done and gone, we headed east, driving five hours, twenty-two minutes, and thirty-five seconds, before stopping at one a.m. at a motel in St. George, Utah. The Institute GPS tracker had indicated Peter and the rest had stopped too. They had been in the same position since I'd entered their codes into the tracker from the data I'd taken off the Institute computers. I'd studied the tape, every face. I'd known them all either my whole life or their whole lives . . . starting at the age of three. If you were three, you were old enough to sit quietly at a desk and learn, said the Institute. You were also old enough to fathom the consequences if you didn't. That was something the Institute didn't say—it proved.

And where were the ones younger than that? I tried hard not to think about it. Raised by foster-type families, Stefan had guessed. Or by their own family if they were like me and harvested instead of grown in a surrogate. That was his second guess. I didn't guess at all. I would search the Institute's computer files to see if I could find mention of a place, an assassin's day care. I'd look for facts, not guesses. But I'd do that later. Better to take on one impossible crusade at a time.

Peter and the others were in Laramie, Wyoming, at the moment, which was curious. They could've gotten much farther in two weeks. Then again, where were they going? Were they going anywhere in particular at all? Or were they making the entire country their new Basement, their Playground? If the only thing that satisfied you was spreading death, you could do that anywhere. Location, location, location—that meant nothing to a chimera. Anyplace that hosted a single living thing was your Playground.

At the motel, I began to pull my bags from the back-seat of the Ford Mustang we'd stolen off a random exit. The SUV and its GPS we'd driven off the interstate and torched before continuing on. Simple arson wasn't challenging. I hadn't participated. Saul had seemed to enjoy it, however; the same Saul whose hand slapped me on the back as I wrestled the bags out. "How's it going, Mikey? Long time no see . . . in person anyway. E-mails lack that personal touch. By the way, how'd that plane work out for you?"

Saul was Stefan's friend, although they'd both deny it and swear to their graves it was a business relationship only. Saul was also something of an acquired taste, like Brussels sprouts. Our landlady brought us dinner once a week without fail and it always included Brussels sprouts. It was like Lolcats—if people bothered with that tasteless shit or, conversely, with an incredibly bad-tasting vegetable, then there must be a reason. If people ate those disgusting things, there had to be an explanation. I hadn't figured out what it was yet, not after a year of grimly forking down their repulsiveness on a weekly basis, but I'd been determined. There was an answer and I'd find it. The fact that everyone else figured it out when they were eight instead of nineteen didn't deter me one bit. They might get AP credit in Brussels sprouts, but I'd catch up. Geniuses always did.

I didn't have to be a genius to know that Saul was a Brussels sprout. I didn't get what Stefan saw in him. It might take a few more years, but, as with the vegetable, eventually I would. "The plane worked adequately." I heard Stefan snort and ignored him. "It's not Mikey. It's never been Mikey. It's not Michael either. It's Misha now." I hefted one bag and tossed the other over my shoulder. "I'm also two and a half years older, have several degrees, blend in"—although my drug dealer persona needed work—"learned to fly"—more or less—"and I've picked up considerably on my cursing. I think I've been fairly productive."

"Cursing?" I turned with the bags and Godzilla looped around my neck to see Saul's hand immediately cover his mouth, muffling the rest of his words. "Good for you. Next to screwing, cursing is one of life's greatest pleasures."

He was mocking me. He knew what I could do, what I was. Stefan and I had debated long and hard about telling him, but when it came down to his being willing to hire the mercenaries and help us take the Institute back, he did deserve to know what he'd be facing in them. And in me. Yet here he was, laughing silently. I narrowed my eyes. "You aren't afraid of me, are you?"

He dropped his hand. "Sorry, Mikey, but nope. I've seen killers. Hell, I am one myself. I can tell when someone doesn't have it in them—not that there's anything wrong with that."

"There is everything right with that, in fact," Stefan interjected firmly as he passed us on the way to one of the rooms we'd rented.

"So, sorry, bucko. Not afraid of you." The same hand swatted my shoulder in apology.

Not afraid of me. That was . . . irritating.

It shouldn't have been. In Cascade Falls, no one was

afraid of me—of my persona, Parker. Saul should've boosted my belief in myself and my conscience. I didn't want to hurt people, right? I wouldn't kill people, ever.

But I could.

I was the same as a gun. I had my safety on, but that didn't mean I didn't deserve to be treated with caution and respect by those who knew me for what I was. I should be given the consideration of any other weapon. Not by my brother, but certainly by a tantric-practicing, horny old criminal who from the neon bright blue, purple, and green of his shirt was color-blind. Forty-five if he was a day. Definitely old. Practically in senility territory. He might be a vegan, Stefan had said, but there were so many things in the body that could go wrong with only the slightest push. You were never as healthy as you thought, especially with a chimera around. And worst of all, he had called me Mikey. I growled low in my throat and followed Stefan to our room.

When the door shut behind us, I tossed my bags onto the bed farthest from the door. Old habit—before we'd settled in Cascade Falls with rooms of our own, Stefan always slept on the bed between me and the door. "I can make him impotent, you know. Or all his hair fall out. I wonder how he'd like that." Saul had a thick head of hair . . . for his advanced age. That would destroy him. Bald and impotent—no more tantric sex camp; his life as he knew it would be over. I gave it consideration. Close or casual—whichever it was, I wasn't going to admit to it.

"Getting cranky, are we?" Stefan dumped his own bags. "And Saul likes you."

"He called me *Mikey*." And he acted as if I were as harmless as a goldfish.

"He's just yanking your chain. That's what he does to people he likes. People he doesn't like . . ."—Stefan shrugged—"he hits in the throat and crushes their larynx. It's a distinction I think you can make. Besides, you're not a woman and yet he can actually still see you. For Skoczinsky, that's huge."

"He looks like an orange-haired peacock," I grumbled. "I think his shirt destroyed my retinas."

"I remember your first shopping trip. Trust me, your taste wasn't any better than his then." Stefan locked the door and jammed the chair under the handle. It was done as automatically as it had been years ago. We were both falling into the old ways.

I couldn't deny his claim. I'd gone from barely seventeen with shirts portraying Einstein, Freud, Marilyn Monroe, and Marvin the Martian to simple, gray long-sleeved T-shirts, jeans, and a dark brown leather jacket. At first it had been to not stand out. Then it had become routine, and finally it had become me— as buying planes and playing a drug dealer had become me.

I'd kept the Einstein magnets on the refrigerator, though, a memory of my first days free. But they were gone now too—burned to a crisp. Except for . . . I opened up my backpack, pulled out a wad of soft, faded material, and saw one of Marvin's eyes winking at me from the folds. I laid it beside the pillow and Godzilla hopped from my shoulder with a satisfied chirp to curl up in it.

Stefan sat on his bed after stripping off his jacket and

pulling the Steyr out of his shoulder holster to lay it on the bedside table. "Michael . . ."

"Misha," I reminded him. I wasn't Michael. I wasn't one of them anymore.

"Misha," he repeated, aggrieved—only mildly, but. . . .

Aggravation was one of the easier emotions to identify and use. Simple irritability could be escalated to an attention-drawing rage with the few right words. Then, while chaos ensued, you could slip away and be within touching reach of your target within seconds. A chimera didn't need seconds. We needed only the most fleeting of touches.

I blinked and shook my head slightly. Other old habits, pre-Stefan ones, were coming back as well. Not habits, lessons. And I could forget them if I tried hard enough . . . not today or tomorrow. I still needed them, but someday, when freedom was permanent.

"That's three names now, four if you count Parker. One more and I'm just getting it over with and calling you Cher. So, Misha," he said, emphasizing it carefully, sarcasm in every letter, "what do you think they'll do now that they're out? Peter and his Dickensian gang of would-be criminals? What would they want?"

Dickens, Charles. Born 1812; died 1870. I shuffled through my memory. Fiction, boring, gray, and grim . . . unless the orphans were singing about starvation on stage. That might rev it up some, but I had never watched it and didn't plan to, so that was a theory unproved. "Dickensian? I guess they are Dickensian, if Oliver Twist ever made anyone vomit up their own intestines."

No longer irritated, but blank, Stefan looked over at

his gun. It was the kind of emotional vacuum some people—*good* people—needed to do what was necessary. "I know. I don't want to. Hell, they are kids, but, yeah, I know."

But he didn't. He didn't know. He only thought he did and he might as well jump off the Empire State Building if he couldn't do better.

"For the last time, Stefan, they aren't kids," I emphasized. " 'Kid' is a measure of age in the outside world. In the Institute, it has no meaning. Look at what Wendy did, and she's ten. You wouldn't ask a rattlesnake how old it was, would you? Age doesn't matter. From ten to eighteen"—which covered Peter to Wendy—"any of them can and will kill you, given the slightest opportunity. And that is what they want." I stroked Godzilla as he slept, chirring in his sleep, paws twitching. "They're not like me, Stefan. Not these thirteen." It was an unfortunate number, just as history claimed it to be.

"They like what they are and what they can do. They like it more than anything. They aren't going to settle down in some little town." I felt another pang at losing Cascade Falls, shoved it down, and pushed on. "They are going to kill people. And I doubt there will be any rhyme or reason to it. They're out of the assassin factory and in the chocolate factory. Every day is dessert Sunday and everyone they come across is potentially . . ."—I shrugged as unease tightened my spine—"dead meat." I'd almost said "victim," but that made it too desperate, too gut-wrenching. When facing the Institute's best and worst in one, we'd have to be as cold as they were or we wouldn't have a chance of surviving. Pit emotion against a chimera and you would die.

Stefan looked at me with a more familiar expression. He didn't get it, despite what he said. "No, they're not like you. I get that, believe it or not." He got up to move to the bathroom, shoving my head lightly as he passed me. "I'm glad you get it too." He closed the door behind him, and I heard the shower start. I fell back across the bed and stared at the dingy yellow ceiling. No, he didn't get it and he wasn't going to. He couldn't understand Institute-born were never kids, never children. It was the damn age thing; otherwise he would've gotten it and known a murderer when he saw one. I wasn't the only one who'd spent years surrounded by killers. Stefan had done his time too. He was like me in that way.

We were two peas in a poisonous pod—or two peas who'd escaped their pod and were living the life they wanted. Hardworking, good people who wouldn't hurt a fly if they had their way. I noticed Stefan's gun was gone. It would be with him in the bathroom and I remembered the man he'd shot only this morning.

Okay, maybe we fell somewhere in between.

Sitting up, I reached for the laptop in my duffel bag and checked to see if Ariel was online. She kept both late and early hours, the same as I did. She'd once said there was so much to do in life that she would sleep when she was dead. I pointed out she was a Buddhist and would never be dead, only reincarnated. She said I was a smart-ass. And I was smart, but I hadn't meant to be an ass. It was a clear supposition: You can't sleep when you're dead if you're never actually dead. Then she said she was Buddhist only on Tuesdays. She practiced a different religion or philosophy every day. How else could you learn?

It was a good point. I personally thought Buddhism was too challenging. With Christianity, you said you were sorry and poof, you were forgiven. In Buddhism, it didn't matter how sorry you were. If you did the crime, you did the time—boot camp for your soul. That was why I hadn't picked a philosophy or religion yet. I wanted to check out all my options and find the one with the most loopholes combined with the least amount of time consumption. I had things to do. Garages weren't going to blow themselves up, now were they?

Ariel was online. Her icon picture popped up immediately on IM. Instant messaging was a little riskier than e-mail for hacking, but I had so many fake addresses bouncing this and my many e-mail addys nearly a hundred times around the globe that you'd have to be a computer genius times ten to track my location. Institute personnel, except for Jericho, had never had the imagination for that—hacking is an art, not a science. Institute students didn't have access to the Internet, and no World of Warcraft basement dweller-hacker wannabe knew I existed. Security was as good as I wanted it to be.

Where've you been, Dr. Theoretical? We were supposed to watch Tombstone *tonight. I promised I wouldn't mock your preoccupation with horses and testosterone. And then* Ghostbusters *to see who of us could diagram a working proton pack first. I had popcorn waiting and everything.*

We had a standing weekly movie . . . thing. It wasn't a date, definitely not; only a . . . thing. We watched the movies at the same time and IM'ed back and forth, either mocking it or betting we could do it better. The flux capacitor battle had been going on for months now.

Ariel's icon was her smiling face Photoshopped onto a mermaid's body with tasteful shells covering certain areas. Mine, since I'd taken her suggestion to heart, was a floating grin, wide and wicked, and nothing else. The Cheshire cat—now you see me, now you don't.

And to Raynor—now you never will again.

Family emergency, I typed back. *Which means I'll have to turn my paper in early. You're absolutely certain the solution would work giving all the hypothetical guidelines? The surplus chromosome on the extra DNA strand would become inactive?*

Yes, yes. Will you stop questioning my brilliance? There was a smiley face icon, but, like me, Ariel couldn't leave anything alone. The usual yellow smiley face was now pale pink, the eyes had lashes, the bottom had a scaled tail, and the top had a wild pink seaweed mass of hair. It also had Poseidon's trident, which meant she was annoyed. *I'm going with ninety-five percent chance of efficacy. But it's all work, work, work with you, cutie. And worse, you won't share. That chromosome is like nothing I've seen and you've only given me half the information on it and won't tell me where you discovered it. But, hey, I get it. No one wants to share the Nobel.*

I would've laughed at that, but more in resignation than anything else. I couldn't go to a real college and I couldn't practice in a field, not one that attracted science types. The Institute was gone, but day care remained. I had no idea if they had the older children's files or not—my file. For now, it was coffeehouses, bookstores, and in Bolivia, busing tables in a restaurant where tourists tipped as if the money were superglued to their hands. *No Nobels. But if I did get one, I'd share with you. Promise.*

There was a pause; then the icon's trident disappeared and a bowl of popcorn appeared instead. *Okay, you're still my Bernie, but don't forget, there are lots of guys around here who'd love a movie night with me right in my own apartment building, but I chose you and your brilliant-ass lives in Texas! Sorry to hear about your family, though. Hope everything turns out all right.* She didn't pry. That was one thing that had made me so comfortable with her at first—that and her ability to keep up with me in any scientific field. *Same time next week for cowboys and proton pack races?*

Bernie was yet another fake name to go along with Parker and Sebastian, and Texas was a fake home. But movie night was real and I was afraid I was going to miss it for a while . . . if I was lucky—forever if I wasn't. I didn't say that, though. All my life was hiding and living a lie. Ariel couldn't be any different, whether I wanted her to be or not. *I'll bring the butter,* I typed.

The icon bounced and turned red in the cheeks. *Aren't you the naughty one?*

For the popcorn, I typed hastily.

"You are in way over your head, Misha. And tell her it's cotton candy–flavored butter because it makes you think of her hair. See where she runs with that one."

Once again I ended up slamming the laptop shut in midconversation to keep Stefan from bugging the hell out of me. "Would you stop that. And how can I be in over my head?" I added reluctantly. "I'm not a virgin. I've had sex seven times"—six and a half, I admitted to myself, but that was need-to-know information only—"and Ariel is a research colleague and e-mail friend. That's it." I finished the rest stiffly, slightly embarrassed as it wasn't strictly true, in my mind anyway, and I also knew Stefan was more than aware of it. He was also aware as much as I was she couldn't be any more than that, although we had different reasons for that knowledge. I waited for the teasing, but it didn't come—not exactly.

Stefan had one of the towels wrapped around his hips. It hid the ugly scar on his thigh that had come from a bullet from Jericho's gun, which had broken Stefan's thighbone like a brittle winter branch. He limped sometimes now in cold weather or after a long day because of me. He'd taken a bullet trying to save me. That I'd done the same for him didn't matter as it wasn't the same. Couldn't be the same. Chimeras are hard to kill. People are not. He didn't seem to notice when he limped.

I never failed to.

"Yeaaaah. Seven times. It's impressive. I'm getting the number tattooed on my arm I'm so proud." He sat back down on the bed. "But you're a virgin." He held up a hand when I started to protest. "An emotional virgin. You haven't been kicked in the teeth by someone you love yet and Pinky there looks like a girl who could rip out your heart, play tennis with it, stick it back in your chest, and continue to lead you around by your di—um . . . nose. But the first time is the worst. Once you get past that, it gets better."

"She doesn't seem as if she'd do that. She's been helpful." In ways she hadn't planned on being. "And who's to say I wouldn't like being led around by my no—*dick*."

"Fine. You're a cursing machine now." He put the gun back on the table. "Then be extra careful. The nice ones don't play rough, but they don't give your heart back either. And growing a new one takes a long time. Trust me." He stripped, pulled on sweatpants, and slid under the covers of his bed for the night. "But don't trust me much." He stared at the ceiling. "Between being based at a strip club and Nat . . . to hell with it, I don't know shit about women. Or maybe I don't know shit about myself. Either way, just be careful." He turned over, then yawned with an exhaustion that covered body and soul. He'd found out Anatoly had died, we'd lost our home, and now he was thinking about the past. And the past was Natalie. All of that would exhaust anyone.

Natalie was the woman Stefan had loved. Or, as he'd said, as much as he was capable of loving. Searching for me, blaming himself, putting away his morals to make as much money as he could in the *Mafiya*—it had all meant there wasn't much left over for Natalie. She'd known it too. She'd left him and, as far as I knew, he hadn't tried again. If he had an itch to scratch, as he'd phrased it, several of the strippers liked making a little money on the side.

"The side of what?" I'd asked, but that was when I was new to the real world, barely rescued. The Institute didn't spend much time on procreation beyond the very basics. They didn't describe the way it made your brain explode in the best possible way, the almost painful but beyond-pleasurable feeling of ejaculation. It felt as if your life were draining away in a rush of warmth and ecstasy, and you were happy to go with it. If that was what happened with only your body, I couldn't imagine if there was emotion involved. What poured out of your body was warm; what poured out of your heart if someone ripped it in half when they left you would be an ice-cold river of sharp razors and broken glass.

Why would anyone want to repeat that experience? Or risk it to begin with? I looked at the laptop for several seconds before pushing it away across the bed. Then I went to the bathroom, emptied the ice into the sink, and filled the bucket with water. Carrying it to the door, I used my penknife to slice the carpet. Just as I thought. Cheap hotel equaled cheap or no insulating rubber or wood threshold. There was at least an inch between the bottom of the door and the floor. I went outside and quietly poured the water all the way up that nonexistent threshold. Back inside, I closed the door, I went to my backpack for my small case of tools, and knelt before the TV. "Sorry." I sighed with real regret. "I know it's your life or ours, but we need the light." And as with all no-tell motels, that was all we had—a single lamp and the bathroom light.

After unplugging the television, snipping the cord,

stripping the insulation to find the hot wire, usually the black one, I folded the grounding wire back out of the way. Counting my blessings there was an outlet by the small table by the smaller window (in case you brought your own extra lamp—God, I hadn't missed these crappy rooms), I plugged the TV cord in and rested the tip of the black wire in the water that had run a few inches under the door onto the concrete floor that had been under the carpet. There. It wasn't a pipe bomb, but it would do . . . and it wouldn't kill.

"What are you doing? You destroyed a TV. That's like the Holy Grail to you. And you gut it to electrocute the maid?" Stefan demanded, the flat motel pillow folded under his head.

"It won't kill. But it will make you extremely sorry you came knocking at our door." I stood from my squatting position and said, "You might want to call Saul. If he steps in the water in the morning, his beard will bristle like a porcupine getting a prostate exam. Oh, and he'll be thrown a few feet away, wet himself, and will probably scream himself hoarse when he can move again." I grinned. "On the other hand, he's probably already asleep. Let him rest."

He snorted and reached for his cell phone resting beside his gun. "Running for the second time is a damn sight different from the first. Now you're teaching me instead of the other way around." He pressed the numbers. "And you have become somewhat of a shit, too, just like I said. And not so little either."

I thought about that and the pipe bombs, the plane, hiring drug dealers, possibly electrocuting the maid, and more Stefan didn't know. No, I didn't mean he didn't know—I meant, he didn't know because he hadn't *asked* me about them. Semantics can save your soul.

I'd become a shit, my brother thought. I grinned again—nothing theoretical about that.

I really rather had.

Chapter 7

I forgot the satisfaction of knowing my new self and becoming who I was meant to be—a manipulative, slightly amoral shit/genius—when at four a.m. a scream and sizzle/zap woke me up. Preparing for the worst was an excellent hobby. Getting the worst was not as enjoyable. Stefan was already at the door with his Steyr 9mm in hand. He didn't have to tell me to pack. We'd learned last time. You pack before you go to bed for cases like this. "Watch out for the water," I cautioned. "I can't drag a crispy, fried brother to the car and our bags too."

Avoiding the inch or two of water that had seeped under the door, but not unplugging the cord in case whoever was out there had a friend, he opened the door. Half in and half out of the puddle of water, a man twitched convulsively, eyes rolling back in his head. "Well, he's not dead, but I'm not sure he's quite alive either," Stefan remarked.

I raced across the room and yanked the TV cord from the outlet. "Incompetent," I muttered at myself. "Older buildings had a less safe wiring configuration and their electrical insulation isn't always up to code if the owners don't make the investment, which apparently they didn't."

"I'm not crying any tears over it." Stefan lightly kicked the man's shoe with his own bare foot. "See the gun? That is not a particularly friendly gun. It's a Russian GSh-18 pistol, made to carry armor-penetrating rounds. It's what we used to call a *nye ostavtye ni odin jiveaum*, a 'take no prisoners' gun or a Siberian Special." Lingering long ago from the Stalin years (the History Channel cleansed my palate between movies), some older Russians considered Siberia equal to death . . . or Hell. Many had passed on that sentiment. Stefan's grandfather had survived Siberia, but to hear Stefan retell the stories, none of his grandfather's friends had.

"Call Saul. Get your shoes and rat while I check to see if there's anyone else out there." He was out the door, bare-chested and barefoot. He didn't look any less dangerous for it. Five minutes later, the three of us were in the parking lot. The still-twitching guy wasn't *Mafiya* despite the Russian gun, which was at least one less problem. He was one of Raynor's men, loyal beyond his boss's death—I'd checked his wallet. He had the same crappy fake government ID. He was alive but wasn't exactly functional. The three of us went back to our rooms, dressed, hefted our bags, and ran back out to the parking lot.

Saul was equally unhappy. His ginger hair was standing on end, there was a sleep crease on his upper cheek, and he was in pajamas—in a way. He saw me wincing and huffed. "This is what you get. If I don't have a half hour to do it right, I'm not doing it at all. He headed for his SUV, parked several cars from the one we had stolen. Our vehicle had its license plate switched twice over from the fast food place where we'd acquired the Mustang. It paid to take precautions. I started after Stefan when Godzilla jumped off my shoulder after spotting half a discarded Twinkie on the asphalt. I turned, dropped one bag, and caught him in midair to scold him. It was only half a minute, but that was enough time for Stefan to reach for the car door handle.

That was when I saw it.

The lights in the parking lot were dim and old, same as the motel, but I had excellent night vision and it was getting better the more I matured—as were other things. It was good enough now that I saw the oil on the side of the cover over the rear wheel. Fresh and gleaming, two fingerprints of wet amber—as fresh as if someone had just crawled out from under the car but a moment before. And who changed the oil on someone else's car at four in the morning?

No one.

"Stoipah, no!" I dropped my bags and ran. "Don't touch the car!"

But it was too late. His fingers had already hooked under the handle. I'd reached him at the same time and tackled him as hard and fast as I could. I might have been frozen when he had fought the man on the car outside Cascade Falls. I wasn't frozen now. I wouldn't let myself be again.

The explosion wasn't huge; only big enough to take out the car and whoever would've been standing next to it. We weren't. We were fifteen feet away, over a scraggly hedge into the other section of the parking lot. The medium-sized fireball behind us heated the air to more than a hundred degrees; the smoke scorched my lungs, but I didn't care. Beneath me was my brother and although he was wheezing for breath, his face reddened by the heat, he was alive and not tiny pieces spread far and wide for the morning pigeons to peck. "What . . . ?" he said, choking. "How did . . . you know? How . . . did you get us . . . out of range?" It was a good question, considering he had at least thirty pounds on me and all dense muscle.

I pushed up to take the weight off his chest and let him recover his breath more quickly. "I saw the oil on the back of the car. Fresh. Someone had been under it. You don't crawl under a car at four in the morning unless you're planting a tracking device or a bomb." The rest? Mmm. There was truth and there was explanation. Sometimes they could be entirely different things and sometimes they could be the same. In this case, they were the same. "Adrenaline. I'm in my prime. Not a geezer like you. I'm stronger than I was three years ago. I work out with your weights." I didn't. Exercise was boring. "You've seen me." He hadn't, but ordinary people don't recall every detail of every day.

Truth, explanation, and half of a somewhat white lie. I'd tell him the entire truth later, when the time was right, but for now, half an untruth was what I gave him. I felt like hell saying it, but I saved my brother's peace of mind, for now, and his life, for good, I hoped. That made it worth it. The car burned behind us and I felt a hand pat my back vigorously. "Small bonfire," Stefan said with a crooked smile; then, apparently his breath back, he pulled me into a one-armed hug so fierce that even a chimera like me yelped. "Don't do that again, okay? It's my job to protect you, not vice versa. I'm the big brother. Me. Got it? If I blow up, I blow up alone. You go with Saul if that happens."

This time when I pushed up, I stood and held a hand down to him. "No." The sentiment was true and spoken matter-of-factly; I wasn't going to change my mind.

He took my hand and got to his feet. "Misha, this is not a game. It's never been a game. You know that. You almost died for me once. If you actually succeed, don't think I'm going to stick around. I did it for ten years. I can't do it again."

I saw him again as he'd once been: the drowning man. I'd given him what I said I wouldn't: lies. He gave me the truth.

I wished he'd lied instead.

I glared at him, but what do you say to a truth like that? I wasn't going to not try to save him if I had the opportunity, but after what Stefan had given up, it would be like spitting in his face to say I wouldn't try to survive if I could. I couldn't do that—throw away what he'd given me. "If I'm too slow next time," I said grudgingly, "I'll go with Saul. But try not to make that an issue, all right? Be more careful."

He raised his eyebrows at my tone—he was lucky to have any eyebrows at all after the explosion. "I'll do my best," he said with a patience his colleague didn't share.

"You two stop bitching at each other and get over here by the fucking SUV," Saul snapped from down the row of parked cars, some littered with burning debris. "Your TV-fried friend might not have left only one present." He dropped to the cracked parking lot surface and crawled under his vehicle. A minute later he returned. "Nothing." He then checked the engine. "We're good to go. Now, get in the damn car!" People were gawking out of the doors of their rooms and there was the unhappy wail of sirens in the distance.

Stefan and I threw our bags in the back and obeyed. This nighttime Saul was much more frightening than the day version. Ginger and gray chest hair, combined with his pajamas, a pair of tight purple silk boxers and that was it. He looked like an obscenely horny children's dinosaur—but lean and quick with ropy muscle. He charged double for wetwork, he'd said. You can't do wetwork, you can't kill, if you're the size of a four-hundred-pound fake prehistoric lizard.

You could have better taste in clothes and pajamas, though. You could have pajamas, period. Was that too much to ask? The color seared my night vision. I couldn't imagine what it would do in broad daylight. Hopefully he'd cover the boxers up with clothes by then. Godzilla hopped from my shoulder, where he'd returned after the Twinkie incident, to the top of Saul's head, curled up in the bed-hair nest and dozed off. "There is not enough money in the world," Saul ground out.

In the backseat, I gave Stefan a visual once-over. He'd hit the asphalt with a lot of force. I knew. I'd been that force. He'd lost his bandage for the cut on his forehead. I'd been the one to clean the dried blood earlier, determine the need for stitches, apply ointment, and bandage it. I was the house vet after all. It was my job. Stefan had complained he could do it himself, but at the same time I could see the pleased look in his eyes. Missing memories or not, I'd accepted I was his brother weeks after he rescued me, but years later, he didn't take it for granted. Plus I placated him with some cheese and peanut butter crackers while I took care of the wound. The tasty treat worked wonders in distracting cranky turtles, ferrets, and brothers.

I lightly touched the cut with one fingertip to assess how it was healing. It was a thin red line, scabbed over, and much better than before. "So?" Stefan inquired. "Add that one to my other one and I look like some grandma's patchwork quilt, huh?" He didn't sound too concerned. Scars didn't bother him. Vanity wasn't a problem for him.

"Believe it or not, it looks good. Cleaning away all that blood combined with the best prescription antibiotics that can be obtained illegally from Canada"—I shrugged—"it wasn't nearly as bad as it seemed, and I did a fantastic job—as always. Can veterinarians win Nobel Prizes? Although I'd settle for government disability for the permanent damage done to my eyes by Skoczinsky's sleep-spandex."

"I was going to say he hadn't changed, the smug little bastard," Saul grunted from up front as we passed a fire truck headed back toward our motel. "But he has. For the worse. Now he's a smug, full-grown bastard."

I ignored him. I had to or I would've reached up to touch his shoulder and paralyze his vocal cords. While I didn't have a problem with that plan, Stefan might. Leaning back against the seat, I changed the subject. "How many more men do you think Raynor had?"

"Impossible to know. But not any more, I think, or someone would've shot us in the parking lot when the bomb didn't work. I did leave that one electrocuted bastard alive, though. The smart thing would've been to finish him off." Stefan shook his head and let it go. He'd killed, but he didn't like it, and I'd never blame him for that. How could I?

"I'm more worried about how they found us," he continued. "We torched the Institute car. We stole a new one. We swapped out license plates on it. How . . . Ah shit. We didn't steal Saul new license plates. That mall parking lot was full of cameras. He could've tagged us by looking at the security tapes. I didn't think anyone would go to the trouble, though. Hell, I didn't know he had more men to begin with. Raynor was acting as if he was off the radar on this one. He may be the only one in the government who knows about the Institute. Jericho was smart that way. But if I had thought he had any more men, I would've guessed they'd assume you and I took out Raynor. And Raynor would've told them at least enough when he first came after us that they'd know we'd been on the run a long time—long enough to be too smart to steal a car from the same place we'd killed their boss."

And the motel, cheap and sleazy as it was, definitely had cameras too. They probably made half their income off private detectives buying eight-by-ten glossies of cheating spouses, had a Web site with PayPal, and ran specials on double prints. That would be how the guy and his friends, if he had any, knew which car was ours and which one to plant the bomb under. They would've seen us on tape getting out of it. Mr. Fried-and-Crispy would've seen it was Saul who'd killed his boss on the mall security tapes, but Saul was nothing more than an inconvenience compared to what I was capable of. "So that guy was either smarter than we think or we're more stupid than we think," I said thoughtfully.

"Or just smart enough, Goldilocks," Saul added. "Now, get this damn rat off my head before I toss him out the window. We have to find a place to dump the truck and get a new one."

When my fingers brushed his head as I retrieved Godzilla, I made him impotent for approximately a day. He most likely wouldn't notice and it improved my mood tremendously. "Try for a blue one," I said ingenuously. "In feng shui, the color blue aids in success."

Saul snorted. "You are one weird dude."

Saul had no idea what I was, despite what Stefan had told him. Seeing is believing and he hadn't seen. That meant he couldn't accept it, not in his gut where it mattered. He couldn't truly believe. If he stayed Stefan's friend, it would remain that way, which was best for everyone all around. It was certainly best for Saul's continued sexual activity and potentially receding hairline.

We stole another SUV before leaving St. George, hitting a quiet neighborhood where everyone still slept. Then we stopped at several different places— neighborhoods and the 24/7 places like porn warehouses and big-box stores for a stack of different license plates. No more mistakes this time. Then we were on the I-15 to Laramie via Salt Lake City. The sun was coming up. Back in Cascade Falls, I'd be getting up about now, eating breakfast, going to work after stopping down by the river to deliver Ralphy his catered

Alpo. The air would be brisk with a cool bite as I'd get a chocolate-cheesecake Danish from the bakery to top off breakfast. I'd say hi to the people I saw and give them the appropriate smile. Sometimes it didn't feel like the practiced one.

It felt real.

"You know what I miss about Cascade?" I asked Stefan suddenly.

"Everything," he answered without taking a second to think about it.

"You too?" I could all but smell the paint fumes from his clothes when he'd come home from work—the gingerbread man.

"Me too." He tapped on the window glass lightly with a raw knuckle. It was an unconscious habit of his. "Sorry I ruined things for us there, Misha. Sorry I lost us our home."

"It's not your fault. It's Raynor's."

"There is that." He tapped again. "And maybe we both got a little sloppy, but goddamn it, I think we were entitled to a little sloppy. That's what having a home is all about—relaxing. Not being on guard every second of the day."

"Not that I don't feel for you guys, but there are thousands of shit-kicker little towns across the country to find a new home in. How about we concentrate on the pack of killer kids roaming the country?" Saul suggested. "What are we going to do when we find them in Laramie? Tranq them on the sidewalk in front of God and everyone, wait around to see if this cure of Mikey's works, all while the police are arresting us for assaulting a bunch of children and teenagers? Dora the

Explorer could locate a better plan than that up her ass."

My jaw tightened over the "Mikey"—I should've taken his hair too—but he was right. We did need a plan to get them away from people and out of sight. "Leave that to me. I'm working on it," I said.

At the same time, Stefan stated, "We'll find them first, see exactly where they are and what they're doing, and then figure something out."

"I think someone just staged a coup on your ass, Korsak," Saul commented.

Stefan folded his arms as he wedged himself more comfortably in the corner of door and seat and considered me. "Huh. I think he might be giving it a shot." He didn't say anything aloud about my drug-dealing plan that hadn't gone precisely as calculated or the landing that had caused the cut on his forehead, but the quirk of one eyebrow and the corner of his mouth said it as clearly. But I also thought I saw faith there. Brothers gave you second, third . . . more chances than you deserved. I wasn't letting Stefan down.

I rolled on my side, used a sweatshirt someone had left in the back as a pillow, and said, "Wake me up for breakfast. I'm starving." I closed my eyes and pretended to sleep, but instead I planned. Stefan was right in that my plans did need some refinement, but I thought he knew he'd be wrong in thinking any of his would work better . . . not with Peter and the rest of the chimeras. Hence the faith. We didn't think in the same way that normal people did, because we weren't normal people. We weren't people at all. It made us unpredictable. In the end, only a chimera could think like

another chimera. And with Peter showing every sign of
being more intelligent than I was, I was going to have
to work especially hard to do that. We were all
brilliant—Jericho's work had made certain of that, but
I hadn't seen signs that Peter was exceptional above the
rest of us while I'd been his classmate. Somehow I'd
missed it. He had fooled us all.

Peter, Peter, prisoner eater. . . .

Peter, Peter, pumpkin eater . . . It was a nursery rhyme,
we were told. Targets and those between you and your
target told them to their children. It was a fact we
needed to know to appear ordinary and we were given
three examples to memorize, which we did in one reading as required, before moving on to the next subject—
how to mimic the neurotoxic effects of blowfish
poisoning if you happened to have a target in Japan.

I'd been around twelve then—two years older than
Wendy was now. Peter had been close to the same. It
was hard to tell in the Institute. There were no birthday
parties. The Playground, yes, but no parties . . . not the
kind of parties, at least, that anyone outside the Institute would recognize as a celebration. I hadn't told Stefan that the Basement wasn't the only place where we
were "rewarded" for exceptional work. The Institute
knew it was important in raising genetic assassins to
equate death with reward. Death equaled reward
equaled incentive equaled eager students—a simple
psychological loop.

On the nursery rhyme day, Peter had asked the Instructor if it wouldn't be better to kill several other
people in the target's entourage along with the target

by using imitative blowfish poisoning to increase the authenticity of the diagnosis. I had thought the same myself. I couldn't help it. It was a logical and effective way to throw off any signs of foul play. But I hadn't said it; I'd only thought it. Peter wasn't like me, however. Peter was a good, enthusiastic student, and he said it loud and proud. That brought him a reward and the rest of us a chance to watch and see what we were missing by not trying as hard as Peter.

In the exercise yard our class gathered to watch Peter enjoy his prize. It was a homeless girl, a runaway—a teenage prostitute I'd guessed, then. Targets were frequently with prostitutes. It was a fact we needed to know.

She was fifteen at most, this girl, but to a chimera, whether it was man, woman, or child made no difference. Age and sex didn't matter when all you saw was an objective. That was all Peter saw. I knew, because I remembered his smile. He had perfect white teeth—we all did. The attractive were less suspicious than the unattractive. Jericho had made that clear. Targets were all prejudiced in one way or another whether they knew it or not, and a negative reaction to the unsightly was a universal one.

As ugly on the inside as he was attractive on the outside, Peter, with his perfect smile and bright, happy eyes, didn't look like a threat, not to a runaway snatched off the streets by silent men, shoved in a van, and brought to a place that looked worse than any prison. None of us would look sinister to her as we stood in a wide, loose circle around her under a hot Florida sun. She'd cowered on the dirt, crying. I re-

membered the trails of clean pure skin under the trails
of her tears. The rest of her face was covered with thick
makeup, her hair bleached blond with black roots, and
her eyes . . . They kept animals in the Institute labs,
starter projects for the extremely young. Some of them
were dogs. I remembered their eyes. Hers were the
same: soft, brown, and dumb with terror. When she saw
Peter leave the circle and walk toward her, she lunged
at him and shoved him behind her; both fell on their
knees. She hadn't been attacking him. She'd been trying to *save* him.

"Little boy." She'd been sobbing so hard, I'd barely
been able to understand her. "They took me, those bastards." She meant the guards who stood farther outside
the circle, passive and watching. "They took me just as
they took you. What do they want? Did they hurt you?
Did they. . . ." She had swallowed. "Did they touch
you? All of you? Oh God, will they rape me? Will they
hurt me?"

Peter's smile had never faded. "No," he'd said, running a fascinated hand through her hair. Then he'd
kissed her cheek, the same way as we'd seen in movies.
That was all we knew of affection, what we'd been
taught to fake. "They won't hurt you.

"But I will."

And he had. He'd killed her, the lost girl with no
name. He took his time too. When he was done, there
wasn't any part of her body he hadn't toyed with . . .
except two. He'd shut down her kidneys, he'd filled her
lungs with blood, he'd torn her liver into pieces, he'd
twisted her intestines into knots, he'd squeezed her
heart with an invisible hand over and over until, after

four heart attacks, she had finally died. But her brain and her vocal cords he had never touched. He'd made sure she remained conscious and aware throughout it all and he'd made sure she could scream. She had felt all the pain, all the terror, not a second wasted to oblivion, and she had screamed until her throat bled, spraying blood with every cry. The entire time she had spent dying, Peter had chanted softly over and over, " 'Peter, Peter, pumpkin eater, had a wife and couldn't keep her. . . .' "

I hadn't thought Peter was smarter than me, but I'd always known he was more ruthless. His heart and soul belonged to the Way of the Institute if not to the Institute itself, and he'd not take any cure willingly. The sun was bright behind my eyelids as the memory ended. I felt my fists clench, my joints complaining with the pressure. He wouldn't take it willingly, no, but he'd take it all the same. I'd make fucking sure of that and I'd remember those terrified brown eyes when I gave it to him.

Peter, Peter—it was time for you to be *my* reward.

Breakfast was drive-through. I didn't mind. The more greasy and loaded with sugar and salt, the better I liked it. Lunch was drive-through too, or to-go, rather. It was a ten-hour drive from St. George to Laramie and we were making it a straight shot, but while much of me was superhuman, my bladder had yet to show signs of being of more than earthly origin. I had to piss the same as anyone else. We took turns, with one in the bathroom and two to stand watch. I didn't think it was necessary. If Mr. Fried-and-Crispy we'd left back in the motel parking lot improved enough to jump up and tear ass after us, he had nothing to go on now. No license plate number. No description of the car. But I'd heard "better safe than sorry" so many times in the past three years that it could've been my middle name.

"I want a taco."

I was slumped in one bright orange plastic booth with my bag in one hand and a giant Mountain Dew in the other when a hand tugged on my jeans. I was alert—bathroom bodyguard at top form—so I'd seen the kid come across the floor toward me. I hadn't known what he was doing and I hadn't known he was going to latch on to my leg. Children weren't like adults. They weren't as predictable. They hadn't gone through all the stages of psychological development that would mold them into the final product. Children were like cats: You didn't know if they'd bite you, piss on you, or purr. Or demand tacos.

"Taco!"

My hand tightened on the bag; I admit it. I liked food, maybe more than anyone alive. We all have our weaknesses. "No," I said automatically. If he wanted a taco that badly, I'd give him a dollar to buy his own, but my tacos were *my* tacos. I'd already claimed them and imprinted on them like a baby duck on its mother.

He scowled, his small face twisting and turning red. With blond hair and an oversized head, he looked about three, but he hit as if he were age eight at least. His hand smacked mine hard and then he tried to wrestle the bag from it. His skin was warm against mine, too warm. *"Taco!"*

"Oh my God, I am so sorry." A woman, presumably

the mother of the budding Antichrist, rushed over and grabbed him around the waist to pull him back. Her hair was blond too, her skin tan, and she weighed about a hundred and five pounds, which could be why she was unsuccessful. He hung on tight to my hand and shirt, and this time the scream of "Taco!" almost shattered the window and door glass of the fast food restaurant.

Three booths down, Saul, now dressed in more than purple spandex, had buried his face in arms folded on the table and was shaking with not-so-silent laughter, the bastard. The mother pulled again and this time managed to pry the Satan spawn off me. Chimeras I was used to. Normal children who also had the ability to maim and terrify were a new experience. "Sorry, sorry," she apologized again as he began kicking rapidly at her legs. "He has tonsillitis and it's making him cranky. He's having them taken out tomorrow morning."

I edged out of the booth, my bag of food and my Mountain Dew cautiously hidden behind me. "He doesn't have tonsillitis." The screaming became louder. "My father's a doctor," I lied without compunction. "I'd have him rechecked before they do surgery." Again the screaming notched up. She appeared confused, forehead wrinkling, and I tossed a bit of convincing logic to go with the rest. "If he can scream like five hundred demons from Hell, the little shit, I think . . . my father would think if he did have tonsillitis, it's cleared up now." That was when I found out where the kid learned to kick so ferociously.

In the SUV, I sulked and nursed my wounded pride.

The bruise on my shin from the woman's shoe would be faded already and on the verge of disappearing altogether, but my temper remained dark. The little monster deserved tonsillitis. Too bad. I should've left well enough alone. Saul was yukking it up in the backseat while Stefan tried and failed to look sympathetic behind the wheel. "Why did she do that?" I mumbled around a mouthful of chili cheese fries. "I didn't do anything wrong." I'd actually done something right. I'd saved Damien from an unnecessary surgery. I missed my movies, but thanks to that kid there was one I wouldn't miss. All that boy needed was a tricycle, because he already had Satan in his corner.

"You called her sweet little baby boy a demon from Hell. Worse yet, a shit. Moms don't like that." Stefan swallowed his laughter in to the most unconvincing cough I'd ever heard.

"I did not." Okay, yes, I did call him a shit, but not a demon. "I said he screamed *like* a demon from Hell. I didn't say he was a demon from Hell. He's Satan at least. I was assaulted by the Omen and you have no pity at all, do you?" I frowned.

"You faced down the Russian mob and the Institute and you can't handle a toddler?" Stefan grinned. "How much pity do you think you deserve?"

Finishing the fries and with the tacos long gone, I decided now was a good time to talk to someone less judgmental, in addition to one with no knowledge of the attack of the evil taco thief. What was I anyway? Meals on Wheels? His mother had money and taco-buying ability. Obviously she had no foresight or spirit of preparation in the face of the purely sinister demands of her own child, but it wasn't as if anyone could hold me accountable for that.

If Ariel wasn't online, I'd see if there was any suspicious rash of deaths in Laramie, other than the ones I'd already found dated last week. There hadn't been any more yet, but with Peter and the others there, and according to the Institute's GPS tracker they were, it was only a matter of time. I grabbed my laptop and opened it as I tipped back the cup for the last swallow of Mountain Dew. I loved caffeine almost as much as grease and sugar. Stefan took in the sight and drawled, "Greek Gods live on Mount Olympus. Geek Gods live on Mountain Dew."

"Drug dealer, pilot, ex-assassin-in-training, genius, geek, and *hot*." I didn't bother to gift him with a glance. "Can you claim that many talents?" I started typing and hacked into the nearest secure WiFi. The free, unsecured kind didn't last past the parking lot of the coffee shop or bookstore that hosted it.

"That is damn talented," Saul said from behind. "Maybe I should think of hiring you as a subcontractor. God knows I make no moral judgments. I make money. That's it. Things are much simpler that way."

"Simple in the way you assisted Stefan in liberating me from a heavily guarded, virtual fort at the risk of your blindingly horrific neon shirt?" I asked as I zipped through a firewall, typing on. God knew I couldn't forget that shirt.

"It was a lot of mon— You liked that shirt?" I turned my head to see him give a pleased grin and then change it into a scowl as he finished his excuse. "It was a lot of money. It had nothing to do with saving your polysyllabic ass. It was only about the money. It's never about anything but the money, you brat."

I dismissed him, saying, "You're lying. Your voice is half a pitch higher, pupils slightly dilated, you touched your collar twice, and you said never—never means at least once if not always. I could go on. Would you like me to?" Saul had a soft spot to have done what he did, one beyond his friendship with Stefan. I wondered what it was. I didn't ask, but I wondered.

I also didn't give him a chance to reply. Instilling fear in your subject at first opportunity ensures better behavior faster. In this case, better behavior would be Saul no longer annoying me. "Besides your refusal to admit morality, we could talk about your extreme womanizing. Overcompensation and denial so blatant it should require little comment, except to you perhaps." I studied him intensely. "Psychology is a hobby of mine. I could produce some notes for you to study. They might assist in your personal development. Except for your love of spandex. I can't comment on that. It's too horrifying."

"He's shitting me, right?" Saul directed the question to Stefan with more than a little desperation.

"Oh, I very well could and you would never know it," I answered placidly, before Stefan had a chance, and returned to my computer. "I could give you an Oedipal complex in less than three minutes if you want to put it to the test. In six minutes I could turn you into an agoraphobic germophobe with profound hoarding proclivities. Those last two aren't easily combined, but I have faith I could pull it off. It's up to you."

"Yeah, thanks, but I'll pass," Saul muttered; then, more softly, in hopes I couldn't hear, he added, "Brat."

"Grown men can't be brats." I sent Ariel an IM. "We can be bastards, though. Do you like your hair, Saul? And your ability to semi-please women with your equally semi-erections? Do you want to keep those?"

Ahhh, and there it was.

Silence.

The next hour remained blessedly quiet. Ariel wasn't around and Laramie hadn't suffered any clusters of peculiar if natural-appearing deaths for eight days, the same as when I'd looked into it yesterday. Five heart attacks, six aneurysms, and four people who abruptly fell over dead with no cause determined. It had all happened last Wednesday and it reeked of Institute tactics. Leave no sign behind . . . unless your owner wanted to send a message. Peter and the others were following training, but they'd stop soon. Where was the satisfaction in having all that power if you couldn't get the recognition—the *fear*—it deserved? There would be more deaths and they would become more and more bizarre and obviously unnatural. There would be more wings of blood when Wendy cut loose—flocks and flocks of them. She, without any help at all, was perfectly capable of wiping Laramie off the face of the map. There would be red, red wings as far as the eye could see.

Fly away, bird. Fly away no more.

Chapter 8

The tracker led us to a house just beyond the outskirts of Laramie. It was the only one at the end of a long gravel road. Its isolation made me think of our house in Cascade Falls—or what had been our house before it had burned. The isolation was the only thing that reminded me. This house needed painting, but it had no Stefan to paint it. Its wooden shutters were split and on the verge of falling off most of the windows. The weeds that made up the yard were taller than my knees. It was all gray. The unpainted concrete porch, the bare, rotting wood, the grime-covered windows—they were the colors of no color at all.

Except. . . .

There were balloons—red, yellow, blue, green, purple; the helium had them bouncing in the breeze. They were tied to the mailbox at the road as people did for birthday parties. When I'd first seen that, fresh out of the Institute, I'd asked Stefan if clowns lived there. What did I know about celebrations and parties? Peter knew, though. Two weeks on the outside and he knew what it had taken me months or longer to learn. How had I missed seeing that in him? Genius beyond customary chimera genius—he was extrapolating information and customs I'd had to learn and he was doing it with what little data the Institute had given us. He was the chimera Einstein, and that not only made him as dangerous as Wendy, but maybe more so with his maturity level and cunning. I was in over my head. We all were, but there was nothing to be done about it. I wanted my brother to stay safe; I wanted Saul . . . well, out of hearing range, but that didn't matter. We couldn't let death roam in a pack across the country. If we did, I couldn't say how long the country would be left.

We were the only option; I was the only cure.

"I don't think they're in there. Not anymore." Stefan had traded his Steyr for one of the tranquilizer guns. "I believe they outfoxed the tracker, Misha."

I didn't have a lot of doubt about that either. The homemade banner across the front door that read TOO SLOW, MICHAEL. BYE-BYE and the fact that their GPS signatures hadn't moved in more than twenty-four hours were sure signs that too slow was me indeed.

Peter had thought of something else that I hadn't during my escape. Stefan and Saul, not I, had figured out I'd been implanted with a GPS tracking chip. It hadn't crossed my mind then, but it had crossed Peter's. I tightened my lips and headed down the grass-spotted driveway toward the house. I managed two steps before Stefan moved in front of me—no surprise there. "When do I lead the way?"

"When you're sixty, not nineteen, and I'm in the nursing home. And I'm hoping before then we can stop worrying about who goes where first." Stefan had switched the tranq gun to his left hand and now carried his 9mm in his right.

Behind me, Saul said, "You can both go first. No skin off my nose."

"You're bringing up the rear, guarding my flank, aren't you?" I demanded, for Stefan if not for me. It was hard to gain acceptance as being as efficiently dangerous as an ex-soldier, such as Saul, and an ex-soldier of a different sort, such as Stefan, without their seeing me in action. And while I did want their respect, hurting people to get it . . . That situation hadn't come yet. I should hope it wouldn't. Being a man and leaving childhood behind were damn challenging and equally damn confusing.

"I'm not interested in your rear or your flank," came the breezy reply. "You're not a woman into thigh-high boots, thongs, or getting the good parts vajazzled, are you?"

I'd been ready to detect his lie. I was not ready for "vajazzle." I didn't know what it meant. I didn't want to know what it meant. My suspicions alone were ghastly enough, and now was not the time to be distracted. Peter and the others were gone; I was ninety-five percent positive. But five percent could kill you the same as ninety-five. One percent could kill you.

If Wendy was inside, she could kill us all.

Stefan kicked down the front door. I had my own tranq gun up and ready to fire. As Stefan had said, aim for the torso and I'd be fine. And while real guns didn't interest me, I had practiced once with the tranquilizer gun. My aim was more than adequate, and my hand/eye coordination excellent, which was *not* a result of denying myself Sara from the coffeehouse's company and keeping my own company while locked in the bathroom, as Stefan had suggested. That wouldn't have given me good hand/eye coordination, only repetitive motion injury.

Stefan disappeared into the gloom of the house and I followed. My eyes adjusted quickly and I could see the signs of habitation in the here-and-there streams of sunlight finding their way through gaps in the musty-smelling curtains. Full garbage bags were stacked neatly against one faded green wall. The bags were white but transparent enough for an observer to see they held empty food containers. Pizza boxes, empty tubs of ice cream, microwaved potato skins and fried cheese; bag after bag from fast food hamburger places. There was more, but I looked away to continue visually searching the room. Knowing that Peter and the others were like me when it came to taste and appetite wasn't helpful to the situation. Anyone locked in a prison where sugar was a concept, not a reality, would flip in the other direction with freedom. That didn't make us the same, not even close.

Saul darted out from behind me and, moving in a crouch, checked out the rooms off the main one to the right. Stefan handled the one, a dining room, to the left as I made my way to the kitchen. I'd thought the house was abandoned, which was why Peter had chosen it. It wasn't. The ancient refrigerator was humming noisily. The electricity was working and so was the water. I tested the tap—the water ran cold and clear. It would be with thirteen chimeras making use of it. There'd be no chance to get rusty and orange. The kitchen table was as scarred and rickety as ours had been in Cascade but with only one plastic chair. Whoever had lived here, and I was completely certain it was "lived" in the past tense, had lived here alone.

On the table was a chipped mug and in the mug was a pile of small pieces of metal—GPS chips. "They figured that out damn quick, didn't they?" Stefan remarked grimly at my shoulder. "How'd they know where they were? And how'd they get them out? With a butcher knife?" He waved a hand at a butcher block knife holder on the counter. It and the knives were dusty with disuse. Our absent owner wasn't into cooking. No, they hadn't used those knives.

I put the gun on the table and pulled up my sleeve to absently trace a finger across my forearm. Beneath my touch a cut instantly opened. Chimeras, except for Wendy, were bred to block harm from other chimeras, but harming yourself was another story. You had only to open that internal door you kept locked from others like you. "That's how. As for knowing the chips were planted at the base of the spine as mine had been, if you knew you had a chip, you could search and find it within yourself. I didn't know, so I didn't look. Peter's smarter than I am, Stefan. Much smarter than I remember him being. You should know that. You should know that things have gotten more difficult." I pulled my sleeve back down as the cut began to heal. "More . . . lethal. We should send Saul back to Miami."

If Stefan had gone for it, I would've added that he should head somewhere far away too. Let a chimera deal with an impending chimera apocalypse. But that wasn't going to happen. I knew my brother too well there.

"You really should've slept with that girl at the coffee shop." Stefan had both hands full, but he had a free elbow to poke me lightly in the ribs. I didn't know how an elbow could be reassuring, but it was.

"I really should have." I sighed and reached past the mug for a cell phone resting there. There was one voice mail. I thought for a fraction of a second, then punched in the only password it could possibly be: Jericho. The father of us all. Bellucci had been nothing but the most distant of reflections, an ego with nothing to back it up. The phone pinged in my ear and I heard Peter's voice, smooth and convincing as any lawyer on the TV commercials telling you he'd get you millions for your fender bender. "Michael, Michael, how can you be with your family when you can't keep up? Can't catch up? I thought you were better than that. You always lacked a love for the work, but I'd hoped the outside world had changed you. After all, our god chased after you and didn't come home again. No one could have predicted that."

No, no chimera could, and Peter couldn't know I had nothing to do with Jericho's death. Even that monster I couldn't kill. There had been failures before me—chimeras who weren't genetically perfect, not strong enough to kill. I had been the only one strong enough, but I had refused.

"We have things to do, Michael. Many things. Entertaining things. We can't wait forever on you, but I'm not writing you off, brother. If you're worthy, you'll find us. Don't forget you *are* one of us."

The voice mail disconnected in my ear. Peter's voice disappeared.

It wasn't true. I wasn't like them, not in the ways that counted.

And they were not my family.

"Are you all right?" Stefan's elbow nudged me again. "I heard the voice. It was that kid Peter. What did the son of a bitch say?"

"That he wants me to find him, but I'm just not trying hard enough." I wanted to throw the phone against the wall. I didn't. When you could kill with the touch of a hand, when you were taught to want it and do it exceptionally well, you were also trained to not lose your temper. No one wanted to buy an assassin who got pissed off that he was served fish instead of chicken and would exterminate you instead of your enemies. Obedience was a must. The Institute had failed there with me and failed with Peter too. Peter's disobedience had been more catastrophic than mine. I wondered how his temper training had taken.

"There's something in the backyard." Saul joined us. Like Stefan, he had a tranq gun in one hand and a real one in the other. He peered in the mug at the bits of metal encrusted with dried blood. "Yum. There's a new way to get your daily iron. Chug it in your coffee."

"What's out there?" Stefan headed for the window over the cracked and stained sink.

"Looks like a body." Saul shrugged. It was the kind you saw in ex-military people: been there, killed that. "Smells like a body. I cracked a window for a whiff. Someone had to own this mansion before the kiddies moved in."

"Shit." Stefan stared out the window. "Another one

bites the dust. Could be worse. I just hope it's not another Zombie Bob. I'll go check it out. You two look around and see if you can find something, *anything* that points to where they're going next."

"I already have that. I'll explain later." I slipped the cheap phone into my jacket pocket. "So we can all check out the body. I can tell how long they were here by the decomposition rate." The helium in the balloons gave me an estimate as to how long they'd been gone. The bright balls, though still floating, were beginning to dip. They'd left three to five days ago.

"Looking at dead bodies doesn't bother you, Mikey?" Saul asked with a bemused note that thrummed under the words.

You didn't have to be ex-military for that to be true. I shoved the tranquilizer gun into the back waistband of my jeans. "I've dissected dead bodies; I've been surrounded by dead bodies; I've made dead bodies," I said flatly. "I wish they did bother me. *You* bother me, though. One more 'Mikey' and every time you see a woman, you'll piss your pants, then vomit, and maybe, just maybe, lose control of your bowels. Good luck finding a thong lover who's willing to take you on then."

Stefan, who'd also put away his tranq gun but kept his Steyr, grabbed a handful of my shirt and ushered me toward the back door. "Enough. No more jealousy. It's not becoming to a genius. Now, get your ass in gear."

As he hustled me with enough annoyance to let me know I was somehow screwing up, I sputtered internally. Jealous of Saul? Why in the world would I be jealous of Saul? Because Stefan had a friend who was here and now when, for the past three years, Stefan and I had been each other's sole support system, unable to trust our neighbors and fellow employees? That Stefan was family, my family, my brother, my friend, and the only person who had ever been any of those things to me? And that I didn't want to share him because there had to be people out there less . . . challenging than I was—the little brother Frankenstein experiment, and he might realize that if given the chance?

All right, that was completely psychologically healthy. Not fucked-up in the slightest. Stefan gave me encouraging pushes toward other people, and I yanked him back with my background checks and my occasional infliction of gastric reflux on his rare dates. I was a genius and an idiot wrapped into one, but most of all . . . I was a dick. And unlike other things in my life, there was nothing theoretical about that.

"Sorry, Saul," I grumbled. "I won't turn your body and its ability to process Viagra against you." At his elderly fortysomething, he was bound to require it. "Just, seriously, don't call me Mikey, all right?"

A hard smack hit my back and Saul's gloating grin didn't have to be seen—only imagined, clear as a bell. "Sure thing . . . Mikey."

I really did hate him.

The body, a man in his seventies, was sprawled in the tall weeds by a detached concrete building—too big to be a shed, too small to be a garage. The decomposition was more advanced than that of those in the Institute, but Wyoming had had some rare rain over the past week and the coyotes hadn't let some fast food of their own pass by. Both Stefan and Saul leaned in for a closer look and then stepped back a few paces when the smell truly hit them. To me it wasn't any worse than the smell of cooking cabbage coming from the Institute cafeteria—different but no worse, and in some ways, not as bad. Cabbage was disgusting.

"They came straight here from the Institute." I straightened from my crouch. "He was about a month away from a massive stroke. A dead man walking, isn't that what they say? No challenge, no fun. They didn't bother to play with him. One of them simply blew out his aorta and down he went."

"I'd say that's something at least, but I'm not sure it is." Stefan was slowly picking up on these chimeras being nothing like me. That was good. It would make him more careful. "Let's take a look in the outbuilding, then get the hell out of here while you explain how we're going to track down this pack of rabid human wolves and fix them."

"Kids did this," Saul mused. "I know what you guys have said, but it's weird to see."

"This?" I shook my head and tossed him my own phone. "This is nothing. If they had it in them, you could almost call it a mercy killing. Here. I transferred some of the Institute video onto it. Take a look. You might want to see for yourself what all of this really is."

Stefan tried the handle on the metal door. It was locked. He tried kicking it down as he had the front door of the house, but he only ended up cursing. "I think that poor bastard thought Y2K was the end times and planned on riding it out here. You can pick the lock or I can shoot it out."

"How do you know I can pick locks?" I asked suspiciously.

"Assassin, drug lord, bomber, hacker, man of a million identities. Now that you've come out of the closet as a master criminal and not the little brother who can't understand Lolcats, I'm pretty sure there's not much out there illegal that you can't do." He didn't appear pleased at that, only tired. "You grew up to be me. It's not what I wanted, Misha."

"It's not real," I said quietly. "It's not forever. It's only until we're safe for good. And I don't make any money off any of it. I'm a pro bono criminal." I tried to smile. It didn't feel real either. "We're the only ones who benefit from it and that benefit is staying alive. It's not the same as what you had to do." I didn't want to disappoint Stefan, but I didn't want him dead either. I'd do what I had to, just as he had.

I fished inside my jeans pocket for a tiny packet of metal tools rolled up in a piece of felt. As I went to work on the lock, I heard Saul make a sound. If there was a word for it, that particular mixture of horror and disbelief, I didn't know what it was. I could hear the tinny screams from my phone and then Peter's and Wendy's voices. But the time I had the door unlocked, Saul gave the phone back to me. "Okay," he said, brusque and pale under that leathery Miami tan. "I've seen it. I get it now. Let's go." I noticed he'd dropped the phone into my hand without touching my fingers. I had a feeling there would be no more "Mikey's" from now on. I'd wanted respect. I had it. I hadn't wanted fear, but I had that too.

If wishes were horses, they'd kick you in the gut

and, when you were down, dump a steaming load of manure on your head. Why didn't useless homilies ever tell it to you straight?

"We're in." I put away the picks and my phone.

"Good job, *vors*." *Vors*—it meant boss in the *Mafiya*. This time the comment was said with an exasperated light swat to my jaw and a reluctant pride to the compliment. "Sorry I came down on you, kid. You're doing the best you can, which is better than I did." Then the sugary sweet, birthday-cake-frosting moment was over—one of the moments guys aren't supposed to acknowledge—and Stefan was pushing open the door cautiously. It was dark inside, darker than the house had been. Here there was only one tiny window set up high in the back wall. I could make out the shape of a riding lawn mower, some tools against the right wall—a rake and shovel were most likely. I could see the cables running up the walls. This place was wired for electricity. So where was the switch? I had just spotted it, halfway back on the left wall—a stupid and inconvenient place to put it—when I saw something else almost at the same time. Less than half a second separated the discoveries.

It was a girl. She looked four or maybe five; it was impossible to tell in murk this thick. She was standing in a back far corner, facing into it—a bad girl who was sent for a time-out, nose to the wall. She had bright blond hair, but not as blond as Wendy's. It was tied back in two ponytails. There might have been ribbons . . . I narrowed my eyes, and the gloom and shadows lightened. Ribbons, blue ribbons. Her dress was blue as well, her socks pale, probably white, her shoes gone.

She didn't move, didn't say a word. She was a child left to die alone in a locked building, too afraid to turn and ask for help, too terrified to know we were better than the ones who left her there.

Except. . . .

She wasn't crying for help because she wasn't breathing. She wasn't turning toward us and freedom because her heart wasn't beating. I couldn't hear it or sense it. I couldn't feel the life in her because there was no life. There hadn't been any life in her, not for a moment. I knew life. You couldn't steal it if you didn't recognize it and any chimera would know what she was—a fake; a life-sized doll.

A trap.

But Stefan wasn't a chimera. He was a man and a good one. He had been taught by his bodyguard days to be cautious and suspicious, but this was a little girl and not one he'd seen on the Institute video. To him, all he would see was that she wasn't a chimera. To human eyes it was too dark to recognize she wasn't anything at all. Before I could open my mouth to tell him to stop, he was there, turning the toy around. It didn't matter that he felt the plastic under his hand and backed up immediately. It was too late. The wire was tripped and the cloud that billowed was as thick as a summer storm.

Chlorine gas—it was easy enough to make. Rob your kitchen or bathroom of ammonia and bleach and Mr. Charles Darwin stepped in. You could scrub your toilet and die with a brush in one hand and *People* magazine in the other, or you could be a chimera, smarter than you had any natural right to be, and use it. You could gather enough, put it in a container, seal it, connect it to a trip wire that was attached to a doll cute enough to pass for the real thing, and you had a way to kill two men almost instantly . . . or however many men happened to be with the Institute escapee trailing you. It wasn't a good way to go, the gas. Your lungs scarred nearly immediately from the corrosive fumes, then filled with fluid, drowning you. If mixed right, it was fatal.

If you were a chimera yourself, it was mildly inconvenient. We were made to be predators, not victims.

I didn't bother to yell Stefan's name. It would be time wasted. I ran for him, grabbed his arm as he started to stagger, then raced back toward the door. Along the way, Saul was starting to drop to his knees. I used my other hand to grab his shirt, another brain-bleed-colored monstrosity, and yanked him along too. The rectangle of light we'd entered through wasn't far, but in a cage of poison gas, far is relative and time is not your friend. I managed to get them outside, each step seemingly mired in mud as thick and cloying as molasses and quicksand, before dropping them in the grass as I slammed the door shut behind us. Then I grabbed each by the shirt collar and dragged them farther away. Little gas would escape that sturdy metal door, but I wasn't much for playing odds, especially when it came to the lives of my brother and my friend.

I sat between them in the scratchy, high-arching weeds and laid a hand on each of their chests. "It's okay. Chlorine gas is easy to make, but Peter hasn't been out of the Institute long enough to know the Internet is usually wrong. He didn't get the mixture right.

The ratios were incorrect for a lethal blend. It's nasty, but no worse than pepper spray. Take some deep breaths. You'll be all right."

That was when the small concrete building exploded. Interesting fact: Not only could you make chlorine gas out of bleach, you could also make plastic explosive. It was more likely you'd blow yourself up while stirring the pot than succeed in your "recipe," but that was why funeral homes had closed caskets . . . to carry your many varied moronic pieces to Heaven or God or whatever you believed in.

I bent my head, hands on Stefan's and Saul's chests as they coughed. Fragments of concrete flew over and past while the dry grass–weed mixture all around us smoldered and caught fire. It had rained once, but once wasn't enough to save this place. A chip of metal or concrete hit my jaw, then flew on, leaving a jagged slice behind. I felt the clotting begin and the skin knitting back together. There wouldn't be a scar. I'd healed fast at seventeen. Now I healed at a speed I didn't want Stefan to know about. I'd been different long before he'd found me. Now I was different to the tenth power. I didn't want to be. I wanted to be more human, not less. I wanted to be like my brother.

This was one of the less times, but the rapidly disappearing wound on my face wasn't something I wanted him to see or a truth I wanted to spill. Not yet. I'd said it a hundred times to myself over the past year.

Just . . . not yet.

Stefan coughed hoarsely and Saul, whom I might not hate after all, choked out, "Been . . . pepper sprayed. This . . . is . . . worse."

"Pepper sprayed. You." Stefan coughed explosively again, then managed to get up on his elbows. "Not . . . surprised." He looked around, eyes streaming from the gas. "Holy shit. We're on fire."

"Only a little," I said, exaggerating or rather under-estimating some, but it was a triage moment. You had to breathe before you could run. "Catch your breath and we'll make it out of here before we're charcoal." I felt his and Saul's hearts beating under my hands, fast with adrenaline but healthy and whole. There were no arrhythmias. Chances were approximately seventy-nine percent that we would make it out of here without being barbecued as they'd wanted to do to Wilbur. I had a flashback to the Institute and brightly colored videos. What had poor Wilbur ever done to anyone? Or the spider, Charlotte? Or Bambi's mother?

That Disney guy had been an excessively cruel man.

The building blew up a second time, what was left of it. Stefan took matters into his own hands. "Breathe . . . later," he wheezed as he got to his knees and then to his feet—unsteady and weaving, but up-right. "Run now." Saul followed suit. They were tough, for humans, both of them. Strong. It had helped them survive their lives and it helped us survive now. We did as Stefan said—we ran. Saul's khakis caught fire once. I patted out the flame when he would've paused to do it himself and pushed him on. We ran around the house instead of cutting through. Who knew what traps could be waiting in there that we'd simply missed the first time or were waiting their turn.

At the SUV, I climbed behind the wheel while Stefan all but fell into the passenger seat and Saul literally dived into the back, nearly squashing Godzilla. I started the engine and tore down the gravel road as fast as the SUV would go without sliding on the gravel and off the road. I didn't think the house would explode as well, but naturally with all things Peter in the past two days. . . .

I was wrong.

A smoke detector wired to more homemade explosives would do the trick. That was how I would've done it, but with Peter showing himself to be more intelligent than I was, guessing was all I could do. The vehicle rocked, but we were out of range, barely, although part of the roof landed close enough behind us to momentarily lift the back wheels inches off the road. They smacked back down and I kept driving. Stefan was hanging on to the door handle. He hadn't had time to fasten his seat belt—safety first, he'd always told me, the hypocrite. But I would let it go this time. "I guess I should be grateful you stuck to pipe bombs," he said, his voice hoarse from his coughing. "This Peter might not know shit about chlorine gas, but he knows explosives out the ass."

"Sometimes you get lucky," I said darkly, jerking the steering wheel and spinning the SUV in a tight circle at the end of the road—a dead end. Why was life so damn appropriate when you least wanted it to be? I headed back the way we'd come, weaving around the pieces of roof and wall in the road.

"If Peter wants you to catch up with him, why is he trying to kill you?" Stefan finally put on his seat belt after I smacked his arm repeatedly and pointed at it.

"Because if these minor problems stop me, then I'm

not deserving enough to find or join them." I steered around a flaming piece of drywall.

"That was minor? You're kidding, right? Two explosions and not-quite-good-enough chlorine gas is minor?" Saul sat up in the back and rubbed his chest as if it should ache. He took his hand away and frowned as if surprised that it didn't.

"Chimeras can kill with a touch, but other people, nonchimeras"—humans, in other words—"kill in other ways. The Institute taught us all the ways there are to accomplish that, to be on our guard against the weaker . . . I mean, normal people." Chasing daily after those genetically the same as me, if not mentally, made it easy to forget who was normal and who was not. "They didn't get into specifics on how to make those types of weapons. We didn't need to make them—we just had to know what we might be up against. But give one of us chimeras the Internet and we don't have to be in the same state to kill you. We specialize in assassinations that look like natural deaths. Peter isn't interested in whether they look natural or not now. He's free. They all are. Free to kill in any way they like."

"Like a buffet." Stefan exhaled, leaning back in his seat. "They've found new toys to play with and after a virtual lifetime of solitary confinement, why wouldn't they want the different and the new? If it weren't for the trying-to-kill-us part of all this, it would be hard to blame them." His eyes flicked to the rearview mirror to watch the burning foundation of what was left of the house behind us. "You said you had a way to find them despite their removing their chips. I don't doubt your genius, kiddo, but how?"

"There were only twelve chips in that mug." I took a hand off the steering wheel and for the first time in my life ruffled his hair, wavy and thick as a dog's undercoat, in mockery of what he'd done to me more than a time or two when I was younger. Turnabout was fair play. I wanted to see how he liked it. "I'll teach you about counting sometime. I might get you up to twenty if we try really, really hard."

"I'd call you a shit again, but it's not helping with your behavior, so it's a waste of breath I could use. And both hands on the wheel." He didn't swat my hand, though, which was considerate in view of how many times I'd swatted him. "Are you telling me, in your own thoughtful way, that one of them kept a chip? Why?"

"I think Peter is curious about me. With my escape— with me went Jericho. That will make him more curious. Jericho was our creator. It's almost unbelievable he could die. Peter wants a look at me, to see if the outside world has changed me to make me more like him." I turned off the gravel road onto a paved one. It was empty except for us. "That doesn't mean the chip is in one of them—one of them could be carrying it in a pocket for all I know. They could be rid of it in seconds. They might've split up, too, although I don't think that's likely. Peter's charisma, his 'family' brainwashing, and his intelligence are vital to keep them all from going wild and getting noticed. They want to kill and they will kill, as often as possible, but they don't want to be revealed for what they are for the first time ever and possibly put down. They need guidance. Peter is doing that."

"Sounds like a fun guy." Saul had his phone in hand

in the back. "I'd better call nine-one-one before that shit burns down all of Wyoming."

I ignored him. He could save Wyoming, which made him the good citizen of the hour. However, I had other things on my mind. "This is a guess, Stefan. All of it. Keep that in mind, okay? I can't predict Peter. He's not the same as other chimeras and not the same as me. He's—what do they say?—a mystery. He's a mystery."

"A goddamn, arson-loving mystery," Stefan corrected.

"That too," I agreed.

"And same as you said, nothing like you," he added.

"I know." Or I hoped, and hope was the best you could do sometimes.

I drove for an hour after talking Stefan through recalculating the tracker to focus from a mass of chips to only one—it had Wendy's ID code because the universe sucked that way—before I noticed the cop behind us. He was far back but closing fast. With the explosions, I'd avoided the interstate in case of the state police, Hazmat, or fire trucks. What had happened at the house would bring in the federal responders on top of the state and city ones. It was best to stay out of sight. But it turned out a deputy had better sight and intelligence than I'd given the locals credit for.

Instead of joining the circus that had to be surrounding what would be left of the house and building by now, he was out trolling the local country roads for any suspicious vehicles. And with our stolen Utah license plate, we were out of place, off Laramie's beaten tourist track, and that definitely was worth investigating.

"He's sniffed us out." Stefan had swiveled in his seat when he saw my quick look at the rearview mirror. "Smart cops can screw your shit up, especially when you don't have the Family's money looking out for you. Damn."

"Your boss paid off policemen?" I asked. "Like in the movies? As in *The Godfather*?" The same as the movies—it shouldn't have left a type of celebrity tingle down my spine, but I forgave myself. I was going through serious movie withdrawal these past two days.

"In his day, he paid off policemen, police chiefs, judges, senators." Stefan turned a forbidding look on me. "Do not be getting any ideas, Misha. You're already full of enough of them to be Lex Luthor. Now pull over and let's deal with this guy. Saul, don't kill him."

"What am I? An idiot?" came the answer from the backseat. "It's hard to run a business from death row. No, thanks."

I pulled the SUV over just as the sheriff's department car turned on its light and sirens. When the deputy climbed out of the car, his face was blank, but I could see a twitch of displeasure in his jaw. He hadn't gotten to play with his toy car nearly as much as he would've liked to. I already had my fake license in hand. . . . The registration and insurance from the glove compartment wouldn't match, but I expected to take care of our cop problem before it came to that. Or so I thought.

The deputy had drawn his gun and had run from his car to ours, shouting, "Get out of the car! Get out of the vehicle, all of you, hands behind your head, and lie flat on the ground! Do it now!"

"Fuck," Stefan muttered, and, cop or not, he slid his hand inside his jacket for his gun. He'd have good intentions; that was my brother—following those good intentions all the way to an internal Hell, though those intentions had saved me. He'd doubtlessly try for a leg shot, but you never knew what would happen when you were trying *not* to kill someone and you were both armed.

I had planned to touch the deputy's hand when he took my license and put him to sleep. I'd say it was now time to improvise, but chimeras didn't improvise. We moved to plan four. Plans two and three were based on a less aggressive and less intelligent deputy—balls and brains, irritating. I'd already rolled down the window and had to keep my voice low as to not be heard by the Law Enforcer of the Year outside. "Stefan, I have diabetes." I didn't ask if he got it or understood. My brother was smart too.

I opened the driver's door and stepped out. I wavered a little, hands up but too floppy and uncoordinated to cup behind my head. My license fell from fumbling fingers into the dirt where we were pulled off the road. "I . . . I don't feel so . . . where . . . I? What's going on?" As soon as the "on" left my mouth, I bent and projectile vomited, *Exorcist* style. Linda Blair would've given me a ten out of ten for style and a record-breaking eleven for velocity. The splatter of my lunch on his shiny mirror-bright shoes distracted the deputy as I fell to the ground, to the side of my recycled lunch—that much into *The Exorcist* I was not—and began having a full-blown seizure. I flailed, convulsed, foamed a little at the mouth for veracity, and decreased

the circulation to my lips to turn them temporarily cyanotic blue.

Stefan came boiling out of the car. "He's diabetic!
He's going into ketoacidosis. That's a diabetic coma,
you dumb country shit. Help me hold him down." He
yelled back at the car, "Jack, call nine-one-one!"

The deputy had seen a lot of faked illnesses in his
day; that was the nature of being a cop. Fake pregnan-
cies, fake grandpa's-having-chest-pain, fake kid-
swallowed-the-dog's-squeaky-toy, all to get out of a
speeding ticket. But he had never seen anyone who
could vomit and turn cyanotic at the drop of a hat. He
was smart, though. He didn't drop his gun, but he
stepped closer—close enough that one of my flailing
hands smacked his leg. Cloth didn't stop the touch. It
was too flimsy an armor. He went down, loose-limbed
and easy as Godzilla did for his afternoon ferret nap.
Stefan grabbed the gun from his hand as he fell, explaining, "No need for baby to accidentally shoot us as
he goes sleepy-time. Good job, Misha." No *Good job,
Misha, except for risking your life when I could've risked
mine instead and probably gotten shot in the process.* Not
even a *Good job, kiddo.* I couldn't imagine I appeared
proud while at the same time wiping the foam and
traces of vomit off my mouth . . . but I was. Proud as
hell. It was good to be the little brother, but it was also
good to be an equal—a partner.

Stefan nodded at the deputy's car. "Don't forget that
while you're on a roll. You're the computer genius. See
if the car has a camera. Are we on video, can you erase
it if we are, or do we need to blow the damn thing up?"

Computer genius? "I'm the *everything* genius"—I

frowned—"and that seems either your or Saul's criminally inclined abilities are up to something that simple."

Stefan grinned. "You're the newbie in this elite fighting force. I wouldn't want to take away that rite of initiation."

"Initiation?"

"You know," he said, his grin wider and, I thought, more evil, "where we make you do all the scut work while we sit back, drink beer, and criticize your technique. We all go through it. Saul peeled potatoes in the military. I mopped up the restrooms in the strip club. Good times, Misha. Welcome aboard."

"Stop playing around, you jackasses." Saul had his own window down now. "He could have called for backup. Let's get out of here before our secret weapon with a double-oh-seven in puke has to spray the entire sheriff's department."

I was going to have to commit one way or the other on Saul's not being that bad or being a demon from Hell who deserved a thousand agonizing deaths.

But I had scut work to do and that decision would have to wait. While Stefan dragged the deputy off to a safe distance, I blew up the car with the three pipe bombs I had left. It was quicker and more efficient. I also ended up thinking that being a partner wasn't all chocolate pancakes, sex with a smart girl, and late-night movies. How fair was it that the genius had to be the cleanup crew, too? I continued to bitch to myself. I'd worked too hard for this. I'd ride out this "newbie" thing and then it would be all chocolate pancakes, sex with a smart *and* pretty girl, and late-night movies. And if I had to build a state-of-the-art smart and pretty Fembot to make that happen, I'd do it. The real thing was difficult to find while being on the run from killers or chasing killers or both. Maybe I'd give her a pink wig, the same color pink as Ariel's hair.

I'd better stock up on WD-40.

In minutes we were back on the road with yet another explosion in our rearview mirror. I drove several miles until we saw the first opportunity to steal another license plate—Wyoming this time—from an abandoned rust bucket on the side of the road. This time we were headed toward Tucson, Arizona, Wendy's chip beckoning the way. It wasn't a tingle that went down my spine this time. It was a chill.

Icy as winter's first breath and a dying man's last.

Chapter 9

Tucson was well over twelve hours away, which meant another motel stop in Springerville, Arizona. I could've admitted I could go on much less sleep these days and driven on, throughout the night if necessary, but there were other things I needed to do as well. A few hours at a motel to let Stefan and Saul sleep in beds instead of in a car with an increasingly agitated ferret would give me the time to do them. Godzilla wasn't claustrophobic. As with most ferrets, he liked tight spaces to squeeze his long slithery shape into and wreak havoc. But also as with most ferrets, he became bored easily. A change of scenery would give him new things to sniff out, investigate, and then obliterate like a furry missile of destruction. It would be good for him and good for me as I had something to create rather than destroy.

The motel room was the same as the other motel room. The bedspreads were orange instead of bile green, but the rest was identical. Even the landscape pictures over the beds were the same or similarly bad. One was a full moon with what was supposed to be a coyote but looked more like Tramp from that other Disney cartoon—the cheerful mutt they'd had the dog-

catcher drag off to kill. God, I hated that Disney bastard.
If I ever found his cryogenically frozen head, I was unplugging that unit pronto. Funny that it was only his
nightmare creations that the Institute let us watch, car-
toonwise, when we were in the younger group. The
other picture was a dusty trail leading up a dusty hill
with a dusty man riding a dusty horse. The man didn't
resemble Butch or Sundance or Val Kilmer in *Tombstone*, so I had zero interest.

"So why the room with a microwave?" Stefan sat in
the chair at the small table. He indicated the four bags
of cheeseburgers, fries, burritos, refried beans, and two
milkshakes—mine, all mine—with the small brush he
was using to clean his gun. "If I know you and food,
and, Jesus, do I, there won't be a crumb left to heat up."

"Think of it as a science project. All those science
fairs I missed out on, what I'm going to build would've
gotten me an A and maybe laid by the hot science
teacher." At least with Saul around, my use of incorrect
and sexually inappropriate language was improving in
leaps and bounds. I grinned at Stefan's bemusement,
grabbed my bags of food, and spread it out over my
bed, sharing with Zilla when he popped out of the
bathroom, dragging one end of the toilet paper in his
mouth. I could hear it unrolling as he ran. He passed
over the carpet and under the low-hanging blanket, out
the other side, up and over the bed, under again, and
then back up to perch on my knee, turning my bed into
a fairly accurate depiction of a Möbius strip. Spitting
out the end of the one-ply, he accepted a French fry
with a contented *mrrrp*.

"My science teacher was named Mr. Wilfred Wyatt,

but knock yourself out. Do I want to ask what you're going to make or be pleasantly surprised when it explodes, disintegrates the motel, or opens up a black hole and sucks in the earth?" He reassembled the Steyr with practiced ease but didn't slide in the clip. With a curious and thieving ferret around, a loaded gun wasn't a good idea. Stefan slept with the gun and clip under his pillow. He could jam the latter home in a fraction of a second and Godzilla didn't have to face manslaughter charges. It was a win-win.

"I'm not going to blow anything up. Anything else," I amended around a bite of a bacon cheeseburger. It was good, better than good—the perfect amount of grease and cheese and slathered with mayonnaise. The hell with understanding the mystery of the Brussels sprout. I was never touching another one again. "As for a black hole. . . ." I took another bite, chewed, then swallowed before going on regretfully. "If only I could get my hands on the right equipment."

"You're kidding, right? I hope you're kidding. You have enough felonies on your plate. Let's not jump straight to Bond villain." With the gun tucked under his pillow, he lay on his own bed and rubbed his eyes. It had been a long day, especially for someone as breakable as a human. Peter had certainly done his best to break my brother and anyone else with me.

"Black holes are misunderstood. Besides, just creating the conditions a black hole could potentially thrive in. . . ." Those tired eyes were now aimed at me thoughtfully, the consideration of revoking my partner status swimming behind them. "I'm joking," I grumbled. From now on I'd keep my fantasies to myself.

"I'm going to make a microwave beam gun in case we pick up another enthusiastic cop." They existed now, but at around one hundred pounds. I could get that down to thirty, maybe twenty-five easily. "Aim, pull the trigger, and it'll fry the electrical system in his car. You won't have to shoot him. I won't have to blow up his car. And best of all I won't have to roll around in the dirt beside my own vomit again. Trust me, that's worth sacrificing a hunk of metal to the microwave gods. Plus maybe Saul will stop calling me 'double O puke,' because it's getting harder and harder not to maim him. He's the only person in the world who makes me regret I'm *not* a killer."

Saul had been afraid of me when he'd seen the clip of the Institute video, and he'd stayed cautious all the way up to when we were pulled over by the deputy. In the aftermath was when his love of vomit humor overcame his sense of survival.

I was definitely back to hating him.

"The guy does like to give people a hard time, but he thinks it's harmless. He doesn't know he's hitting all the wrong buttons with you. I could tell him." He toed off his shoes and yawned, the skin under his eyes gray with exhaustion. "But that would let him know where you're vulnerable. Psychologically. And theoretically." His lips curled as I snorted at my favorite catchall. "I know how much you love having your weak spots exposed or admitting you have any at all." My snort was much darker this time.

"And this is part of being an adult," he continued. "Figuring out who you like and who you don't. Who's worth putting up with despite some questionable qualities. Learning more about them and finding out those qualities aren't so bad when you compare them to all the good ones they have. Or just tuning it out and forcing yourself to get along. That's life."

"When it rained last week and you couldn't paint, you sat on the couch and watched *Dr. Phil*, didn't you? Admit it. I renounce you. You are no longer my brother." I went to work on the bean burrito and fed Zilla a bite out of pure spite. The ferret flatulence in the car in the morning might be enough to take out Saul. It would be my own form of chlorine gas. I'd be guilt free—hands clean of anything but innocence and cheap motel soap.

"Am I wrong?"

"Go to sleep already." I pelted him with a fry. "You're twenty-seven. Almost as old as Saul. I'm pulling the weight in this geezer parade. You need your rest."

"Nineteen and already you don't want my advice. They grow up so fast. Like a stake through the heart. Sharper than a serpent's tooth. Soon you won't let me hug you in public anymore."

He was unbearably smug and I had no problem with tossing another fry at him. "Ass. I never let you hug me in public. We're guys. Even Institute-trained know better than that. Did you ever hug anyone in the *Mafiya*?"

"If by hug, you mean choke into unconsciousness . . . all the time. I'm not afraid of my emotions, Misha. Embrace yours." The words were dripping with enough amused sarcasm that I knew there was no winning this one. I finished the last burrito, balled up the final paper sack, and headed for the microwave with my tool kit.

"You're a disgrace to mobsters and ex-mobsters everywhere." I unplugged the unit, put it on the floor, sat next to it, and started to strip it down to its basic components. As I worked, I finally admitted, "But I'll always listen to your advice. You know that, right?" Stefan had led me through almost three years as if I were blind, and basically I had been. The world had been an illusion inside the Institute. Stefan had been my guide through the reality of it; he'd taught me to be part of it. I wasn't sure I'd have made it without him. Hell, I knew I wouldn't have. I tossed the microwave door to one side and repeated, "You know that, right?"

A quiet snore answered my question. I studied him for a moment, sprawled on the bed—a very dangerous man who was anything but that to me. The shadows of weariness stained his face. I got to my feet and walked over to him, my hand hovering over his chest. He was healthy and whole. I could feel that sensation running through me, tickling my nerve endings. He was fine. He needed rest; that was all. I went back to the microwave and kept working. A half hour later I was at the door. As soon as I turned the seventies-style knob, Stefan woke up. "Where you going?" he muttered, his hand moving in an automatic reach for the gun under his pillow.

"To the vending machine outside. I need more parts." I shrugged off my backpack—great for hiding said parts—and pulled out a heavy roll of cash. I waved it at him reassuringly. "I'll leave money inside what's left of it when I'm done to reimburse them. I'm not a thief." I was everything else under the sun, but not a thief.

That had Stefan's eyes opening wider. "Jesus, Misha, how much do you have there?"

"Oh," I shrugged, "a couple of hundred thousand. It's escape cash I kept tucking away every few weeks from the offshore account. If we're on the run, we can't always rely on finding a bank that accepts wire transfers from the Cayman Islands. You have to think about these things."

He stared at me as if not certain he wasn't dreaming . . . or having a nightmare; it was a difficult thing to interpret which of the two when it was someone else doing the wondering. He then sat up and jammed the clip home in his gun. "Okay then, Mr. Prepared. Let's go defile that vending machine."

"I don't need a bodyguard. I'm the Grim Reaper walking, remember?" I stuffed the cash back into my bag. No sense in paying until I saw approximately how much I was going to rip out of the machine.

"Yeah, a pacifist Grim Reaper who uses his sickle to hang wet laundry on. Scary shit. I think I'll go along for the ride anyway." He swung his legs over and stood. "And bring the rat with you."

Godzilla? "Why?"

"Because when you're not around, he pisses on my bed. Why do you think I keep my bedroom door closed at home? To keep him from sneaking in to read my *Playboy*s? Take the damn rat."

Picky, picky, picky. I scooped up Zilla and draped him around my neck, and the three of us spent the next fifteen minutes cannibalizing the vending machine for parts and Ho Hos. The parking lot was empty except for cars, and all the windows were dark. No one saw us. Back in the room, I finished the microwave gun while Stefan sacked out again.

When it was done, I had a fleeting wish I was home and had access to some nice paint that would go over metal—metallic blue or candy apple red. But it was functional and that would have to do the trick. I peeled off the necessary cash to pay for the vending machine and started back outside. I paused at Stefan's bed where he lay flat on his stomach, buried in the deep sleep he needed more than I needed a body-guard. I touched the back of his calf with the lightest graze of a fingertip. It would keep him sleeping through the noise of my opening the door. Looking over my shoulder, I whistled lightly and Godzilla bounded off my bed, climbed my leg, and curled up in the pocket of my jacket. Stefan wouldn't be happy when he did wake up if he had ferret urine soaking his sweatpants.

I opened the door, stepped outside, and walked the fifteen feet down to the vending machine. I was consid-ering more sugar—candy bars this time. I reached a hand into the guts of the machine and then . . . nothing.

The night gobbled me up and took me away.

All those monster movies had been right. You shouldn't go into the dark alone.

I woke up instantly, not in fits and stages. Once I healed, I returned to fighting form immediately. Jericho would've been proud of how I'd managed to accelerate the process and how I'd perfected what he'd begun. The thought left a bad taste in my mouth and when I opened my eyes, that bad taste went straight into an extremely bad mood as my pupils adjusted to the low light.

"Raynor," I said flatly. He was the government's dog panting at the end of the Institute's leash. He'd tortured and murdered Anatoly, ruined Cascade—our home—and yet, after we assumed we were free of him after Saul had killed him in the mall parking lot, he was back for more. "Even death doesn't want your malevolent ass."

I recognized him from the sliver of profile I could see from where I was slumped against the door behind the passenger seat of a car humming smoothly over concrete. The pictures I'd taken of him off the Internet had been crystal clear and his threatening to shoot me in the mall parking lot even more so. He turned enough to reveal the short dark hair brushed forward, a faint pallor under his skin, and his impeccable suit's collar open to show a half-inch tracheostomy tube in his throat. The tube was covered with a small, clear Passy-Muir valve that let people with trachs talk. Raynor tapped it. "Thanks to your friend, I'll be needing this bugger for a while." His voice was perfectly understandable, if hoarse. "My bad luck. Your bad luck happened to be an eager-beaver doctor with a penknife in that parking lot. Your extremely bad luck indeed." He shifted his attention back to the road. "Did I mention that an impromptu tracheotomy whilst not under anesthesia isn't particularly pleasant? No? Perhaps we'll discuss it more later."

I looked down to see handcuffs around my wrists and a chain securing them to the metal bracing under the passenger seat in front of me. I had four to five inches' slack at the most. I was strong, but not strong enough to shatter metal. And Raynor, more careful now than before, had also shackled my ankles. I could dislocate both of my thumbs and slip the cuffs, but there was nothing I could do about the restraints holding down my feet. I looked back up to see the car clock reading 4:23 a.m. Stefan would still be asleep. He wouldn't know I was gone. If Raynor had used a silencer, and I knew he had, neither would Saul.

"Speaking of pain, how's your head? I was a good ways down the parking lot when I made that shot, but a rubber bullet would fracture the skull of anyone normal—anyone human. Kill them outright most likely. But I know how you chimeras heal and I crossed my fingers for you, although you were out for a few hours. When I dragged you into the car, I gave it a feel. And there it was—a nice fracture down the back of your skull. Not a hairline one either. A definite kill shot, again, for anyone normal. Yet here you are. You didn't disappoint, Michael. I have to give you that."

If I'd been out for two hours, he had come close to killing me. It was a hard thing to do, but not impossible and the brain was a delicate organ in a human or a chimera. I didn't have enough reach to lift my hands and feet, so I bent my head low and ran fingers through my hair. It was spiky with dried blood. He wasn't lying. He'd shot me while I'd been contemplating Milky Ways over Three Musketeers, damn it. He'd shot me right in front of the vending machine. . . .

God.

He'd shot me while I stood fifteen feet from our room where I'd left Stefan asleep—where I'd made sure he would *stay* asleep, unguarded and unconscious, an easy target. I hadn't locked the door on my way out because I was only fifteen goddamn feet away. "Stefan," I demanded. The blood in my hair was dry, but the tinfoil taste of it in my mouth was fresh. Invisible blood for a not-so-invisible desperation. "Where's Stefan?"

"Ah, Stefan Korsak, your brother." The way he said "brother" told me he knew something.

Knew too much.

"I killed him," he went on matter-of-factly. "Real bullets this time. I'd say it was painless, but I don't think it was. I shot him five times in the gut. You've not seen true pain until you see someone die of that. The trauma. The shredding of the intestines. The acid pouring from the stomach and eating away at everything it touches. But unfortunately my time was short. I let him suffer in excruciating agony for a moment or two, then finished him with one to the head. Like putting a lame horse out of its misery. I do occasionally have my kinder moments. You may thank me at your convenience." I turned away from him, away from it all, and rested my forehead against the window glass.

Stefan.

Thank God.

Thank fucking God.

Raynor was lying. Unless he'd rolled Stefan over in his sleep to shoot him, that whole story was, as Saul would say, bullshit with a side order of day-old crap for flavor. The story didn't matter, though. I would've known he was lying without it. He'd taken psychology classes with the best and the brightest of the CIA, but he was just a human. Institute training trumped CIA training and chimera trumped human. The most minute of facial expressions, pupil dilation, the heart rate I could sense speeding up slightly . . . I didn't care. I didn't care how I knew, only that I did know. My brother was alive. Through sheer luck or Raynor's need to make his escape with me quickly, Stefan was alive.

No thanks to me.

I'd thought I'd known best. I'd thought I was doing him a favor by helping him rest. I should've thought I was a dangerous idiot with the skills and a lifetime of training but not the experience, because that was what I was. The glass was cool under my forehead and I closed my eyes. But now Stefan would wake up and I would be gone. He'd search for me, but Raynor had proved, for a human, he was a formidable and cunning opponent. I had no idea how Stefan could hope to find me now. That might kill him the same as Raynor's imaginary bullets. And it would be my fault the same as if there had been a gun and I'd been the one pulling the trigger. I had done this to my brother. Raynor didn't matter. It had been me.

If I lived at all, how was I going to live with that?

There was a stirring in my jacket pocket and I slivered my eyes to see Godzilla poke his nose out. He knew danger when he smelled it and had obviously stayed hidden while Raynor wrestled me into his car. I gave a low hiss of warning, inaudible except to ferret ears, and he instantly disappeared back into my pocket. If Raynor found him . . . I didn't want to think about it. I didn't want to think about my failures, my screwups, my fuckups. I didn't want to think about anything right then.

I didn't get my wish. Big surprise.

"Ah, don't be like that. It'll make for a boring trip. We've had the Institute, which can be rebuilt as we have the day care to supply it. But you—you and the others are a problem we haven't faced before. Therefore, a new place shall be created for you and them— what should we call it? Probation? Detention?—where naughty little assassins are taught their rightful place." Raynor's gravelly voice was far too cheerful for me.

"But you look down in the mouth at that news." He *tsk*ed, the sound odd through the trach valve. "I know—let's bring your friend up. You'll have company. That'll put the pink in your cheeks. You might work up the curiosity to ask me precisely what they'll do to you when I have the probationary program fully staffed. I hate it when I concoct devious plans and no one can be bothered to ask me about them. My ego becomes quite bruised. Since I'm going to stop, are you sure you don't want some Tylenol for that formerly fractured head of yours?"

"No, thanks," I said without any emotion he'd be able to detect. "I'm not deficient. I'm not weak."

"Like me, you mean?" The car had pulled over into what had once been a rest stop. It was now a deserted, crumbling place except for us. "I suppose I should be offended by that, on my behalf and on humanity's behalf as well, but, Michael. . . ." He put the car in park and smiled at me. It was full of gloat and triumph. "This deficient human has certainly put you in your place, now haven't I?" He opened the driver door, but paused to gift me with a last few words before exiting. "Your place in the grand scheme of things is slave, chimera. An obedient, servile *slave* and I'll make damn sure you never forget that again."

He slammed the door behind him. I didn't bother to think about being a slave again, because I'd die before that happened. I did think about what he meant by bringing my friend up. What friend? Saul?

I heard the thump of the trunk, muffled sounds of outrage, and then the other door to the backseat was flung open. I saw pale skin, a flash of long legs under a short purple, blue, and green filmy skirt, lavender sandals that had ties that crisscrossed up the calf to tie in a neat bow just under the knees, and toenails painted pink—cotton candy pink.

The same as the girl's hair.

"Ariel?"

"Yes, your Easter egg–colored girlfriend from New York." Raynor tore away the duct tape that served as a gag, taking strands of pink hair stuck in the adhesive. "She was so worried about you that she showed up in Cascade Falls looking for someone who matched your description with the rather boring name of Bernie. Instead, she found one of my men. Mercenaries. You kill one, I simply hire another. I didn't think you'd go back to the Falls, but you never know. And while I didn't catch you, I did catch another little fish in my net, or rather one of my men did. She's quite a loud fish too but a perfect way of keeping you in line, along with the chains."

Her wary and suspicious blue eyes focused on the finger he wagged in her face. "Now then, scream again, little fish, and I'll hurt you. And trust me when I say that I'll enjoy it. Might even make a hobby of it. So let's use our inside voices, shall we?" He closed the door, the overhead light going dark again. Back behind the wheel, he hit the childproof locks and we were on the road again. "And do keep in mind, Michael, while I can't do much to hurt you in the more permanent sense without losing a large profit, to her I can do anything I want. My imagination in that area is vast and impressive."

I didn't face Ariel, not yet. I had a question first, the same question for both of them, but I asked Raynor first. "How did you find me?"

"Oh, I have a tracker too. I found the house in Laramie the same as you, but as I flew, while suctioning out my new tracheotomy—quite pleasant, thank you—I beat you. I saw the discarded chips inside the house and I knew you wouldn't be far behind. I waited out of sight and shot your 'borrowed' SUV with a magnetic tracking disc. Hands-on operation, that's what I'm about. And I don't care for my mercenaries to know too much about what I'm doing. Then I followed you and waited for a chance at you alone, without your rather shady companions. Lucky me, I stumbled across one fairly quickly."

Again, thanks to me. Now I looked at Ariel. Despite the dark and with the help of the occasional passing headlights, I could see that her usually smooth pink bob was a tangled mess. The faint glitter of light purple eye shadow and mascara was smeared. Her standard pink lip gloss was gone, the same pink as her short fingernails that decorated the hands that sat in her lap.

The hands didn't have much choice. Her wrists were restrained with the same plastic ties the police used. She looked lost, confused, and vulnerable . . . right up until the moment she lifted her bound wrists and smacked me hard across the jaw with them. "Liar!" Then she leaned back far enough to plant one purple sandal in my left ribs. "You are such a filthy liar, Bernie! Or is it Parker? That's what they were calling you in that tiny little town. And this maniac is calling you Michael. So which is it?"

Strands of hair had fallen in her eyes and she blew them out of the way to gauge that perfect aim one more time. The sandal slammed me again. "When we get out of this, when I kick your brainiac ass, I want to know exactly what name to call you, and it damn sure won't be Dr. Theoretical."

She was petite and slender, but she could kick like a mule. With four inches' reach thanks to the chains, there wasn't much I could do about it either. She kicked me one more time before giving up to glare at me. I seized the moment of silence to ask her what I'd asked Raynor. "How did you find me?" Or rather, how had she found out where I had been before going on the run again?

"Oh, please. I'm every bit the genius you think you are and then some." The tiny mermaid tattoo beside her eye seemed to flick its tail at me in displeasure. "You can bounce your Internet signal around the world a hundred times, but I can still trace it back to the source. It did take me six months. You were awfully thorough, but I have a brother who hacked the Pentagon when he was eleven." She gave me a last disgusted glance, then used her fingers to awkwardly try to smooth out her hair. "I've known you didn't live in Texas forever, but you seemed like such a good guy that I thought you might have your reasons to lie. And when you disappeared after a few weird e-mails and mentioned a family emergency, I started to worry." She shifted shoulders under a sparkling top—I'd call it light green, but she'd probably call it sea foam. "So . . . I went for a surprise visit. Because *I* worried. Because *I'm* a good person."

"And, my, I'll bet you were surprised, weren't you, darlin'?"

She lifted her foot to kick the back of Raynor's seat, but then thought better of it and paid him no attention instead. "I flew into Portland using up *all* my frequent flier miles, rented a car, and when I got to Cascade Falls, I found out there was no Bernie. I shouldn't have been surprised, since you lied about where you lived." She was back to glaring at me. "But some coffeehouse bimbo recognized your picture." She blushed as pink as her nail polish. "One that I happened to have with me. No big deal. I have one of my pet rat too." Her expression said I was about ten rungs below rat, and not a pet one either. "The bimbo said your name was Parker and you're soooo sweet and such a doll and couldn't be cuter and you worked at the coffeehouse."

The glare was white-hot now. It could've cut metal like an acetylene torch. "You're watching movies with me every week while flirting with some brainless wonder serving up caffeine, lying about your name, lying about getting your PhD. Lying about everything. But I try . . . *try* to give you the benefit of the doubt. Fake name, fake job when you are smart enough to have two PhDs by now; you love the escape of movies because maybe that's the only escape you have. You could be in the Witness Protection Program. I liked you so much, I was willing to turn off my own brain cells and go along with that ridiculous excuse."

This time she did kick the back of Raynor's seat. "Until this asshole has some goon grab me, toss me into the trunk of his car, put me on a private plane, fly me out here, and throw me into *another* car trunk. That is not Witness Protection. Homeland Security, Gitmo, or plain criminals, that I can see, but not Witness Protection."

"You're right about that, but kick the back of my seat again, girly, and I'll but a bullet in that pretty little foot of yours," Raynor warned.

The threat didn't intimidate her—I wasn't sure anything would—but she used common sense and tucked her feet under her in an impossibly flexible move. "And now this dick says your name is Michael." The fury faded from her eyes and transmuted into speculation. "Well?"

"Well what?" I asked cautiously.

"What's the truth? What's your name? Who are you? What's going on? That 'well.'"

She was every bit the Ariel I'd come to know over the past years . . . and more. That should've made me happy. Taking into account the situation, I was anything but. "Oh. You're done. I wasn't sure," I said. "I thought you might go on for a couple more hours."

"Do you want me to kick you for hours, because that

I can do. I take yoga. My stamina is profound. Absolutely goddamn *profound*, got it?"

I got it. "My name's Michael, but I go by Misha, and I was in hiding. That's kind of obvious." I shook my chains to demonstrate. "That was why I lied to you."

"And?" she asked when I stopped.

"And that's all I can tell you."

"That's all? What do you mean that's all? After you used me? Because that was what it was, wasn't it? You were using me for. . . ."

The next words out of her mouth were going to be "genetic research," and that was the last thing I wanted Raynor to hear and be thinking about. It would muddle things and have him ordering someone to make a run at Stefan to get my case with the delivery system of tranquilizer guns. That was not going to happen. I couldn't kick her, in turn, to keep her quiet, not with my shackles.

I went with the next best thing, cutting her off with a brusque, "Fine. Okay. I used you for computer sex. I typed with one hand and jacked off with the other. When I wasn't screwing Sara from the coffeehouse and was home bored, you were better than porn. All right, another lie. You were almost the next best thing to bad porn. If you'd shut up once in a while, I could've moved you up a rank or two. The Internet is full of horny guys. Don't tell me I'm the first one you've come across." I slid down in the seat. "Jesus, Raynor, you couldn't do better than kidnap my computer hump-day special?"

I took back everything I'd said and thought about

Saul. Channeling his perverted ways had created the perfect excuse to fit the situation.

I heard the faintest of choking sounds beside me and slanted my gaze toward eyes that, despite the gravity of the situation, were luminous with suppressed laughter. *Liar, liar, pants on fire,* she mouthed silently. I almost smiled. She was right. There wasn't a chimera born who didn't know how to lie.

Not the kind who lived very long.

We were headed north. I could tell that easily enough. But where? After an hour I gave in and asked. "Aren't you the curious thing?" Raynor said. "And I do mean 'thing.' We're going to Montana. I already have contractors in place building a new Institute and an adjoining rehabilitation facility. Busy, busy, busy. I've a lot to do and I was never one to let flies light on me."

Ariel opened her mouth when he said Institute, her smooth brow under pink bangs creased. I shook my head at her and she remained quiet. "And you think you'll be able to catch the others the same as you did me?" I said.

She started to open her mouth again when I gave the same shake of my head. You'd think being kidnapped would have anyone afraid, man or woman. So far, I'd seen her pissed off, highly pissed off, extremely pissed off, and entertained by my lies, but I hadn't seen fear on her face once. She showed what the old movies called moxie or spunk. She would know. She had watched those old movies with me from across the country, every week.

"Then why don't you let Ariel go? She won't be any use to you at a new Institute."

"I told you. She's my assurance you'll behave. You're a very naughty young man, Michael, what with trying to kill me and all. Not to mention we will need a starter kit, so to speak, for the new Basement. You can't have a Playground if there's nothing to play with, can you? I think she'll do nicely."

"How much assurance do you think that is?" I asked flatly. "She's better off dead here than in the Basement."

Her eyes widened slightly and this time when I shook my head, she kicked me again. I was lucky to be a chimera or my ribs would've been sore for a month. "I like you, Misha. I really do. I always have. You're special and brilliant and quirky and one of the most amazing people I've ever known, but if you try to shut me up one more time, the next kick will be to your face. It's a pretty face too. I especially like your eyes . . . fox green, but a fox that would never eat a chicken or clean out a henhouse. A vegetarian fox. You have nice teeth too, probably a killer smile. Try to not make me kick it in, all right? If I want to talk to the psycho, I'll talk to the psycho. And since you won't tell me anything, the psycho is my only other option."

This time it was me opening and shutting my mouth, and not at a shake of the head, but at the lift of a sandaled foot. "Psycho," she said, realizing I was going to obey the Foot of Doom, "what the hell is going on? You're government, I can tell. I've worked government contracts before. You're too megalomaniacal to be a cop or a crook and too egotistical to be another country's spy. So who exactly are you? CIA? FBI? Or my first guess—Homeland Security. That's it, isn't it? You have the attitude. Didn't you asses ever bother to think Homeland sounds a lot like the Fatherland or the Motherland and none of those things worked out too well for Germany or Russia?"

If Raynor had pulled the car over and pistol-whipped her, I wouldn't have been surprised. Fortunately, dealing with Jericho and his successor had taught him patience; either that or he was impressed. I knew I was. She was like a force of nature—a whirling pastel-colored verbal tornado cutting down anything in her path. Then there was the Basement, a worse punishment than any pistol-whipping, shooting, or roadside torture.

"I'm all of those things, little girl." I saw the reflection of his grin in the rearview mirror. "But I'm also more. You might say I'm a government agency of one. The blackest of ops and every conspiracy nut's worst nightmare. I'm going to take your boyfriend here, who now happens to be my personal property as everyone else who could lay claim is dead, and I'm going to torture him at great length, brainwash him, turn his mind and soul inside out until he does exactly as I say. And if that doesn't work, I'm going to put several bullets in his brain." There was the grin again, colder and sharper with anticipation.

"Being that he's actually worth something to me in the monetary sense and you are not worth a dime," he continued on with Ariel, "you might want to think twice about what I could do to you. I can find an off-ramp, a deserted road, and carve the tongue right out of your smart-ass mouth. That would shut you up. Of course, once I get started, it is difficult to stop. We all have our vices."

I'd thought Raynor was smart, and he was, and from his files I knew he did love interrogation. That might have been his problem. He was used to torture, used to victims already put through more than any mind or body should have to suffer. He was used to the broken.

Ariel was not broken.

She was an adamantine spirit who'd just been told the best she could hope for was a miserable death here or something worse in someplace called the Basement. You didn't need to be a genius to figure out it was better to die quickly than pick behind what was beyond those two doors. You didn't need to be a genius, but she was one.

A genius who took yoga.

She raised her hips off the seat, lunged forward, wrapped her long legs around the metal extension of the driver's headrest, and proceeded to do her best to choke Raynor to death. Having had a tracheotomy, he was down by ten points already. He couldn't scream through his mouth and he couldn't scream through his speaking valve either. Her knees—damn sexy knees—covered that completely. I could see her thighs ripple with muscle as she tightened the grip.

The fact that I was looking at her thighs while the car was careening across the interstate was not my fault. Her skirt was short to begin with. Now it was up around her waist as she did her best to save our lives. The saving-our-lives part should've distracted me from her panties, tiny and green with pink bows on each side, but it didn't . . . and were those rhinestones glittering below her navel and disappearing under her panties? I had the feeling I now knew what "vajazzled" meant.

That was when the car hit the guardrail and flipped. There wasn't anything I could do to prepare myself, chained as I was, except for bracing my legs against the floor. My head slammed against the window, then against the seat in front of me. I hung upside down briefly, the cuffs tearing at my wrists. My skin gave way where the metal didn't. Abruptly we were back upright. Outside I saw tufts of dried grass and I guessed we'd gone completely over the rail and down a mild embankment. Raynor was unconscious and Ariel was now in the front passenger seat. Whether she'd been thrown there or had climbed didn't matter. She was making the most of the moment.

"Where's the key?" she demanded, her skirt fluttering back down into place. For the second time in days I was damning gravity. "Misha, this is an escape, okay? Stop looking at my ass and tell me where this son of a bitch put the key to your chains."

I avoided the ass issue—there was no correct comment for that. If I was looking at her ass, then I was too perverted to care about saving my life, and if I wasn't looking, then she'd want to know why I wasn't looking. I went with the simple truth. "I don't know. I was unconscious when he put them on me." More like three-fourths dead, but we didn't need to go into that. "Check his suit pocket, then his pants pocket."

"Oh, fun for me. Having to stick my hand next to a psycho's wienerschnitzel." She searched his suit jacket pockets first and found nothing. "Wonderful," she snapped before gamely going into his pants pocket. "Whoops, I was wrong. Not a wienerschnitzel. Closer to a cocktail weenie. Doesn't it figure. Massive ego, teeny weenie. Ah ha!" Triumphantly, she held up the keys, reached across him to undo the childproof locks to the doors, and had me unchained in less than three seconds. "Don't look so worried, Misha." She wrinkled her nose. "I'm not an S&M queen. I worked as a magician's assistant one summer. I can also hold my breath for three minutes under water. You wouldn't believe how popular that made me when I turned eighteen."

I could imagine all right and now wasn't the time for it, but for once my body didn't obey me. I found out it was not impossible to run with an erection, but it was somewhat uncomfortable. We headed away from the interstate. No one was going to pick up two people hitching for a ride at four in the morning and I didn't want to run into any police. That was a complication to avoid. I hated leaving Raynor alive, but if I had been the killer I refused to be, I couldn't kill him in front of Ariel anyway. That would be a much bigger complication than the police.

That meant we ran. If only two hours had passed since Raynor had kidnapped me from the motel in Springerville, we were still in Arizona. All we had to do was find a phone and have Stefan and Saul come get us. However, in the ambient light of a sickle moon, it looked as if we were in a popular Arizona attraction, the Petrified Forest. There weren't a lot of phones there. Petrified or otherwise.

Chapter 10

Ariel leaped over fallen stone tree trunks with as much grace and style as if it were an event in the Olympics and she were being judged. All tens. She also didn't stumble a single time. Considering we were away from the highway lights and going by the limited light of the moon, that was impressive. I didn't stumble either, but chimeras had excellent night vision and mine had only become better as I matured, the same as everything else.

"You have great night vision," I said as we ran, neither of us winded so far.

"You have no idea. My brother, not the hacker, but my other brother, is a pilot. His vision is twenty-ten. My whole family is freakishly talented, apart from my sister. She's four and tells everyone she's an alien or a visitor from an alternate dimension, depending on her mood. She collects toy horses, then covers them up with little blankets for bedtime, except she covers them all up—including their heads. Her room looks like a fluffy pink horse morgue. She also wants to design shoes made out of human hair. She doesn't say where she's going to get the human hair, though, so when I go home to visit, I tend to lock the door. By the way, I was going to ask if that was a ferret in your pocket or were you just happy to see me, but I already saw the hard-on, so I'll just go with nice ferret."

I grinned. With Ariel, there was no point in being embarrassed or you'd spend every minute of the day bright red. "Thanks. His name's Godzilla."

"The ferret or your penis?"

"I'll let you guess." I stopped to get my bearings. Looking up at the position of the stars, I started running again, bearing to the right.

"With my night vision and the ability to visually measure to within approximately one centimeter, do you really want me to?" She was laughing again. Not many people laughed after being kidnapped, being involved in a car wreck, and having to use yoga skills to choke out an evil son of a bitch.

Godzilla poked his head farther out of my jacket pocket and chirped curiously. "I think I'd rather you didn't. Godzilla, meet Ariel. Ariel, meet Godzilla. He bites pretty much every chance he gets. I think the Visitor Center is this way. We can call for help."

I didn't say call my brother. I'd been careful not to give out any details about Stefan or to mention that he even existed when e-mailing or talking to Ariel. I'd been taking a risk with her from the beginning by investigating the genetics issue, and growing to know each other hadn't made the risk any less. I hadn't been willing to add Stefan into that mix. When she asked about family, I told her my parents were dead and my sister had been in the Peace Corps but died in a plane crash in Africa. That tended to limit questions and made me as sympathetic an orphan as a grown man could possibly be.

"It is? How do you know? Have you been here before? You know, when you weren't running from a crazed psychopath with deep, dark, and mysterious designs on you that you haven't bothered to explain yet?"

Since I'd met Ariel online, I'd noticed she never used one word when five hundred would do. Just as she never wore one color when there were at least seven right at hand. "Yes, I've been here before." I picked the question that could get me in the least amount of trouble. And saying, no, but I had memorized the maps of every state we'd passed through so far in case escape routes were needed wasn't something I was willing to offer. It wasn't as if I could pass it off as an interesting hobby.

"So, if we find the Visitor Center"—she sailed over another petrified tree—"and we break in to use their phone, who are we going to call? That guy's government, the kind of government that the government itself barely knows exists. He can eat police for breakfast and make prisoners disappear forever. The police can't help us with whatever bizarre thing you're involved in. Oh, hey, my little sister would kill me if I didn't ask: Are you an alien? This is just like all the movies where peaceful aliens come to Earth and the evil government tries to dissect them. Although I highly doubt any alien would come here. I believe in aliens. Trillions upon trillions of galaxies; we can't be the only intelligent life out there. But with all our fighting, wars, disease, poverty, and reality TV, we're like the meth–central, white-trash trailer park of our corner of the Milky Way. No alien would stop here to gas up. And who could blame them?"

There'd been a question in there somewhere. Now, what had it been again? Right. Whom were we going to call. "I have a friend who lives close to here. I'll call him."

It turned out I didn't have to call Stefan. He pulled into the Visitor Center at the same time we made it in. He didn't look pleased. He didn't look pleased in the way Rabid Zombie Werewolves from Mutant Hell—it was a real movie; I'd seen it—weren't pleased. He opened the door of the SUV and stepped out. There was the subtle motion of him putting his gun in the back of his jeans that no ordinary person would notice, twenty-ten vision or not. "What the fuck happened?" he demanded. He could've said more, considerably more. Out of nowhere it was my Internet friend from New York. I was in the middle of a park instead of asleep in my motel bed. I'd left everything behind, including my phone . . . everything except Godzilla. He had a bubbling volcano full of questions and he couldn't ask any of them in front of Ariel.

I had some too, the main one being how he had found me.

"This is your friend? Is he psychic or what? How'd he know where we'd be? And why's he so angry? What a temper. I don't know that I'd be friends with someone with that kind of temper." That was a good one with the way she'd done her best to break my ribs in Raynor's car. "And could someone kick in the door to the Visitor Center? I have to use the ladies' room, and I don't want to go around back and get my ass stung by a scorpion."

Saul stepped out of the other side of the vehicle. I pointed at him. "He'll kick it down for you. That's Bubba, my other friend."

It was almost worth Raynor's being left alive to kidnap and plot to see the contortions Saul's face went through when he was labeled with the fake "Bubba."

"Yeah, sure, chiquita," he said dubiously. "I'll kick it down for you." It took him a few tries, but once they were inside and I heard the bathroom door slam, both Stefan and I went at it.

"Raynor's alive. I was out putting money in the vending machine," I started to explain—I supposed we'd have to leave money to pay for the Visitor Center door too; being a good citizen was frequently frustrating—"and he shot me in the head with a rubber bullet. I woke up, chained, in a car going north. He's building a new Institute in Montana and was taking me there. One of his goons stumbled across Ariel in Cascade. She was worried about me and had tracked my IPS, although I bounced it around the globe a few hundred times. She's apparently as smart or smarter than I am." Which everyone lately appeared to be. "He thought she'd be insurance on my good behavior. She figured out he's government of some kind. She thought my name was Bernie, but she heard him call me Michael. We escaped when she choked him out with her legs—she takes yoga—while he was driving. The car flipped and we escaped. She doesn't know I have a brother. I said I'd call a friend from the Visitor Center for help. That's it." My short time in person with Ariel had taught me how to spit out a lot of information in very little time. It was useful.

I pointed at him. "You. Go. How'd you find me?"

He stared at me. I remembered when he used to have to look down to meet my eyes. Now that we were the same height, the stare was somehow more intense and as ferociously amber as one of those Rabid Zombie Werewolves.

Shit. I'd been so busy explaining what had happened that I'd forgotten *how* it had happened.

"We're on the run and you were shot in the head when you went outside without me," he said, his voice unnaturally calm for what I knew of my brother.

"A rubber bullet. He might as well have hit me with a Tic Tac." That wasn't quite true, but downplaying it was my best hope.

"When you went outside without me."

"You were asleep. You needed the rest," I pointed out.

"Without me."

I opened my mouth, found nothing and no words that were going to turn this around, and closed it.

Stefan apparently approved of the move and answered my question. "I found you because I woke up when your friend Peter the Pied Piper of killer kids called on that phone he left you." I'd kept it in case he did. It was too cheap to be GPS enabled and he wanted us to find him anyway. "When that happened and I discovered you were gone, I used my own tracker." He bared his teeth in a savage smile. "They're like iPhones, right? Everyone has to have one."

"Your own tracker?" Despite the smile he'd used only against people he was about to beat up or shoot, I was curious—guilty as hell too, but curious. "What'd you track? I know you didn't plant anything in me when I wasn't looking."

"Your rat. One day when you were at work, I took him to the vet and had him chipped. I know it'd break your damn heart if he ran off." His smile was no less pissed off.

No, what he knew was that at least fifty percent of the time Godzilla was with me and if we ever had to run again, it would be one hundred percent of the time. He'd outthought me when I hadn't had a clue he was thinking about having to run at all. "That is devious as hell. That is Institute devious," I said with reluctant admiration.

"You bet your ass it is." This time the smile disappeared. Lines bracketed the side of his mouth and I could tell he was more tired now than when I'd "helped" him sleep. "What did you do, Michael?" There was no Misha now. He knew what I'd done. I'd used my genetic abilities on him, though I was doing it for him. It was a violation, a huge one. That deserved my Institute name. "I would've woken up when you opened the door. After the mob, after what you and I lived through before, I would've woken up and we both know it."

I was an ass. I hadn't meant to be. I'd tried to do a good thing, but we were in a situation where there were no good things, only the right things. I hadn't done the right thing. I'd been careless. "You were tired. I was only going to be out there two minutes. I wanted you to be able to sleep. I thought I was helping, but clearly I fucked up."

He stared at me for another second. "Fucked up doesn't begin to cover it." He headed back to the SUV. "Let's go. We have to get rid of your girlfriend somehow and get back to finding Peter and his goddamn posse. And we have Raynor back on our asses. I assume he's not as dead as we'd hoped or you would've told me."

I'd disappointed him. There hadn't been a time Stefan had been disappointed in me—until now. I felt as if I'd been kicked in the stomach, a kick much worse than the ones Ariel doled out. I would've rather he went back to being angry with me. "Stefan," I said quietly, "I'm sorry. I'm. . . ." I was what? What else was there to say? He'd thought he'd lost a brother again and if my healing abilities hadn't quadrupled since I was seventeen and if he hadn't chipped Godzilla, he might have. He was right. Fucked up didn't cover it and neither did "sorry." Nothing did.

I walked in silence behind him. I had issues. Anyone raised at the Institute would, but I hadn't felt this worthless and guilty in my life. Each step I took felt mired in quicksand. He was the sole family I had and I'd let him down.

Where was my genius now?

Stefan exhaled, stopped, turned; then he hooked an arm around my neck and squeezed. "Still your brother, Misha. I love the hell out of you, jackass. We'll write this off as lesson learned, all right? Now, get your girlfriend. Apparently she has a black belt in yoga but takes as long as a ninety-year-old woman to pee."

My shoulders slumped in relief at his willingness to forgive. "Why is it men piss and women pee?"

"Okay, loving you a little less," he snorted. "Go."

I started to, but paused. "Wait. You said Peter called. When you answered instead of me, what did he say to you?"

He shook his head. "You don't need to know. You tried to do something for my own good. I *know* this is for your own good. So go get the girlfriend." He checked his gun, replaced it, and covered it with his shirt. He didn't know he'd done it. The move was completely automatic, caused by the memory of what Peter had told him. Peter said he was curious about me. Peter was not curious about Stefan in the slightest except in how many varied ways he could dispose of him.

That wasn't going to happen.

"Go without you? What happened to lesson learned?" I leaned against the SUV beside him. "I think I'll stick around. 'Bubba' can hurry her up."

Stefan's lips twitched. "What if he flirts with her?"

"First, he's in his forties. That's disgusting. Second, if she did take him up on it, she'd kill him. His heart would give out before the Viagra kicked in."

"There's something to be said for dying a happy man," he commented, eyebrows raised.

"No, there's not." My mood at being forgiven abruptly deflated.

"No?" The eyebrows went a fraction higher and his lips twitched again.

"No," I said darkly, moving to the hood to see inside the Visitor Center.

Seriously, how long did it take someone to go to the bathroom?

I worried about how we were going to explain to Ariel how Stefan and Saul were waiting for us before we had a chance to call them. Despite her comment, she wasn't going to buy psychic. Her four-year-old sister with the horse morgue and human hair shoes might buy it, but not a woman who was, I couldn't deny any longer, more intelligent than I was. But it turned out not to be a problem. I was given a humbling example of how experience in duplicity edged out genius without trying.

They said nothing.

In the back with me, Ariel, Dr. Ariel Annabelle Mac-Leod, verbally poked and prodded Saul and Stefan relentlessly for two hours on how they'd known where we were. Neither of them said one word. The louder and more persistent she was, the denser the silence became. At one point, Stefan dozed off while Saul drove, which was the equivalent of sleeping through a tornado siren two feet from your ear. That was when Ariel turned her frustrated attention back to me, but it was too late. I'd learned by example. Everything she asked about Raynor, the Institute, if the two up front were indeed "fucking psychic Men in Black," if the sky was blue and the grass was green, I smiled, shrugged, and kept my mouth shut. I half expected another attack with purple footwear, but it didn't happen. She finally gave up, folded her arms, and started reciting Pi. If we were going to ignore her, she could do the same, but she was also Ariel. She could ignore us and annoy us, except for a snoring Stefan, by assaulting our eardrums all at the same time. She was up to the eight-hundred and seventy-fifth decimal—I wasn't intimidated as I could go up to a thousand—when Saul decided he needed a bathroom break of his own.

How did I know since he wasn't talking? I could feel, literally, his bladder aching. When little kids read their comics and wished for superpowers, I couldn't imagine any of them wishing for that one. *Wolverine, Magneto's distracted. He needs to piss like a racehorse. Make your move!* It wasn't as if I could feel every ache and creak of a person's body, and I had to be extremely close to them to feel anything at all, but if it was painful enough and the proximity was there, I could often feel more than I wanted.

Like now. Thank God he didn't have prostate problems yet.

He picked an off-ramp on the trail back to Tucson, and Peter, and stopped at a McDonald's packed with the breakfast rush. We looped the building twice before finding someone pulling out and taking their parking spot. The second we stopped, Ariel opened her door and said the first thing since she'd started on Pi. "I have to go to the bathroom and I'm starving. That government asshole took my purse. So one of you as-yet-indefinable assholes hand over some cash."

Saul grunted but handed her a five. She flipped him off with a perfectly appropriate doctorly finger and said, "Thanks, big spender. That might buy me a sausage and biscuit but no OJ. I'll be sure to name my scurvy after you." Then out of nowhere, she turned and kissed me. It wasn't a long kiss, but it was warm and firm with the sweet taste of tongue, and abruptly she was gone, flouncing her way into the restaurant. I wasn't being sexist when I said flouncing. Ariel didn't flounce. She walked with a strong and determined gait, but her skirt flounced. It couldn't help it. It looked made of filmy scarves. If you're a scarf, you don't have much choice: flutter or flounce. Between the kiss and the flounce, I smiled. I couldn't help myself.

Saul sighed as Stefan yawned and straightened. "Okay, Smirnoff, now that you slept through the make-out session, what are we going to do with the mouth that ate the continent? Send her home? Bury her in a shallow grave? What?"

Stefan tilted his head to look back at me at Saul's news. I shrugged again. It had worked for me so far for the past hour. He was caught between a teasing smirk and a frown, I could tell, but settled on a frown. "Raynor took her," he said. "He has her ID. He knows who she is, where she lives. If we send her home, there's a chance he might snatch her again to get at Misha. We'll have to stash her someplace. With someone we trust until this is all over. She damn sure can't come along." He left it unsaid that it would be more dangerous than sending her home.

He rubbed his face. I could hear the scrape of his palm over the bristle of his beard. "You know anyone out here you trust, Saul?"

Saul yawned himself, his bladder complaining more. "I have people that subcontract for me, sure. I have people like that all over the country. But someone I trust? In my business? Yeah, right. How about you? You have anyone you trust?"

Stefan groaned, low and resigned. "Besides the two guys sitting in the car with me? No. Shit."

Saul undid his seat belt. "Well, keep thinking. Gotta shake the snake before I explode." He got out and disappeared inside after Ariel. The difference was twofold: His clothing didn't flounce—blinded, but no flouncing. The second difference was that he came back. Ariel didn't.

Stefan and I went in to search for her, but she was gone. I checked out the women's restroom myself. That was one good thing about growing up without ingrained social customs. You didn't care when you were caught doing what traditionally you weren't supposed to do. And naturally I was caught peering under occupied stall doors and was summarily hustled back out into the parking lot. Compared to the whole of my life, I had no problem with being called a pervert and a line cutter. I knew I was only one of the two.

Stefan stood with me on the asphalt. "She must've gone out the other side. Hitched a ride maybe. I don't know, but she's gone. I ran the perimeter. I'd have seen that pink hair if she was on foot, but nothing. She's just . . . gone."

I nodded. "I'm not surprised." And I wasn't. I'd rather expected it. "Can you go back in and get me something to eat? I've been banned."

He studied me, more than baffled. "You're not worried about her? Pretend all you want, but I know you like her. You're not worried Raynor will catch her again?"

I more than liked her, but that wasn't the issue. "She's smart, Stefan. Smarter than I will ever be, and if

I'm saying that, with my ego, you know it means something. If she doesn't want to be caught, she won't be. You think I make great fake IDs? If she wants to make any, they could blow mine out of the water." I no longer wondered if that was the correct phrase. I knew. A few days of chasing Peter and running from Raynor and my brain was in overdrive. Cascade Falls had been good, better than good, and I missed it, but it hadn't stretched me; it hadn't pushed me. I was learning much more now because I had to. Necessity wasn't the mother of invention. Desperation was. "Ariel will be fine. Probably better than we'll be. And she'll be safer than with anything we could do for her."

If anything, he was more bemused than before. "You believe that?"

"No, I know that. I've known her for two years now. It doesn't matter if it was on the Internet or with video cams. With my psychological and profile training, I would know her—genuinely *know* her, her personality, what she would do, what she wouldn't do, everything that makes her her. I would know all of that even if we'd only written letters once a month. She will do the smart thing and that is to not be with us, near us, or anyone we might think we could trust with her. Trust me on this, Stefan. Just . . . trust me." I gave him a light shove toward the restaurant. I'd said all I could say for now. "And I'll see Ariel again someday. I can guarantee it. One hundred percent." It wasn't a lie. I believed it wholeheartedly. I knew it as I knew her.

"Pancakes and biscuits and gravy," I ordered to get him moving. "Oh, and hash browns. Four of them. And

I know they don't make milkshakes this early, but maybe could you bribe the manager? Chocolate?"

He narrowed his eyes but started walking. He knew I wasn't lying. I liked Ariel too much to lie about that. It was embarrassingly plain to see. But he also suspected I wasn't sharing everything. He let it go, though, and did what I asked him. He trusted me. "You are one weird kid, Misha."

"I'm not a kid, remember?" And for the first time since I'd been complaining about the term, I knew it was true—I knew it for an absolute fact. I wasn't a kid, not compared to my twenty-seven-year-old ex-*Mafiya* bodyguard brother, not compared to the ancient Saul, not compared to anyone. I wasn't a kid. I would never be one again. I also knew now you shouldn't wish your youth and pseudo-innocence away.

You'd never get it back.

Chapter 11

We found Peter in Tucson.

He was waiting for us. If he was losing confidence that we'd catch up, I didn't question the logic. But we had other things come up and they would come up again. Raynor couldn't track me . . . or Godzilla, being in the dark there about ferret chipping, but he had to have an Institute tracker of his own. He would be following Wendy's chip the same as we were. Peter and the rest of the chimeras, us, and a government sociopath—it was a parade no one wanted to see.

Outside the SUV's window, I could see the city. I didn't need a map to know we were in South Tucson. I'd already memorized the map I'd Googled on the computer. It wasn't Cascade—not a coffeehouse or bakery in sight. There were crumbling buildings and cold, hard faces. I knew why Peter had chosen this particular place in the city. The old man they'd killed in Laramie hadn't been a challenge. Now Peter was looking for one, or at least more entertainment value.

Stefan was driving now and he clicked the locks shut. "We're too busy to kick some wannabe-carjacker's ass right now," he explained. "Dealt with that crap all the time in Miami. Wannabes. It gets real boring real fast kicking the baby fat off some fifteen-year-old gang-banger with an HK. You have any people working down here, Saul?"

He blew out a puff of air ripe with disgust. "Nope. I tried recruiting some locals a few times, but they kept getting whacked after a few weeks or months. A waste of time. This is a kill zone, pure and simple."

Peter's kind of place. I glanced down at the GPS tracker. "Turn left, then left again. They're less than three blocks from here on the right." I gave him the address. Discarding the tracker beside me, I pulled the case with the tranq guns out from under Saul's seat and started unloading them.

"You know that if we park here and live to tell the tale of how we cured a horde of psychotic murdering kids, we'll have to walk home. The SUV will be gone the instant we're out of sight," Saul said.

"That won't be a problem." I handed him one of the oversized tranquilizer guns and Stefan the other as he steered with one hand.

"No?" Saul questioned skeptically. "Why is that?"

"People know. Normal people too. They're in that building up there." I pointed at the windshield toward the corner ahead of us where a two-level pueblo-style building squatted in a precarious heap at the intersection of two streets. "And everyone in that building is dead. The people around here might not smell them yet or maybe they do, but either way, anyone who was in there is dead. The most oblivious person in the world couldn't walk past it and not know. They'll cross the street to avoid it. Instinct. It's left over from a time when instinct was the only thing that kept early man from being eaten by a giant *Canis dirus*. No one will come near the building or bother the car."

"A *Canis* what?" That would be Saul. Again.

"A dire wolf. A big-ass Pleistocene wolf. A three-hundred-pound people-eating puppy. Woof, woof." I took a gun of my own out of the case and then closed it.

"Smart-ass." Saul shifted the tranq gun to one hand while pulling his own gun with the other, once again prepared for any situation. "Why are we trying so hard to save these kids? They killed an entire building full of people. They kill and they love it. If they were normal people, we'd wait until they were old enough, slap 'em on death row, and give them their last booster shot. Jesus, Stefan, Michael, they're too dangerous to let live. They're too dangerous to try to cure. That Wendy kid killed the possibly salvageable ones; you said yourself. Why are we risking our lives for murderers without an ounce of remorse?"

"Because they weren't just born that way. It wasn't an accident of nature that produced a rare sociopath. Someone made them this way, through genetics and training and brainwashing. They're monsters, but that's because a monster mirrored his own ego in them. They deserve a chance, even if it's not much of one or the monster wins. Jericho wins and that's not acceptable." I put my hand out, ready to open the car door. "Let me go first. It's Wendy's chip. If she's there with them, Stefan, you need to stay outside until you hear me yell for you. Saul, you go around back in case a few try to escape." I doubted sincerely that would happen, but I had to plan for all eventualities. Because of Wendy, I needed to go in first.

Wendy was a new kind of monster. We were all chimeras, a name from the creature of mythology—two-in-one—but Wendy was something else. Wendy was a chimera with a fucking cherry on top. She was another creature of legend.

Basilisk.

Mythology said if one saw you, you died. One look and your life was over. Wendy was that myth, born to reality and walking the earth for the first time.

"What makes you think you're immune? You said it yourself; Wendy is the only chimera who can hurt other chimeras." Stefan, like Saul, had his gun backing up the tranq one. He parked the SUV on the street two buildings down from our target. He and I got out and headed for the front of the squat box of a building while Saul headed around the back.

"Peter is running the show and Peter wants something from me. He won't let Wendy kill me. And," I muttered low and fast, "I've been practicing."

"Practicing? What do you mean you've been—"

The door to what had once been a pawnshop, but was most likely a meth lab now, slammed shut behind me. I'd been quick, because I was that much quicker now—quicker than any human. The door cut off Stefan's voice and I concentrated. Inside it was quiet. The walls and floor were covered with years of dust and grime. There were bars on the windows, the glass itself covered with newspaper to hide the interior from prying eyes. There were cots all over the one big room. The bodies of several Hispanic men lay dead on them—not because they died peacefully in their sleep, but because there was so little space between them they couldn't fall to the floor. There were some exceptions where a few cots had been turned or tipped over by death convulsions. Most had guns or knives in their hands or laying by them. They had all, to a man, gone the Basement way. Not one had died easily.

The one closest to me had gray rubbery streamers of flesh spilling out of his gaping mouth—part of his lungs. You couldn't cough up both of them at once, or just one, but you could cough up pieces of them until you choked and asphyxiated or died from another lack of oxygen: lungs blown to tatters. Either/or. Another man lay on his back, his brain matter having spilled out his ears, nose, and mouth. Someone had crushed his skull.

The next victim was shirtless and curled on the floor, his abdomen split neatly from breast bone to below his baggy jeans somewhere. His arms were curled around the large pile of intestines that had poured free, as if he could push them back inside and hold himself together. The man closest to him had shot himself in the head with his own gun to escape his torment, but first he'd ripped off his pants. His penis and testicles. . . .

I stopped cataloging the carnage. It was nothing I hadn't seen before—nothing new under the sun that could be done outside the Institute that hadn't been done inside. The one difference was this wasn't a reward for excelling; this was freedom.

I could smell anhydrous ammonia fumes wafting down from the top floor. Meth lab—I'd been right. I was also right in not expecting Stefan to listen to me. The door opened and shut almost silently behind me, but he didn't say anything—battle ready.

"Michael, finally." The voice echoed in the still air. There was the sound of one footstep.

"It's been so dull waiting for you and your . . . pets? Isn't that what you call lesser creatures you keep with you and alive for no apparent reason? I've seen them being walked in parks and down the sidewalks in rhinestone collars and pink leashes. Did you forget this one's leash? Will he bark for a treat? Will he piss himself at what he sees here?"

Peter had drifted nearly soundlessly down the stairs against the back wall. Now he sat, midway down, and dangled one hand over the rusted wrought-iron railing. He was the same as he had been on the Institute tape—cheerful, charismatic. He had changed from the white pajama-style uniform to a black shirt and jeans. Dark shirt, dark hair, shadows clinging to him—Death himself. "So. Look at you, Michael. You have changed. Having seen what was outside our walls, I think all of us would change. Will change." I didn't raise the tranquilizer gun yet. I wanted to know more. What did he want with me? Where were the others? Stefan, now beside me, followed my lead. He knew violence and he knew it well, but in this particularly vicious subcategory, I was the expert.

Peter leaned to rest his forehead against the thin metal banister. His eyes were chimera eyes—one blue, one green. He hadn't bothered to conceal that with contacts as I had. Ordinarily those colors would be the calm pastels of a spring morning. Somehow on Peter they seemed almost blind. He was blind in a way, seeing only what he wanted to see, and what surrounded us now was all he wanted to ever see—destruction. I didn't see his mask; I saw what was behind it.

"I have to say, Michael, I'm rather surprised. We all knew you wouldn't graduate. You were days at best from dissection. Strawberry jam in a jelly jar. In the refrigerator you'd go. Yum, yum. Good eating." His grin was friendly and happy as a golden retriever's. In two weeks he'd picked up the language, the casual nature, the obscure phrasings we'd not been taught. I was only now coming into my own after almost three years.

How had I not seen him before for what he was?

"But now you're different." His eyes went distant as if he were listening to inner instruction, his brain studying the peculiarity that was me. "You have bite to you now. Inside. Before, you would've let them walk you down to that metal table, obedient. . . . No, not necessarily obedient, but passive. Passive to the end. Now, however . . . now I think you would fight."

He was right. I would. I wouldn't kill, but you didn't have to kill to fight and try to escape. "You're stronger." Peter stood, arms lazily resting on the metal as he bent over as if to get a closer look at me in the dim light that struggled through the paper-covered windows. With our vision, it was an act to make me associate him more with humans, therefore harmless, than with chimeras. It was a good move to put me off my guard. Trained powers of observation can be used against you. Lifelong associations of one thing to another are difficult to break. "You're a better chimera, but are you good enough to join us and be accepted into the family?"

"Where is the rest of the 'family'?" I asked in a detached tone, letting him know his trick, good or not, wasn't working.

Calm. Cold. Being Jericho. The first naturally enhanced chimera, born with increased healing and strength. He couldn't kill. That was his gift to us. Despite his genetic inability to dole out death, he had remained the ultimate chimera in his mind. He feared none of us . . . until the end. And at that he was far more proud of his Wendy creation than wary of her. Jericho had been living, breathing ice. I would be too.

"Here, there. Around." He rocked back on his heels. "Dull and boring as things were waiting for you to slog along behind us, we thought we'd help you out and give you a chance to catch up. That pathetic bag of bones in Wyoming wasn't worth our time, of course. So the next time we stopped, I thought it would be interesting to find something more spry. I love that word— 'spry.' The definition of walking around when nature should've already taken you down. A very optimistic word. Before I killed her, I asked that nice, spry lady at the gas station when we came into town where the most dangerous people hung out." He laughed, derisive and sated all in one. "And here they are—with their guns and their knives. They were like us in a way. They liked to kill too. Murder, rape, and they couldn't wait to teach us some manners when we came knocking at the door."

He reached down and picked up a gaudy red plastic rose I'd dismissed earlier as unimportant. He must have gotten it at the same gas station where he'd killed the woman who gave him directions. He tossed it over the rail to land on one of the bodies. "But these dangerous people were writing checks their antisocial tendencies couldn't cash. They said they were, how'd they put it, 'pure evil motherfuckers who were going to fuck up our baby-ass shit.'" He imitated a deeper, hate-filled, older man's voice perfectly. "They give out the label sociopath so easily here in the real world. No one has to truly earn it. Isn't that a shame? It devalues the meaning and the purpose . . . our meaning, our purpose." He sighed, pulling on a pensive mask, but the glee leaked through. He took a step upward and then one more. "It won't stay that way. Give us time and we will change the word and the world. Mass murder with a lollipop for these ignorant, oblivious wastes of genes. Are you up for that, Michael?"

At his first step I'd raised the tranquilizer gun. "No one is here but you, are they?"

"No," he smiled. He pulled a black cord necklace out from under his shirt. Attached to it was a tiny cloth bag. It would hold Wendy's chip perfectly.

"And you don't want me for your Manson Mein Kampf family dream-come-true, do you?"

"He catches on." He applauded once. "Want you? *Hardly.* You've changed, but not enough. And even if you had, this isn't what it's all about. We never wanted you, Michael. We want to punish you. You've done a very bad thing and you have to pay. And, Michael, you are going to fucking pay and pay and pay." He was moving up again at a run, but Stefan, who'd had his gun up long ago, had already pulled the trigger. The cartridge hit Peter in the upper leg. He didn't stagger, much less fall. My cartridge hit the wall he disappeared behind.

Damn, I was certain the dosage would be high enough to knock him out. I started after him, weaving between cots, and then skidded to a stop. Stefan heard it at the same time I did. Half a step behind me, he grabbed my arm and ran, yanking me along with him. He didn't need to. I was as fast, and running over the top of bodies and their various crushed organs didn't faze me. Stefan, despite his mob background, flinched slightly but didn't let it slow him down either. We hit the right wall of the room simultaneously with the semitrailer that crashed through the front of the building. Stefan was knocked to the floor by a falling piece of ceiling. I was thrown forward by the slam of an upended cot against my back.

I'd known the building was structurally unsound by looking at it when we arrived, but I'd underestimated its instability. Perfect for an explosion, I'd thought, and it was a meth lab. I'd been on the alert for trip wires, any evidence that the lab upstairs would be blown. But that would've been a repeat of the last attempt on our lives—the establishing of a pattern. Patterns were to be avoided; they ignited suspicion in the authorities. Bought and paid-for indentured assassins were taught to avoid that. But I knew to listen and watch for other traps as well. I was facing down my own who'd received the same training as I had. The instant I heard the full-throttle roar of an engine, I knew. That Stefan knew too didn't surprise me. The longer we were together, the more I saw how similar our lives had been in the things we'd been taught to do and the things we'd actually done.

It sucked for us both.

It sucked more when the building collapsed on top of us.

"Get away from him, you son of a bitch. Touch him again, and it'll be the last thing you *ever* do."

Stefan. . . .

Only Stefan could put that much grim promise in the word "ever."

Hazy . . . everything was hazy, lazy, dazy, wavy. No . . . no z's in wavy. It was dark and bright and red and dark again. The rapid switch didn't improve the hazy, lazy, dazy any.

"Sir, we're trying to help him. He could have a crush injury to his chest. That can be fatal, do you understand? He has a pneumothorax—one of his lungs is deflated. He probably has blood building up around his heart. We have to stabilize him now or he'll die. You got that? He'll die. Now, get the hell back. Lenny, where the hell are the cops? We need them on this guy."

Cops. That would be bad. That had the haze fading faster as I felt my adrenaline increasing on its own, doing what a chimera's body was built to do. I helped it with what I'd learned in the past years. I increased the adrenaline tenfold. That much would be detrimental and lethal to a human; to me, it was fuel accelerating the healing.

"Jesus, he's going into some serious sinus tach. What the fuck? Four hundred and fifty beats? Jackie, the cardiac monitor is screwed. Get the backup monitor!"

We chimeras would not be good for the mental health of EMTs, paramedics, or any other medical personnel because we made all their medical knowledge useless. I knitted the hole that had been torn in my lung back together, causing massive numbers of cells to rush to meet one another. The three broken ribs would have to wait. I flooded my system with endorphins to dull the pain. There was some small amount of blood around my heart. I had my blood vessels reabsorb it. Opening my eyes, I lifted a hand and pulled the irritating endotracheal tube used to intubate me out of my throat and whacked the EMT on the head with it. It wasn't very polite of me, as he was trying, in his mind, to save my life, but the only thing he could do was slow the process down and do more harm than good. Stefan knew that, which was why he was threatening to beat the shit out of my would-be angel of mercy.

Said angel of mercy was a balding, chubby man, and I'd left a red mark on the top of his shiny head with the tube. I felt guilty about that until I heard more sirens in the distance. Cops. Either the cops weren't enthusiastic about coming to this part of town for a truck running into a building, or any other reason, or the fire station was closer. I sat up on the gurney and put my hand out. Stefan, covered in dirt and blood, instantly clasped my arm and lifted me to my feet. The ribs twinged, but that was all. I might've overdone it with the endorphins, nature's morphine. I gave Stefan a loopy smile. "Did a building fall on me?"

"No." He had his arm around my shoulders and was helping, if helping was half carrying, me to the SUV waiting for us two buildings down. It hadn't seemed far when we'd parked. It seemed a half-hemisphere walk now. I vaguely noticed his other arm was pointed behind us as he crabbed us along sideways. He was holding his gun on the EMTs. None of them was inclined to die to take me to the hospital for a Snoopy Band-Aid. "You were hit by a semi *and* then a building fell on you. You are incapable of doing things the easy way, aren't you?"

"Hit by a semi and lived." My grin stretched wider.

"Clipped," Stefan elaborated. He had no grin or smile.

I ignored him. "I'm indestructible." The *s* in indestructible was slurred, but I didn't mind. I was the king. I told Stefan so. "I'm the king. All hail the king." I decided I felt too good to walk and gave up. Forget the cops; napping on the sidewalk sounded like a great idea. We were about ten feet from the SUV when I decided that. Stefan half lifted me with one arm and carried me like a sack of potatoes the rest of the way, which was no way to treat the king, while Saul opened the door to the backseat from inside. He put his hands under my shoulders and eased me in while Stefan slammed the door behind me. Saul jumped behind the wheel and Stefan reappeared at the other side of the SUV, climbed in, and lifted my head to rest in his lap.

"Get us the hell out of here, Saul."

"Yeah, like you had to tell me that, oh great master criminal. Jesus." I could feel the SUV already moving and moving fast from the screech of tires. "What is it with these damn little psychotics and destroying buildings? I nailed one in the chest as he was coming out the back. He had black hair, about eighteen. I think it was that Peter kid. He came out the second-floor window, flipped up over to the roof, and then jumped to the next building. Like goddamn Spiderman. He was weaving, though. I was going to go after him, but then Rome fell. I think you need to juice up your tranq-cure, kid."

"You've no . . . idea." The sun through the window sparkled in a thousand colors. I didn't know there were a thousand colors. "He grew up, same as me. Stronger now. He's not a rhino anymore. He's four or five rhinos. Up the dose. Definitely. Up. Up, up, and away."

Stefan's thumb gently peeled back my eyelid. "Been practicing, huh?" I had said that, hadn't I? Before we'd gone into the pawnshop. "On the healing, I'm guessing. Not even chimeras can fix a deflated lung and blood pooling around your heart in minutes. And somehow you're doped to the gills, though I didn't let that guy give you anything. Your pupils are huge."

"That's the adrenaline for healing and the endorphins for . . . I'm hungry." I tried to sit up. Stefan held me down easily with a hand on my forehead and one on my chest. I wasn't simply hungry. I was starving. I'd pushed my body to extremes I'd hoped I had in me but hadn't been completely sure about until now. It took massive amounts of energy to do what I'd done, and I needed to replenish it. But when I tried to explain, replenish sounded more like plenrish. I said it several more times until it was less of a word and more a mouthful of oatmeal. That only made me hungrier. Oatmeal . . . Ariel liked oatmeal with brown sugar, cinnamon, and maple syrup. Ariel was hot. Not just hot . . . what'd they say . . . yeah . . . smoking hot.

Did Ariel think I was hot?

"Am I hot?" I asked Stefan. "Smoking hot? Think Ariel thinks I'm smoking hot?"

"Yeah, you're the sexiest motherfucker on the planet,

Misha." There were so many emotions behind the blood on his face, but right now I could read only two of them. Exasperation. Worry. Too much worry. "Now enough with the endorphins. You must have more in you than you'd find swimming around in fifty marathon runners combined. Cut back on them enough to be lucid, would you?"

The sirens behind us were louder and closer. Who needed to be lucid to know that wasn't good? "Shit." Stefan twisted his head. "I made it through the mob years without having to shoot at a cop once. Doesn't it goddamn figure? Think I can hit the tires of three police cars?"

"Gun." My tongue felt thick, but I could do the little words. Cake of piece. Or something like that. "Micro. Wave. Gun."

"Okay, that I approve of. Beats pipe bombs by a mile. Where the hell is it?" He leaned over me, careful not to rest any weight on my chest, and dug around in my duffel bag. "Damn it!" I saved my sympathy. He'd packed the bags when they'd come after Raynor, Ariel, and me.

"Forget? Old. Senile. We need a drugstore . . . adult diapers."

"Misha, seriously. Dial down the damn endorphins. Jesus, finally." He yanked the microwave gun out of my backpack, rolled down the window, and, holding me against him with one hand as we rose up off the seat, he leaned out and fired. "Christ, it worked." As if anything I built wouldn't work. He fired two more times and there were no more sirens. Easing back inside, he dropped the gun in the floorboards.

"Way to save our ass, kid," Saul said from the front. "You done good."

"Always do good. I'm brilliant. The most brilliant genius to. . . ." I lost my train of thought and then caught a more important one. "Still hungry."

"Saul, emergency kit." Stefan lifted his hand from my chest and caught the bag that sailed back. Stefan didn't go anywhere with me, on the run or living our once peacefully mundane lives in Cascade, without food. I didn't know if chimeras in general required more calories than humans or if it was merely me, but I outate Stefan three times over.

Outate.

Which reminded me again.

Food.

Now.

Hungry.

Stefan had a ham sandwich half—unwrapped. I snatched it clumsily from his hand and took huge bites, swallowing without chewing. While I ate, I did what Stefan suggested and eased back on the endorphins, although I hated to see the rainbows in the streamers of sun disappear. They were nice. They reminded me of home. There they arched over the river and the dam almost every week. It was the reason the bridge that topped the dam was called the Bridge of the Heavens. It made more sense than a golden ladder.

But I wasn't dead yet, so no Paradise for me.

As I finished the sandwich and eased back on the production of the endorphins, I began to notice things. The pain that stabbed my ribs was gone. A point against lucidity. Stefan was the other thing I noticed. When I'd woken up, I'd seen him covered in dirt, dust, and blood. He hadn't been hit or clipped by a semi, but a building had fallen on him as it had on me. "Are you. . . . ?" I grimaced and braced my ribs with my hand. "Are you all right?" My body wasn't close to full capacity yet. I couldn't feel if he was hurt or not. My lingering damage took precedence and I couldn't change that. The body's self-preservation overrode what my mind ordered it to do. I raised my other hand and swiped at the blood-dust paste on his face to see the damage. There were several cuts and scrapes, but they weren't bad. The blood was from them and his nose. It didn't look broken, though. It was all superficial, but that was nothing compared to what could be going on inside him.

"I'm all right," he assured me. "Sore and getting less and less male-model material all the time, but I'll live."

I wouldn't be satisfied until I knew for myself. Lucid and determined, both made me inescapable. "More food," I demanded grimly, opening my eyes. I went through three more sandwiches and two Gatorades in five minutes. It helped. My ribs were healing, but not instantly. Bone was slower to repair than anything else. After eating, I lay quietly, Stefan's legs remaining my pillow. With my eyes shut, I concentrated on stretching my limits further. Damn stubborn bone. "Does your back or neck hurt? Your abdomen, chest, head?"

Stefan had explained while I was eating how part of the ceiling had dropped, one end resting on top of the semi and the other landing on top of him where he'd been flung to the floor. It had been what had shielded us from chunks of the second floor and saved our lives.

There'd been barely enough room for him to grab and drag me with him as he tunneled through tangled cots and debris to crawl under the semi and out the hole it had knocked in the front wall. He also was filling Saul in on what had happened with Peter when I'd interrupted with my woefully inadequate attempt at a diagnostic.

"I'm fine, Misha," he reiterated. "I'm a muscle-bound human. You're a skinny chimera who lies like a dog." He gave me a napkin to wipe his blood from my hand. Some of it, along with dirt and dust, had ended up on the sandwiches, but I was too ravenous and too set on feeding the healing process to care. "Of the two of us, who do you think is going to walk away?"

I wanted to snort, but I knew what my ribs would think of that. "I'm athletic, like a runner."

I had the self-esteem to know that was true. The six and a half times I'd had sex, no one had any complaints about my body. In fact, they'd enjoyed the look of it and definitely enjoyed what I could do with it. I had read up on the subject beforehand. I wanted to do it right and from the reactions, I thought I had . . . excepting the half time, which had been my first. The books said that was normal too. "So what if I'm not a walking triangle of steroids," I added. That, however, was completely untrue, but if I couldn't have endorphins, I could sting my brother . . . and distract him. He was joking with me, but there was no humor in it. In less than twenty-four hours I'd been kidnapped, in a car wreck, hit by a truck, and had a building fall on me. As brothers went, I was high maintenance.

As an apology, when I asked for a candy bar, I broke off half and gave it to him. With my obsession with

food, there was no higher gesture. He accepted it with
all the gravity it deserved. Or he was mocking me. Either way, the graveyard shadows in his eyes receded
and that was enough for me.

Godzilla, curled on my stomach, had been chirping
nervously. As I was giving the ferret a peanut from the
PayDay bar, Saul put down the visor against the searing
Tucson light that sunglasses couldn't handle and said, "I
don't get it. You said they killed all those gangbangers in
there. That punk-ass teenage Jim Jones said this wasn't
about Michael's being good enough to join up with their
Sesame Street serial killer family after all. Why weren't the
rest of them there? Besides the one driving the truck?"
Who had gotten away so quickly Saul hadn't seen
whether it was a girl or a boy. He hadn't seen anyone
period. "Why didn't they stay put and try to kill us or, for
God's sake, give us a chance to do the same to them?"

"Because they're not done playing yet." My muscles
tightened. The moment was coming. I'd put it off as
long as I could—too long. This came from a combination of Institute-ingrained secrecy and something else.
Once I was free, I'd picked up quickly the practice of
denial. Inside Institute walls, it was impossible. Outside them, it was a drug—mental heroin. The more you
did, the more you'd do. I was headed straight into cold
turkey rehab now.

"Peter didn't say play. He said punish," Stefan said
quietly, but without yielding. He'd been patient with
my evasions these past few days, giving me the chance
to prove I was the man I said I was. That patience was
over. "Why do they want to punish you? What did all
Peter's bullshit mean?"

The moment was closer, its consequence-laden breath on the back of my neck.

I sat up slowly, Stefan's hand bracing me. Godzilla slithered to the floorboards in search of more peanuts. I settled against the seat, giving my ribs a chance to get used to the change of position and increased pain. It was all done slowly, but not as slowly as I answered Stefan. "It means Peter knows more than he's saying."

"He's not the only one, is he?"

The moment was here.

"No," I said, "he's not."

It was time for the truth and I told it—the majority of it. There was one thing I held back. Among other things, I told them Peter knew about the cure. What I didn't tell was the truth of the cure itself. I had to. If I hadn't, the only cure for the chimeras would be a bullet to their brains. Killing thirteen teenagers and children, murderous or not, would be on Stefan's and Saul's consciences for the rest of their lives. I wasn't going to let them carry that with them, especially when I couldn't take part of that weight myself.

I wasn't a killer; it was a vow to myself—not one that I wouldn't break, but one that I couldn't.

Not a killer, never again.

I was a liar, though.

And a manipulator.

A deceiver.

A hypocrite.

What good is a conscience if it lets you commit every evil under the sun save one?

No damn good at all.

Chapter 12

After the two-hour drive to Phoenix, we stayed at the first nice motel—*hotel*—I'd been in. Saul checked the three of us in while Stefan and I made our way cautiously along the shadowy recesses of the lobby. There were potted trees, fresh flowers, and furniture—the kind you could sit in without catching a venereal disease. An art deco–style chandelier of brightly colored blue and purple glass gave the large room an underwater feel. If a dolphin had gone swimming by, I wouldn't have been surprised.

Or a girl with a mermaid tattoo.

Keeping our heads down, we waited for Saul by the elevators. We'd changed clothes in the car and cleaned the blood and grime from our hands and faces as best we could with napkins and bottled water. We couldn't do anything about the hair, though. Pouring bottles of water over our heads at a rest stop had the mess going from dusty mop to matted, clumped hair that made the homeless on the streets the salon poster children for great hair care in comparison.

Saul met us and handed us a key card. "You don't have to go through with this, Skoczinsky." Stefan was carrying his duffel bag as well as mine, my backpack,

and my laptop. The ribs would be better than new in a
few hours, but the pain, dull and insistent, hadn't left.
That was why we'd stopped, although there was plenty
of daylight left to keep going. The chip, which hopefully remained around Peter's neck, was headed west
toward Los Angeles. Stefan had said if they went on a
wild, crazed murdering spree there, it wasn't as if anyone would notice. LA, after all, was crazy central. We
couldn't do anything about it anyway. We needed time
to stop and recuperate.

By "we," he meant me. Here, I could sleep in a real
bed and not in the back of an SUV bumping over every
pothole in existence. I could shower in hot water, lie
flat, sleep, eat more. The hunger had faded, but it
would be back. I hadn't forced myself to heal this fast
before. But I'd never had anything close to these inju-
ries since I'd learned to speed the healing process.
When I was seventeen, I couldn't control my healing
very much at all. No chimera could. Your body healed
at its own automatic, albeit, accelerated rate.

But as I'd gotten older, my body matured, and that,
combined with relentless exercises in healing myself of
self-inflicted cuts and burns, turned me into an athlete
of healing—the best in the world. I wasn't invulnera-
ble, but I was harder to kill. Or that was what I'd
thought before I'd been run down by a semi and had a
house dropped on me. It was a wonder that passing
Munchkins hadn't sung a song and stolen my shoes
before running for it up the Yellow Brick Road.

I wondered if I could genetically engineer a flying
monkey.

I jerked back to the subject at hand. This time the

mental meandering was from exhaustion, and with not too many endorphins. "I wouldn't blame you," I said. "Thanks to me, you didn't come into this with open eyes."

He considered Stefan first. "Having a friend is a pain in the ass. But you're easier, Smirnoff. You pay me big bucks for the really entertaining illegal work. The rest of what I do—find someone, lose someone, suggest a reputable hit man, break a kneecap on a slow day, obtain and deliver rolls of plastic, duct tape, and three identical khaki green shirts when all the stores are closed during a Miami hurricane; the usual crap—it gets boring and before you know it I'm watching *The Real Housewives of Beverly Hills* to see whose skin is stretched the tightest. But you? Lots of money, a yearly Hanukkah card, and occasionally crazy, wild shit that Spielberg would find unbelievable. You keep me on my toes."

Saul zeroed in on me next. "As for you, you played things close to the chest, but so do I. Occupational hazard. And despite everything, it doesn't change our plan or hopefully the end result. If anything, it gives us an edge we didn't have before. Besides, dropping your ass means dropping Stefan, and I like his money too much." As the elevator dinged—a low, expensive sound that could've been an ancient Tibetan gong— Saul grinned and shot me with his finger. "Looks as though you're stuck with me, Mikey."

Skoczinsky giveth and Skoczinsky taketh away.

The elevator was paneled in dark, rich wood, intricate crown molding, and a bench against the back wall covered in sedate black and gold striped cloth. The small discreet TV above the doors was the single exception to the British library look. "And books," I muttered. "What's a library without books?"

I didn't realize I'd said it aloud until Stefan told me to hold it together; we were nearly at the room. Adept as I was at reading people, a murderous mind is a terrible thing to waste; I had no idea what he was thinking. Since telling him and Saul almost all of what I'd held back, I'd been waiting for my brother's reaction. He hadn't shown one. He'd given me one last sandwich, had asked frequently how I was doing, had eased me out of the vehicle as I kept my arm wrapped around my complaining ribs, and had taken all the bags, but mainly he was quiet, deep within himself.

When the moment had come, it hadn't come alone—but hand in hand with a trail of consequences. It wasn't the truth that made a man, but standing face-to-face with the cost of deserting that truth. Whatever that cost was, I'd accept it. I took the key card from Stefan and opened the door wide, both of us visually checking out the room. That was the best I could do. Stefan could look under the beds for chimeras or bogeymen. My reserves were running out and I needed to save them. Saul's door to the room beside ours shut, but not before I heard him on the phone arranging for a massage.

Eat, drink, and be massaged, for tomorrow we may die.

I went into our room. The beds were huge and the color orange was nowhere in sight. There were white puffy bedspreads. When the motels we stayed in had the option of charging by the hour, a white cover would last all of five minutes. There was a TV hidden away in a massive entertainment center, a refrigerator, coffee-maker, microwave, and the bathroom had a whirlpool tub and a shower. I saw it all in one swift scan. There was the soft snick of our door shutting, but I didn't move out of Stefan's way for him to dump our bags. Instead, I put my hand on his forehead, his chest, and then his abdomen. My ribs were a work in progress and my body fought my mind, but I was close enough to being whole that I was able to wrench enough control to assess Stefan. Normally I could've touched him on his arm and felt all of him at once. If there were anything wrong anywhere within him, I'd have sensed it. But close to whole wasn't whole and I had to put more effort into it.

"You're a human MRI, huh?" It was a comment, but the emotion behind it was impossible to interpret.

I nodded. No concussion, no brain damage. I moved my hand to his heart. "Improving my own self-healing wasn't enough. All those sick animals I found, all the blind turtles, birds with broken wings"—and the chipmunks that escaped foxes but not soon enough. The rabbit with a broken leg, probably from a stray dog—"I fixed them. I'd thought for a long time: If I can take things apart, why can't I put them back together? It's the same principle, the same ability to manipulate cells. On the first day we moved to Cascade, I found Gamera in the woods, blind as a bat. That's when I started to practice." Last, I put my hand on his stomach. Good. There was no internal bleeding. He had bruises and cuts, but he was all right. He'd walked away from a collapsed building and I hadn't. Human 1–Chimera 0. Life loved to mock our egos.

I wanted to go to bed and sleep for a few years, but in this place, I couldn't imagine getting a speck of dirt on their immaculate bed. I headed for the shower, but I kept talking. "I thought it would be simple, but it wasn't. It's always easier to destroy than to create; easier to break something or someone down than to build it up. Luckily, Gamera was in no hurry." I stripped down and neatly folded the clothes I'd changed into to try to pass as something more than a guy who lived in a box on the street. "It took six months to cure Gamera of cataracts—basic, simple cataracts. A doctor could've done it in less than an hour." I stepped into the shower, pulled the curtain, and turned on the water.

It was hot, almost scorching, and good—too good. It loosened every muscle in me and I decided to take the shower sitting down. I should've used the whirlpool tub, but I wanted sleep more than jets to ease any residual aches. Washing my hair with one hand, I let the other one lie idle. No more aggravating the now-cracked ribs. No longer broken—bones were difficult—but I was getting there.

"I'm listening."

I moved to scrubbing the dirt from my neck and chest. The EMTs hadn't wasted any time in cutting my shirt down the middle to slap on the electrodes hooked up to the cardiac monitor. "You are? I thought you were putting on a wig and grabbing a butcher knife. I keep waiting for the other shoe to drop."

"Norman Bates? I doubt I could find an old lady's dress that would fit my manly shoulders. Think the Terminator instead, and, yeah, I'm listening." There was the creak of the door frame as he leaned against it.

"You told us the rest, but the healing thing, but you were pretty succinct. You don't seem a hundred percent sure about that. As you're most often one hundred and fifty percent positive about everything you set out to accomplish, it seems weird. And no bragging on your brilliance? That's not you. You're your number one fan."

One hundred and fifty? I was one hundred percent positive on the cure, seventy-five at best on being able to deliver it. "People are different from birds and chipmunks. They're bigger and I haven't healed one before." Belatedly I remembered this wasn't quite true and added, "Except for the kid in the taco joint. I cured his tonsillitis, the little monster. I should've left him as he was. Oh . . . and I worked on that cut on your forehead from the plane crash. I barely gave it a boost, enough so you won't have another scar with my name on it." Another memory popped up. "Ahhh, yeah, and you and Saul. The chlorine gas in Laramie was the real thing, not a weak version. I didn't exactly tell the truth on that one either."

"You don't exactly have telling the truth down to an art, do you?" he commented mildly. I'd have felt better if he'd growled it. I was still waiting on that other shoe. "Regardless, whether you can heal other people a little or a lot, that seems like a good thing to me."

It did? I sat in a puddle of water as the dirt ran off me in streams. I'd told him, but not clearly enough. "The healing isn't about healing, Stefan. It's good to have, but that's not why I learned how. It's about Wendy.

"If we can't get the drop on Wendy, surprise her and

take her down before she knows we're there, then I have to be able to protect us. This was the best thing I could think of to try." We'd always planned on rescuing those left in the Institute and I'd known all that time it wasn't Bellucci we had to worry about. It was Wendy.

As Wendy's abilities were purely destructive, I might be able to keep her from killing us at a distance by blocking her with the same ability, only turned on its end. Reconstructive. Opposites collide and cancel each other out. All we needed was a second to shoot her with the tranq gun. Three years I'd been thinking and practicing. If I managed to buy us that one second, I'd be damn grateful. Hard work had made me more than Jericho could've guessed and three years of fully maturing on top of that made me ten times what I'd once been. My chances seemed good . . . until I thought of what three years of growing up might have done for Wendy.

I was hoping practice made perfect.

I leaned my head back against the shower wall and let the water beat down on me. My eyelids drooped and I was headed fast for sleep when Stefan spoke again. "And the cure? If you have some doubts about Wendy, what about this cure? Will it work—now that you've included me in your need-to-know circle that was formerly you and the ferret?"

I winced and it wasn't my ribs. Exhaling, I put a hand on the edge of the tub, heaved myself up, and turned off the shower. I caught the towel he tossed me and dried off. When I looped it around my hips, I repeated what I'd been thinking. "The cure is one hundred percent effective. If I have a chance to give it, it'll work. There's no question about that."

"None?" He moved aside to let me out. I took the few steps necessary, dropped the towel, and climbed under the covers and cool sheets. They felt better against me than any clothes I owned. If we did survive, I was sneaking more money from the Caymans for better sheets. I rolled carefully onto my stomach, increased my endorphins enough to take away the remaining pain, and closed my eyes. "Peter looked goddamn perky as he ran off with not one but two darts in him," he pointed out.

"I'll quadruple the dose. I promise you, Stefan. It will work." The world was slipping slowly away. Cocooned in warmth and darkness, I didn't mind.

"You want me to trust you on it?" Right before I heard Stefan shut the shower door, I heard him murmur, "When you think why I should, Misha, you let me know."

He'd trusted me time and time again, but I'd lied time and time again—calling it anything but lying to fool myself. When was too much? When did that last straw come along? It was lucky that I had time to sleep on it, because right then I didn't have a good answer for his question or mine.

The only one I had, the only true rebuttal, neither of us would want to hear.

Days ago I'd been thinking I wouldn't lie to my brother, but I had been, more or less, for three years. Call them lies or omissions or secrets—all the things we said we wouldn't do—but at the end of the day we never failed to. Sometimes they were a convenience or a habit or at times the only kindness you could give someone. Stefan should know that.

He had a secret too and it colored every part of his life.

And mine.

I woke up to the smell of eggs, bacon, coffee, and pancakes. I savored the moment: soft bed, sheets that weren't comparable to one-ply toilet paper, and no pain. My ribs were whole and healed.

"Room service. I know that has to be high on your list of the most incredible things invented in the history of time," Stefan said.

"You can't eat a pyramid." I opened my eyes and sat up. Through the curtains, I could see the sun rising. "I slept that long?"

"Hit by a truck and a building. That sort of thing deserves a few extra hours. Give yourself a break." He was already at the table, munching on bacon. "And if you want any food, you'd better hurry. I've had too much fast food lately."

I climbed out of bed, dressed, and took a seat to rapidly fill my plate. He wasn't serious, but food was just below sex in life's great pleasures. I wasn't taking any chances. "I thought about what I said last night." He started, pouring more coffee. The scrapes and tiny cuts on his face were going to make shaving a bitch this morning. "And I was an asshole. Your badass mobster big brother got his delicate feelings hurt and I projected."

He covered the smile, faint but there, with his cup of coffee. After he swallowed, he added, "See? I listen to all your psycho-techno babble. My eyes glaze over, yeah, but I listen." He picked up a triangle of toast before dropping it, interest gone. "It's not that I don't trust you, Misha. It's that after all this time, you don't trust me. Buying planes, recruiting drug dealers, the pipe bomb thing—*Jesus*, the pipe bombs—the healing and, damn, that's the least of all the rest you told us. You didn't tell me any of it."

I leaned back in the chair and pushed away my plate before I took a single bite. It took one painful topic to kill both our appetites. "I didn't keep it to myself because I don't trust you. Well, except for the pipe bombs. You never would've gone for that. It was because I want to be normal, Stefan. I want to be like my big brother. Isn't that what all younger brothers want? When they're little, they tag along. When they're grown, they want to be half the man their brother is."

I ran fingers through my bed hair and made it worse by ruthlessly scrubbing my scalp. "Keeping you up to date every day on my progress at becoming more different and less human wasn't my idea of a good time. I'm not like everyone else. I'm not like you, but I wanted to pretend I was. I wanted you to, hell, forget that I'm not. *I* want to forget I'm not."

"So we're both idiots." He pushed my plate back in front of me. "No, you're not like me. You're better. A better person, a better goddamn everything. Now, eat your breakfast. And if you open your mouth to say you aren't everything I know you are, I'll stuff a bagel in it. Plain. Without cream cheese." Healthy food—the ultimate threat.

"We are idiots, aren't we?" I took a bite of the blackberry pancakes covered in syrup and butter. "In the future, if I do sort of accidentally keep some things to myself, will you know it has nothing to do with trust? That it's not you; it's me."

""It's not you; it's me.' Jesus. You're something else." The grin was quick. "We're not breaking up, Misha. And, yeah, I'll know. Eat."

Now that my secrets were out, it was time to work on Stefan's. I had another bite of my pancakes before moving on to the bacon as I sidled into the subject slowly. I'd made bombs. Stefan's secret was one I was going to have to defuse.

I'd worked on finding a cure for years, the second I managed to get a computer and a stack of books on genetics. That was where the cure had to be. Jericho had genetically altered us to add the ability to make human bodies our psychokinetic playgrounds, and that meant genetics would be the only reasonable assumption to reversing it. I read and I researched. I learned, and I didn't like what I found out.

It was impossible to take a person, a natural human chimera already born with no supercharged healing or killing abilities, and change his genetics to become what Institute chimeras were. My kind of chimera had to be built from the ground up. The process had to start at the very beginning. Once one cell became two, the work started. There was no other way.

I hadn't mentioned it then, when I discovered the truth, but as we might not survive Peter and the others, I wanted . . . I wasn't sure what I wanted—a different type of truth, maybe, the only kind that mattered, that one being the one between Stefan and me. I'd once

asked Stefan how he thought Jericho knew I was a chimera ripe for scooping up for the Institute. He'd said
probably through a pediatrician's office or the hospital
where I'd been born. I'd been fresh out of the Institute
then. I hadn't known much about the real world. Now
I did. They didn't do DNA tests on healthy children
born in hospitals surrounded by Mylar balloons and
blue teddy bears. DNA tests were rare, unless you were
sick, and many times a DNA test wouldn't show a
chimera—not a human one. It took several tests, testing
several different sites in the body.

It was time to ask again. "You know, I've wondered
for a while how Jericho found me. They don't do DNA
tests on babies at hospitals unless they think there's
something wrong with them."

Stefan went with the abrupt change of subject so
smoothly that I knew he'd been doing some thinking
about it himself—for a while; almost three years I
would guess. Picking up his toast again, he said, "It
was a long time ago, but I think I remember Anatoly
and Mom having trouble getting pregnant with you.
They probably had fertility treatments done. You know,
in case I had to be replaced."

"Replaced?" I frowned.

He shrugged. "The *Mafiya* needs sons to run it and
life expectancy on those sons isn't the best. No father
would want all his eggs in one basket, so to speak."

That was good, about the *Mafiya*. Extremely good. I
could fact check it on the Internet, and it was aimed at
distracting me by pissing me off that Anatoly didn't
think Stefan was enough. The fertility clinic was better
than good. It was brilliant, a place where DNA testing

was as common as dirt. He'd done his research. As I'd
learned from Stefan, he'd learned from me. But almost
three years of psychological training compared to nineteen of the same plus interrogation classes? He didn't
have a hope in hell.

"What kind of treatments?" That was me, intrigued
by any kind of science. Nothing suspicious at all. Pay
no attention to the man behind the curtain; the Great
and Powerful Oz examining his brother's psyche.

In the midst of all this—chimeras, Raynor, and digging at the inherent nature of family—I made time to
miss my wall of movies. Why not? Another form of
denial.

Stefan shrugged and slathered up part of his egg
with the toast. "I would've been six. I was more into
watching *The Transformers* than wondering where babies came from. As far as I knew, they found me under
a cabbage leaf in the backyard. Your cabbage leaf was
apparently at some clinic somewhere. That reminds
me, I used to tell you babies came from sitting on dirty
toilet seats. And boys could get pregnant too. It took
them four extra months to potty train you because of
that."

The last wasn't a distraction. It was a memory and a
knife to the heart all in one.

"That's most likely what happened." I accepted it
and gave him a few slices of bacon. The man was a fool
for bacon, and that knife . . . it was in his heart. "Jericho
might've wanted to see how one of his chimeras, engineered with our parents' respective egg and sperm,
would behave in the outside world for a short while.
All good experiments need a random blind study. I

could've been that study—chimera on the loose. And, P.S., you suck ass on the potty-training thing."

There hadn't been a fertility clinic, no blind studies. Before I'd come to the conclusion that all of Jericho's children were born in a petri dish, I'd already sent my DNA to Ariel. Natural chimeras had the two different types of DNA scattered throughout their bodies for the most part. Jericho's chimeras had the two in every cell. That was impossible for a human chimera. It was the last nail in the coffin. It wasn't long after, to double-check my suspicion, I'd done my own DNA testing. Every drugstore had them now. Whozurdaddy? Whozurmama? I took one of Stefan's hairs from his brush and proved what I'd already come to know.

I'd seen the pictures. I looked like Stefan's brother, Lukas. I had the eyes—the universe being ironic again as all Jericho's chimeras had those eyes—I was about the same age and I'd been within a hundred miles of where he'd been kidnapped. Another irony or my salvation. Stefan's too.

He knew I wasn't Lukas now. He hadn't always. When he'd rescued me, he didn't second-guess it once. I was his brother. He believed it so deeply that I believed it too. In the face of his pure faith, I'd finally had faith myself. I'd accepted my lack of memories being some form of traumatic amnesia or caused by the fall on the rocks during the original kidnapping on the beach.

Some time after that, though, he'd found out Lukas was dead. It had to be from Anatoly. Looking back, I'd first noticed the difference at the beach house with his father. The difference wasn't that he'd treated me as less than a brother, but that he'd insisted on it even more fiercely. That and he would do anything, once he'd been able to get out of bed after being shot by Jericho, to keep me from being alone with Anatoly. I'd thought the change had been because we'd both almost died. He'd nearly lost me again. And keeping me away from Anatoly . . . once I knew what Anatoly was, made sense. Another monster, another killer in our lives, but a useful one. But Anatoly hadn't told me anything . . . other than to be kind to Stefan, that he deserved it.

And Stefan did, because for all his searching. . . .

Lukas was dead.

If he wasn't, Stefan and I would be scouring the earth for his other brother. Not his real brother. I was as real as Lukas had been. I knew that. Almost three years with Stefan—there wasn't a doubt in me about that. But if Lukas were still alive, we'd have searched until we found him and Stefan would've had two brothers. I thought I would've liked another brother. From all the stories Stefan had once told me before he knew the truth, trying to prod my memories—memories that weren't mine—Lukas sounded as if he'd have made a great brother. Stefan didn't tell those stories much anymore, now that he knew Lukas was gone. I'd start asking again once in a while. I wasn't Lukas, but telling the stories would bring a part of him back to Stefan, if only for minutes or an hour.

I'd finally found that different kind of truth—a lie that wasn't a lie at all. Stefan knew I wasn't Lukas, but he knew I was his brother, the same as I knew that he was mine, that being brothers had nothing to do with sharing the same blood. He wouldn't ever tell me about

Lukas and he would hope I'd never find out. He wouldn't risk that I'd again feel those doubts that I had following my rescue or that I would think he considered me any less of the brother he'd been born with.

That was Stefan.

And that was fine. That was better than fine. Some things didn't have to be said aloud.

I also knew that while Lukas was gone, he'd given me a gift, although he'd never known me . . . or rather had never met me. He'd given me the memories of sun, wind, and horses to warm me in a place as cold as death itself. It was his best memory. Galloping up and down the beach, the ocean's roar loud in his ears, the wind in his face—it was his best memory and mine too, although I hadn't actually experienced it. Yet Lukas made me feel as if I had. Tangible and real as any other memory I had had in the Institute, that memory had kept me sane.

More than that, Lukas had given me a brother to pull me from that frozen sterile prison and set me free. Lukas had died, but he'd given me life. And as logical and scientifically minded as I was, I didn't question the mysterious nature of that. It was as true and real as the sun and the sky above.

"How does it feel?" I asked, taking from his plate a jam-loaded biscuit to replace the bacon I'd given him.

"How does what feel?" he asked with a trace of caution hidden behind the words—hidden to anyone but a genius like me.

I grinned. "To be a free, off-the-shelf baby when they spent big bucks making me? I was the Cadillac of infants. You were barely a Volkswagen."

He let me have another one of his biscuits, this time fired directly at my head. I caught it. I wasn't going to duck and waste a perfectly good biscuit. "You're an ass."

"Thanks for the lessons in that. They've been invaluable." I continued to grin as I took a bite of the biscuit.

The moment that had descended on my yesterday hadn't been the best of my life—not the worst, thanks to the Institute—but not the best either. This one was—this was the best moment I'd had. At peace with my family . . . where I belonged.

And then Peter called and turned the moment into a memory. Memories are good too, but they're only shadows of moments—a sepia photograph of what you saw, heard, felt. Once a moment is gone, you don't get it back.

Peter's cell phone rang again.

I was really beginning to hate that son of a bitch.

Chapter 13

"You're alive, Michael. Good. It's difficult to keep punishing you if you let a simple building falling on your traitorous head take you out of the game."

I sat on the edge of the bed and wished Peter were there so I could shove the cheap phone down his throat. As for his calling me traitorous, I didn't ask him what he meant. I knew—as did Stefan and Saul now that I'd come clean. Peter wanted to punish me because he'd learned of the cure. "It's even harder to punish me, Peter, when you keep running away. You wouldn't be afraid of me, would you?"

"In the outside world for three years and you haven't learned how to play a game yet. It's rather sad how you've wasted your freedom. I feel sad for you, Michael. I honestly do."

Peter hadn't felt sad in his life and while he knew the meaning of honesty, he was incapable of it. "What do you want, Peter? I'm done with following you around. I don't have to. There are other people out there who want to catch up with you more than I do. I'll let Raynor do what he does best and maybe I'll go on vacation. Hawaii. I've always wanted to see a volcano."

He laughed. "Raynor. The Institute's invisible pet pit bull. None of us knew he existed until you escaped, and suddenly he was at the new one we were moved to all the time. Checking up on Bellucci, who, as it turned out, did rather need some checking up on, didn't he? Too bad, so sad, but Bellucci didn't learn what Raynor constantly told him about lax security." His voice hardened. "But that's all over now. Turn on your TV or your laptop. Find a cable news channel. You might see my bright smiling face. Do it now, Michael. The games are over. Next time I see you, it'll be in Heaven."

The phone clicked and went silent in my ear. I tossed it onto the bed and took the remote from the bedside table that not only turned on the TV but also slid back the entertainment center doors. I was not going back to a thirty-eight-dollar-a-night motel as long as I lived.

"What'd the bastard want now?" Stefan growled, joining me in front of the TV.

"I think to tell me it's time to meet at the OK Corral. He's ready for the showdown." I cycled through several news stations until I found what Peter had wanted me to see. In Eugene, Oregon, more than a thousand blackbirds had fallen from the sky, stone dead. The screen showed people milling about and looking in confusion at the carpet of iridescent black that covered their streets and yards. Only one person didn't seem puzzled. There was only a short glimpse of him before the camera panned elsewhere, but it was Peter. He was waving before pointing at the sky with his finger and pulling an imaginary trigger. It was Wendy's work. Fly away, birds. Fly away no more.

"Eugene." Stefan started to rub his hand over his

jaw and stopped, remembering in time the lacework of cuts and scrapes that crossed his face.

"Wait." I studied him, concentrated, and then said, "Okay, you're good now. You can even shave if you want."

He ran his hand lightly across his face, then harder before moving into the bathroom to check the mirror. "They're gone. I can't tell they were there at all. That's . . . Damn, Misha. Unbelievable."

I had done it. I'd healed without touching . . . as Wendy killed without touching. That made our chances of survival better, and made me feel more like her, a hundred times the freak I had been seconds ago. But I could deal with being a freak if it meant I was able to live through this.

"If I can heal a blind, evil-tempered hundred-year-old turtle, a few scrapes are no problem. How'd it feel?" I asked. I was curious. I knew what it felt like when I healed myself with my new accelerated ability, but I didn't know what it was like for someone else.

"It tingled some, and weirdly enough, I knew it was you. I could feel the, I don't know, the Misha of you. It was better than a tetanus shot in the ass, that's for sure." He turned away from the mirror.

"I can fix your leg too. Bone takes forever to work with, but give me a few days and you won't limp in the winter anymore."

"Hell, kid, I never cared about that." And because he was who he was and it had been for me, he hadn't, but I did. It would be a Jericho memory I could bury forever: the one of him shooting my brother to take me back to Hell.

"We'll see. And don't call me kid." I turned off the TV. "They're in Eugene, or they were."

"They're going to Cascade Falls. They'd know that was where you were living. Raynor would've told Bellucci and God knows Bellucci would've told them anything they wanted before he died. And if Peter wants to punish you. . . ."

Wiping out a place I'd considered home would be one of the harsher punishments I could think of. "He said he'd meet me in Heaven."

"The Bridge of the Heavens. On top of the dam. That scenario has nothing but nasty and suicidal written all over it. Too bad we can't really let Raynor handle it. I know you have the cure, but even cured, give these kids guns and knives and they'll do it the old-fashioned way."

"Raynor's smart and he did manage to capture me, but I'm only one. He doesn't know it, but he's out of his league. They'll roll over him like a tank." I planned on being there to see it too. No one deserved it more.

"Yeah, I know, but it's nice to dream once in a while. Pack and get us tickets to Portland. I'll go wake up Saul and make sure he has one of his guys meet us with some weapons and a car at the airport. Damn, what about your tranq guns? There's not much sense in going if we can't take the cure with us."

"They're plastic and disassemble in three minutes. Then I reassemble them into a larger gun that is nothing more than a toy. I also have stickers that say TOY, MADE IN CHINA, and SUPER-DUPER MEGA-MACHINE that go on the side. The tranq cartridges we can drop in a bottle of shampoo. We'll have to check one bag, but no problem. Don't tell Saul that, though. Tell him we have to smuggle them the only way God and the TSA have left to us." I grinned. "Tell him it'll expand his sexual horizons and he should try not to walk funny through the scanner."

He snorted. "You are pure evil."

I shrugged. I had no problem telling the truth when I couldn't get around it and that meant I didn't have a right to be offended when I heard it. "Somebody has to be."

Jokes aside, by the end of it all, that could be more true than Stefan imagined. Someone had to do the only thing left to do. I hoped he could live with that.

I hoped I could too.

The flight was long. I'd commented that if they let me do the flying, it would be much shorter. Stefan accepted the statement with all the forgiveness and love one brother had for another. He popped me one in the shoulder, hard. Considering I'd learned to fly using the Internet and a few DVDs and the crash was minor, in my opinion, I'd think that he'd let it go, but no. I had a feeling I was grounded, quite literally, for a very long time.

When he was handing me his peanuts, crackers, chips, and soda, he said, "You're planning on Raynor's being there to help out, aren't you? Not intentionally, but you think he can provide some sort of distraction."

My lips curved as I took his food. I used to try to make sure we both had equal shares on the run or at home, but we'd both come to realize that despite his doing it out of big-brother instinct, I actually needed more food than did either he or your average four-hundred-pound sumo wrestler. I'd stopped protesting then. In this particular case, anyone sane would have considered it a favor that someone else had taken the inedible airplane snacks off their hands.

"He does have an Institute tracker, the same as we do," I said. "And I don't think Peter likes him any more than he likes me." I opened the bag of peanuts and sighed as they spilled out stale and rock hard into my hand. Saul had the aisle seat and I leaned over Stefan to say in a low tone, "Is the you-know-what still with you?"

"You son of a bitch. I didn't buy that for a second. I know more about the *S* word than you ever will." He couldn't say smuggling. There are no secrets on airplanes. Sound travels and passengers these days were more than willing to take off their belts and try to strangle an orange-haired would-be terrorist/smuggler or a man who simply liked to walk around with a tranquilizer cartridge concealed in his rectum for no special reason.

"Sure you do, Saul. And you weren't disappointed that you didn't have to bend over and take it like a man." I'd learned that phrase on TV when I was fresh out of the Institute and Stefan had choked on his dinner when I'd asked him to explain it to me. "I believe you." I went back to my peanuts and the SkyMall catalog. Godzilla, in his carrier under the seat in front of me, had his pointed muzzle through the crosshatch of metal bars and was vengefully biting the toe of my shoe. Flying didn't seem to be anyone's favorite activity today.

"How many plans do you have for how this can go down?" Stefan asked. "It's not as though there are too many hiding places on a bridge. I've been able to come up with one plan on this. Two if Raynor shows up."

I turned a page. They had the most absolutely needless inventions in this magazine. It was hypnotic. "Two."

"Not your usual ten or twenty? I think I'm unnerved."

I glanced over at him. His tone was light, but his face was serious, grimly so. "Only unnerved? I'm scared shitless." And there was nothing theoretical about that.

One of Saul's subcontractors met us at the Portland International Airport—not that it looked international, but I supposed the designation was true. The FAA doesn't let you lie about things like that. We had a car and enough guns for Saul and Stefan to take on an army, so all was right with their world if not Godzilla's. He was still biting the carrier's cage bars. Air flight had not agreed with him. If ferrets were meant to fly, as Stefan had commented midflight, then I would let him throw Zilla out the window.

Before his man left, I asked Saul, "Could he take Godzilla? In case . . . just in case." I dug through my backpack for our money and counted out a thousand. "And find him a good home if he has to?" I handed the guy the carrier and the thousand dollars.

The man looked at Saul and at the money and replied in a drawl that originated far from Oregon, "I don't mind. Hell, my sister does animal rescue. Has a houseful of furry critters."

"Give us at least a week to come back for him," I

warned, putting a finger through the bars to rub his
small head. He promptly bit me and I smiled. It was
two predators bonding, not a good-bye, because that
was what I chose to believe.

Once again we were supplied with an SUV. I didn't
have anything against the environment, but when you
hauled around as many weapons as Stefan and Saul
needed to feel comfortable, you required a roomy vehicle. "I'll drive," Stefan said.

I claimed the passenger seat. Saul could sit in the
back all but buckled into an infant's car seat for once.
"His sister rescues animals and he sells guns to anyone
with the cash. People are strange," I said, slamming the
door behind me as Stefan began to navigate our way
out of the airport parking garage.

"Says the genetic superman riding around with an
ex-mobster brother and an international criminal mastermind," Saul pointed out.

I didn't know about the mastermind part, but the
rest was true enough. It didn't change the fact that people were strange. In our case I liked to think it was a
good kind of strange.

It was an hour and a half from Portland to Cascade
and in that time I told them my plan, which, compared
to all the other plans I'd engineered in the past years,
was beyond simple. We went to the bridge, I did my
best to stop Wendy from killing us, we shot the chimeras with the tranq guns, everyone was cured, and we
went back to another nice hotel. And if Raynor showed
up, he could simultaneously distract the chimeras
while we shot them, again with the tranq guns, and
Stefan could beat him to a pulp afterward.

"Sad to say, that's my plan too," Stefan admitted. "But it's a crappy plan. We're on a bridge with no place to hide or set up an ambush, although since I imagine they'll be waiting for us, that's a point in our favor. At least they can't ambush us either. If they were ordinary people, weak, puny, and not too bright like Saul and me"—he punched me casually in the arm—"I'd say our chances were good. Saul kicked ass in the military, I kicked ass on the streets, and you are the self-proclaimed Einstein of our times."

"I'd say that's an accurate description," I agreed without a hint of a smirk, although I'd seen couples at night cross the street if they saw Stefan coming. Hell, I'd seen three or four men cross the street. Weak and puny he was not. He looked not like what he was all the time, but like what he was capable of being any-time—a wolf in human skin.

"A suicide run with a couple of smart-asses," Saul mumbled. "I hate my life."

Stefan continued. "But they're not like Saul and me. They're like you, Misha. They're fast and strong and smart as fucking hell. And Peter has them doing what-ever he says, which makes him something even more than them."

"Except for Peter and maybe Wendy, they shouldn't be as fast and strong as I am. That comes with maturity, and the rest of the chimeras are years younger than Peter." Except one. "And Raynor is smart as well. In a different way and in this case it might be a better way," I said. "We're trained to take out targets, usually one—maybe two or three. We didn't need to worry about defensive tactics, because no one would suspect us. Someone falls over because of a natural death and a cute sixteen-year-old waitress who was serving him dinner goes into hysterics. Who's going to blame the waitress for a heart attack because her hand brushed his when she handed him his glass of water? No one. When Raynor kills people, chances are everyone in the area is going to know it and Raynor is vulnerable. He can be killed much more easily than a chimera. Don't think he doesn't know that and that he doesn't value himself very highly."

Stefan nodded. "I wondered if you'd see that. You know, then. Raynor won't be coming alone."

"You were testing me?" I scoffed. "The fully trained assassin?"

"You said it yourself. Chimera warfare is different than human warfare. You're like a single bullet, elegant and deadly. Humans are like ten thousand NASCAR fans, each one with his own tank. If our lives are at stake, we are bringing all we have, all we can borrow, and all we can steal. Raynor is definitely not coming alone. Whoever he brings won't know a damn thing about chimeras. That's Raynor's secret. But they'll be shooters and the kind that don't mind mowing down a kid or two to get the rest to cooperate. Not to mention Tasers, the rubber bullets like Raynor used on you." He tapped a finger on my head. "Not as hard as it seems. Who knew? Raynor goddamn knew, Misha. So if something happens to me or Saul, remember that. Raynor is more than a distraction to be used. He's a genuine threat."

He was. He was human, but I couldn't dismiss that he'd caught me and had me chained in his car. '"I'll remember, but nothing is going to happen to you."

"Hello? I'm along for the ride too. How about nothing is going to happen to me?" Saul complained.

Stefan ignored him to say, "And Saul and I might not have USDA-grade assassin stamped on our asses, but between the two of us we've killed a shitload more people than you care to know about. So don't be so quick to jump between me and a bullet this time. If you can keep Wendy from doing her creepy thing, I can take care of myself. Okay?" He waited until I confirmed it.

"All right."

"If we're lucky, we'll all get out of this in one piece," he finished. Then he gave me a hell-on-wheels grin and quoted my favorite word: "Theoretically."

I tried to grin back, but I didn't feel it. I planned on this working, but I thought that Butch and Sundance had planned on eventually leaving Bolivia in one piece too. I wished now I hadn't given us their names while we'd lived in Cascade.

As omens went, it wasn't a good one.

Chapter 14

It shouldn't have felt like coming home with Peter and the others waiting to punish me, and if "punish" wasn't to kill slowly and painfully, then my imagination wasn't all that I knew it was. It did though—it felt like coming home. We'd been gone only a few days, but I'd missed it. It didn't stretch my mind, make me learn faster, soak up more knowledge, instinctively fit in better as the adrenaline rush of being on the run did, but it was a nice place all the same. It felt the same as when I watched one of my favorite movies for the fifth or tenth time. I knew every line of dialogue, every explosion, every wave that crashed against a sinking ship, every gunshot, but it was as good as the very first time I watched it . . . better almost. It was warm, familiar, and safe. I'd not had a moment of that in the Institute. I learned the value of it when I'd escaped.

The Bridge to the Heavens was blocked off on Cascade's end by the sheriff's car. Sheriff Simmons was dead on the road beside it, and I saw Jess Quillino, his deputy, her legs showing beyond the bumper from the other side of the car. Other than that, there were no other people around—none alive. The bridge over the dam didn't go anywhere too important, definitely not to an infinity of heavens. If you crossed it and drove about forty miles on a single-lane road, you'd get to a town small enough that it made Cascade seem like New York City. Hardly anyone made the trip from this direction and if they were coming from the other direction, that end of the bridge was blocked by the Institute bus, long GPS disabled; I was certain.

I passed out the tranq guns, tightened my lips, and went with one hope—that I didn't get us all killed. "Stoipah, Saul, just remember one thing. They're not kids. They never were. If something goes wrong, they'll kill you and they'll laugh while they do it. If it goes bad, use your guns, not the tranq ones. And be sure to shoot them in the head. So—" I inhaled, exhaled hard, and opened the car door. "Let's go."

We walked around the sheriff's car and I didn't look at the body too closely. He'd been a nice enough man. He'd given me a break with the fake tourist. He'd played pool with Stefan. He had a wife and a little boy. If we'd never come to his town, he'd still be alive. Those thoughts weren't helpful at the moment and I shoved them down as we headed onto the bridge.

They were waiting halfway across. We stopped forty feet short. The thirteen of them were waiting in various poses. Some stood, some sat cross-legged on the road, Wendy—my eyes locked on Wendy—sat on the three-foot-tall concrete wall that kept cars from plummeting into the river boiling at the base of the dam. Dressed in a small blue sweat suit with a spray of rhinestone flowers across the top, she was kicking her feet idly against the concrete, her fair hair lifted in the wind. She waved at me. "Hi, Michael. Hi, hi, hi. Did you see the birds? They fell like they were a part of the sky at night. Black, black everywhere. I did that. That was me."

"I know." Keeping her in view, I turned my attention to Peter who stood in front of them all. Peter who'd led us on this chase, had tried to kill my brother and my friend over and over, who had taken down the Institute from the inside practically on his own. Peter, Peter, pumpkin eater. Peter, the Pied Piper of death. "I'm here, Peter. Now what? How are you going to punish me?" I was tense on the inside, tense enough I could feel the sharp ache of it . . . of waiting for Wendy to try anything aimed at Stefan, Saul, or me.

Peter smiled at me, that same charismatic, smug smile I was sick to death of. He said nothing. "All of this and you're going to stare at me like an idiot? This is it, Peter. You said I had to pay. I had to be punished. Where's your big punishment?" I wasn't waiting. This was a perfect chance and I was taking it. Without their leader, they'd be confused if only for a fraction of a second. It would have to be enough. While I was still talking, I shot Peter in the chest with the tranquilizer cartridge at the new dosage. He had the speed—my speed—to avoid it, and I was ready to keep shooting until I hit him.

But he didn't move—not before the shot, during, or after. He simply stood and the smile slowly fell off his face.

He looked down at the dart, puzzled, and said, the words already slurring, "What do I say, Wendy? What do . . . I . . . say . . . now?" He dropped bonelessly to the concrete, unconscious.

"Poor Peter," Wendy chirped before her voice hardened to stone. "He was always so hopelessly stupid."

She stopped the kicking and leaned a little as if to study me more closely. "The same as you, Michael. You reek of stupidity. You always did. You're soft and worthless as a human, even worse than one actually because you have the gift. Not much of one, but enough. You never had the will, though."

"You. God, I should've known. Peter was nothing special other than loving to kill, but you—you were always special." She'd fed him every line, every word, all along. Every action that had been taken, the entire plan, the rebellion, it had all been her. I'd grown. I'd become a man. Wendy had grown and I had no idea what she had become.

As Saul would've said, we were well and truly screwed now.

"As special as they came, that I am. And that was a problem. A very large fucking problem." Her voice had gone from little girl to adult and now it went to as rich with hate as a death row inmate. "I was bored. I'd been bored forever and they kept running out of people for me to kill at the Institute. They also started thinking," she said, her smile coldly vicious, "and they should have. What would happen when I was bored and the Basement and animal labs were empty? I couldn't let them think about *that* too long, could I? Because they knew what would happen. I wasn't Jericho's favorite anymore. He was gone and Bellucci—he was always afraid, from the first day he took Jericho's place. But even if they hadn't been starting to think I was more than they could handle, it wouldn't have mattered. I was bored, bored, bored, and there weren't enough people in the Institute to entertain me. The world, though, the whole, entire world—how much fun would that be?"

I saw something I hadn't guessed at when Wendy and I shared a prison. "You were never obedient, were you? Of all of us, some more than others, you never were at all." I thought she had been. Their goal and hers were the same—death. She had appeared perfectly happy and content. But I'd been blind. The likes of Wendy wouldn't bow to anyone—not even to her own creator, if he'd lived.

"When I was young, I pretended. Now that I'm not . . . I stopped pretending." She was ten years old and she thought—she *knew* she wasn't young anymore. Her face, rosy pink from the wind, hardened. "They should've graduated me when I was three, because even then I was the best of all of you in every way." She kicked again. It was to be shocking in its cuteness, to entertain herself by making our brain rebel at the incongruity of what she was, the inner and the outer mismatched enough to make your stomach churn. "Bellucci wasn't Jericho of course. Security became lax. Lax, lax, lax. I like that word." She smiled, pretty as a picture. "Until one day there was a new researcher—an older woman with a deeply buried maternal instinct that would've had Jericho screening her out simply by looking at her. It took a while, but I am sweet and adorable and she, like you, Michael, was stupid. I asked one day if she'd show me how to play a game on her computer. After I popped a few cells in the decision-making part of her tiny brain, she could see no harm in that." Chimeras were never allowed on or near a computer that could access the Internet—with good reason. "That was that."

All it took for her to learn a way to reach the outside world was one woman who wasn't quite as soulless as the rest of the faculty. She'd have obtained her password. Gotten access to "play games" now and again, but now and again was all Wendy would need.

"I learned how much more lay outside the Institute than they ever told us. How many more people. Endless numbers of playthings. I also found a friend." From her lips, "friend" was a word in an incomprehensible alien language. "I found one of us who'd taken care of their owner, brutally I hope, and found freedom. It made me think. What would I do if I were free?" Her smile was hideous. "What wouldn't I do?" She looked past us. "Lily One, come say hi, hi, hi to your boyfriend."

Stefan and Saul shifted their stance enough to see whose footsteps were coming up behind us . . . although they already knew. I'd told them. When I'd told them about everything else, I'd told them this too—that she was a chimera. It had been one reason I hadn't worried when she'd disappeared at McDonald's. No one could take care of themselves as she could. She stepped into sight, her smile more natural and familiar than Wendy's. Her eyes, now chimera blue and green instead of just blue, were clear and happy. She was as she'd always been: glorious.

"Ariel." I nodded. "I was wondering when you'd turn up."

"Misha," she scolded, her pink hair mixing with the

blue of the sky and the green of the trees like an Easter egg. "Way to turn a girl's smile upside down. I wanted to surprise you. You're no fun at all." In one hand she held a metal cylinder about seven inches long and three inches in diameter.

Wendy didn't like not being the center of attention. "Bellucci told us you were in Cascade, Michael. We could've killed you much sooner for your presumption without all this running around, barely playing at all, but we were waiting for Lily to finish up with her work and make her way out here. Did you plant it, Lily? Is it done?" Wendy asked.

Ariel nodded. "In the Portland International Airport." She gave the "international" portion of the title a roll of the eyes, the same as I had, although my eye roll had been internal. "It's barely international, but good enough for a test run, to see if the theory works."

"A theory is useless without proof," the twelve other chimeras all murmured. I caught myself before I did the same—another Institute rule; another Institute lesson.

"What did you do, Ariel?" I demanded.

Her smile was dreamy this time. "Remember SARS, the bird flu, swine flu? They all had people in a panic, didn't they?" She tapped a pink fingernail against the metal cylinder. "This will have them too dead to worry about panicking. I whipped it up in my lab. It's airborne, has a seven-day incubation time so people can travel far and spread it wide, and a thirty percent mortality rate. I could've made it higher, but then who would we have to play with? You can't break all your toys. That wouldn't be very bright of us, would it? The one in the Portland airport will go off at eleven a.m. tomorrow morning. There are quite a few travelers at that time. I wonder how far it will go. How much of the world we'll touch."

"They'll shut down the rest of the airports," Stefan said.

"If they find the mechanism, but they won't. I didn't even go through security before I planted it. And if they did find it, did discover it was a man-made virus and not a new, natural version, which they won't with the work I've done, they can't shut them all down forever, can they? I thought it was a little much, so many people. I play, but on a smaller scale, but Wendy insisted. And when she said she'd free the rest of us, I thought it was worth it." She frowned, only now seeing how few chimeras there were. "This is all that survived the rebellion?"

"This is all that survived Wendy," I said quietly.

"These were the worthy," Wendy snapped. "The rest would do as they were told, but they didn't have the heart or the hunger to be what we were born to be. We are the birth of a new race and only the best will be part of that birth. Only the best shall have the world as their new Playground."

"But why?" It was Saul this time; Saul who'd seen war and worse, and this was beyond him. "What's the point to all of this? Just killing for killing's sake? And soon you'll get bored of that too and kill the entire world?"

Wendy didn't answer him. Wendy didn't talk to humans. "As for why I came after you, Michael, you have to be curious. You know you're not important enough for my attention . . . except . . ." She did her little-girl repetition again. I didn't know whether she was aware she was doing it or doing it for the same reason of making us psychologically ill watching and hearing her. "Except, except, except, that when I found Lily One, she told me what you were up to. She knew you for what you were from the beginning." She hadn't been the only one. "You've gotten as negligent as Bellucci's security and have forgotten your training. I wanted you, Michael, for one reason only. You dared think you could cure us. You *dared*," she said, her face crimson with fury now, "when the only cure needed is for the weak and pathetic previous stage of evolution that covers this world now to die. It's our turn now and you thought somehow you could stop your betters. That you should stop them. You're broken, Michael. Perverse. Traitorous. Sick. And the sick need to be put to rest, especially the sick with egos bigger than their abilities."

I shook my head at Ariel. "You shouldn't have told her about the cure." She shrugged. It was a pretty shrug and the smile was dazzling, but there was more unease in her eyes as she glanced again at Wendy, then at the small number of chimeras, and then at me.

"Misha," she said, "you know there is no cure."

"You've more than earned your punishment." Wendy was done batting around the mouse. Now it was time for the kill. "And what could be a better one than for you to watch this town, its miserable people, and your unnatural attachment die from Lily's concoction. Then, naturally, I kill you, the cherry on top of my sundae. I love sundaes." The tip of a pink tongue touched her upper lip. "They're almost as good as *this*."

I had an attachment to this town, but I had a stronger one and she knew it. Raynor had told Bellucci, and Bellucci had spilled his guts literally and metaphorically all in one. She knew Stefan had rescued me, that I'd lived with him since my escape from the Institute, that he was my family—a word she'd put in Peter's mouth and in the other chimeras' brains, but that she'd never understand herself. Understanding didn't matter, though. She knew where she could hurt me the most.

I felt the shimmer of power hit him. Wendy, the first chimera who didn't need to touch to kill—Wendy who had only to see or know you existed; Wendy who was trying to kill my brother right now. Trying to rip him apart from the inside out.

She failed.

He fell to his knees from the pain of cells frozen for the smallest measurement of time until I set them free again. There was a trace of blood dripping from his nose over his mouth, but he was alive. He was fine. That was until Wendy tried again. This time Saul and I fell to join him. I held her off, held her back, but I was losing ground and the other chimeras were moving forward, except for Ariel.

I thought I could do it. I genuinely believed I could. But I'd been wrong. Wendy was death incarnate. I could try until the end of my days and I would never be what she was now . . . at ten years old. I had seconds, maybe less, left before she overwhelmed the healing protection I had thrown up over the three of us. The pain was agonizing. I couldn't lift the tranquilizer gun. I couldn't move at all, and Saul and

Stefan . . . I could feel how much worse it was for them. They couldn't lift a finger, much less a hand with a gun in it.

Yet a shot cracked clear and loud all the same.

As the material over Wendy's chest blackened, then turned red, her eyes widened—the cat suddenly finding out what it is to be the mouse—and she tumbled backward over the edge, lost to the lethal churn of water at the base of the dam. But not before I heard screams in the hills beside the river, fainter than the rifle shot but as fatal. Wendy had taken her killer and his waiting comrades with her.

I staggered to my feet, yanking at Stefan with one hand, then at Saul, and started firing my tranquilizer gun at the chimeras who had halted at Wendy's fall, milling about, momentarily lost. But as I thought at the Institute, they were the varsity team. They were the ones who lived and breathed to kill and they didn't need a Wendy to do that.

With all three of us firing, several fell, but they were quick . . . like me. Smart . . . I didn't think so much of that about myself anymore. They were predators from the moment one cell split to become two. This was what they were born to do and no one on Earth was better at it than they were. I tried to keep between them and Stefan and Saul. They couldn't hurt me. But, as I'd thought, they were smart. One tackled me to the road, taking me and my gun out of commission for a few seconds until I touched him and he fell at my side. I didn't have to touch now, except Wendy had drained me, and touching was much easier and faster until I recovered. He didn't move again. I'd done what no chimera before Wendy had been capable of—I manipulated the cells of my own kind.

I wasn't Wendy, but I wasn't Michael either, not anymore.

Back up on my feet, I fired at another chimera, another Peter . . . Peter Three. He stumbled and collapsed and I turned. . . .

Too late, I turned. Stefan had turned too. It was only a tranq gun, and the boy was nine at best. He could've walked right out of *The Brady Bunch*, one of those old TV shows that had been on cheap hotel TVs as early-morning reruns when we'd been trying to escape the Institute the first time. The same curls, freckles, happy smile, but with a hand that struck faster than a cobra. It hit in the center of Stefan's chest and I felt it. I felt Stefan's heart stutter, I felt it stop, and then I felt it tear in half. I felt him die. I'd worked so hard on blocking Wendy's type of deadly ability, I hadn't had the resources to block the usual chimera kind as well.

Saul shot the boy in the back and he probably shot more. I didn't notice and I didn't care. I ran, dropping my gun and falling on my knees by Stefan's side. When this had all begun days ago, I'd imagined Raynor's fake tourist shooting Stefan, I'd seen the image of his eyes, turning from the brown I knew to the gray of the clouded sky. I'd imagined wrong. They stayed brown, the brown I saw over a breakfast table, that laughed when I did something idiotic or clever or pretty much anything at all, the brown of a brother who hadn't taken one day of our years together for granted. It was the brown of a brother who wasn't going to leave me, no matter what he or God or reality thought.

I wasn't going to let that happen.

I put my hand over his chest in the same spot the other chimera had snatched his life away and closed my eyes. If he'd just stopped Stefan's heart, it would've been simple. But he'd torn it apart and that wasn't simple at all. Ragged edges—I couldn't see, but I could feel. They had been viciously torn. How could I join those back together again? God, how?

No. *No*. I had to remember what I'd learned.

It was flesh, not bone. Bone was difficult; flesh was easy. Wasn't it? Hadn't I said so? Hadn't I proved so? And a heart, that was merely—shit, Stoipah, don't— that was only the engine that kept the entire body running. You could do without one of those for a good four or five minutes without brain damage; if the body was cold, hypothermic, then longer. I dropped his body temperature like a rock as I carefully put his heart back together, bit by bit. It had to be right, had to be perfect or it wouldn't work. It wouldn't. . . .

I stopped thinking and healed—that and nothing more. I poured every ounce of my ability from me into him. I did the impossible. I made his heart whole again but it didn't beat.

I raised his temperature back to normal but it didn't beat.

I was terrified, desperate, desolate, and fucking pissed off, and I gave it the biggest bio-electrical jolt I could manage. I gave him everything I had and felt the blackness creeping around the edges of my vision as I slumped across his unmoving chest.

You never let your brother down. You never let your brother down. You never let your brother down.

Until you do.

The darkness was complete. I didn't know for how long, but when I opened my eyes, I felt a hand patting my back and saw breakfast brown eyes smiling at me. "You're a miracle, kid. Did I ever tell you that?"

"Don't call me kid." I swiped at my eyes, which weren't wet; I didn't care what anyone said. "Ah, Jesus. Call me kid whenever the fuck you want."

If I let my big brother hug me, I wasn't going to admit to that either.

Theoretically.

Saul helped us both up. Stefan was steadier than I was, but that was from all the energy I'd expended. Big boys don't cry and all that manly crap. Around us all the chimeras save one were down and unconscious. Saul shrugged. "She didn't try to attack us. She didn't do anything at all. I thought you might want to talk to her before whacking her with the cure." Both he and Stefan stepped back, not too far, but enough to give us the illusion of privacy.

"You really weren't surprised?" Ariel tilted her pink head, curious. "You knew?" Her gaze, the lifelong familiarity of blue and green—there was a brilliant, almost explosive shine of life behind those eyes. She had a love of life—her own. It was too bad there was no love for humanity.

"I gave you a clue, you know." I gave a rueful smile. "My fake name. Bernie. Short for Niccolò di Bernardo dei Machiavelli." I wouldn't admit to myself I'd hoped she would pick up on that and leave this all alone, disappear, and save herself. Stefan wondered when his father died if someone could love a cold-blooded killer.

Now I knew.

"Oh, that was clever. Clever, rotten, and sneaky. I love it." She gave me an admiring salute with three fingers, all bearing brightly colored rhinestone rings. "But tell me, Misha, what did I do? How's a girl going to learn if she doesn't know where she went wrong? What made you suspicious?" Beneath us, the river roared as it hurtled over the dam, a monster of nature ready to gobble whatever fell into its maw as it had gobbled up Wendy. With so many monsters gathered in one spot, the natural and the unnatural, it was enough to make a skeptic like me believe in fate.

"Nearly everything. You were too good, Ariel. You're smart, far too smart. You would've come to the same conclusion that I did with the information I gave you and the genetic samples themselves. There's no way to synthesize a drug to cure a chimera, but you lied. You agreed with me, questioning a few things once or twice to make it more believable, but then you 'helped' me find the nonexistent solution." This was how Wendy had found out I'd tried to make a cure and why she was so intent on punishing me. Ariel had told her.

"Anyone as intelligent as you would've known there wasn't one. You're also too psychologically adept," I said. She preened as if it were a compliment. Hell, it was. "You asked questions that seemed innocent on the surface but actually tunneled deep beneath it." She did it better than I could and I'd been a star pupil in the Institute's psychological interrogation class.

"You used verbal and physical cues to make me automatically trust you. . . . That was why you were so insistent on the video feed. When I talked, you looked at me as if I were the only other person in the world and as if every word I said were the most fascinating thing you'd heard or would hear." All the best con men could do that, and con men were nothing compared to a chimera. "You dilated your pupils to indicate arousal." We hadn't been taught to follow through with seduction; we weren't taught why seduction *was* seduction; we were only taught it was bait and a way to get a wary target close enough to touch and kill. That was all the Institute needed us to know—enough for that one touch. More than that was a waste of time and profit. "You did lead into it a little early, though."

"It couldn't have been real? Dr. Theoretical, I think you underestimate me." Her pale pink lips curved playfully.

"It could've been." On my part I knew. On hers I could only guess. "But you were too good at it. Not off by a single note, not once. And then there was this." I pointed a finger beside my eye to indicate where her mermaid tattoo was. Temporary or permanent; that didn't matter. It was Disney, and that did. She apparently had fonder memories of those cartoons from Institute days gone by than I did.

"Too good." She laughed as I'd heard her do many times before, but this time I was positive it wasn't an act. "Undone by my own brilliance. I do like you, Misha. I really do. It took being with you in person to find that out. Which is why I let Raynor 'catch' your girlfriend. I wanted to meet you, know you in real life, not just as pixels. Before that, I honestly didn't know I could like someone. I didn't know how. None of us do, do we?"

"No weakness. No limitations. No mercy," I said.

She nodded, her hair swinging at her jaw with the motion. "Jericho would be so disappointed." She smiled, the dimple flashing beside her wide mouth. "The bastard, which makes liking you more fun. I was his first; did you know? That probably confused you, that you didn't recognize me from the Institute. I'm not twenty-two; I'm twenty-nine and his very first success. He had a run of bad luck after me, batch after bad batch, before he finally had production going smoothly. Assembly-line assassins. I graduated when I was seventeen and you were this tall." She held down a hand to indicate. "I killed my owner when I was seventeen and a half and walked away. I liked being free.

"Speaking of like, did you like me back? Though you knew I was lying to you? And especially now you know that I'm an older woman." She smiled again. Happy. Always happy. Happy to watch movies and chat online; happy to kill. She didn't see the difference between the two. Not yet . . . even with her doubts now regarding Wendy. Not yet and maybe not ever.

"At first. Then I sort of loved you. I still do." Unlike her, I didn't sound happy. I wasn't. Loving Ariel wasn't a love to savor or cherish. Loving her meant I might not love again. She was a sociopath and as she'd said, she liked me, but that didn't mean she would or could learn to like anyone else. A friend? A neighbor? Fun was fun, and toys, like her engineered superflu, were hard to give up. Like Wendy, Ariel wouldn't tolerate tedium. Loving her didn't mean I didn't know what she was. It was why I kept e-mailing her, kept in touch, kept her thinking I was on *her* hook, because all chimeras had to be cured—even Ariel.

"How many people have you killed since you dropped your owner and ran? How many people did you kill when you weren't ordered to or forced to? How many people, Ariel, did you kill because you liked doing so? How many people, not counting the ones you'd kill with what you made in your lab, will you kill in the future if I don't cure you?" I asked.

"Please. So serious. People are like potato chips. You can't kill just one," she said, radiant with humor. When I didn't comment, the dimple and smile disappeared. "Why does it matter? That's what we do. That's who we are. We are evolution in progress, Michael. Everyone else"—she gave a shrug as pretty as her first one and utterly dismissive—"their time is over. Our time is now. Why shouldn't I have fun with them?"

"How many people, Ariel?" I repeated.

She stared at me. She didn't understand. She couldn't understand; she was psychologically incapable of it—at least now. And now was all we had. The water was louder now. Nature knew evolution better than we did. It knew a wrong turn and we were that. "You do have a cure, don't you?" she asked slowly, for the first time seeing something in me that was similar to what she'd been wary of in Wendy, something to be feared.

"I do," I said quietly.

"And you'd use it? On your own kind?"

"As Wendy had killed our own kind, I will. There's no other way."

"I didn't know that about Wendy. That she would kill her own, kill one of us. I hope you believe that." She shook her head then, denying it. "Whatever it is, you know it's not a cure, Misha. It's a poison, to strip us of what we are." She took a step back from me.

"No, it is a cure, but not for you or the others. It's a cure for the human race. We're not right. We're twisted. We were made that way. We're a malignant cancer and, as with any cancer, the cure *is* a poison. You won't be able to kill anymore." I hesitated, because it was dark and ugly, but it was necessary. She'd lied to me; I'd lied to her. I'd lied to everyone for all my good intentions and promises to the contrary, but that was over.

"And you won't be you anymore. You'll still be intelligent, that won't change, but Ariel will die. Someone will take her place. Someone who doesn't care what color her hair is or that she likes mermaids and short skirts or purple sandals. She'll be a new person— not an interesting person; brilliant but not clever; alive but she won't care particularly if she is or not. She won't have hopes and dreams, and fun will be only a word to her. But she won't kill again and that's the best I can do. We're not the next step in evolution. We're a mutation created by a madman and brainwashed to be monsters. Monsters belong in those movies we watched, Ariel, not in the real world."

That was when Ariel chose to take herself out of the world. She spun on one heel, spread her arms wide, and sailed over the low concrete wall. For a moment she seemed to hover in the air, a butterfly in color and light, too much a part of the air and sky itself to fall. But fall she did, with a graceful dive that would take her into the same thrashing crush of water that had swallowed Wendy.

It was beautiful, that incredible soaring flight and inevitable plunge, and I hadn't taken a step to stop her. Sometimes the cure is worse than the disease, and more rarely the cure is worse than death itself. Ariel couldn't be anything less than she was and she made her choice. But she took the virus canister with her. Metal, it would sink to the bottom of the river and the airborne virus would never see the light of day. Ariel's last gesture wasn't a gift to the world or to Cascade Falls; it was a gift to me.

She wanted to surprise me. I let her.

With that surprise, that gift, she redeemed herself—in my eyes at least, and my eyes were the only ones that counted.

"She took yoga and ballet," I said, more to myself than Stefan or Saul. "If anyone could fly, she would be the one." I didn't go to look over the side. It made it easier to believe.

Fly away, bird. Fly away always.

Then there was work to be done.

Energy already recharging, I knelt beside the nearest chimera. He had fallen facedown when the tranquilizer dart had hit him. I rolled him over. Dark blond hair, light-skinned; it was Michael Three. It seemed somehow right a Michael would be my first. I laid my hand on his forehead. What I was doing was almost as complex as putting Stefan's heart back together. The physical connection helped.

"What are you doing?" Stefan squatted beside me. "You just said there was no cure."

"Not a genetic one, no." The cartridges we'd shot the chimeras with hadn't held a mixture of "cure" and tranquilizer—another lie. They'd been nothing but pure tranq, because there was nothing else to mix with it. "I'm basically destroying a good deal of their amygdala and a particular portion of their frontal cortex and hypothalamus." I felt the cells die in Michael's brain, leaving a lesion of darkness I could've seen if I'd closed my eyes. I moved to the next one—a Lily. She had brown hair and dark skin—Lily Four, then. "I'm giving them highly improved lobotomies or a variation of an amygdalotomy combined with other procedures. They should retain almost all of their emotions, except aggression."

"Almost"—it was a word that encompassed more than a person could imagine.

"You said chimeras naturally blocked other chimeras from damaging them? And if that's what you're doing, won't they heal?" He didn't like this. I didn't blame him. I didn't like it either.

"All that practicing I told you about, all the healing I did on the animals and myself for almost three years every day, it increased what I can do tenfold. We weren't taught to try to be more than what we were. I don't think it crossed any of the researchers' minds that we could actually increase a genetic trait by exercising it, but I did. I worked Jericho's gene until I could make it do fucking backflips." Lily went quicker than Michael and the third even faster. "If you can build something up, you can tear it down more easily and efficiently— even if it is a chimera." It was a simple logic and I thought the only reason Jericho hadn't thought of it was that healing others and building, not manipulating, wasn't part of his mental wiring.

I looked at all the fallen chimeras around us. "They couldn't stop Wendy and they can't stop me now. They can't heal what either of us does to them. They're not strong enough."

"There was no cure, was there? All along there never was." Stefan stood, his hand resting on my shoulder.

This was my last omission from all that I'd told Stefan and Saul. I wasn't going to say it was my last lie. I knew better now.

"I am the cure." I raised my eyes to him. "There's no way to turn off the gene Jericho gave us. It would fight off any attempted gene therapy, any bone marrow transplant. And I can't stop the gene from functioning either, not without killing them. It's an intrinsic part of our DNA, not an extra chromosome. Not something we can do without. I turn the gene off, I turn them off, permanently. This"—I rested my hand on the next forehead—"is the only answer." That was one lie I hadn't told. I had researched for a way, which was how I'd found Ariel. I'd had hope, but I was a child of Jericho and that meant reality and ruthless necessity always trumped hope. When I finally accepted the truth, I used the time to become what I was now. I found the cure inside of me, not in an outside world nowhere near ready to scientifically understand what we were, much less change that.

"Misha. . . ."

The sympathy in his voice was strong. He knew. I knew. It didn't have to be said aloud. I'd pledged day in and day out that I wasn't a killer, but I was a thief of souls. The twelve that remained here, they might as well have been the Four Horsemen, bringing death and despair to the world. They had to be stopped. But which is worse? To take who a person is, for good or bad, and erase his free will, or to kill him? If I'd asked them, every one of them would've chosen the same fate Ariel had. I didn't give them that choice. I did what I thought was best. I played God . . . just as Jericho had.

But with him dead, someone had to.

"They can't murder without aggression," I said, "and they can't have aggression if I destroy the part of the brain that births it." It was the best I could do—a very poor best.

I rested my hand on the forehead of the last one—Peter. He'd played genius and villain well, while all the time Wendy had been pulling his strings and feeding him his lines. He was a killer too, same as the others, but he wasn't what I thought he'd been. He was both predator and prey, because there was nothing in his mind now except silence. Wendy's last act before falling away, besides killing the sniper who had shot her and his companions, had been to turn Peter off as if he were a toy she was done playing with. Only his brain stem worked now, keeping his lungs inflating and deflating, his heart beating, but the rest was dark and dead. He was brain dead. She'd made a true puppet of him, empty and hollow. It would've made her laugh, the irony, even with a bullet in her small chest. Peter was gone and I couldn't fix that. The other chimeras wouldn't be able to undo what I'd done and I couldn't undo what Wendy had done. She and I were a new breed of chimera—with a new balance of power.

Ariel had been a chimera, able to survive a good deal, but the unquenchable hunger of water at the bottom of the dam? No. I had no hope there. Wendy, though . . . the Grim Reaper himself would be afraid to touch her long enough to take her life. Fine. If I saw her again, I'd do it for him.

Somehow.

Chapter 15

For the second time in his life Raynor was going to do some good. The first had been having one of his men shoot Wendy, because Raynor knew as well as anyone that Wendy wasn't viable for sale, profit, or life in general. He'd saved Stefan or Saul from having to do it—if they could've lifted a hand to do it. It didn't matter how evil a ten-year-old little girl was; putting a bullet in one would haunt your nights for years to come—unless you were Raynor. The only regret he would have was a lack of a commemorative photograph to hang on his wall.

"Well, chaps, it looks like you've done my work for me." He had walked around the sheriff's car and was heading toward us, his gun up and aimed at the cluster of the three of us. "One, two, four . . . twelve unconscious chimeras wrapped up in a bow and ready to go to rehab. Learn to mind their masters." He didn't know what I'd done to them and I wasn't inclined to tell him. I didn't know what kind of life they would have now. The ability to kill remained within them, but they wouldn't use it. They couldn't. With a complete lack of aggression, they wouldn't be able to kill, even in defense. As I'd told Ariel, they'd be smart as they'd been before, but they'd be blander, milder, less interested in life in general. When they woke up from the tranquilizer, my best guess was they'd keep the Institute story to themselves—they'd know by now that would only end them in a psych ward. They'd wander off and do as Ariel had done; as I'd done. They would make fake IDs, get jobs, live their lives—but without flavor or zest. They would be gray people in a gray world, but without leaving a trail of torture and murder in their wake.

Raynor would say you have to break some eggs to make an omelet. Raynor was a dick.

"Stefan," I said.

Stefan shot him in the right shoulder. It was his right hand that held his gun. Raynor dropped it as he clutched his shattered and bleeding shoulder. Saul whistled. "You're fast. How'd you get so damn fast? I was in the rangers and I'm not that fast."

"I think Misha juiced me up some. Either that or you were a piss-poor ranger." Stefan walked over and swept Raynor's legs out from under him. "All your men up in the hills are dead now, Raynor. A couple months' paychecks and all you have are a pile of dead mercenaries to show for it, thanks to one little girl. And I'll bet my last dollar they're mercenaries because you wouldn't share the Institute with anyone else in the government. Too messy and much less money for you." He kicked him in the stomach next. "I hear you shot my brother in the head with a rubber bullet. Not nice, asshole. Not nice at all." He kicked him again and air whistled out of Raynor's trach tube as he doubled over. "Nice. Maybe I can get you to whistle '"Yankee-fucking-Doodle Dandy'" on that thing." He kicked him once more, in the ribs, and harder this time. I had the feeling, if I let him, he would go on kicking Raynor until he was dead. I didn't mind that too much, but we needed him for something first—that second good thing he could do.

"Stefan, we need him," I said, catching his arm before he launched another kick. "We could call it in ourselves, but no one knows how intelligent a chimera can be, especially one like Ariel. We need him to find the bomb."

"Bomb? What are you prattling about?" Raynor spat blood onto the road. "Don't try to distract me from the merchandise, and that's what you all are and were always meant to be, Michael One. Merchandise. Don't ascribe to delusions of grandeur and think you're a person. A regular human being. You're not. In fact, the Institute would've tattooed a price on you lot if your value didn't keep going up."

"All these chimeras loose on the world for weeks now, Raynor." I bent my knees so I could stare him in the eyes. "Do you think killing an old man and gangbangers was all they were up to? They built a virus bomb and planted it somewhere in the Portland airport. It's airborne and set to go off at eleven a.m. tomorrow. No one will even notice what's happening. The incubation time is seven days. It will kill thirty percent of the people it infects and Portland airport is an international airport. You know what that means, how far it will go. You're the one with the capacity to think like a chimera if you have to. Find it and stop it or you may be one of the ones it kills." That was the one argument that would have him cooperating.

"It's a silver metal cylinder this long and this big around." I demonstrated with my hands before resting my hand on his unwounded shoulder. "Since you're Homeland Security, I hope to God you can do something about it. But before you go, tell me how you knew where to look for us. How'd you know Stefan was my brother?" I wanted to make sure he was, as Stefan guessed, the only person in the government who was after us.

"Your brother?" I tightened my hand on his shoulder and I gave him pain, considerably more pain than was in the shoulder pierced by a bullet. He shuddered beneath my touch and went from white to gray. He cleared his throat, the trach and its talking valve bobbing as he swallowed convulsively. "Yes, I . . . for whatever reason, Jericho didn't bother to document that Korsak was your brother. He was an arrogant bastard about sharing information. We had to wait until he died to even see his files on the kids. That's how he wanted it. Only when the top man is dead are the files automatically sent to a chosen successor."

He took a few more breaths to recover. "Perhaps Jericho didn't think it was important. When you were taken from the Institute, Jericho went after you, and I was in charge of finding out how anyone knew the Institute existed at all." His breath wheezed in and out of the valve. "I thought it had to be someone military or with law enforcement. The raid was too well planned. I visited the offices of the local cops and FBI, and that was when I saw it. A top Russian mob boss had been offed and Korsak was the main suspect. They had their whole murder board covered with pictures of the families. Even down to a picture of a boy kidnapped ten years before. I could see how certain incorr—" I let him feel the pain again, the exquisite pain of careful wording. What Stefan and I knew, voiced or not, was ours only. No one else needed to know. And that included Saul. Raynor winced and went on. "I could see how certain conclusions could be drawn. I drew mine and have been chasing Korsaks since then. Any one I could lay my hands on."

"Like my father," Stefan said without question.

On that, Raynor remained silent. It was for the best.

"Then I was an idiot and got my fingerprints on file and you found us."

Raynor looked up at me uneasily and nodded at Stefan's comment. "No one else knows about us?" I asked.

"No one." He shook his head.

"Are you telling me the truth, Raynor? I want you to look at those chimeras. You shouldn't worry about collecting them. They're not killers anymore. No use to you. What I did to them," I said, thinking I'd let him wonder exactly what that might have been, "I can do to you, but for what you've done and allowed to continue and wanted, I could leave you the very goddamn picture of drooling subintelligence. Someone would have to change your diapers for the rest of your life. With your dignity and vanity, I don't think you'd like that." I leaned in closer until he could feel my breath on him. I made it cold—the touch of a corpse. "On the other hand, leaving you alive and sane if you're cooperative means nothing to me either. Only results matter. So go find that cylinder and save lives, including your own." I took my hand from his shoulder. "I'm not like you, Raynor. I'll always be better, because I'm not a killer."

It was a lie.

I had killed him—the moment I'd let go. I'd weakened a vessel in his brain and destroyed all the pain receptors in the meninges. They wouldn't register the pressure of the leaking blood. There'd be no headaches to warn him. He had three days maximum and when he died, death would be in a split second. He would never know it was coming.

As I'd said, I had killed him for what he'd done and what he'd allowed to be done at the Institute, but more than that, I had killed him for what he knew. He knew about Stefan and me. But his successor wouldn't. There'd be no murder board of a mob murder Stefan hadn't committed to be stumbled across. There wouldn't be a picture of a little boy with bicolored eyes like mine. His successor wouldn't know Stefan existed, but Raynor did. And he'd come for us again. At least for me, and Stefan might die trying to protect me. Raynor might wait a few years, but he'd come. Men like Raynor didn't give up. Men like Raynor, Jericho, Bellucci, they never gave up. Monsters didn't.

Stefan had done his best to keep me true to myself, although he'd been clear that self-defense was justifiable and to go for it if I had to. I'd refused all that time. I'd told him I wouldn't be the killer they had made me. I'd said I wouldn't kill, not even to save my life.

But there was one life I would kill for. I'd been blind because I'd wanted to be. There had been that false image that had fooled my mind of Raynor's man killing Stefan when we'd first fled Cascade. In my mind's eye I'd seen him pulling his trigger, yet I'd refused to let it go any further, that thought. I'd seen it and then I'd unseen it. Felt it and buried it. Saw its face in intimate detail, yet couldn't tell you a single feature.

I hadn't let my own brain recognize this choice would come, undoing everything I had built the new Michael/Misha on. The games I played in my head where thoughts could be knotted and hidden away ended as one of my own kind had killed Stefan when he was less than ten feet from me.

I wouldn't kill for myself, but I would kill for my brother.

And I didn't regret it, not for a moment. It didn't make me a monster or a freak, saving my family. It made me what I'd wanted to be all along.

It made me human.

Epilogue

Raynor did as I told him, if only to save his own life from Ariel's work. He died two and a half days later. I checked the obituaries. He had a nice-looking picture and an Armani suit. I wasn't surprised. Saul went back to Miami and if he blocked our numbers from now on, I wouldn't blame him. We took our time in picking another town. It didn't matter where it was really, only that it was home. We chose different names and jobs. I went with Wyatt, and Stefan was John Henry. Although Doc Holliday was rolling over in his grave at Stefan's poker skills and I still didn't care much about guns, my love of Westerns and Western aliases would never die. Instead of being a house painter, Stefan was a car salesman and surprisingly good at it despite his wolfish looks. Once he pounced on them in the car lot, I thought people were afraid to *not* buy a car from him. He was employee of the month more than once, which embarrassed the hell out of him. I had a copy of the picture made and hung it in the living room to give him shit. That's what brothers do—give each other shit.

And we were brothers. What he knew and what I knew in the privacy of our own hearts didn't change that.

I had two jobs. I worked at the library part-time and spent four days a week at what had to be the last video store left in America—what could be more perfect? I could both feed and entertain the mind. I'd moved movie night from Wednesday to Sunday, but I didn't give it up. I loved the fantasy of movies, maybe more so now.

After all, what had reality done for me lately?

Stefan watched the movies with me now that Ariel was gone, provided he didn't have a date. I'd gotten over that no woman was good enough for my brother and stopped giving the ones he asked out acid reflux on date night. He was surprised at how much easier dating was here than it had been in Cascade Falls. I didn't clue him in. Of all the lies I'd told or truths I'd omitted, I could live with that last one. The brotherly ass kickings were still in full force after what I'd pulled on the dam at Cascade Falls. While they were deserved, taking it on myself to be a cure for my fellow chimeras when there was no other, I'd skip further punishment if Stefan found out what I'd done to his dates in Cascade. Besides, if he missed a movie or two with me, it wasn't that bad. Godzilla took his spot and hogged his share of the popcorn. And if I missed someone who was a killer, a sociopath, and had a smile I'd not forget until the day I died, that was my right.

It was five months later that I finally admitted defeat, finishing what I'd started more than half a year ago, and was at my laptop, hacking into Lolcats, crashing the site, and removing any mention of it from the Net. It was evil. It had to go. My eye was caught by the sudden flash of a white IM box at the bottom of my screen as I typed. It flickered blankly for a second; then a question appeared in flowing pink and green script with a familiar winking mermaid as punctuation:

Hey, sexy, want to watch a movie?

About the Author

Rob Thurman lives in Indiana, land of cows, corn, and ravenous wild turkeys. Rob is the author of the Cal Leandros novels; the Trickster novels; the Korsak Brothers novels; and a story in the anthology *Wolfbane and Mistletoe.*

Besides wild, ravenous turkeys, Rob has a dog (if you don't have a dog, how do you live?)—one hundred pounds of Lab/Dane mix. She has the bark of twenty German Shepherds, a head the size of a horse's, teeth straight out of a Godzilla movie, and the ferocious habit of hiding under the kitchen table and peeing on herself when strangers come by. By the way, she was adopted from a shelter. She was fully grown, already house-trained, and grateful as hell. Think about it next time you're looking for a Rover or Fluffy. Rob also has two other dogs who are slightly more invested in keeping their food source alive.

For updates, teasers, music videos, deleted scenes, social networking, and various other extras, visit the author at www.robthurman.net.

Read on for an exciting excerpt from
the next Cal Leandros novel,

DOUBLETAKE

by Rob Thurman

Coming in March 2012 from Roc.

Family . . . it is a bitch.

The thought drifted out of nowhere.

Or maybe it didn't, considering my current situation. There was no denying that it was true. Everyone thought it sooner or later, didn't they? If there's only you, you're good—lonely maybe, but good. You can't fight with yourself. If there are two of you, it can still be good. Your options are limited. You make do and appreciate what you have, unless it's the stereotypical evil-twin scenario. Then you aim for the goatee and blow his ass back to the alternate dimension he popped out of.

A Kishi hit my back. I flipped him over and put a bullet in the back of his head.

Yeah, normally two was a doable number. It was when you hit three and higher that things started to go bad. That's when the bitching and moaning started, the pitting of one against another, the slights that no one forgot. No one could tell me that Noah didn't pitch a few of his relatives kicking and screaming off the ark long before the floodwaters receded. It was no familial *Love Boat* and I believed that to my core.

Which brought up the question: Did that wrathful

Old Testament God kill the sharks? I don't think he did. You can't drown a shark. I think they were snacking on biblical in-laws right and left. Noah, Noah, Noah . . .

I swung around and kicked the next Kishi in the stomach as I slammed another clip home before putting three in his gaping, lethally fanged mouth as he jumped again. It sounded easy, but considering the one I also had attached to my other leg, it was a pain in the ass.

Family-wise, I had no pains in the ass. I was lucky. I had one brother and he was a damn good one. Once we were on our own, I'd escaped the curse of screaming Thanksgiving dinners—now I had a turkey pizza; Niko had a vegan one. No bitter arguments around a Christmas tree—each year Niko gave me a new gun; I gave him a new sword. Absent was the awkward discovery of first cousins shacking up at the summer family get-togethers at the lake. I didn't have to wait for summer. I saw my brother every day when he winged my sopping towel off the bathroom floor at my head or I asked—after the fact—if I could use his priceless seventeenth-century copy of some boring book no one but him and the author had read to prop up a wobbling coffee table.

Summer vacations . . . if you thought about it, what kind of people actually gathered together at a lake with cabins and all that crap anyway? Hadn't they ever watched *Friday the 13th*? Jason? Hockey masks? Machetes? A good time for me, yeah—oh hell yeah—but not as much for the members of your average Prius-driving middle-class family.

Stupidity is everywhere.

The rest of my life might be challenging in some areas—like at the moment, with an adolescent Kishi either trying to eat my leg or hump it to the bare bone—but family? I knew I had that under control, had no reason to worry about it or dwell on it. I watched my brother's back; he watched mine. We were a Hallmark card dipped in blood and made of unbreakable steel. I'd never had a doubt about my family and I never would—no matter what the Kishi, who had brought the topic to mind to begin with, were doing to annoy me on the general subject.

No, it was all smooth sailing, rather like this current job, until my cell phone rang. "Niko," I said, shooting another adult Kishi with jaws stretched wide enough to swallow my entire head. He had leaped downward at me from a fire escape of a condemned tenement building long crumpled in on itself—no demolition crew needed. Gravity worked for free. "Can you get this one off my leg before I need sexual-assault counseling?"

Niko said to not kill the babies, although at one hundred and fifty pounds, "baby" was pushing the definition, but I was doing my best, more or less, to be a good boy. Although it would've been much easier to be a bad boy.

So very bad. So very fun.

For my brother, however, I reined in that part of me—that nonhuman half of me, choke-chaining it with a practiced grip. It was the price I paid to keep my brother satisfied. Bearing in mind that if it wasn't for him, I'd be dead or sanity-challenged ten times over, I

owed the man. I was also fond enough of his bossy
anal-retentive ass to die for him.

More importantly, to kill for him.

And choose the darkest of roads to make that happen.

All that made ignoring a giant baby with an equally
giant bite easy enough. As I fished for my cell, Niko
was less than awed at my babysitting skills and said so.
"If you can't do a minimum of three tasks at once, I
have failed you with all my training and instruction.
I'd blame myself, but clearly it's entirely your fault—
your laziness, your total ineptitude."

Not that we shared the fraternal fondness out loud.
How manly would that be?

It wasn't as if I hadn't heard that all before. If adults
heard lullabies when they slept, Niko's admonish-
ments would be mine. I shook my leg again, then shot
another Kishi that was bounding down the side of the
next building, which was equally as dilapidated as the
first, putting three bullets between his blazing silver
eyes. They shone brighter than any streetlights in this
part of town . . . until the Kishi's life seeped away and
left only the dull gray of death. I felt bad for the Kishi—
almost—but they had turned a block that had once
hosted scavenging homeless, thriving drug dealers and
sullen hookers into a desolate wasteland. I didn't have
a preference for one over the other, Kishi or human.
The mayor wanted the city cleaned up. The Kishi Clan
was doing the job one block at a time . . . even if it
meant eating quite a few people.

Were those people good people? If I knew anything,
I knew that these days I wasn't in the position to make
the call on whether certain people were worth saving

or leaving to the predators. That I left up to Nik. I simply stepped over their bodies and went on with the job.

Regardless of whether they were good or evil, those people belonged, whether they knew it or not, to the Kin. The Kin, the werewolf mafia of New York City, weren't pleased to be sharing their money or their snacks with Johnny-come-lately preternatural hyenas from the depths of . . . um . . . I should've paid attention to where those depths were—maybe Africa?—during the premission rundown, but Niko knew. That was enough. I didn't think it mattered much. They were encroaching on Kin territory, and the wolves didn't like that.

Unfortunately for the Kin, the Kishi, as a race, howled at a decibel level that would have any Kin wolf's ears within ten blocks bleeding. Curled up in homicidal furry balls, moaning for their mommies, they hadn't had much success in taking down the Kishi. Luckily for Niko, me, and our bank account, human ears couldn't hear notes that high.

And although I wasn't entirely human, my hearing was. That made us the go-to guys for this job. It had seemed easy from the hiring and from the half of our fee that was slapped into my palm—if it hadn't been for Niko's research, finding out the Kishi were highly intelligent, if extremely malevolent. That meant the adults were fair game, but the younger Kishi we had to pat on the head and then find a goddamn supernatural foster and rescue organization for murderous fur babies that would raise them right, socialize their asses, put rhinestone collars on them, and take them off our hands.

How many of those do you think were in the phone book? Nada? Good fucking call.

But the bottom line was, it was all about family. The adult Kishi were taking down prey for their young—which luckily only numbered one at this point—feeding him or her, setting up a nest, claiming this place for their own. They were doing what evolution had bred them to do. They were killers—predators to the bone. They would slaughter anything they thought they had a chance of bringing down—but to give them credit, they looked after their family.

That's where family became a bitch in yet another way. You eat people for your family; you piss off the Kin for your family; you die for your family.

As a random bastard had once said to me when I was a kid in the fourth grade as he demanded my sneakers and backpack, life isn't fair. I agreed with him by punching his annoying teeth down his equally annoying throat. If that's what the world wanted to be, I'd go along. I didn't make the rules. I only played by them.

Since when?

Since never.

This wasn't a schizophrenic voice—at least I hoped not—this was just my subconscious, or half of one. It was the bad thoughts people think—normal people, too—that they shouldn't, don't like to admit to, and don't act on. But as I wasn't normal and wasn't exactly the Webster's Dictionary definition of a person, my bad thoughts were much more bad than most, and I did sometimes act on them. Sometimes or often or frequently or very frequently, depending on my mood . . . no judgment needed or wanted.

They were almost as much of a bitch as family could be, with the inner squabbling, but I'd learned to mostly tune them out. Slowly they were beginning to taper off. Not because *any* part of me had less to say, but because two halves were becoming a whole. Two genetic and mental halves melding into one. Out of the way, Sybil, there was a new nearly cured crazy in town. Many psychotherapists would be proud of my progress—the ones who hadn't met me and, if they had any sense, wouldn't care to.

Soon I wouldn't be good or bad. I'd only be me.

They'd have to invent a new adjective for that.

I shook my leg futilely one more time and exhaled in irritation at the molten mercury eyes, the dark red coat dappled with silver spots, the milk-white teeth—as large as a German shepherd's adult teeth—that continued to gnaw at my thigh. "Three seconds and he's a rug under the coffee table. Your move, Cyrano."

Did Niko have a proud, hawklike nose? Yes, he did. Did I give him hell over it? What do you think?

I answered my still-ringing cell phone as I shot the last Kishi that leaped through a boarded-up window. Wood split, glass shattered, and bone splintered. The combination made for one dead Kishi whose stomach was rounded and full with its last meal, which, I was guessing, had been the last occupant of this street. From the hypodermic needle the parahyena coughed up in its dying throes, that meal had most likely been a tweaker.

They say drugs kill, but does anyone ever listen?

"Yeah, Leandros," I said into the phone. "Death and destruction by the dollar. The meter's ticking. Go."

I hadn't had a chance to check the incoming number, not with Kishi Junior both seducing and making a meal of my leg. But it didn't surprise me to hear a familiar voice. Five people total had my personal number. Our work came by referral only these days. "Kid, thank Bacchus," I heard the relieved exhalation. "I need you and Niko at my place now."

The three seconds was up and I had the muzzle of my Desert Eagle planted between toddler Kishi's moon eyes as he gnawed harder at my lower thigh. I had a high pain tolerance—you learned to in this business, but to balance it out, my tolerance for nearly everything else in the universe was low. *Damn* low. Too bad for baby. It was night-night time. I might as well stop the pattern now. The same as his parents, he would grow up to be a killer anyway.

Like you did?

As if I didn't know that.

But I was a done deal; the Kishi wasn't, not quite yet. "Goodfellow? You in trouble?" I started to put pressure on the trigger and tried to ignore the shadow of guilt I felt. It *was* a kid. A killer kid, but a kid nonetheless. Couldn't I relate? On every single level? Then again, did I care if I could relate? Was I Dr. Phil? Hell, no. I was, however, Niko's brother. That had me yanking harder at my internal leash while frowning crossly at Niko as I gave him a few extra seconds to move over, slide his katana blade between my leg and the Kishi in order to pry the creature off in one efficient move.

"You owe me," I grumbled at him.

While the last Kishi squealed, barked, yowled, and laughed hyena-crazy through a toothy muzzle, Niko threw him down and hog-tied his preteen fuzzy ass. My brother—he wasn't a bleeding heart. There were more dead monsters and people in whatever version of hell you wanted to believe in who'd testify to that. He did like to give a break when he thought one was due, though—or when he thought their birthright shouldn't automatically condemn them.

He'd learned that raising me and adjusting to my birthright—a lifetime of habits, right or wrong, was hard to break.

Robin's voice was in my ear, catching my attention again. "Am I in trouble? Ah. *Hmmm.* It's more like everyone else is in trouble with the exception of myself," he hedged. "I'd rather explain it in person and give you the keys to the bar. Ishiah left them for you."

Ishiah was my boss at my day job/afternoon job/ night job—whenever I wasn't out doing what pulled in the real rent money: kicking monster ass. He owned a bar called the Ninth Circle, was a peri—a winged human-type creature that had spawned angel legends— and was generally neutral on whether he should kill me or crown me employee of the month for making it a week without icing a customer while serving up his or her liquor of choice.

Why would he want to kill me? We had a lot of unpaid tabs because I once hadn't made that said employee of the month. But hand held to the empty, godless space that filled the sky, if I killed you, you usually had it coming. Or you just weren't that quick. In my world, the two were practically the same.

"The keys? Why did he— Ah, hell with it. We'll get the story when we get there." I looked down at Niko crouching on the street, rhythmically rubbing the Kishi's stomach. He crooned mournfully, my blood on his teeth, the silver of his eyes surrounded by the white of fear. "Fuck me," I sighed. Before I let Goodfellow off the phone, I added, "By the way, do you know anywhere we could drop off a baby Kishi to be raised up all good with God? Religious, righteous, and true? Oh, and nonpeople eating?"

"Your imitation of a Southern drawl is pathetic and, yes, drop him off here." He rattled off an address. "They take in strays all the time. But you better do it in the next hour or they'll be gone."

"Gone where?" I asked.

"Who knows? I t doesn't matter. They'll all be gone. Everyone. Now hurry the hell up. I'm paying your bill this time. I'm a puck, a trickster, and a used-car salesman. Don't think I won't squeeze every penny out of Niko's well-shaped ass if you don't perform this job to perfection." His phone disconnected in my ear.

"Who was that?"

I grinned down at my brother. "Robin is hiring us for a job, and I'm thinking seriously about taking a dive in the fifth, because it's your ass on the line if we screw up."

"Goodfellow will be a good client. He wouldn't cheat us." Niko finished the knot on the rope and slitted his eyes at me. "And let us leave my ass out of it. Why I claim you as my blood, I will never know."

That wasn't true. I didn't know why he put up with me, but I took it on faith that Niko knew something that made me worth keeping around. Niko knew extraordinary things that most others didn't know and wouldn't ever know. He was like that. Then again, very rarely, Niko screwed the hell up, wasn't the infallible older brother—because no one was infallible. No one. I hadn't kept count before, of the times he was wrong, but if I'd known what was headed our way, I might've starting adding them up now.

Number one was a little over sixty minutes away and headed for us like a freight train.

Tick-tock.

ROB THURMAN

CHIMERA

Ten years ago, Stefan Korsak's younger brother was kidnapped. Not a day has passed that Stefan hasn't thought about him. As a rising figure in the Russian mafia, he has finally found him. But when he rescues Lukas, he must confront a terrible truth—his brother is no longer his brother. He is a trained, genetically-altered killer. Now, those who created him will do anything to reclaim him. And the closer Stefan grows to his brother, the more he realizes that saving Lukas may be easier than surviving him...

**Available wherever books are sold or at
penguin.com**

R0080